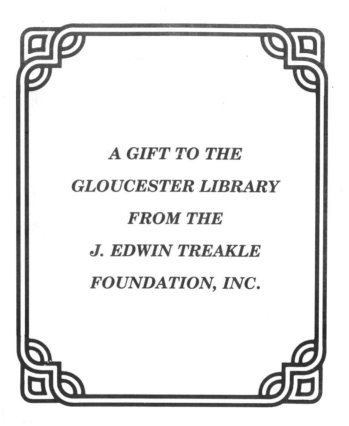

PRAISE FOR MELANIE DOBSON

Hidden Among the Stars

"Star-crossed, forbidden love and the disappearance of family members and hidden treasure make a compelling WWII story and set the stage for modern-day detective work in Dobson's latest time-slip novel. Exquisitely penned, with strong faith elements, *Hidden Among the Stars* is Dobson at her best."

CATHY GOHLKE, Christy Award–winning author of *Until We Find Home*

"A stunning family mystery, this novel is poignant, resonant, and long after the last page, its breathtaking twist will have you asking, 'What would I have done?'"

SANDRA BYRD, author of *Lady of a Thousand Treasures*

"*Hidden Among the Stars* is a glorious treasure hunt, uniting past and present with each delightful revelation. Dobson celebrates faith and the strength of human spirit in true-to-life settings, high-stakes decisions, and heart-gripping characters. It's must-read historical fiction that left me pondering well-crafted twists for days."

MESU ANDREWS, award-winning author of *Isaiah's Daughter*

"With great skill and grace, Melanie Dobson weaves the past and present together in a beautiful story of love that goes far beyond the superficial. A master at storytelling, Dobson leaves readers with an unpredictable and completely satisfying ending."

HEIDI CHIAVAROLI, award-winning author of *The Hidden Side*

Catching the Wind

"Dobson creates a labyrinth of intrigue, expertly weaving a World War II drama with a present-day mystery to create an unforgettable story. This is a must-read for fans of historical time-slip fiction."

PUBLISHERS WEEKLY, starred review

"Dobson skillfully interweaves three separate lives as she joins the past and present in an uplifting tale of courage, love, and enduring hope. A strong choice for historical fiction fans who appreciate well-developed characters and settings."

LIBRARY JOURNAL

"A beautiful and captivating novel with compelling characters, intriguing mystery, and true friendship. The story slips flawlessly between present day and WWII, the author's sense of timing and place contributing to the reader's urge to devour the book in one sitting yet simultaneously savor its poignancy. A hint of romance supports the plot yet never overwhelms it."

ROMANTIC TIMES

"A childhood bond, never forgotten, leads to a journey of secrets revealed and lifelong devotion rewarded. Readers will delight in this story that illustrates how the past can change the present."

LISA WINGATE, national bestselling author of *Before We Were Yours*

"Another captivating weave of great characters, superb storytelling, and rich historical detail from talented wordsmith Melanie Dobson. A story to remind us all that resilience springs from hope, and hope from love."

SUSAN MEISSNER, author of *As Bright as Heaven*

Shadows of Ladenbrooke Manor

"Masterful. . . . Mysteries are solved, truths revealed, and loves rekindled in a book sure to draw new fans to Dobson's already-large base."

PUBLISHERS WEEKLY

"[This] poignant mix of historical and contemporary family drama . . . delivers a beautifully redemptive love story that will appeal to a diverse audience of readers."

SERENA CHASE, *USA Today*'s Happy Ever After blog

Chateau of Secrets

"Amazing characters, deep family secrets, and an authentic French chateau make Dobson's story a delight."

ROMANTIC TIMES

"A satisfying read with two remarkable heroines."

HISTORICAL NOVEL SOCIETY

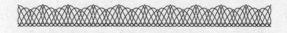

HIDDEN AMONG THE STARS

MELANIE DOBSON

HIDDEN

AMONG THE

STARS

Tyndale House Publishers, Inc.
Carol Stream, Illinois

Visit Tyndale online at www.tyndale.com.

Visit Melanie Dobson's website at www.melaniedobson.com.

TYNDALE and Tyndale's quill logo are registered trademarks of Tyndale House Publishers, Inc.

Hidden Among the Stars

Designed by Gearbox

Edited by Sarah Mason Rische

The author is represented by the literary agency of Natasha Kern Literary Agency, Inc., P.O. Box 1069, White Salmon, WA 98672.

Matthew 28:20 and Revelation 21:4 are taken from the *Holy Bible*, New Living Translation, copyright © 1996, 2004, 2015 by Tyndale House Foundation. Used by permission of Tyndale House Publishers, Inc., Carol Stream, Illinois 60188. All rights reserved.

Job 19:25-26 is taken from *The Holy Bible*, American Standard Version.

Judith 9:11, Psalm 27:1, and John 15:13 are taken from the *Holy Bible*, King James Version.

For information about special discounts for bulk purchases, please contact Tyndale House Publishers at csresponse@tyndale.com, or call 800-323-9400.

Library of Congress Cataloging-in-Publication Data

Names: Dobson, Melanie, author.
Title: Hidden among the stars / Melanie Dobson.
Description: Carol Stream, Illinois : Tyndale House Publishers, Inc., [2018]
Identifiers: LCCN 2018007552| ISBN 9781496428295 (hardcover) | ISBN 9781496417329 (softcover)
Subjects: LCSH: World War, 1939-1945--Fiction. | GSAFD: Historical fiction. | Christian fiction.
Classification: LCC PS3604.O25 H53 2018 | DDC 813/.6—dc23 LC record available at https://lccn.loc.gov/2018007552

Printed in the United States of America

24   23   22   21   20   19   18
7   6   5   4   3   2   1

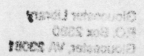

TO MICHELE HEATH

My amazing first reader and forever friend
Thank you for teaching me how great hope can
be found in the midst of suffering

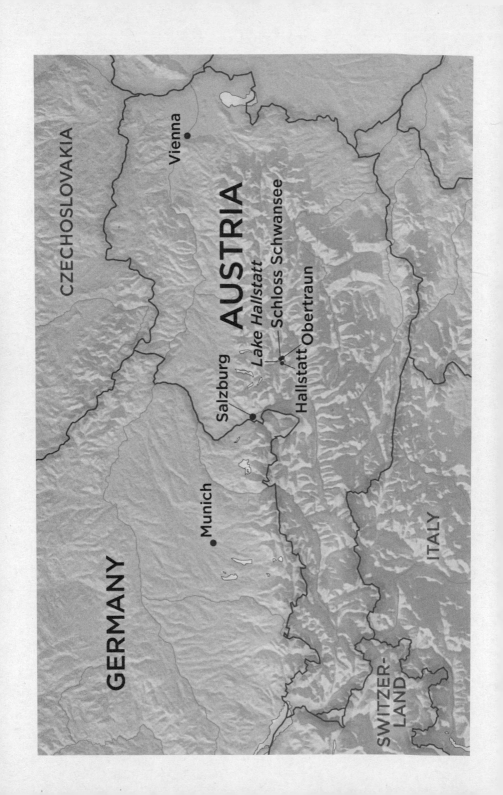

For thy power standeth not in multitude

nor thy might in strong men:

for thou art a God of the afflicted,

an helper of the oppressed . . .

a saviour of them that are without hope.

JUDITH 9:11 (APOCRYPHA)

CHAPTER 1

ANNIKA

LAKE HALLSTATT, AUSTRIA
MARCH 1938

The blade of a shovel, cutting through frosted grass. That's what she remembered most from the spring of 1938. In the year that followed, on the darkest of nights, she could almost hear the whisper of digging again. The sound of Max Dornbach calling her name.

"Annika?" His confident voice bled into the fluid sounds of that evening, but her heart took on a rhythm of its own, twirling like the feathery seeds of dandelion caught in an Alpine storm.

How did Max know she was hidden behind the pines?

When she peeked between the branches, he was looking straight at her. Reluctantly, or at least attempting to appear reluctant, she stepped out from her haven, into the cast of blue moonlight, Vati's winter coat buttoned over her calico chemise.

Temperatures had dipped to near freezing again, but Max wore a linen shirt, the sleeves rolled up to his elbows. Strength swelled under those sleeves, arms that had rowed a wooden *fuhr* boat around Lake Hallstatt nearly every summer of his seventeen years, carving his muscles like the fallen birch her father liked to shape into benches and chairs.

"What are you doing out here?" he asked, though she should have been the one questioning him. He'd awakened her when he snuck by the cottage she and her father shared in the woods.

At first she'd thought it was Vati who crept by her window, on his way to the tavern, but then, in the beam of light, she'd seen the threads of blond in Max's brown hair, the shovel resting against his shoulder as if it were a rifle readied for battle. She liked to think he'd purposely rustled the branches because he'd missed her these winter months as much as she'd missed him.

"You woke me." Annika took another step toward him. "I didn't know you'd returned from Vienna."

"My parents wanted a holiday."

The Dornbachs visited at Christmastime, but rarely in the spring while Max was studying in *Gymnasium*. Unlike Annika's father, his parents thought an education with books and such was important.

"I'll tell Vati you're home," she said. "He can light the furnace."

"It's not necessary." Max stomped the heel of his boot onto the shovel to remove another pile of earth. She imagined the rust-colored clumps yawning after their hibernation this winter, shivering in the frigid air. "My father already lit it."

She hadn't realized Herr Dornbach could do such things on

his own, but then again, even after living fifteen years—her entire life—on this estate, Annika knew little about Max's parents. Neither Herr nor Frau Dornbach bothered to befriend someone beneath their rank. Certainly not their caretaker's girl.

Annika scanned this knobby plot of land, harbored between the pines. "Why are you digging at night?"

When he shook his head, refusing to trust her with this, her heart wrenched. She'd never told another soul any of his secrets. Not about the dent in Herr Dornbach's motorboat four summers past or the gash in Max's leg that she'd helped wrap or the evening he'd cried when he lost Pascal, the pet fox he'd rescued from the forest.

Pascal now rested peacefully in this piece of earth along with numerous rabbits, four cats, two squirrels, and a goldfinch, each grave marked by a pyramid of stones that Max collected from the cliffs on Hoher Sarstein, the mountain towering over his family's estate.

When they were younger, Annika had helped Max conduct a service for each animal, solemnly crossing herself as they transferred the care for these animals over to *Gott*. Once a laugh slipped from her lips, as they'd been reciting the words from Job.

"But as for me I know that my Redeemer liveth, And at last he will stand upon the earth: And after my skin, even this body, is destroyed, Then without my flesh shall I see God. . . ."

They'd been burying a beetle named Charlie in the dirt, and the thought of this creature standing before a heavenly being, his six spindly legs trembling in awe, made Annika laugh. Looking back, it wasn't funny—irreverent, even—but she was only eight and quite nervous at both the thought of death and the unknowns surrounding the afterlife. All she could see was a frightened Charlie, feeling as small as she would feel under the gaze of the almighty God.

Max hadn't invited her to another funeral since that summer, seven years past. She thought he'd stopped burying his pets, but apparently he'd been burying them in the night, when no one would ridicule him.

She moved closer to the hole. A cloth seed bag rested near the shovel, partially hidden behind Max. "What are you burying?"

"Oh, *Kätzchen*," he said, shaking his head. He'd called her *kitten* since she was in kindergarten. As if she were one of his pets.

Annika's hands balled into fists, and she buried them deep in Vati's pockets. "I am not a kitten."

Max resumed his work. Blade against earth, determined to conquer the soil. When she lifted the bag, he swatted her away. "That's not for you."

"Did you lose another animal?" she asked, still holding the cloth rim. It was heavier than she'd expected.

He shook his head again, this time more slowly. "I fear we're about to lose everything."

This new tone frightened her. "I don't understand."

He scooped out two more mounds of dirt, and she dropped the bag into the hole. Then he pushed the dirt in and smoothed his shovel back and forth over the ground as if he were trying to iron out the wrinkles. "Come along," he finally said, hiking toward the wall of pine trees that separated this plot from Schloss Schwansee, his family's castle.

"What's wrong, Max?"

"The parliament approved our annexation into Germany."

"I know," she replied, glad she was already privy to this bit of news. "Vati is pleased."

"The German Reich is no longer willing to tolerate the suppression of ten million Germans across the border."

That's what Hitler had said on the wireless last month. Salvation was what he promised, the rescue of Austrians who'd been mistreated. *Anschluss*—as he called it—was prohibited by the Treaty of Versailles, but their new Führer didn't seem to be daunted by treaties or the fact that the Austrian chancellor wasn't interested in a union between his country and Germany.

Her father had celebrated the *Anschluss* at the beer hall. He'd fought as a foot soldier in the Great War, and this new union, he thought, not only would revitalize Austria, it was reparation for their empire's bitter losses twenty years ago. This time, Vati said, no one would defeat a unified Germany.

Max stopped at the edge of the trees, light from the castle's windows filtering out onto the lawn, erasing the blue haze of moon. "Your father's pleased because he isn't Jewish."

Annika shrugged. "None of us are Jewish." Except her friend Sarah, but Hitler would hardly concern himself with the Jewish Austrians who lived back in these Alps. Only summer tourists—and the occasional skier—visited their mountains and lake.

Max planted his hands on her shoulders, anchoring them so she couldn't shrug again. She tried to focus on his eyes, but his touch electrified her, a jolt that ricocheted between her fingers, her toes.

"Adolf Hitler isn't a savior. He's the devil incarnate." Max's eyes flashed, the fierce edge in his voice frightening her. "And he won't be satisfied with the devotion of our country, *Kätzchen*. He'll want the hearts of our people, too."

She'd heard the stories about Hitler and his thugs, about the years Hitler stirred up trouble in the streets of Austria, but still she protested. "Hitler's home is in Berlin now."

Max released her shoulders and stepped out from the mantle of pine. "It won't stop him from trying to build his Reich here."

Annika shivered as she followed him toward the cottage she shared with her father, though she tried to pretend that the trembling deep inside her, flaring across her skin, was from the cold. She'd never heard Max speak of politics before. Usually he talked about his animals or school or the music he loved in Vienna. She, his devoted audience, listened to his stories every summer and in the winter weeks when he came to ski.

To her right, the gray slate on the castle's turrets glowed in the moonlight. Back in the seventeenth century, the owner of the local salt mine had built this place as a fortress between the mountains and the lake. The upkeep and expansions kept her father and now her employed year round, though one day she dreamed of being the mistress of this castle, sipping tea in the parlor instead of scrubbing its floors.

Max tucked his shovel into the large shed where Vati kept his tools and equipment. "You'd best go home. Before your father begins to worry."

Annika dug her hands into the coat pockets. "I'm glad you're here."

"It's only for a day."

"Still, I'm glad."

He lifted her right hand from the warmth of her pocket and pressed his lips against it. "Don't let one of Hitler's men steal your heart, Annika."

He released her hand, but it stayed before her, suspended in the air.

Shouting erupted inside the main house, Herr Dornbach swearing. And then the voice of Frau Dornbach stole through the open library window, yelling back at him. Max moved quickly through a side door that led into the castle, and then he closed the window to silence the fight, at least to her ears.

Annika shuffled across the ice-glazed grass, to the lakeshore. Birch benches were scattered across the property, but this bench near the reeds was her favorite.

Sitting, she pulled her arms out of the large sleeves and wrapped them tightly over her chest. Tiny clouds rose with her breath, each one climbing in the air as if it wanted to scale the mountain ridge that curled around the lake, a glorious sea creature guarding its den.

Moonlight shimmered on the water, and several lights flickered on the other side of the lake in the village called Hallstatt. When they were children, she and Max had dreamed about one day swimming across this expanse of lake together, racing to see who would win. They'd never done it, of course. Vati wouldn't have cared if she tried, but Frau Dornbach took great care in keeping her only son safe.

Why had Herr Dornbach been yelling tonight? The arguing between him and Frau Dornbach had escalated this past summer, their words escaping through the windows and finding Annika in the garden or hammering nails into a board as she helped Vati build a bench or fix a wall.

Herr Dornbach yelled at Vati last summer as well, though usually because Vati didn't arrive early enough for work, too sluggish after a night in the beer hall.

Sometimes she wondered if her parents would have fought like the Dornbachs if her mother had lived. Or perhaps Vati wouldn't drink if her mother were still alive. Sometimes her father still called out to Kathrin—her mother—in his dreams, his sorrow a storm that shook the cottage rafters and pine walls.

When her father woke, he often called Annika's name, but only because he wanted her to bring black coffee to chase away the fog in his brain.

She closed her eyes, the cold settling over her face as her thoughts returned to the young man who'd been digging in the forest. If only Max could have seen her with her hair properly curled, dressed in the pale-pink summer frock she'd sewn for his return, instead of lumped up inside Vati's ragged coat.

Her gaze wandered back over her shoulder to the light on the ground floor of the castle, to the library where Max enjoyed reading one of the many books that trimmed its shelves. Was he looking out at the lake like her? Or perhaps he was missing whatever he'd buried.

The thought of buried bones made her stomach roll, but these animals were important to Max, so they were important to her—just as important as keeping his secrets.

A breeze rustled through the branches, stirring up the depths of this lake before her and the longings in her heart. And her mind wandered back to Max's hands on her shoulders, his lips pressed against her hand.

No one else could steal her heart because it had already been stolen. And nothing could ever change her love for Max Dornbach.

Nothing at all.

CHAPTER 2

CALLIE

People tuck the strangest things into the pages of their books. Dried flowers. Birth certificates. Twenty-dollar bills. One time I found a baby's tooth crammed down the spine of *Ginger Pye*. I'm not entirely certain what type of person stores a tooth in a children's book—perhaps a boy or girl saving it for the tooth fairy.

The owner of a book, I've discovered, can be as intriguing as the author. And owners often lose more than someone else's story when they give away their books. Sometimes they give away a part of their story as well.

My story is the same as any other in that no one owns it except me. And it's filled with threads of achievements and regrets, seemingly random bits of plot that meander across the pages of my everyday even as I sell other people's stories, the sort neatly sandwiched between two covers with a spine that's either stiff or slightly worn, smelling of musty leather and ancient ink.

Below my bedroom—a bedroom where, at this very moment, I'm supposed to be asleep—is the bookstore owned by my sister and me. Some nights, like this one, sleep is fleeting as my mind tumbles the unpolished pieces of my story over and over, trying to smooth out the edges.

When I realize there'll be no respite from the tumbling, I decide to seek the company of friends and their secrets. A mug of chamomile tea in hand, I slip down the back steps of my loft apartment.

More than fifty years ago, Charlotte Trent opened Magic Balloon Bookshop on the ground floor of this colonial brick building, next to her husband's ice cream and soda shop so kids could enjoy a treat along with a new or used book. The Trents were never able to birth children, so they welcomed an entire village into this store as their own, including my sister and me.

When I was younger, I'd spend hours here after school, reading books that took me to the faraway places I longed to see. Now, as a bona fide adult, I can go down and read whenever I like, including these late-night hours while everyone else in our small town is asleep.

While some might proclaim the death of the print book, every day dozens of kids still tuck themselves away with a book on beanbags or in the hidden spaces of the two-story castle that my sister's carpenter husband, Ethan, built for us. The kids of Mount Vernon and the surrounding county now know me as Story Girl, a role I've embraced since my fifteenth birthday, when Charlotte gave me a pair of red-striped socks and a copy of L. M. Montgomery's novel about a girl who entertains a group of children with the most fascinating tales, some true, some not.

Charlotte's gift changed my life in more ways than one. In *The Story Girl*, the children find a picture of God portrayed as a fierce, cruel man and take this picture to a minister, crying as they ask if that is what God truly looks like—a face of hatred instead of love.

The minister's reply is simple, but his words affected me in a profound way.

"God is infinitely more beautiful and loving and tender and kind than anything we can imagine of Him."

In my own tears, a new picture of God began to form, a smile on His face instead of an angry scowl. Montgomery's words, the truth ingrained in them, stitched themselves into my teenage mind. God wasn't cruel like my own father had been. He loved me, Calisandra Anne Randall, a girl who craved beauty and kindness and, more than anything, a family who cared about me.

After reading *The Story Girl*, I realized that I wanted to spend the rest of my life working with books, helping change and expand the perspective of others through the power of a great story.

A few years later, Charlotte gave my sister, Brianna, and me another present. After she retired, Charlotte gifted us with the keys to her bookstore and then she moved out of the apartment over the shop, into a condo east of town. I still have my striped socks. And a decade after Charlotte handed over the keys, Brie and I still own this shop.

A cramped office in the back of the store hosts Charlotte's antique desk—a giant walnut piece with carved braiding around the edges, fancy Queen Anne legs, and iron pulls on the eight drawers. The desktop is covered with papers, a computer cord, and paper clips, along with two pictures of my sister with Ethan and their four-year-old twins, Owen and Oscar. Two boys who I'm pretty sure worked together to hang the moon with their dad's hammer and nails.

Books line shelves above the desk and spill over the edges of cardboard boxes on the carpeted floor, filling in all the spaces of this room. The bottom desk drawer holds the thick album that Brie and I have been compiling since we took over the store, the forgotten items left in the stacks of used books sold here.

With one swoop, I push aside the clutter on the desktop and open the album to see if Brie has added anything new to our collection. Stored inside the fifty or so vinyl sleeves are letters, theater tickets, and all sorts of pictures—formal ones dating back a hundred years alongside Polaroid prints and more contemporary pictures of birthday parties, beach trips, and one of a family visiting a medieval church somewhere in Europe. But there's nothing new inside.

Brie is two years younger than me, and she's the chief book collector and manager of our little shop. I'm part-time sales clerk, website manager, blogger, and Story Girl, though my name should probably be Story Lady since I'm fast approaching my thirtieth birthday. The income for all the above is miserly, but my apartment comes with the job, and I have a bicycle and two good legs to pedal wherever I need to go in this town. And if I want anything else—I lower the voice of my mind as if I might offend these walls—I can buy it online.

I'm the curious one of the Randall girls—Curious Callie is what Brie used to call me after our favorite little monkey, though my curiosity is fueled by purpose these days. I research and post articles about children's authors and then spend my free time updating the expansive Lost & Found section on our Magic Balloon Bookshop website.

When Brie and I first took over the bookshop, I tried to find the previous owners of the bits and pieces we discovered in our collection of used books by contacting whoever sold us the book. Now when we find something, I post the item online instead.

The postings generate a lot of traffic from other curiosity seekers like me, but in the past eight years, no one has ever emailed or called to collect a letter or photograph or that tooth I found in *Ginger Pye*. Still I post, driven by the hope that one day I might actually reunite someone with a significant item they've misplaced. Restore what was lost to its original owner.

At least once a month Brie and I also find money hidden in the pages of a book, but we keep mum on the cash lest we have a host of people calling to claim it. While kids and adults alike often view their books as safety-deposit boxes, my sister and I have started a real savings account with this extra money in a bank down the street. It's our own secret stash, more than two thousand dollars now accumulating interest.

I jump at the sound of rustling behind me. Inkspot, our resident cat, hops onto the desk and knocks his tail into my tea, the drops splattering across the vinyl pages of the album. A swift whisk of my sleeve wipes up the liquid, and then I pet his white fur and the perfectly formed black splotch between his ears.

Sometimes I wonder if he's down here at night with his super vision, reading about poor Tom Kitten or perhaps the Cat in the Hat. Like me, he's found refuge inside these walls.

Some books, I think, can be like cats. No matter where they're sent, they have this uncanny ability to find their way back home.

Turning, I lean over and lift a hardcover book from a recently delivered box. It's a newly printed edition of *Djibi*, the tragic story of a cat who liked adventures.

I ordered four books to read as I research for my next monthly post about a children's author, this one an Austrian man named Felix Salten who wrote in the 1920s and '30s. Salten wrote stories about a variety of animals, some of the creatures pursued by hunters. Sadly, as a Jewish man, he became the hunted one when the Nazis took over Austria.

"You can read this one later." I nudge *Djibi* toward Inkspot, tapping the cover illustration of a gray cat. "Assuming you know how to read."

He doesn't mew in response, but he eyes the cover.

Under *Djibi* are three other recent editions of Salten's books, all of them translated into English. *The Hound of Florence. Fifteen Rabbits. Florian: The Emperor's Stallion.* After I publish my blog on Salten, I'll put all these books on our shelves to sell.

A much smaller box sits beside the one with the Salten stories. The tape is dangling off the edge, and I peel it back to remove another of his stories. Instead of a new copy, this worn, early version has the ruby-red sketch of a deer embossed on its cloth cover, the deer's eyes seeming to search for a friend.

Bambi: A Life in the Woods.

A 1931 edition, according to Roman numerals on the copyright page, printed in Vienna. It's a classic I've read before in English, a story that bears little resemblance to Disney's version. I didn't order this book, but Brie knows about my featured post for July. Perhaps she's planning to surprise me with an early edition for my birthday.

Nothing sparks my imagination more than the discovery of an old book in any language. Like an abandoned house, I wonder at the many stories it could tell of its journey, beginning with its birth in an Austrian printing shop almost ninety years ago.

The clock on my phone reads a quarter past two, but I'm still wide awake so I wander out into the bookstore, the old *Bambi* edition under my arm, and settle into a blue twill beanbag sized for an adult.

Light from the streetlamps filters past the display of books in the front windows, streaming between the shelves in this room. I flip on the bronze sconce high above the castle gate and glance across the shop. Colorful Japanese lights bubble above the front window, and curved bookshelves ripple like sea waves across the carpeted floor, around the dozen or so beanbags that stand like stones in the tide. A hot-air balloon, pieced together from papier-mâché, dangles above the castle, beside the loft. To my left is the front counter with its antique cash register alongside a modern iPad and white Square.

When Charlotte first opened this store to supply readers with French, German, and English resources, she thought it vastly important that children read books that would grow and expand their minds, stories they could cling to as friends when others weren't friendly. Brie and I followed suit when we took ownership, only buying books for the store that we'd let our own children read. Or read eventually. I don't have any kids yet, and Brie's twins prefer picture books over ones with actual words.

In the back corner of the shop is a platform with a puppet theater. I'm no good at puppets, but I sit on that platform every Saturday for my weekly appearance as Story Girl to read the brilliant words of authors such as Dr. Seuss, Robert Munsch, and Doreen Cronin. Lately I've taken to wearing a cherry-red cape to match Charlotte's striped socks since my younger audience members are convinced I'm somehow related to WordGirl from PBS. The youngest kids also think I can fly.

I've never bothered to explain that the only time I've ever flown is in my dreams, on the nights I'm able to sleep.

Inkspot settles in beside my beanbag on a pink square of rug, and I open the cover of *Bambi*. Inside is an inscription, written in beautiful script. Thanks to Charlotte, I can read some German.

Annika Knopf
Schloss Schwansee, 1932

I push down one of the corners, bent from wear, as my brain tumbles the words into translation. *The Castle of Swan Lake.*

Underneath the name of the castle and date is another inscription, simple and yet deeply profound.

Mit all meine Liebe, Mama.

My fingers against the page, I can almost feel the lingering heat from this mother's love, and my thoughts travel back to the woman who birthed me and then thought it witty to name me Calisandra, after herself and the abbreviation of her favorite state—a woman who moved to Santa Monica when I was two and left me behind with the man who never got around to proposing marriage. A man who died fourteen years later. Sandra Dermott friended me on Facebook while I was in college. She has a family in California now, four children whom she clearly adores.

What happened to the girl who once owned this book in my hands? Did she treasure her mother's gift for the rest of her life, or give it away?

The pages are smudged, worn. In the first section are illustrations of Bambi and Faline, and then pictures of the stag and Man.

The book was written a decade before Hitler came to power, but Hitler, I'd read in my research, amplified the anti-Semitism already rampant in Europe. Perhaps Salten saw the scribblings of persecution long before they coated the walls.

Turning the pages, I begin to notice something different about this version of *Bambi*. In black ink, under the original German print, are extra lines on every other page as if someone decided to add to the story. I recognize many of the German words in the story, but none in the handwritten lines.

My eyes finally heavy, I close the book and lower it to the carpet.

Brie and I have found plenty of books marked up in the past, but I've never seen handwriting like this at the bottom of the pages, as if the words were part of the original story.

Who marked up this valuable edition, almost a hundred years old? An aspiring author, perhaps? Or had someone tried to leave a message hidden in the pages?

My skin tingles at the thought.

Charlotte's ability to read German has faded in her twilight years, but it's not gone. Tomorrow, after my appearance as Story Girl, I'll ask her to help me translate these lines. Perhaps there's a simple explanation for the additions.

My hand slips down to find Inkspot's fur, but it lands on the *Bambi* book instead. And I fall asleep right there, dreaming of old books and balloons and cats who like to fly.

CHAPTER 3

"'This is George.'" I hold up the picture book so every child seated on the carpet can see. "'He was a good little monkey, and always very curious.'"

I slowly turn the page as I tell the story of the monkey and the mysterious man with the yellow hat, on their way to camp in the wilderness. The man warns George not to wander off, but when he turns around, it's too late. George is already gone.

My audience scoots closer, several dozen children anxiously waiting to hear what happens to the monkey they love. And I, in my red cape and silly socks, unfold the story for them.

In this day of unlimited screen time, countless games and movies, I've often wondered if this next generation of kids will be the one to turn their back on books. So far I've seen no evidence of a rebellion. They come in droves to the store and—usually—listen without interruption. Perhaps it's a testament to their parents' love of the written word.

After I finish George's adventure, one of the younger boys in the front row raises his hand, whipping it around like a flag caught in a storm.

"Yes, Michael?"

"I'm wearing new underpants," he announces confidently, as if everyone will be just as excited as he is by this news. "Spider-Man."

I quickly reach for the crate where I store my reading books. "Very good."

He stands, turning to the children behind him. "Do you want to see them?"

Thankfully his mother rushes forward before I have to intervene. "No one wants to see your underwear," she says in one of those mortified mom whispers meant for a crowd.

I march my fingers quickly across the book spines in the crate and pick up one that I hope will redirect, ASAP. We have ten minutes left, plenty of time for Dr. Seuss. "Anyone ever hear about the fox who wears socks?" I lift one of my legs for a visual of my striped pair.

A few of them raise their hands.

I open the book and repeat by memory. "'Fox. Socks. Box. Knox. Knox in box. Fox in socks.'"

The front door chimes, and I'm hoping it's Charlotte so I can ask her to help me translate the lines in the *Bambi* book. But when I glance up, I choke down a groan. Kathleen Faulkner and her six-year-old son, Jack, walk into the store.

Focus—back to the blue-socked fox in my hands, my words slurring a bit as I continue with the story.

Kathleen seems like a perfectly nice woman, and her son is

adorable—but I am a victim of the smallish-town curse where every resident's path seems to intersect everyone else's at one point or another. And I can't very well turn away the wife and stepson of my ex-fiancé from a reading of Dr. Seuss. I'm only grateful that not once in the past two years, to my knowledge, has Scott Faulkner stepped through the front door.

Jack squeezes into a space beside my feet, Kathleen joining the lineup of adults curled around the outskirts.

"'Let's do chicks with bricks and clocks, sir. Let's do tricks with bricks and blocks, sir.'"

"You messed it up," Owen, my nephew, shouts. Then he grins as if he's done my audience a great service by correcting me.

Unfortunately, the tongue-twisting in this book only gets worse from here, and I've lost my momentum.

I start to read the next page about stacking the chicks and bricks and blocks, but it's a disaster. Perhaps I should ask if Michael has anything else he'd like to share.

"I hate to interrupt," my lovely sister says from behind the parental wall, "but I have it on good authority that chocolate-chip cookies taste best when they're warm, and I've just taken a batch out of the oven."

With those words, the fox and his socks are forgotten as my audience surges around the castle steps, up to the counter with the cookies and hot chocolate that Brie has waiting for them every Saturday. Next week, I'll take a mulligan on the book about the quirky fox.

"Have I told you lately how much I love you?" I say, slipping beside my sister. About two minutes have passed since she made the call, but only crumbs remain on the ceramic cookie tray.

Brie collects the paper cups that line the counter and wipes her hands on her polka-dotted apron. Her brown shoulder-length hair is newly streaked with lime green. "I've got your back, Callie."

"You are the best of sisters."

As Brie pours several more cups of chocolate, handing them out to the children, I glance around the busy store until I find Kathleen and her son in the loft, snuggled together on a couch. Surely she knows that Scott once proposed marriage to me, but the fact that he was seeing both of us at the same time in the weeks before our wedding day doesn't seem to bother her in the least. Unlike me, who can't seem to move past the betrayal. The colossal failure in the spotlight of our town.

Two years come and gone, and I'm still stuck, wondering about what might have been while my ex-fiancé has clearly moved on.

"I wish you could let it go," Brie whispers, and I worry for a moment that she might break out into song.

"It only bothers me when I see Kathleen around town." And when I'm trying to ignore the bump swelling across her abdomen.

"The wounds of the heart take the longest to heal," she says.

"But one day they heal, right?"

"You just have to meet the right man."

I swipe one of the remaining cups of hot chocolate and step back before she starts listing the available men in our church and across Knox County.

When I was in my early twenties, I longed for a husband and children to love, a family who loved me back. But that would require dating again, and I have zero desire to expose the fragments of my heart and past to another man. I haven't gone out with anyone since Scott, at least not more than one date and only at Brie's insistence. Brie thinks a good man will steal my heart one day, but I doubt any decent thief would want the shattered pieces of it now.

Brie checks out two customers, slipping their books into white bags designed with a bouquet of balloons. Kathleen and Jack are moving toward the top floor of the castle.

"I'm done talking about men," I whisper after the customers leave.

Her lavender-glossed lips pucker. "That's good because I was planning to ask you about the box you broke into last night."

I lean back against the papered wall. "Technically, it was already open."

She sighs. "I wanted to give you that book for your birthday."

"I promise to be surprised."

Her head tilts slightly to the right as she assesses me. "At least you'll be surprised when I give you your other gift."

"You don't have to give me anything else, Brie." A little boy whizzes past, holding a book like a paper airplane in his hands. Sometimes I wonder how we make any profit at all. "Where exactly did you get that *Bambi* book?"

"From a dealer in Idaho."

I sip the overly sweet chocolate. "I found something inside it."

Her eyebrows rise. "Money?"

"No."

"More pictures, then?"

"Wait here." When I return to the counter, I open the worn cover for my sister and point down at Annika Knopf's name.

She shrugs. "We find names in most of our used books."

"But we've never found this." I turn to the third page. "There are extra lines on some of these pages. The handwriting looks almost like the font in the printed text."

As Brie examines the copy, I watch Kathleen's son emerge from the slide at the bottom of the castle. His mother descends the spiral stairs to meet him, the bump under her shirt clearly visible as she reaches for his hand. Jealousy rears somewhere deep inside me, peeking its ugly head up over the wall that circles my heart.

"Did you translate any of this?" Brie asks, and my gaze falls back on the page.

"I tried, but I couldn't make out the words."

She hands me the book. "I wonder where Schloss Schwansee is located."

"I couldn't find it online."

"So you're off to Charlotte's . . ."

"This afternoon, if you don't need me here."

"Have at it," Brie says before greeting another customer. Her interest in the German notes has come and gone, but me, I'll obsess until I know what they say.

Annika Knopf, I suspect, has probably passed away by now, but every time we receive a book with something unusual inside, I want to reunite the item and book with the child who once owned it, as if I could return a piece of what I hoped was a happy childhood. In this case, perhaps Annika's descendants would be intrigued by whatever she wrote inside this book. In my story-world optimism, I can help provide a happy ending for their search.

Then again, it's entirely possible that Annika's descendants sold this book even though they knew about the handwriting. The money might have been more important than preserving a family heirloom.

Kathleen reaches for her son's hand, and before I can escape to the back room, they are beside me. Jack in his pressed shorts, button-down shirt, and a clip-on tie. Kathleen in white capris, a sage-green blouse, and heeled sandals. I, on the other hand, resemble Raggedy Ann, except my curly hair is light brown and I'm wearing black-framed glasses with my striped socks and blue sundress.

"I'm sorry we were late for story time," Kathleen says, sounding genuine with her apology.

"No worries. I'll be here again next Saturday."

Jack eyes the cape tied around my neck. "Are you Superwoman?"

I swallow my sigh, deciding in that moment that Superwoman is better than Raggedy Ann. "Perhaps."

"I like your socks," he says.

"Thanks. I like your tie."

A stack of new books in their bag, Kathleen and Jack walk out of the store hand in hand, headed north toward the roundabout—known in our town as the square—where the annual Memorial Day festivities are about to begin.

Watching Kathleen through the window, my thoughts drift again to how different my life would be if Scott hadn't met her. I'd be married like Brie, perhaps even have a child of my own. No wandering around a bookstore in the midnight hours for me. I'd be content in my own home, with my own children, not trying to reunite lost items with their owners.

Drums thunder in the distance, followed by the crashing of cymbals. In seconds the bookstore empties, our customers pouring out onto the sidewalk as they wait for the bands and floats to roll by, the candy raining down from the sky.

Inkspot curls around my ankles, and I tuck the old *Bambi* book under my arm to pick up the cat. Together we watch the grand marshal, the mayor of our town, marching toward us, the high school band and color guard close behind.

In our celebration, we remember together those who served our country around the world, those who lived to tell their stories and those who died fighting against tyranny. And we remember with hope for peace against the tragedy of war, hope that none of my Saturday-morning kids will have to leave their families to fight.

CHAPTER 4

MAX

VIENNA, AUSTRIA
MARCH 1938

Gray cobblestones pressed into Max Dornbach's knees as he knelt in an alley near Heldenplatz and scratched Frederica, the stray tabby cat he'd befriended, behind her ears. A peaceful ruler, her name meant. And right now, they desperately needed *der Frieden* in Austria.

Frederica liked it when he scratched her ears, but even more, she liked sharing whatever he brought for her in the rucksack that held his lunch and books for *Gymnasium*, a rucksack he carried even on days like today when the schools were closed. She mewed when he retrieved the strip of bacon along with a chunk of mild Drautaler cheese, devouring it rapidly from his palm.

He could almost hear his mother's voice, scolding him for feeding a stray, but secretly she liked animals as much as he did.

She wasn't in Vienna to scold him anyway. Instead of driving back to the city last night, she'd opted to stay at their summer estate for another week.

A roar erupted from the heart of Vienna, rippling out into the corners of its districts. Crowds had gathered on the lofty road called Ringstrasse, buzzing like a thousand hornets around a nest. Many of them waved flags and belted out the lyrics of a Nazi anthem as if they'd been National Socialists all along.

"For the last time, the call to arms is sounded!"

"For the fight, we all stand prepared!"

Freedom, the Viennese sang—they were finally free from bondage. As if they'd been caged up.

Max's stomach turned at the thought of Nazis descending upon their beautiful city today. Vienna's elegant streets, with their budding tulips and gilded facades, darkened by the shadow of Adolf Hitler, the old cobblestones contaminated by the boots of his henchmen.

Dr. Weiss had sent Max a telegram while the Dornbachs were at Lake Hallstatt, asking him to visit after the parade. If only he could retrieve the man's daughter as well and retreat to the lake.

Much had changed in Austria in the past four weeks. Luzi Weiss and her family, no matter how much Max begged, would never receive an invitation to the Dornbachs' summer home, even if Frau Weiss and Max's mother were old friends. Dr. Weiss's father was Jewish and so were both of Frau Weiss's parents.

This hatred of Jewish people already ran deep in Vienna, but the Nazi Party and their blatant anti-Semitism had been banned in Austria until last month. Now with Chancellor Schuschnigg's arrest, everything had tipped on its head.

Much of Vienna was celebrating this new alliance with Germany, the new Führer a savior of sorts. As the general director of the Mercur Bank, Max's father was expected to celebrate as well—front-row seats for the Dornbach family when Hitler ascended to Hofburg Palace for his victory speech today.

Max refused his father's offer for a seat of honor, but he'd promised to attend the parade. School had been canceled, businesses closed, so Austrians could crowd the streets as they waited for the Führer to make his grand entry. A much different entry than when a penniless Hitler had attempted to attend the art academy here thirty years ago.

"Stay away from the parade," he told Frederica as he brushed the dust off the knees of his trousers. "Too many stomping feet."

Max moved toward the boulevard, standing in the back of the crowd, trying to block out the rancid chant in a city that prided itself on beautiful music.

Couldn't they see that fighting alongside Hitler would imprison them all?

"He's coming," someone shouted.

Cheering replaced the song, and his heart sank further. A woman next to him began crying, joy instead of sorrow streaming down her cheeks. This new chancellor was worshiped in these streets as if he were a god. But a god of what? What virtue did he bring?

Reconciliation, some might say. Hitler was able to verbalize like no one else the anger many Austrians already had toward the Jews, a hatred that had been boiling for centuries.

About eight hundred years ago, Jewish refugees had arrived in this city, and over the centuries, they'd been repeatedly expelled, welcomed back, and then expelled again, their synagogues burned as they fled. Not until the last century were Jewish residents finally given full Austrian citizenship. Many Jewish families had garnered wealth and prestige among their fellow Austrians in these years, but not everyone celebrated their achievements. Many, the jealous ones, wanted to expel them again.

A motorcade of open cars crawled up the boulevard with uniformed men marching solemnly beside the vehicles. And then Hitler was there, in the front seat of a Mercedes-Benz, grand marshal of the parade with his black hair slicked back under a brown hat, an awning of a toothbrush mustache over his lips, the sleeve on his overcoat outstretched as he saluted the soldiers lining the streets. His mouth was set in a firm line below the mustache, a hairline crack in the face of stone.

Austrian hands waved in unison as he passed, hailing high even as they sank low to worship the German Führer who'd promised salvation for Austria.

"Salute, Max."

Max glanced over his shoulder to see Ernst Schmid, his chest drowning in a black suit coat as if he were going to the orchestra instead of a street rally. Ernst was a year younger, still more boy than man with his short hair sticking out in all directions in spite of a generous coating of hair oil.

Max didn't reply, but his arms stiffened at his sides, hands in his pockets.

Ernst's arm was fixed forward like the others, but his eyes remained on Max. "Heil Hitler," he barked as Hitler saluted the crowd.

Max still didn't move. The motorcade passed by, and the crowd followed after it, clamoring toward Heldenplatz to hear Hitler speak.

"Heil Hitler," Ernst repeated, this time to Max.

Max's hands burrowed deeper into his pockets. "Heil Austria."

Ernst stayed beside him as people swarmed toward the plaza, and he eyed the rucksack slung over Max's shoulder before glancing back out at the street. "It's time for you to grow up, Max."

"I don't need to cling to a man like Adolf Hitler to make me feel important."

Ernst sniffed, appropriately offended. "Why didn't you salute our Führer?"

"You're not my superior, Ernst, and he isn't my Führer."

"He is all of our Führer." Ernst's rigid chin inched up. "And in time, I will be superior to you."

Max shook his head, disgusted. The man was the son of the Dornbachs' former housekeeper in Vienna. Frau Schmid had been released about three years ago for stealing, but Ernst had hated Max long before his mother's dismissal. Ever since they were children, Ernst had tried to torment Max, stealing things that were his. Max wondered still if Frau Schmid's purported theft had really been Ernst's doing, his mother taking the fall.

"Perhaps one day you will salute for the sake of Fräulein Weiss," Ernst said, sounding as if the thought gave him great pleasure.

Max wished he could slug Ernst right here, as he'd often wished when they were younger. Though he was vocal about his distaste of anyone with Jewish blood, Ernst was obsessed with Luzi. Max had seen him watching her at the Dornbach parties, when Ernst was supposed to be helping Frau Schmid serve the food, but it wasn't admiration in his eyes. He looked more like a bird of prey ready to attack.

Ernst would probably be first in line to become a member of

the notorious *Schutzstaffel.* Germany's bullies. Hopefully Hitler would send him far away to train for the SS.

"Yes, Max." Ernst clipped his shoulder. "You will salute, for the Fräulein if nothing else."

"I'll never salute," he said.

⁂

A footbridge crossed the Wien near Hietzing, and Max followed the street over the river, into this southern district of Vienna. Luzi and her family lived in a coral-painted villa; Luzi's father practiced medicine on the ground level, and their family lived in the flat above.

Music spilling from Luzi's violin streamed out their window, pooling over the street and the park behind their home, beckoning him forward. He could imagine the gentle sway of her body as she bore the weight of her music, cradling her violin. Then the passion in her face, her lips pursed in concentration when she brushed the strings with her bow made from Pernambuco, wood taken from the heart of the tree.

Luzi didn't just play music. She *was* music, embodying a song from her chin down to the black heels she wore for every performance. The same heels her mother once wore when she performed.

Before he saw Luzi, he must speak to her father.

The door to Dr. Weiss's office was unlocked, and when Max stepped inside, the violin music drifted down from the back staircase, into the office. Dr. Weiss looked up from the shelf he was rearranging by his desk. He was about forty years old, a few years younger than Max's parents, but his dark hair had begun to thin. In a frame above the desk, the only decor in the room, was his medical diploma from the University of Vienna.

Max had rarely been here when there weren't patients crowding the front, but with the parade today, he suspected that most men and women were either waiting for Hitler's arrival or hiding out in their homes.

"Thank you for coming," Dr. Weiss said.

Max leaned back against a post. "I hid the things you gave me. They are—"

The doctor waved his hands. "Don't tell me."

"Safe, Herr Doktor. That's all I was going to say."

"Where are your parents?" Dr. Weiss asked.

"Mother stayed behind at the lake, and I suspect my father has forgotten all about me by now."

"One of my patients—the Nazis tore apart his house, looking for his family's jewelry."

"It is safe," Max assured him.

"Already I have more things." Dr. Weiss opened his medicine cabinet and took out dozens of glass bottles. "They arrived yesterday."

Max held up his rucksack. "Will they fit in here?"

"I believe so."

The doctor glanced toward the window at the front of his office before removing a burlap bag from its hiding place behind the jars. He slid it underneath the remaining food and a schoolbook that Max brought with him in case anyone asked why he needed the rucksack.

"Did your family attend the parade?" Max asked.

"Frau Weiss would never celebrate the arrival of that *schlimm* man." He'd never heard Dr. Weiss call Hitler by any name other than evil. "I was required to go, but I didn't stay long." He pounded his chest. "In here I'm not celebrating."

"Nor am I." Max looked at the ceiling. After a short pause, the music started again. "Will Frau Weiss let me see her?"

A smile slipped across Dr. Weiss's face. "If you inquire nicely, Max. Like a house cat instead of a lion."

Nothing seemed to irritate Frau Weiss more than someone, particularly Max, stepping between Luzi and her violin. "You won't ask for me?"

"Miriam will do as she sees fit."

He hadn't spoken to Frau Weiss about his intentions, but Dr. Weiss knew. One day soon, if Luzi would have him, he planned to marry her.

He strung the strap of the heavy rucksack over his shoulder and climbed the steps in the foyer to the second floor. Nina, the housemaid, answered his second knock, her knee propped as a barrier against the edge. Through the slat, he could see her graying hair pulled tight in a bun, the blue plaid apron over her dress.

"Hello, Herr Dornbach," she said, but she didn't open the door any wider.

Behind her were two upholstered chairs and a couch in the sitting room, but no one was seated there. "I'd like to speak with Frau Weiss."

"One moment." Nina slid the bolt across the door as if he might try to break down the door.

When Nina returned, she opened the door wide enough for Max to squeeze inside and directed him into the sitting room. His gaze trailed toward the hallway as he listened to Luzi's violin. A private concert, he imagined, just for him.

"What does your father say about the *Anschluss*?" Frau Weiss asked as she stepped into the room, her waved hair skimming the collar of her starched white shirt. Suddenly the papered walls surrounding them felt more like a boxing ring.

Max straightened in his chair, trying to appear as if he weren't preparing for a fight. "He doesn't talk to me about such things."

Frau Weiss sighed. "We will continue on here, minding our own business."

Max feared what would happen, though, when others started minding their business as well. "I've come to see Luzi."

Frau Weiss shook her head. "She's practicing for the Opera Ball."

"That's not for two more months!" He sounded more like a lion now, but Frau Weiss infuriated him. He and Luzi had grown up as friends, but for the past year, her mother had thwarted every attempt he made to see Luzi outside a formal social engagement, as if he might harm her.

"She needs every waking minute to prepare, and you, Max, will only distract her."

"Just a few minutes," he begged. "Please."

The door at the opposite side of the sitting room opened, the private staircase leading up from the office. Dr. Weiss joined them in the ring, a stethoscope draped over his white lab coat. "I believe what Max meant to say was that he has the utmost respect for Luzi's talent and that he is kindly requesting to spend five minutes encouraging her in her endeavors, not distracting her."

Frau Weiss glanced between the men, and Max attempted to smile in the kindest way possible so that Luzi's mother didn't think he was a cad who expected to get everything he pleased. Or a man who would misuse her daughter's heart.

A baby's cry broke through the music, hijacking the beauty of Luzi's song. It was Marta, Luzi's only sibling.

"Nina?" Frau Weiss called toward the kitchen.

The housemaid peeked her head through the door, nodding. "I'll get her."

Frau Weiss turned back to Max. "Five minutes," she said sharply.

Max thanked both Frau and Dr. Weiss before rushing down the hallway. Near the end of it, he stepped into the library, a room devoted to both music and books. Luzi stood beside a tall window, the violin fixed between her jaw and shoulder as she played, her ash-brown hair swept back in a loose chignon.

The stand before her was layered with music sheets, but instead of reading the music, her gaze was focused on the park behind the apartment as if she could will its flowers to bloom.

Their city might be unraveling, but Max was content right here. "Hello," he said quietly, not wanting to frighten her.

Stepping away from the window, she lowered her bow, but the violin remained cradled over her arm when she smiled at him. Her eyes were a pale green, the color of spring. "You are here."

"Indeed."

She gently placed the violin in its case. "How did you convince Mutti to let you in?"

"Your father convinced her for me."

"Ah . . ."

"Five minutes is all she gave us, but it's enough for today."

How could anyone hate someone as beautiful and talented as Luzi Weiss, no matter her heritage? For that matter, how could anyone hate another person because of their ancestry?

If only he could scoop Luzi into his arms and steal her away to the lake, hide her from men like Ernst Schmid.

"Did you attend the parade?" she asked.

"Yes, so my father can tell whoever he must that his son was there."

She sighed. "I wish I could go outside with you, if only for an hour or two."

"I'll ask your mother."

When Luzi shook her head, a soft strand of hair fell forward across her white blouse. "Mother thinks only of the music."

His fingers drummed against his leg, aching to brush that strand back over her shoulder, but he reached for her hand instead. "I think only of you."

She blushed.

"One day soon we must leave this city."

"My parents will never let me go."

A picture ran through Max's mind of him and Luzi hand in hand, husband and wife, taking a train to Czechoslovakia or south to Italy. Far away from Hitler and all those who seemed to worship him.

"I have a friend who can make papers for us," he whispered. "A wedding certificate and passports for Herr and Frau Dornbach, married this year."

Luzi glanced toward the door before focusing on him again. "Father has started making inquiries for our family."

"To emigrate?"

She nodded. "Don't tell anyone."

"I'll accompany you—"

"Away with you now," Frau Weiss interrupted them as she stepped into the room, carrying Marta. The baby's cheeks were red and streaked with her tears. "Luzia must practice."

Max slowly released her hand before turning toward Frau Weiss. "It hasn't been five minutes."

"Clearly you are not a musician, Max."

"No." He smiled. "But I have the deepest appreciation for the violin."

Luzi laughed and then quickly choked back the laughter when her mother stamped her foot.

"You shall hear her at the ball."

He waited a moment, hoping that Luzi would contradict her mother, but her eyes were focused on the music stand.

Baby Marta squirmed in Frau Weiss's arms. "On your way now," the woman said, shooing Max again. He glanced back at Luzi. She'd placed her bow on the strings, preparing to play.

He lingered by the door, hoping to hear Luzi's voice one more time.

"May I hold her?" Luzi asked her mother.

"Another hour, and then you can rest."

The memory of her violin trailed Max through the streets as he turned toward Vienna's old town. What would it be like to move with Luzi and her family to a place like England or America or even South America, where other European Jews had gone? A place where Luzi and her family would be safe?

They would have to leave soon. He would be eighteen in December, the age of conscription. Like so many students in his city, he'd been planning to join the Austrian Army to fight against the invasion of Nazi Germany, but their army never shot a single bullet to ward off Hitler.

Max would never salute, and he would never fight for that man.

CHAPTER 5

ANNIKA

Two aspirin and a piece of toast. Annika placed both beside the percolator of coffee as Vati's snores rattled down the hall of their cottage, shaking the wood counter, oven, and lump of a refrigerator in their kitchen space.

The snoring thundered louder as she snuck along the hallway and inched open her father's door, the cigarette smoke in his clothing searing her nose. The key to the castle's front door dangled from a hook near his bureau, and she quietly swiped it, folding it into her palm.

As she stepped outside their home, she buttoned her woolen sweater over her white blouse and the waistband of her blue coarse-cotton skirt. Her father's head would be pounding when he finally awoke, like one of his hammers against a nail, and she preferred to be far away when he started shouting her name.

The spring air awakened her swiftly, much more than a cup of coffee ever could, and she heard the song of a bird weaving through the boughs of a conifer. She searched the knobby cone buttons and fur coats of the trees, but the bird evaded her.

Swallows were prevalent in Austria—the one songbird that preferred the sky to the trees or marches. A bird that the local *Vogelfreunde*—the bird friends of their region—couldn't catch. But this was a crossbill singing, she guessed. The parrot of the Alps.

The *Vogelfreunde* prowled through the woodlands and meadows with their nets every autumn in search of the crossbill, goldfinch, bullfinch, and siskin that often roamed low to the ground. During the winter months, these men and women cared for the birds and then sold them at their spring exhibition. Any unsold birds were released into the forest for the summer months.

Had the *Vogelfreunde* released their catch for the spring, or had this bird managed to maintain its freedom?

A branch rustled, and this time Annika caught a glimpse of the bird, his russet head coloring the winter branches like a cranberry garland on a Christmas tree.

"Fly free," she whispered. The *Vogelfreunde* never harmed their prisoners, but still she thought neither the songbirds nor the silent ones should be locked in cages for the winter.

The crossbill's song of freedom played in her head as she skirted out of the trees and around catkins fringed over the lakeshore, past buildings that housed cows and horses long ago. In the yard beyond her, the medieval Schloss Schwansee towered like a cathedral on the land between the mountain and the shore. Lake

Hallstatt mirrored blue below it, its glassy surface broken only by the village's candy-colored reflection across the water.

Schloss Schwansee was smaller than other nearby castles like Hohenwerfen or Schloss Mirabell, but it was every bit as intriguing with its three turrets, each one topped with a cone of slate. Dormer windows lined the attic with a much taller tower standing at its side, a former bell tower perhaps, and a family chapel linked to the rear through a narrow corridor.

Like most of the outbuildings, the chapel was typically locked when the family wasn't home, but during this last visit, Herr Dornbach had asked Annika's father to build something inside the chapel. Or at least that's what she'd overheard when Vati was talking to her friend Hermann, the youth he hired to help with all the construction projects. When Vati had seen her, he'd asked for lunch.

Between the lake that lapped up against its front lawn and the mountain wall on the other side, the house would have been well protected in centuries past from any warring enemy, but someone in the past generation had cleared a lane through the forest, connecting with a country road that led into the nearby town called Obertraun.

Herr Dornbach and Max had already taken the train that stopped in Obertraun back to Vienna, but Frau Dornbach had lingered here another week. Now that Frau Dornbach was gone as well, Annika would spend her morning sweeping floors, dusting the furniture, scrubbing the porcelain in the bathrooms with Domestos like her mother used to do.

This role of housekeeper was only for a season, but it was a role Annika wore like a badge trying to honor both Max and her mother every day with her work. If God ever allowed Mama to glimpse down from the heavens, Annika hoped that she'd see her taking good care of both Vati and this castle.

One could only polish so much silver, though, sweep and scrub so many meters of floor. In the winter, Annika would go for weeks at a time without cleaning a single room until Herr Dornbach's secretary sent a message via telegram to say the family would arrive soon. Then she'd air the musty smell out of the house, make all the beds, stock the icebox with food from the grocer.

She unlocked the front door, and inside, the carpeted staircase dipped down into a hall floored with polished marble, the vast space between the walls built to entertain aristocrats from Vienna and local men after a hunting party in the hills.

The staircase split at the landing, and she climbed up to the left, each step groaning as if its back were on the verge of breaking, its joints aching with four hundred years of service to the Dornbachs and other families who'd called this castle home.

Others, like her mother, had spent their lives serving this house—and sometimes its inhabitants. Annika had no intention of giving up her entire life for a house, but each time Max left, it felt as if her heart were on the verge of breaking like these steps. A deep thundering ache that made her tremble on the inside.

A giant portrait of Max hung in the corridor above a wrought-iron tripod empty of its flower vase. She didn't linger there. His handsome face was so firm in the painting, his lips pressed together in a way that made him look cruel. Like his father could be.

The door into Herr Dornbach's bedroom was beside his wife's, both rooms overlooking the lake and village and rugged Alps in the distance. Max's room was in the back of the house; the view from his window faced the forest and fortress of a mountain.

She always saved the cleaning of Max's room until last.

Some nights, when Vati left for the beer hall, Annika returned to the house, though she never cleaned in those late hours. Sometimes she riffled through the clothing and records in Max's room, as if he'd left part of himself there. Other nights, she'd settle into the library on the ground floor and read one of the many books neatly lined on the shelves. Sometimes she even borrowed a book or two, carefully replacing them before the Dornbachs returned.

Vati would have her head if he knew she snuck in while he was away, pretending to be the lady of the house, but it seemed to her that he often forgot his role as well, propping himself up, in his mind at least, as the king of this castle.

Annika retrieved the cleaning supplies from the hallway closet and stepped into Frau Dornbach's bedroom. Instead of portraying family members or landscapes, the oil paintings on her walls were swirls of odd colors and shapes, contrasting with the worn chintz curtains that draped over the windows, a marigold-yellow and green design topped with marigold fringe to match the bedcoverings.

Why the mistress pulled these heavy curtains over the windows was beyond Annika, especially with the view of the boathouse in the reeds below and the village of Hallstatt across the lake with its dual church steeples gleaming like two bronze candlesticks.

The Catholic church was posted like an elegant stamp in the right corner, but next to it was the creepy *Beinhaus* filled with hundreds, if not thousands, of bones, dug up from graves after their ten-year lease expired. Or at least that's what her friend Sarah Leitner said after she'd visited this house of bones.

Perhaps that was why Frau Dornbach closed these curtains. Perhaps she didn't like the Beinhaus either.

While Annika no longer laughed about death, it still made her nervous. In fact, it terrified her. After she died, she hoped her bones would stay intact and that someone would bury her near her mother's grave on the hill.

Annika rested her broom and dustpan by the dressing table and placed her bucket of rags and jar of Domestos on the hardwood that rimmed the carpeted floor. Then she tied back the curtains and opened the windows to flood the room with mountain air, mollifying the remnants of dust and mold that had accumulated over four hundred years. Generations had lived and died in this house, but mold clung to the place like the salt buried deep in the mine above Hallstatt.

A Victrola stood near the bureau with dozens of vinyl records in a case beside it. Annika selected one of Bruno Walter conducting Beethoven's Emperor Concerto with the Vienna Philharmonic Orchestra and let the music permeate the room as the crossbill's song had the forest. Along with the sunlight, the melody brightened the room, and she wished she could stay here all day.

Her duster in hand, she stepped toward the bureau, but the shoe boxes in Frau Dornbach's dressing room seemed to call out to her. Dozens of them packed neatly into an antique armoire, many acquired during Frau Dornbach's trips to England and France.

The cleaning, Annika decided, could wait.

The orchestra playing in the background, she began unloading and neatly restacking the boxes in a separate pile near the door, so she could put each one back where it belonged. Frau Dornbach's shoes were beautiful, but Annika didn't spend time opening all the lids. She only wanted the one at the bottom, the pale-green box striped with ivory and stamped with *Georgette of Paris*.

Even a box seemed more glamorous when it was from Paris.

Instead of shoes, the box now housed ten envelopes stuffed with photographs. She shouldn't know this, of course, but over the years she'd learned plenty of things about the Dornbach family that were supposed to be secret.

Annika carefully thumbed through the contents of the box, careful not to disturb the order or leave smudges on the pictures. Sometimes she wondered why Frau Dornbach kept these photographs in a shoe box, but she could never ask. Neither the Dornbachs nor her father could ever find out exactly how nosy she'd been.

Some of the photographs inside the envelopes were taken on a vacation to the Mediterranean coast while others were of the Alps. One was of Max on snow skis when he was about ten. He'd wavered over the years about things like music and books, but he'd never wavered in his love of skiing, whether it was cross country through the valleys or down the groomed slopes.

But these photographs left her empty, teasing her with Max's presence when she couldn't speak to him.

One of the envelopes contained several sepia-colored photographs that she'd never seen before, each about twenty centimeters long. One showed an older couple standing beside a carriage, the woman pretty but stern looking, her dark hair pulled back in a knot. The man beside her held a top hat close to his waistcoat, his long beard cascading down over his chest. Relatives, she assumed, from decades back.

Max never talked about his extended family except for an uncle who had immigrated to the United States and an aunt who'd moved to Paris with her French husband. Then again, Annika never talked about her family either. The grandfather on her mother's side had died in the Great War, and her grandmother followed soon after. The grandparents on her father's side lived in Linz, but the Knopf family never visited. Vati had some sort of falling out with them when he was younger.

Under the photographs were other mementos. A lock of blond hair, probably from Max. She brushed her fingers over it and then cradled it for a moment against her cheek. There was a piece of blanket in the box and white booties with pink strings. Those she assumed to be from the baby girl Frau Dornbach lost in the early 1930s. If they'd given her a name, Annika didn't know what it was. Max only talked of his sister once, and then he seemed to bury the memory with his animals.

Max loved well, but then he let go. Annika, on the other hand, clung to the people she loved as the Vogelfreunde did with their prized birds. Except she never released them.

Perhaps her clinging was more like the salt in the mines. Once hardened, it remained until someone flooded it from the chamber with water or broke it away with a pickax.

At the bottom of the box, she found something else new. A star necklace, the six-pointed gold pendant ringed with diamonds. It reminded Annika of the necklace Sarah wore. The golden Star of David. Though Sarah referred to it as a shield instead of a star.

She'd seen this symbol in the papers as well. The Jewish athletes in Vienna, they stitched the shield to their uniforms.

But why did Frau Dornbach have this symbol of the Jewish people in her box?

She pressed the necklace into her palm, her back against the armoire. Perhaps one of Frau Dornbach's ancestors had purchased it from a Jewish jeweler. With its gold and diamonds, the worth of it must be . . . She couldn't imagine how many schillings one might pay for a necklace like this.

The chain dangled down her sleeve, the gold threading the forest green in her sweater.

One day, would Frau Dornbach pass this down to Max's wife?

Annika lifted the necklace to her throat, clasping the chain around her neck, closing her eyes. In this quiet space, she could see Max in Vienna, his gaze wandering out of his classroom window. Was he thinking about her as well?

"Annika?" It was Vati calling her name, the sound muffled in these walls.

She gasped, reaching for the necklace clasp underneath her braid, trying to release its hold before her father found her with it. When the clasp finally gave way, she dropped it back into the shoe box, but before she slammed the lid, the stench from cigarette smoke filtered through the door. And then her father was in the dressing room.

She shoved the Georgette of Paris box away as if it were an ember that had leapt out of its fire. Unfortunately, Vati watched its flight across the dressing room floor. Then he surveyed the rest of the shoe boxes stacked beside the antique bureau.

"What are you doing?" he demanded.

"Nothing, Vati."

His voice escalated. "You're rummaging through their things?"

She shivered. The photographs, even though they left a void, were her only connection with Max when he wasn't here. Her father must never find out about those. "They are shoes, Vati, nothing more. Some of the prettiest ones I have ever seen."

"You are not to touch Frau Dornbach's things."

She nodded furiously. "I won't ever look at them again."

"You're supposed to be cleaning the rooms. Like your mother . . ."

"I know." Her voice sounded small, like the squeak of a squirrel, and she wished she were stronger like Max or even Sarah. Neither of them were scared of their fathers. "I will clean now."

"Hermann has arrived. We need your help in the chapel as well."

She'd known Hermann Stadler since they were children and liked him well enough, but she hated the chapel. The walls felt as if they were smothering her. "I'll come, after I clean—"

"Now, Annika."

The Georgette box was sitting on its own, under the canopy of hanging clothes. She lifted another box to return to its original place, hoping to distract her father, but he stepped over her and snatched up the Georgette of Paris box. Then he opened it and dumped the contents onto the carpet.

"What is this?" he whispered, lifting the star pendant.

She shrugged, trying to calm the pounding in her chest. "Just a necklace."

A dangerous necklace with all its diamonds, the symbol of a people who increasingly needed a shield.

Vati's eyes changed before her. Angry at first, turning wild and gray like a wolf's, and then narrowing with greed. As if he'd found a trunk filled with gold. "In Frau Dornbach's room . . ."

She scrambled to her feet, following him out of the dressing room. He held the necklace up to the window and the diamonds and gold glistened in the light.

Was her father planning to sell it? Surely not. The Dornbachs would release him from his position for thievery, and he and Annika would lose everything. The cottage and the milk from the goats. The samlet from the lake. The birds that sang to her in the spring.

Unemployment, she'd read in the papers, was already rampant in Austria. Her father would never be able to get another position.

Annika held out her hand, her voice gaining strength. "Give me the necklace, Vati."

A strange smile crawled across his lips—the most awful smile she'd ever seen. "I knew it," he muttered more to himself than to Annika.

Her hand dangled in the air like the hook at the end of a fishing rod. "What did you know?"

Instead of answering her question, he dropped the necklace into his shirt pocket, and she feared this necklace would find trouble in her father's greedy hands.

"Please, Vati." She reached out her hand. "Frau Dornbach will find out that we went through her things."

He glanced out the window again; then he turned back toward her, the eerie smile still pasted on his lips. "She'll never ask about this piece."

CHAPTER 6

"Remarkable." Charlotte traces her neatly trimmed fingernail, polished with a pearly white color, under the script on *Bambi*'s third page. "The print is almost identical to the original text."

My fingers clench the velvet arms of the chair beside her, my sandals tapping the Oriental rug in time with the classical music playing softly through Charlotte's speakers. "What does it say?"

She inches her reading glasses closer to her eyes, their rims pressing against her silver-white bangs. Then she checks inside the front cover—a familiar routine for her, this searching for the owner's name inside a used book.

"A lovely tribute," Charlotte says quietly after she discovers Annika's name and the words from her mother.

Even as she says the words, I know she's thinking about Nadine, her deceased mom. Charlotte's mother was French, but as a German teacher living on the border between France and Switzerland, Nadine spoke both languages to the daughter she adopted postwar.

There'll be no magical reconciliation between my biological mother and me, but at least I know my story—our story—as broken as it is. Charlotte doesn't know where she was born or to whom. Family connections, I've discovered, go way beyond blood, but I've always wanted to find Charlotte's biological family for her.

I glance over at the worn blue spine of *Hatschi Bratschis Luftballon* by Franz Ginzkey on a bookshelf near Charlotte's piano, the magic balloon book that shaped her childhood and inspired the name of her store. It's also the one item that Charlotte has left from her early years, the only clue to her past.

The German classic has never been translated into English, but when we were younger, Charlotte translated the story as she read it to Brie and me. Hatschi Bratschi swipes little Fritz from his village in the magic balloon, and in the following pages, they travel the world until the wizard, searching for more children, falls off the balloon. Fritz enjoys the rest of his voyage until he reaches the wizard's castle. There he discovers more kidnapped children and valiantly returns them all to their homes at the end.

The story is harsh compared to many of the books for American children, but I've always been fascinated by Fritz. Not only with his ability to escape from an evil wizard, but his incredible journey around the world.

I look between the *Bambi* book in Charlotte's lap and *Hatschi Bratschis Luftballon*. Both books—one about tragedy and the other about triumph—written by Austrian authors in the same era, except Felix Salten fled from the Nazi Party while Franz Ginzkey joined its ranks.

Charlotte turns to the handwritten text on the third page again, studying the words. "The Germans banned this book during the war."

I nod. "Felix Salten was Jewish."

"They thought he'd written this story as an allegory about those who wanted to kill the Jewish people."

I shiver, thinking about the antagonist called Man, hunting down the innocent deer for sport. I haven't been able to find much useful information about Felix Salten for my post, so I've requested several articles from the National Archives of Austria. The researcher there, a woman named Sophie, said she'd send me one later today.

Charlotte looks up, her short hair combed neatly behind her ears. "Where did Brianna find this?"

"From a seller in Idaho." I dip my spoon into a bowl of fudge ice cream and savor the sweet chocolate. "She wanted to surprise me for my birthday."

She turns the page. "My mother read this story to me when I was a girl."

And then she seems to slip away as she stares at the page.

She's done this ever since I've known her, losing herself in the pages of a book. Once she told me that books were her own magic balloons, the words and stories transporting her to another place, often back to her home in France.

Someone renamed her Charlotte when she first arrived at the orphanage east of Lyon. It means "free woman," a new birth in a sense. After the war, Nadine had wanted her newly adopted daughter to embrace that name and embark with her on a journey of freedom.

Charlotte loved her mother dearly, bringing her to the United

States almost sixty years ago following Charlotte's marriage to a soldier from Ohio named Marshall Trent.

After Nadine died, the Trents searched for Charlotte's biological family but found no record of her birth in Lyon or the surrounding towns in France, so they crossed the border to search the civil registrar's office in Geneva. When that proved unsuccessful, they moved on to Germany. No central registry office recorded German births, so they combed through records in civil registration offices in several of the larger cities.

Later I tried to help Charlotte find her family as well, searching online in the catalog of the Family History Library. Though her biological parents were probably deceased by now, I was hoping to find a brother or sister or even a cousin who remained behind. Someone to fill in the gaps of her story.

But none of us have been able to locate the record of her birth. We need the name of the town or city where she was born in order to find any information about her family.

Charlotte remained at the orphanage near Lyon for about five years until Nadine rescued her, and then she emulated Nadine's kindness when she met Brie and me. Not orphans exactly, but two girls who desperately needed a mom. Or at least an auntie who could help guide us across the mountains and valleys of life. Charlotte filled in these missing gaps for us.

When Charlotte looks up at me again, her dark-green eyes are confused. "It seems to be a list."

"What sort of list?"

She shakes her head. "I'm not certain."

Brie and I have found plenty of forgotten lists tucked between a book's pages—usually cataloging groceries or things to do—but none inscribed in the copy. This list, it seems, was meant to be remembered permanently by either its author or the recipient of the book.

"Can you translate any of it?" I press.

Charlotte pats my leg. She's known me since I was eight and knows very well that sometimes I push too hard. This tenacity, she once told me, was also a gift, but not everyone appreciates it as much as she does.

How Charlotte saw my determination all those years ago as a child empowered me in a sense, making my grit a blessing instead of a curse. Even today, my perspective on myself often evolves to match the view from her eyes.

She reaches for the bowl of cherry cordial that I brought her from the ice cream shop once owned by her husband and digs her spoon into one of the three scoops. In all these years, I've never known her to waver on books or ice cream.

After taking two bites, Charlotte returns her bowl to the glass coffee table and looks at the book again. The words come to her slowly as she scans the lines on one of the first pages. "Gold necklace, ruby brooch, and six silver teacups with—" it takes her a moment to translate the last word—"saucers."

I glance over her arm, studying the script again. "Perhaps someone recorded their family heirlooms."

"There are two initials at the end of the line," she says. "R. L."

"Strange."

"Maybe Annika was trying to hide her secrets in plain sight. If she didn't want an adult to find it . . ."

"No better place to hide than in a children's book."

She nods, pushing her reading glasses back over her short hair. We've commiserated over the years about how few adults actually open books written for younger people. The older population, we both think, would learn a lot about children by reading what intrigues them. And while I'm admittedly biased, some stories written specifically for children are light-years more entertaining than what's marketed toward their parents.

The author of the list certainly valued precision in her script, taking the time to do her work well. She seemed to care deeply about what she was recording, and I wonder if it was Annika Knopf trying to hide something between these pages or if her mother wrote this list for her.

I glance again between the two books—one on the shelf and one in Charlotte's hands—and wish they could both tell me about their journeys.

"I can't read any more today." Charlotte lowers the book to her lap.

This time I pat her leg. "It's okay."

"My mind is still sound, just not my recall."

"Your mind is even sounder than mine."

Charlotte continues flipping through the pages, scanning the illustrations of Bambi playing with his cousin Faline, hiding with his mother in the forest. Some of the illustrations are printed in bright colors, others in black-and-white. Then she looks back up at me. "Did you see the picture?"

I scoot toward her. "What picture?"

She slowly rotates the book, and I see a yellowed photograph, torn from a newspaper and attached to a page near the end of the book with about a dozen pieces of clear tape. It's a picture of a young man, seeming to gaze into the eyes of a woman cut from the photograph, though her gloved hand is resting in his. He's striking, with light hair and a smile that must have stirred the hearts of many young women in his day.

The caption's missing as well, but I can read the name of the newspaper and the date above the photograph.

Neues Wiener Tagblatt. 6 May 1938.

"The Vienna newspaper," Charlotte says.

"Perhaps Annika was from Austria as well."

Charlotte closes the book, staring down at the cover. "I was baptized in 1938."

Elbows on my lap, I wait silently. She rarely speaks about her memories from the orphanage or the tragedies of a great war that spared no one, including the children.

"I wish I could find your family for you, Charlotte."

She reaches for my hand; her skin is so soft, so thin, that I worry about bruising her. "It's much too late for a reunion now."

"Do you still want to know what happened to them?"

"Sometimes I do." Her voice shakes. "Other times, I'm afraid to find out."

"Everyone should know their story."

Closing her eyes, Charlotte rests her head against the chair. "Hopefully this Annika left Europe long before the war began."

Charlotte's hand nestled inside mine, I allow her the space she needs to drift away. I would never do anything to hurt her, but I wish I could gift her with something good from her story.

CHAPTER 7

MAX

VIENNA, AUSTRIA
MAY 1938

Chandelier light glowed on the gilded walls of the ballroom as Herr Krause, the conductor, lifted his baton. Then the members of the orchestra filled the chambers and balconies of the *Rathaus* with the flush of music. The marble columns lining the room vibrated with their song, the German flag fluttering behind them.

The ensemble comprised eighteen players—trumpeters, flutists, a cellist—but Max only had eyes for the woman in the second row, third seat on the left. The violin cradled against the pearl sleeve of her gown, her long skirt almost touching the ground. She, like all the women on the platform, had dressed in her finest attire instead of the black frock she typically wore to perform.

The opera last weekend had been canceled after Bruno Walter left Austria, but no one canceled this dance at the lofty town hall even if a majority of the musicians playing tonight were Jewish.

The Viennese would be hard-pressed to put together an orchestra without Jewish players. An impossibility perhaps. And what was Vienna without music?

Dozens of formally suited men lifted their arms as they prepared to dance; then the beaded gowns of their partners began twirling in unison between the columns, creating their own percussion from the silk and satin in their skirts.

The world seemed to have gone mad right before Max's eyes. The rioting in Vienna's streets, fighting with both words and clubs. Yet hidden behind the armor of these golden walls was a respite of beauty and peace. Here, for the night at least, Austrians danced together instead of fought. Celebrated the music that once mended their fractured differences.

Herr Neubacher, Vienna's newly appointed mayor, swept past Max, dancing with the wife of a philosopher who'd recently returned to Austria, part of the group expelled over the years for supporting National Socialism. In the past month, Nazi supporters by the thousands had flooded back into Austria, marching across the welcome mat that Hitler had laid out for them.

Many aristocrats in this room wanted to fold their identity into the greatest country in the world, even if it meant losing their beloved Austria. The humiliation of the defeat two decades past had flamed their pride, the fire burning hotter within them every passing year. Many who fought and lost that great war as young men saw the opportunity for victory now. An opportunity to show the world that they would no longer cower.

"Max." His mother stepped in front of him, her blue satin gown glowing in the chandelier light. "Aren't you going to dance?"

He nodded toward the orchestra. "My partner is currently occupied."

"As she will be all night. There are many other women who'd like to accompany you."

"I don't want to dance with anyone else."

When his mother glanced back at him, her lips were pressed together in disapproval. She liked Luzi well enough, and she certainly liked Frau Weiss—the two of them had been friends since their days studying at Vienna Conservatory, bonding over their love of composers such as Ludwig van Beethoven and Johannes Brahms. His mother seemed to disregard the growing animosity toward the Jewish people in Vienna. She loved music, and most of the musicians in Vienna happened to be of Jewish descent. The only time she disparaged a musician was when one appeared too lazy to hone his or her craft.

His mother didn't disapprove of Luzi, but she didn't want him to make any commitments before he finished school. However, it didn't seem to him that he would be going to *Gymnasium* much longer if the new government was going to force him into the Wehrmacht when he turned eighteen.

His father moved up beside them, nodding toward the floor. "We should dance the next one."

Klara Dornbach gave a brisk nod. "Of course."

Max stood behind his parents, watching the dancers over his mother's shoulder. Both his parents stood solemnly, displaying the air of their aristocratic bloodlines. As if they would protect themselves in the future by reminding others of their heritage.

They'd been arguing again before they left the house tonight, his father insisting that Mussolini was still going to defend their country, his mother saying that if the Italians were planning to help, they would have done so months ago.

Both his parents knew well what was expected of them in the old Austria and had tried to impart the importance of these expectations to Max as well. But Hitler, it seemed, didn't put much stock in the bloodlines of aristocracy, though the man they called Führer was very much focused on the blood pumping through veins if it happened to be Jewish. Max had spent most of his life focused on the future, but the past was all that seemed to define people under this new regime.

The music ended, and a new set of dancers, including his parents, stepped onto the floor. Max's gaze settled back onto Luzi. If she saw him, she didn't give any indication, her eyes focused solely on the music stand in front of her. He inched to the front of the crowd, and when the maestro finally rested his wand, Max moved forward to escort Luzi to the refreshments in the next room. She tucked her violin into its case and clasped it shut, protecting the instrument until they began playing again.

"I wish we could dance together," he said.

She glanced toward the floor, empty now as the dancers poured into the side room. "Not tonight, Max."

"But at least we can eat."

Luzi shook her head. "I don't want any food either."

"You must be famished."

When she smoothed her hand over her sleeve, he saw it tremble. "My nerves can't tolerate it."

"But your body needs it."

"Please, Max, don't make me fight."

He reached for her trembling hand and tucked it into the crook of his arm. "I wouldn't dream of fighting with you, Fräulein."

Her hand clutched his arm at first, and then it began to relax as he guided her through the crowd, out onto a balcony that wrapped around the grand city hall, overlooking the park below. They both leaned across the balustrade, breathing in the balm of cherry blossoms that sweetened the breeze.

Max smiled at her. When he was with Luzi, all the hostilities in Vienna, all the secrets, seemed to disappear. "You are playing beautifully."

She shook her head, her dark hair glistening in the golden light that seeped through the open door behind them. "I'm playing like someone who's forgotten most of the notes."

"You can pretend, Luzi, but I know full well that you played every note to perfection."

She sighed. "I don't know how I played. I was lost in the music."

"As was I." He turned around, leaning back against the balustrade so he could see her eyes. "Where are your parents?"

And then he wished he couldn't see her eyes, at least not the sadness in them before her gaze fell to the tree-lined walk below. "They were uninvited."

Blood rushed to his face. "What?"

"They received a letter yesterday rescinding their invitation."

The hairs on the back of his neck stood as rigid as the soldiers who'd escorted Hitler into their city. "But they didn't rescind your invitation?"

"No, they needed someone to play. I almost refused but . . ."

"Your mother?"

"She thinks the music will carry us away from here."

He clenched his fists, anger erupting inside him. "It's wrong, Luzi."

"I know," she said, her voice small. "But what are we to do?"

"We fight it."

"Not on our own." She turned and stepped away from the railing. "I must return to my seat."

"A few more minutes," he begged. "I don't know when I'll see you again." His parents would insist that they leave before the musicians finished playing, at a time deemed fashionable by his father.

She smiled at him. "I've no doubt it will be soon."

And then he heard the melody of flutes inside the hall, followed by two violins playing "Village Swallows from Austria," a piece written by Josef Strauss to accompany the Viennese waltz.

Luzi stepped forward, her smile gone. "They've started without me."

"It's too late to join them now," Max said, reaching for her arm.

She shivered, rubbing her hands together. "Herr Krause will be livid."

He watched the women inside the ballroom lift the hems of their long dresses, preparing to dance. It was a political waltz for their city, meant to communicate freedom for all.

"Please, Luzi," he asked again. "Just one dance."

She closed her eyes, as if listening for the answer in the music.

"We'll pretend that we're an empress and emperor," he said. "Sisi and Franz Joseph."

"Only part of a dance," she finally relented. "I must return to my seat before they begin the next song."

"Part of a dance, then."

She slowly picked up the hem of her dress, and he took her hand. "Let's show them how to waltz."

It seemed to him as if the gates to heaven opened up, joy raining down as the angels themselves sang in his mind. Luzi was in his arms, following his lead as they circled the floor to music that once defined all of them in this room.

If only they could dance all night together.

Dance for a lifetime.

"I feel as if all of Vienna is watching us, Max."

"Not us." He grinned down at her. "They only have eyes for you."

She smiled back at him, radiant. "Sometimes I think you must be blind."

"No, but I only have eyes for you too."

The music was coming to a close; he could feel Luzi releasing her hold. He didn't want this to end, but he guided her toward the orchestra and then reluctantly released her. Herr Krause glared at him, and the moment the music stopped, Luzi found her place.

But no one's glare could erase Max's smile. He'd danced with Luzia Weiss, and she had smiled back at him.

CHAPTER 8

LUZI

The conductor's lecture lasted until long after the guests were gone, chastising Luzi—rightfully so—for dancing instead of joining the other musicians on the stage. Then Herr Krause dismissed her with a wave before he marched across the floor.

Luzi lifted her violin case and walked slowly toward a side door that led down into the courtyard. One of the flutists was supposed to drive her the seven kilometers home, but it seemed that Daphne had left with the rest of the orchestra. Only the waitstaff remained behind, bustling around the ballroom as if they didn't see her, hadn't heard the conductor screaming about her negligence.

But still she smiled at the memory of her dance. For a moment tonight, it had felt as if she were in a dream. As if all of Vienna were celebrating her coming out as a debutante, an event that would no longer happen next year or probably any year—at least for her.

Were the aristocrats, along with the Gentile bourgeoisie, whispering about the Jewish girl in Max Dornbach's arms? Or did they wonder why she wasn't playing her violin? Most of them knew her parents, and many of them knew her name as well, but these days, she doubted if they wanted her dancing among them.

Her mother would be irate at the conductor for keeping her so late, at Daphne for leaving her behind . . . and at Luzi for succumbing to Max's charms. She didn't doubt that Max cared for her, but her mother said that much of Vienna was closing their doors to the Jewry here, and she wanted her daughter to be known above all else for her music.

As long as Luzi could lose herself in her music, everything would be fine.

The door at the bottom of the Rathaus staircase opened into a rectangular courtyard boxed in by a portico. The scent of spring—flowers and grass—wafted through the arched corridor on the other side, from the park that separated city hall from the University of Vienna.

Spring—the warmth of this season made her heart full.

Her violin case clutched in both hands, she lifted the bow in her mind and began to play a piece from *Die Jahreszeiten*—Joseph Haydn's oratorio about the seasons. The music sent sparks of light through the dark yard, chased away the miserable thoughts that wanted to repeat—*da capa al coda*—in her head.

Al fine.

She'd already rehearsed what would happen when her mother found out about her dance. Now she needed to focus her thoughts on reaching University Ring, the road beyond the park.

Her heels clicked against the stone pavers in the courtyard, like the hooves of horses that pulled the grand carriages around this city, her mind teasing her with its tricks in the absence of music. There was nothing to fear. . . .

Like the swift flick of a match, the bitterness of cigarette smoke invaded the scent of spring. Luzi bristled in the dim lantern light, searching the portico on both sides of her for a face. It must be one of the staff, she told herself. A waiter or custodian who'd come outside to smoke.

Still she walked faster, to the corridor across the plaza, leading into the park. On the other side of *Rathausplatz*, she'd hail a taxi to take her home. Or catch the tram if it wasn't too late.

Her gaze focused on the chamber of light beyond the courtyard as she began replaying the music about seasons in her head.

Something shuffled on her left, and a shadow grew where the lantern light spilled on the ground. Her first thought was to retreat into the hall, but the door had locked behind her. So she rushed forward, focused on the arch above the corridor, on the sliver of open space on the other side of these walls.

A man stepped out of an alcove, and fear clenched her chest, talons pressing through her skin. At first she couldn't see his face, but then she recognized him. It was Ernst Schmid, the man once employed at Max's home.

Did he know that she was playing tonight? He might have seen her name in the newspaper announcing the event.

Luzi turned away, trying to pretend he wasn't there, pressing one heel after the other on the stone even as her mind yelled for her to run. But where would she go? It wasn't like the last time he'd found her—this time no one was around.

Ernst stepped in front of her, blocking her exit through the tunnel, and her mind flashed back to memories that she wanted to leave buried.

When she was fourteen, she'd stepped into a bedroom in Max's home to rest, escape the party outside for a few moments. Ernst found her there alone, but instead of excusing himself like a gentleman, he had cornered her. She'd screamed, and she remembered so clearly the shock in his eyes at her protest. Then the anger. He'd fled from the room as if she'd been the one to accost him.

She hadn't told anyone what happened, but she'd seen him several times after that event, and each time she could feel his gaze. Not pleasant like when she caught Max stealing a glance at her. Nor friendly. It was as if he was biding his time.

She clutched her violin case to her chest as if it were a shield and veered around Ernst. Her heels clapped loudly on the stones as she rushed under the arch, through the corridor, trying to cling to the echo of song.

Ernst didn't say anything, but she heard his feet falling behind her, keeping pace. She wanted to run, but suspected it would only encourage him, like a panther hunting its dinner. He might only toy with her, but then again . . . she didn't want to think about what else he might do.

She rushed along the tree-covered walk in the empty park, the chaos of traffic in the distance, honking horns and squealing brakes replacing the music in her head. The noise was a beacon to her, the promise of a crowd to ward off this man.

"Luzi," Ernst said behind her, her name like a growl.

She walked even faster, toward the streetlights she could see beyond the trees. Surely, even at this hour, some students would be walking the sidewalks of *Universitätsring*.

Ernst grabbed her arm, whirling her toward him.

"What do you want?" she demanded, wrestling against his grip. She tried to remain strong, but she felt like one of the strings on her violin about to snap.

He tightened his fingers. "Why are you out so late?"

She straightened her shoulders. He knew exactly where she'd been tonight, and he would have been at the ball as well if he'd been invited. "I'm on my way home."

He pulled her closer, and the stench of his breath, the stale alcohol and smoke, gagged her. The canopy of branches overhead blocked out most of the city lights. "It's as if you wanted me to find you."

"That's not true."

"Perhaps you were hoping for Max Dornbach, so the two of you could sneak away."

"Max is a gentleman," she retorted, her arm throbbing under his grip.

"Then I'll show you what Max is too cowardly to do."

If she screamed out here, no one would hear her with the noise of the traffic, so she shook her arm again, praying for deliverance under her breath, but he didn't release her.

He forced her to turn toward him. "And I'll protect you from the Nazis."

She cringed. "I only need protection from you."

He laughed as if she'd made a joke.

"Let me go, Ernst," she said, harsher now, trying to evoke the courage of her father, a man who'd fought a war to stop foreigners from bullying them.

"You don't want me to let you go, Luzi. Not really."

"Yes, I do."

"Think what I could do for you."

Her violin case was lodged between them, and she feared what would happen to the instrument if she dropped it, almost as much as she feared what Ernst might do. "I don't want anything from you," she insisted.

The heat from his breath burned her neck, seared her skin. With one hand wrapped around her waist, he yanked up her gown, pushed it up her thigh.

She pulled away, slamming his chest with the case. "No—"

"You don't have a choice."

"I distinctly heard the Fräulein say no." A man half a head taller than Ernst stepped from behind the trees, dressed as a gentleman with the air of someone accustomed to being in charge. A blonde woman wearing a sweater and short skirt stood beside him.

Ernst dropped the hem of Luzi's dress, but he didn't release his grasp on her arm.

The man moved closer. "Must I call for the *Polizei*?"

Ernst snickered. "The police won't care."

"Any assault against a lady will greatly concern them."

"This one's not a lady." He lowered his voice with contempt. "Nothing but a Jew."

The blonde woman tugged on the gentleman's arm, and when he took a step back, Luzi was afraid they would leave her. "I was playing with the orchestra tonight at the Rathaus," she blurted, wanting him to know that she was a musician. That she was human.

The man didn't reply.

"He has no right to me," Luzi pleaded.

Ernst traced his finger down her neck, lingering on her collarbone, and she felt as if she might be sick all over his shoes. "I have every right to you."

If this couple walked away, she had no doubt Ernst would force himself upon her. And her life . . . it would be forever ruined.

"Go home, lad," the gentleman finally said.

"Leave us alone, and I will."

The man lifted his arm and punched Ernst in the nose. Ernst reeled back, holding his hand over his face, but before he bolted away, he spit on Luzi as if she'd betrayed him.

"Are you hurt?" the man asked her, though it seemed that he'd lost some of the confidence in his voice.

"I'll be fine."

He glanced at the path. "Do you live nearby?"

"No," she said, her entire body shaking. "I was planning to take a taxi home."

He responded with a brisk nod. "We'll follow you out to Universitätsring, to make sure he doesn't return."

"Danke."

Her body was still shaking as she climbed into the cab, down to the toes hidden in her mother's narrow dress shoes.

"Number 69 Elisabethallee," she told the driver.

"You shouldn't be out by yourself," he said as he turned south.

"I know." The conductor shouldn't have made her stay so late at the hall, but she couldn't blame him. Max shouldn't have distracted her, and she never should have danced with him.

She must stay focused on what was best for her parents and her sister, not what her heart might urge her to do. Music, she prayed, would be her family's ticket out of Austria.

The taxi stopped, and after she paid the driver, Luzi looked both ways before stepping onto the sidewalk, as if Ernst might have followed her all the way home. But she didn't see him, nor did she smell cigarette smoke.

She rushed into the building, up the steps. Inside their apartment, her mother waited for her in the sitting room, hurrying toward her with arms outstretched. "We were so worried."

"I'm sorry I'm late." Luzi set her case on a chair, her voice sounding as hollow to her as the belly of her violin.

"The ball was supposed to end two hours ago."

"I was delayed," she said simply. Tomorrow she would tell her mother about Max, but she'd never tell anyone about Ernst. Her father might retaliate, and if he did, she feared no one would fight for him.

"Where's Papa?"

"He took the trolley to the Rathaus to look for you." Her mother scrutinized her. "You've stained your gown."

"Have I?" She looked down at the brown stain near her waist, the place where Ernst had spit on her.

Mutti stepped back. "I'll get some soda and water to clean it."

As Luzi moved toward her bedroom, ready to change out of her dress, she began humming "Village Swallows from Austria," trying to remember the dance.

She prayed that her mother was right. The music would carry her entire family, migrating like the swallows of Austria, across their country's borders and perhaps across an ocean as well. They would get their visas, and then they'd all be safe from men like Ernst Schmid.

CHAPTER 9

The desk in my apartment overlooks Mount Vernon's Main Street, quiet now after this morning's parade crowd has returned home. When I'm not helping Brie with the store downstairs, I'm typically sitting here by the window, researching and writing posts on children's authors like Felix Salten who use their life story as fodder for their writing.

More than ten thousand people follow the Magic Balloon blog—librarians, kids, parents, other bookstore owners. Readers, I've discovered, enjoy hearing about the successes of their favorite authors like J. R. R. Tolkien, J. K. Rowling, and Theodor Geisel (aka Dr. Seuss), but even more, they like to read about their failings.

The failures give hope to people both young and old. And the biography posts, along with our Lost & Found page, generate enough traffic to our site that Brie and I have managed to supplement our sales income with a bit of advertising.

I tap onto the bookmark for our website, and a colorful bouquet of balloons lifts off from the bottom of my screen, the balloons floating to the top of the page and then dividing neatly into six topics—*About, Blog, Shop, Lost & Found, Events*, and *Contact*. The site, with all its whimsical colors and moving pieces, is designed to appeal to kids, but Brie and I want people of all ages to be able to navigate it.

After logging in to the dashboard, I click on Lost & Found to update the page. Each item is listed with a bullet point—a Roger Clemens rookie card, a silver ring, an assortment of letters, photographs, and certificates. Visitors can click on each piece for a description of the used book, lost item, and sometimes a photo.

I don't include photographs of the valuable items; if anyone emails me about being the potential owner, I can ask for specifics. Plenty of people have responded to my listings, but I've never matched anything with its original owner.

Under a new bullet point, I type, *Unusual list found inside German edition of* Bambi. Then I link the headline to a full description.

Early edition of Austrian book, Bambi: a Life in the Woods. *Owner named Annika Knopf, dated 1932 by her mother. Unique list inscribed on the pages.*

I leave off the info about the photograph and Schloss Schwansee—those will help me identify the original owner or her family if someone does inquire.

My online search for an Annika Knopf has revealed several contemporary women, but between the publication date of the book and the mother's inscription along with the neatness of the script inside, I'm fairly certain Annika lived most, if not all, of her life pre-Internet. Back when people of all ages treasured their books and spent hours practicing their handwriting.

Perhaps Annika was a girl with a grand imagination. Or perhaps she was keeping a list of her family's heirlooms or things she wanted to buy one day. If I could reunite her book with her family, that would be the happiest ending of all for me.

Rain begins channeling down my window, and when I glance outside, I see a family of five crossing the street, each of its members clutching an ice cream cone and smiling in spite of the weather. I turn quickly back to my iPad screen.

At the top of my inbox are two articles about Felix Salten from Sophie, the Vienna researcher I've connected with online. With the help of Google, I begin translating the first one.

Salten was born in Hungary, the grandson of an orthodox rabbi, but his family moved to Austria soon after his birth because the government in Vienna began granting full citizenship to Jewish immigrants in 1867. Salten wrote *Bambi* in 1923, and it was such a huge success that he sold the film rights a decade later to an American director for a thousand bucks. This director later sold it to the studio of Walt Disney, who released it in 1942—ironically, while Salten and his family were exiled from their home.

The second article says Salten fled Vienna soon after Hitler annexed Austria to Germany. Many Jewish people tried to leave Vienna during the following year. Salten and his wife attempted— and failed—to obtain a visa through the American consulate, but their daughter helped them immigrate to Switzerland before the war began.

In the novel, Bambi's mother tells him not to look back, and I wonder about his creator—did Felix Salten ever look back? Surely he must have grieved the loss of the city he'd once loved and the thousands there—about sixty-five thousand Jewish brothers and sisters—who were killed during the Holocaust.

I have a little over a month to finish my article on Salten and then start gathering info about another author for a new post, one with a happy ending, of course. People like to hear about the failures, but most of them read children's books because they also want to read about their favorite characters fighting to overcome whatever obstacles are in their way, triumphing in the end.

I thank Sophie for her help, then send one more request, asking her to find the Vienna newspaper from May 6, 1938.

Someone knocks on my door, and I fold over the cover of my iPad before crossing the hardwood. It's my sister, her apron still streaked with chocolate from this morning, her hair strung back behind her ears.

"You want me to take over?" I ask.

"Yes, please." She loops the apron strap around her finger. "Ethan said the boys are about to drive him mad."

"From one zoo to another for you."

My sister lives a mile away from the store, in one of those Victorian homes on Gambier Street with their high ceilings and winding staircases. The house keeps Ethan and his carpentry skills quite busy, with the added benefit of offering plenty of space for the twins to play. On cold or stormy days, they've been known to roller skate across the cement floors in the basement and play leapfrog down the foyer.

She checks the time on her phone. "It's only an hour until close."

"I've got it." With my declaration, Brie unties the chocolate-splattered apron and holds it out, but I decline her offer. "I'll collect some dinner for us after I finish."

She tilts her head, skeptical. "On your bicycle?"

"Pizza delivery. Extra pepperoni for the boys."

"Thank you."

But really I should be thanking Brie because Saturday nights with her crew are the highlight of my week. I'll spend an hour cheering while the boys play hoops to give Brie and Ethan some much-needed couple time. A win all the way around.

My iPad propped on the counter downstairs, the store empty, I begin writing an email to the bookseller in Boise, inquiring about where she obtained the copy of *Bambi*. It's a favor I'm asking—most sellers won't give out this information—but Brie said she's purchased books from this lady before. Perhaps she'll tell me as a courtesy.

I start searching again for articles about Schloss Schwansee, but I'm obsessing now, hunting for answers I don't need. Moving on is what I need to do, at least in my mind, or I'll be stuck here all night.

Slipping around the counter, I begin shifting beanbags back into place, reshelving books that have wandered. Inkspot is asleep in the corner, probably exhausted from the dozens of hands stalking him all day. I understand. Too many people, for too many hours, exhaust me as well. My sister and Charlotte are the only adults who don't wear me out after an hour. And they are the only ones who understand that I still adore them, even when I need my space.

Family, I guess, is supposed to be like that.

Brie and I have the same father, but we have different moms. Brie's mother ran away in the middle of the night, about six months after Brie was born, and never seemed to look back. I remember her vaguely, an apparition who haunted my mind until I found out that she wasn't my biological mom.

I don't look anything like Sandra Dermott, the woman who gave me life, nor do I look like my father. But Brie and I, as different as we are, look just like sisters.

Rumors fester and grow in a town like ours, but if people whisper any longer about the Randall girls, I'm not privy to it. Unless their parents have told them stories, the kids who crowd my floor each Saturday don't know about my broken family, and most of the students from Brie's and my school days have since moved to the big city or a state farther south where the sun shines warmth for most of the year.

When Brie and I were kids, our father was on the road most of the week and often weekends as well, driving a tractor trailer. On my eighth birthday, he decided that he didn't have the extra cash for frivolous things like child care while he was traveling. For that matter, he didn't have much time to care for his kids when he was in town, but at least an adult was home those nights and brought us an occasional bag of fast food.

So I moved into the mother role for Brie, out of necessity. In hindsight, the state should have stepped in, but back then I didn't know that kids could borrow another family for a season. I made up all sorts of stories when adults asked about my father, because I'd somehow gotten it in my mind that Brie and I could end up in prison for being home alone.

Charlotte—Mrs. Trent to me then—never once shamed us. She offered Brie and me a safe place to spend our after-school hours. On Sundays, when the bookstore was closed, she invited us to church and into her home. She and Mr. Trent didn't have children, and for all intents and purposes, Brie and I didn't have parents. A match truly made in heaven.

When I was ten, Mr. Trent passed away, and after his funeral,

I marched into Magic Balloon and informed Mrs. Trent that I'd decided to adopt her into our family. Ridiculous, looking back, but she didn't laugh at me. Instead she said that it wasn't often someone had the privilege of being adopted twice.

Our dad died when I was sixteen, Brie fourteen, and Charlotte invited two bewildered teenagers to come live with her. We both helped her with the bookstore each afternoon during high school. That switched to full-time after I graduated, working at the store to pay for my tuition at a local university called Mount Vernon Nazarene.

It took me six years to obtain my degree in English, but late into the night, when I couldn't sleep, I delved into web design so I could launch a site for the store. The web experience proved to be just as valuable as my degree. Instead of leaving Mount Vernon like my high school friends, I opted to stay working here, helping Magic Balloon thrive. Brie headed up to Michigan for college and returned home four years later with a husband who adored her.

I'd so wanted a family of my own, like Brie, but men had terrified me during my college years. I deftly warded off any potential dates by proclaiming the supremacy of my busy life, and I think I terrified a few college men as well by seeming indifferent to their interest. Anyone who knows me knows that I'm protective of my heart, not indifferent, but during my early twenties I didn't waver far from that facade.

Five years ago, Scott stopped by Magic Balloon in search of a gift for his niece. He worked remotely for a tech company, and our website, he said, needed some work. After I assured him that anything Fancy Nancy would jockey him into position for uncle of the year, he gave me a few tips on how to update our site. Then he invited me to dinner.

Initially, with our conversations focused solely on the website, Scott and I became friends, but as the weeks went by, we fell into something else. I thought it was love—and he declared it to be so. But I was wrong, and the loss just about crushed me.

The shopkeeper's bell rings, an old-fashioned chime to remind our customers that we retain old-fashioned customer service. Several children walk through the door.

Two tween boys ask me about a creepy kids' series they say they're dying—lots of snickering—to read. I explain politely that we don't carry any books in that genre. We have to draw the line somewhere, I tell them, and we've decided that there's enough horror in real life for some children. No more reason to add to the fear.

One of the kids, the older boy with bangs hinged up like a ladder, pushes back, saying there's no problem with pretend scary. Smiling, I start my well-rehearsed lecture for such a time as this.

"Books are a lot like food," I begin, stepping between the boys and the exit. "First is the healthy stuff that most parents want their kids to read. Some of it tastes great, others perhaps not so much, but it's good for the body and mind."

Hands stuffed in his pocket, the hinged-bangs boy is not buying it, so I continue on. "Next there's brain candy, the sugary sweet stuff that tastes good going down, but turns into a bellyache if you binge. . . . And then there's the poison."

He rolls his eyes.

"Kids need to eat real food for their bodies to grow, not the pieces of poison left out for, say, rodents."

"There's nothing wrong with rodents—"

"I think some books for kids can damage a perfectly good brain."

At least, they can kill the hope that flickers inside it, stamp it out. Those books begin to define their readers.

"This store is a refuge," I finish, "for a young person's body and mind."

The boy and his friend rush around me, fleeing for the door, and another child, about two years younger, taps my arm tentatively, asking me if we have *The Humming Room*. I direct him straight to the section for middle grade.

When the store clears again, the telephone rings, and I rush toward the front counter.

"Magic Balloon Bookshop," I answer. "This is Callie."

"Callie Randall?" a man asks.

"How can I help you?"

"This is Josh Nemeth, from Ohio State," he says as if I'm supposed to know who he is.

"Did you order a book?" I watch Inkspot skulk around the perimeter of the room, checking to see if the kids are gone.

"I'm calling about the book you found. The one owned by Annika Knopf."

I lean against the back wall, surprised. "I just posted that."

"I have an alert set up," he explains. "I've been searching for information about an Annika from Austria for years."

I want to reunite this book with its owner, not someone else searching for her. "I don't know that she's from Austria—"

"But the book is printed there?"

"Yes, in Salzburg," I say, reopening my iPad.

"My uncle met a woman named Annika near Salzburg, after the war," he says. "He never told me her last name."

Google leads me straight to Dr. Nemeth's biography on the OSU website. He's an assistant professor, researching and teaching modern European history.

After skimming Dr. Nemeth's bio, I study the photograph. He's a nice-looking man in a rugged sort of way, reminding me of Ryan Gosling in *La La Land* with his stubble beard and a melancholic look in his eyes as if he's thousands of miles away. In Austria, perhaps.

"Why exactly are you trying to find Annika?"

"She told my uncle a story, a long time ago . . ." He pauses. "My uncle's gone now, but I'd like to find Annika or her family, so they can tell me the ending."

And I want to know as well, Annika's story, but first I need to make sure we are talking about the same person. "Her mother wrote about a castle in the inscription."

"If it's the same Annika, the castle would be Schloss Schwansee."

Goose bumps trail down my arms. It must be the same woman.

"It's on the banks of a lake called Hallstatt," he says.

Dozens of images replace Dr. Nemeth's profile on my screen. Bluish-green mountains surrounding a pristine lake, medieval houses in a village called Hallstatt hugging the shore. And there's an ancient castle on the opposite side of the water, no name listed, but it's near a village called Obertraun.

Poetic descriptions accompany the photographs. Sun-painted mountains. Jagged cliffs. Ghostly fog creeping across the jeweled lake. What would it be like to see a place like this, hike around an alpine lake instead of perusing it from my computer screen?

"This list inside . . . What exactly did it say?" he asks.

"It's written in German." I'm not ready to tell him about anything that Charlotte translated. "We bought the book from a seller in Idaho."

"Where did the seller get it?" His voice has changed, tightened, with this question, and I wonder if he's intrigued or angry.

"I emailed her today and asked that very same question."

The bell above the door rings again, and Devon Baker, one of my Saturday morning regulars, tromps inside, tugging on his dad's hand. His father is a local, but almost a decade older than me. While I attended school with his younger sister, I can't for the life of me remember his first name.

"She has it, Daddy," I hear Devon say, dragging Mr. Baker toward me like a magnet about to attach itself to the steel counter.

"I'm sorry, Dr. Nemeth. I need to call you back."

The man doesn't seem to hear me. "Can I borrow Annika's book?"

Hyper-focused, just as I suspected.

Devon rounds the counter and gives me a hug. Then he rushes off toward the castle.

"Just one moment," I whisper to Devon's dad. He looks irritated about having to wait, especially since no one except us and a cat are in the store. So much for customer service.

Turning slightly, I try to hide the telephone under my long hair as if Devon's father won't see it.

"I can pick it up—"

"No." I don't want this man I don't know to show up at the store. "I'll scan the marked pages and upload them to Dropbox."

Then again, I'd like to meet him before I hand over Annika's list, and hear his uncle's story. Mr. Baker glances at me again, and I know I'm about to lose a customer if I don't end the call.

"I'll bring it to you," I blurt. Instantly I wish I could take back my words. I don't want to drive to Columbus or attempt to navigate the crowds at Ohio State.

Devon catapults off the slide, and after his father retrieves him, the man takes a step back as if he might bolt for the door.

"Did you translate any of the notes?" Dr. Nemeth asks, clearly not relenting.

"I'm sorry. I have to go."

"When can I meet you?"

"Email me at the store's address," I say. "We'll figure out a time."

He begins talking again, but I disconnect the call.

"Now—" I lean toward Devon—"what can I help you find?"

Devon smiles, his freckles climbing upward. "A Magic Tree House book."

"I suspect you have a specific one in mind."

He nods. "The one about the sabertooth."

I curl my fingers, pretending they are claws. "It's a fierce saber-tooth."

"I like fierce."

"Very good then. Let's see if we have a saber-toothed tiger in stock." I guide him toward the base of the castle, the section crammed with dozens of Magic Tree House chapter books and decorated with the cutout of a sturdy tree. Devon plucks the saber-tooth story off the shelf, and his dad agrees to buy it along with two more in a series of more than fifty books now.

While Devon climbs up the castle steps again, presumably to ride down the slide one more time, I take his books to the counter.

Mr. Baker hands me his credit card. "Devon thinks this place is his second home."

"I understand. It's been my second home since I was about his age."

Mr. Baker's gaze falls to my left hand, as if someone might have slipped an engagement or even wedding ring on it since story time this morning. Then he smiles at me, any lingering frustration about his waiting gone.

I pull my hand back to reach for a paper bag under the counter. Single men make me nervous enough, the expectations often unclear, but the married ones who like to flirt—nauseating.

"How is Mrs. Baker?" I ask, packing up Devon's books.

"She moved to Wisconsin a few months back."

"I'm sorry," I say, though I'm not entirely sure that's the proper sentiment.

Mr. Baker pushes his glasses up his nose. "We've been separated for more than a year."

I eye the front door, wishing another child in town would have a sudden book crisis. Or an adult for that matter. I'd be fine with just about anyone, except perhaps Scott, walking through that door. "Hard for everyone, I'm sure."

"Not so much," he replies. "We fell out of love long ago. She's engaged to someone else up there."

Ten seconds, that's how long it would take me to sprint to the staircase by the office and be halfway upstairs. I don't like the way he's looking at me or the way he's announced his ex-wife's engagement as if I'm supposed to rejoice at this news.

"Thank you for shopping here, Mr. Baker." I hand over the bag. "I hope you and Devon have a good night."

"My name's Nate."

My nod is sharp, dismissive. "Thank you," I say again, though I don't want to acknowledge his first name. It's old school, I know, but titles are not only a form of respect; they keep a safe distance between me and any man who threatens to step into my space.

"Devon and I are having dinner at China Buffet," he says. "Care to join us?"

Brie's right. I'll never marry if I continue to run from every man who expresses interest in me, but then again, I'd rather stay hidden away upstairs for the rest of my life than marry someone who could fall out of love.

"I'm afraid I can't." I glance at the clock behind the counter. "I have to work until six, and then I have a date afterward." No need to tell him that the date involves hanging out with my nephews.

His smile falls slightly, but he's not deterred. "Perhaps next weekend."

Devon squeals as he zooms down the slide.

"Let me know if there are any other books you'd like me to order," I say, escorting both Devon and his father toward the door before Devon decides to climb back up.

He swipes the bag from his dad's hand. "Thanks, Story Girl."

"Next weekend," Mr. Baker reminds me before stepping toward the door. "We'll go on some sort of adventure."

I lock the front door and head back upstairs to prepare for an adventure of my own through someone else's story.

CHAPTER 10

ANNIKA

LAKE HALLSTATT, AUSTRIA
JUNE 1938

Annika had learned how to read in *Volksschule*, in the years before Vati decided that she needed to stay home and work with him. Instead of schoolbooks, she now read every word of the newspapers her father brought home to feed the fire in their kitchen stove.

These days Annika almost wished she didn't know how to turn letters into words or words into the haunting stories that the Vienna newspaper was celebrating these days—the arrival of Hitler into the country that he'd renamed Ostmark, the plunder of shops in Judenstrasse, the mass burning of Jewish and Marxist books in Salzburg, the arrest of Jewish people attempting to leave

Vienna, and the expulsion of renowned Jews like Bruno Walter from their positions.

How could the people of Vienna celebrate when some of their innocent neighbors were being arrested and others were being denied the privileges to shop, read, and work?

Annika sipped her coffee, creamy with goat milk, and turned the page as the clock ticked to half past eight. She had more time these days—the only animals on the estate now were chickens and the two goats who feasted on the lawn and rewarded the Knopfs with milk, and Vati had locked the castle after he found her looking through the shoe boxes. The next day he'd monitored while she finished cleaning the rooms, and then hid both the key and the star necklace, probably in his pocket because she'd searched the house while he was gone at night and couldn't find it.

Perhaps he'd already lost or sold the necklace in a drunken state. Then the Dornbachs would have nothing to fear.

Soon she would begin frying ham for Vati's breakfast. He was still asleep after another night at the beer hall. He spent most of his evenings there now, probably to avoid being with her or alone with his memories.

The older she grew, the more she reminded him of his deceased wife. Or so she'd heard him say to Hermann when they were working on the chapel.

Sometimes she thought Vati blamed her for her mother's death, though she would never, ever have done anything to harm the woman she'd loved more than anyone else in her entire life. When she was eleven, she'd stepped away from school, thinking it was only for a season as she nursed her mother and cared for the estate. But in spite of the medicine and rest, her mother grew even more ill. While Vati continued to work, Annika took her mother by train to Salzburg once a week to see a specialist who was never able to diagnose exactly what was stealing her life away.

Then Annika had stayed with her in the hospital, feeling as helpless as Vati. He couldn't stand to see his wife in such a state, and near the end, when Kathrin Knopf was sleeping most of her days and nights, Vati stopped visiting altogether. Mama told Annika that he was grieving, that she must understand his pain as well. She tried for her mother's sake, but she never understood how he could abandon his wife in her last days.

Sometimes she missed her mother so much her entire body ached. Other days it seemed there was nothing left to feel, as if she were completely numb to the pain. But the grief always returned. Mama had been gone for almost four years now, but some mornings when Annika woke up, she pretended her mother was still here.

Mama would have sent Annika back to Volksschule—her own schooling had ended at the age of ten, and she wanted her daughter to learn everything that she had not. But no matter what Annika said to try to convince her father, he thought school was a waste, as was the weekly service in Hallstatt's evangelical church.

She turned the newspaper page again and scanned a spread of pictures, the members of a much higher society dancing at a Viennese ball.

Her gaze froze on the picture of Max Dornbach at the top of the page. Her Max with his warm smile, the one he'd displayed whenever they played in the lake.

Yet he was dressed differently than she'd ever seen him, and in his arms—he was guiding a stunning woman around the dance floor, a woman with dark hair and a pale silk gown that shimmered with an entire galaxy of sequins in the light, as if she were a meteor shower on display. A woman who looked at Max as if her world revolved around him.

Annika pressed her hand against the fold of the paper, deciding right then that she didn't like sequins.

Max's name was listed on the right column of the page with the names of others in the photographs. Luzia Weiss—that was the name of the lady dancing with him.

Leaning back against the chair, Annika closed her eyes and forced her frizzy hair into a braid, the tip of it brushing her collar. She wished it were long and silky like Luzia's hair, perfectly smooth. Wished she had a long gown to wear to a ball.

What would it be like to dance "The Blue Danube" with Max? His hazel eyes, the color of sun and pine, gazing down, her own face flushed from his attention even as her feet kept time with the music. In the sea of dancers that swept through her mind, she pretended that Max was smiling because he was dancing with her.

The stove crackled before her, begging for more fuel, and she reached for the scissors on the counter and cut out all the photographs around Max and Luzia, crumpling the paper into balls before feeding one of them to the fire.

She looked at the photograph again, at Max focused on the woman beaming in his arms. Then she cut Luzia out of the photograph and burned her portrait in the flames with the other old news.

The picture of Max and a roll of tape in her hand, she tiptoed down the narrow hallway and opened the door to her bedroom. Inside, she knelt beside her bed and pulled out a metal box, removing her worn copy of *Bambi: A Life in the Woods*, a gift from her mother. She used to read about the author, Felix Salten, in the papers. A Jewish writer who lived in Vienna.

Had he left Austria now like Herr Walter?

She tugged the book to her chest.

Bambi was a sad story in one sense, but she related deeply to the roebuck whose mother died, growing up with a father who remained distant for most of his life. A novel about those who chose to kill for power and even entertainment.

Sometimes she liked to think of Max as a strong roebuck, herself as Faline, whom he loved. It didn't end so well between the deer in Salten's book, but it would be different for Annika and Max. They shared a history that stretched back much longer than any girl he met in Vienna.

If Vati ever found this photograph of Max, he'd be so angry at her for entertaining silly thoughts about the Dornbach son. He'd probably rip up the photograph like she'd done with Luzia's and feed the scraps of newspaper into the stove.

But Max would be safe in these pages—Vati never opened any of her books.

She taped the picture of Max to a page near the back of her book, and after saying a prayer for him, she slipped the box under the bed.

Today she would pretend she was Luzia Weiss. And that Max Dornbach was offering her his hand, smiling down at her.

꙳

"It's a fine day for a swim."

Annika squealed as she turned from the goat, throwing her milk pail to the ground before almost knocking Sarah Leitner over with her hug.

"I've missed you," Annika said. They'd been the best of friends in school, and until this summer, Sarah had visited often when the weather grew warm, wanting to swim together. Annika's bathing suit was still folded in her bureau, waiting for Sarah to return.

"I've missed you as well." Sarah was dressed in a floral summer dress and sandals, her hair neatly curled. And she held an olive-green knapsack in one of her hands, hidden partially behind her back.

"Oh no." Annika tried to brush the dirt from Sarah's dress, but that only seemed to spread it around. "I've messed you up, haven't I?"

"I don't mind being messed up for a hug," Sarah said. "My brother said you came by twice last week."

"I was hoping you could swim." Sarah's brother had said she was working at a nearby farm this summer. In Sarah's growing up, Annika wasn't certain her friend would be able to play in the lake anymore.

"Is Hermann here?" Sarah asked, looping a strand of hair behind her ear.

Annika shook her head. "He's not coming today."

"I—I have something for him."

Annika reached out. "I can give it to him tomorrow."

Sarah clutched the straps of the knapsack closer to her chest. "I'll find him later."

Annika sat on one of the wooden stools outside the barn. The sun had tipped over the Alps on the other side of the lake, chasing the morning fog away. "Everything is quiet here," she said. "Too quiet. Even the Dornbachs haven't returned."

"Perhaps they will stay in Vienna this year."

She couldn't imagine it, an entire summer without Max. Nor

could she let her mind wander to what he might be doing in the city with Fräulein Weiss or another young woman.

The days and hours seemed to spin around her, spiraling out of control. So much kept changing—the rhythm of her life, the people she loved, the news that streamed out of Vienna. If only she could press the cone of the spinning top until it tumbled over, giving her a chance to breathe before the world shifted again.

Sarah sat on a second stool, glancing at the cottage before leaning toward Annika. "Is your father still asleep?"

"He went into Obertraun today."

"People say he's working with the Nazis."

Annika shook her head. "There aren't any Nazis in Obertraun."

"Nazis are everywhere."

A layer of ice seemed to creep across Annika's arms, and she rubbed her hands over them. "Just for today, let's pretend there are none in Austria."

Her friend glanced out at the lake. "Then we must take a swim."

Sarah pulled her bathing suit out of her bag and the two of them changed in the cottage before diving into the lake together, shrieking when the cold water swept over the heat of their skin.

They raced out to the depths but didn't swim far before they returned to play near the shore as if they were ten again, splashing each other, diving under the surface to see who could stay submerged the longest, their lungs begging for a breath.

When the sun began lowering toward the western edge of the lake, Annika followed Sarah back onto the shore, the weeds and mud in the shallows oozing between her toes. "Must you go?" she asked.

"I'm afraid so."

Annika sighed, wishing this day never had to end.

They changed in the boathouse, Sarah transforming back into

the young woman she was expected to be, her knapsack strapped over her shoulder, but she didn't seem to want to leave either. Together they sat at the edge of the dock for a few more stolen minutes, their feet dangling in the cold water.

Annika pointed toward Sarah's throat. "You forgot to put on your necklace."

Her friend shook her head. "My mother won't let me wear it anymore."

She almost told Sarah that she'd found a similar necklace in Frau Dornbach's room, one encrusted with diamonds, but it seemed the star was something to hide these days. "You used to be so proud of that necklace."

"It stirs up unnecessary trouble now."

"Your mother's words?"

Sarah nodded.

"She takes good care of you and your brother."

"Your mother used to take such good care of you, too." Both of them looked across the lake to the outline of the cemetery on the other side. "Do you still miss her?"

"I'll always miss her," Annika said. "Will you come swim again soon?"

Sarah lowered her bag into her lap. "Things are about to change for our family."

Annika shivered. She didn't know if she could bear another change.

"My father lost his position in the mine," Sarah said, "and now all the Austrian Jews are being summoned to Vienna."

"Will you go?"

Sarah shook her head. "We're moving to Bolivia to live with our cousin. He's already found Father a job."

Tears sprang from a well deep inside Annika, spilling over onto her cheeks.

"It's warm enough to swim all year in South America," Sarah said, talking faster as if to convince herself along with Annika. "And we won't have to worry—"

"I don't know what I'll do without you."

"I'll write," Sarah promised.

"And I shall write you."

Sarah hugged her. "Friends for life."

"*Geh mit Gott,*" Annika said, trying to be strong.

Go with the blessing of God.

But even as she said the words, her heart was bleeding. No matter how many extra schillings she saved from their grocery money, hiding them from Vati in her metal box, she'd never have enough for passage to South America.

Sarah slipped into her canoe, and sadness washed over Annika as her friend paddled away.

Perhaps it was time for her to say a final good-bye to that wide-eyed girl who wanted to play. Perhaps it was time for her to grow up as well.

CHAPTER 11

"I'm late, I'm lost! I'm late, I'm lost! I'm going to miss my own wedding."

Well, not my *wedding*, but the panicked words from Robert Munsch's *Ribbon Rescue* loop through my head as I attempt— quite poorly—to traverse the metropolis known as Ohio State University, searching for a parking space to house Charlotte's Prius.

"What time is Dr. Nemeth's class?" Charlotte asks from the seat beside me, her eyes hidden behind Jackie O sunglasses, her silver-white hair curled with soft waves.

"Four."

She checks her cell phone. "It's three fifteen now."

"We're close," I say, trying to reassure both of us that this road trip wasn't in vain.

In hindsight, perhaps I should have accepted Dr. Nemeth's offer to drive to Mount Vernon, but Charlotte has been asking to shop in Easton, and at the time, it seemed like a good idea to visit those stores and Dr. Nemeth on the same day. I hadn't wanted a man who'd found me via the Internet to come to the bookshop either, but it wasn't like Dr. Nemeth couldn't visit on his own—the address to Magic Balloon is right on the website.

Charlotte's phone rings, Bach's Minuet in G major interrupting my thoughts. She quickly mutes the ringer.

"Who's that?" I ask.

She shrugs. "Probably a telemarketer."

I nod toward the phone. "You can answer it."

She tucks it into her navy-blue handbag instead.

We pass century-old brick buildings, one with a clock tower, and then modern ones enclosed in glass. A reflecting pool. Shady buckeye trees. The gray perimeter of the football stadium and Grecian columns on the library. No time for it now, but I wish we could escape into the library for an hour and peruse the books.

I groan as we drive past the clock tower a second time. "I should have met him someplace else."

"We'll get there," Charlotte says, gently resting one of her hands over my fingers, which have begun drumming a beat on the steering wheel. We stop and wait for a horde of students to ramble across the street.

It's three forty by the time we find a visitor's space, at least two blocks from Dr. Nemeth's office. Charlotte holds on to my arm as we rush toward the sprawling brick edifice that houses the history department. The admin at the front desk directs us to Dr. Nemeth's office, but even though the light is on, his door is closed. And locked.

No surprise, I guess. It's now two minutes after four.

Through the window, I see Dr. Nemeth's desk cluttered with papers and notebooks and an assortment of scattered pens. Hanging above his desk, perfectly centered, is an eight-by-ten photograph of him with a stunning woman at his side and a toddler in his arms. The woman has straight blonde hair, and she's wearing a floral sundress that matches her daughter's attire. Picture perfect in the frame.

I lean against the doorpost in defeat. "I don't know if he'll come back to his office after class."

Charlotte glances down the hallway. "We'll have to find out where he's teaching."

"I'm not storming into his class!"

Charlotte puts one hand on her hip. "We came all this way, and now you're going to quit?"

"It's not quitting. I'll just connect with him later."

But Charlotte's not waiting until later to find out about Annika and her list. "I'm going to speak with that young lady at the front desk."

She turns away, but she doesn't walk far. An older man, a fellow professor I assume, wheels his chair to the edge of his office door. "Are you the woman with the German book?"

I step toward him. "My name's Callie."

He doesn't seem to care about my name. "Josh said to find him upstairs in room 240."

Charlotte flashes a triumphant smile, and I thank the professor before following her back down the hall and then up a narrow flight of steps. Charlotte props open the door to the lecture hall as I eye the stacked rows of students. Several hundred of them.

At the bottom of the hall stands Dr. Nemeth, his brown hair swept to the side. His jeans, oxfords, and tan T-shirt make him look more like a student than a professor. He doesn't seem to notice as Charlotte and I slip into the back row and fold down plastic chairs.

"Austria's Salzkammergut was a mountain retreat for Nazi officers during World War II," he tells his class, one hand on the side of a wooden podium. "The Nazi elite built villas on the shores of the seventy-six lakes in that district to entertain their mistresses. They also tested submarines and underwater rockets in the deepest lakes, three hundred or more feet below the surface."

Charlotte seems to be as immersed in his lecture as the rest of the class, her chin propped up by her fist, the sleeve of her pale-pink blouse on the armrest. And I wonder—were Annika's parents members of the Nazi Party? Her mother might have been the mistress of an officer, gifting Annika with the *Bambi* book before it was banned.

"The Nazis stole and then hid countless pieces of art from the Jewish people, along with gold bullion and other relics, in their quest for wealth and, more important to many of them, power. The salt mines and tunnels in these mountains served as a sort of depository for such treasures during the war, but what happened after the war is just as shocking."

No one moves in the room, and I wonder at the magic of this professor. He's waved a wand of sorts, hypnotizing with his words. A map of Austria appears on the screen behind Dr. Nemeth, and he sweeps a circle around Hallstatt and several surrounding lakes with his hand.

"The Nazis planned to build a Fourth Reich here in what they dubbed the Alpine Fortress, but when the Allies infiltrated their fortress, they began throwing stuff in these lakes. Crates and crates of gold, weapons, thousands of counterfeit British banknotes that Hitler planned to use to destroy the British economy during the war."

What if the Nazis used Annika's book to record what they hid?

But then again, what Nazi, rushing from the Allied troops, would take the time to write out a detailed list in a children's book?

Dr. Nemeth glances up at our row, and I lift my hand in an awkward wave. He nods and then returns to the matter at hand. "Some people call this region the Devil's Dustbin, for it seems as if the devil himself swept across Austria and dumped whatever remained right here."

I've done some research about the Nazis in both Germany and Austria over the years, in particular how they treated Felix Salten and other Jewish authors among them. My favorite monkey wouldn't have existed if the Nazis had their way. His German authors, Margret and Hans Rey, were also Jewish. They fled by bicycle when the Nazis invaded their refuge in Paris, taking their treasured drafts of the *Curious George* manuscript with them.

But I've never read anything about the Nazis hiding treasure in Austria's lakes.

Dr. Nemeth gestures toward the region one more time, and I run my hands over the stone-colored tote in my lap, a cocoon of sorts for *Bambi*.

Is it possible that Annika found treasure in one of these lakes or in a mine near Hallstatt? And if so, what happened to it?

"Let's take a five-minute break," Dr. Nemeth announces to the class. Chatter ripples across the room as he turns off the projector and hikes up the stairs, his hand stretching toward me as I stand. "You must be Callie."

"That's me," I say, shaking his hand. "I'm sorry I'm so late. I—"

"No need or, frankly, time for apologies." He's looking at me, but he doesn't see me, not really. His gaze is focused on the tote strung over my arm.

"This is my friend Charlotte Trent," I say, redirecting him for the moment. "She helped me translate part of the list."

Charlotte smiles at him. "My eyes aren't as cooperative as they used to be."

He shakes her hand. "A pleasure to meet you, Mrs. Trent."

Reaching inside the bag, I pull out the book for him. He finds Annika's name inscribed in the front, tracing the word with his finger. Then he turns to the second page, and his eyes widen when they land on the handwritten listing of the gold necklace and ruby brooch.

"You know German?" I ask.

"A little."

He flips through the pages quickly as if he has to catch the writing before it flies away. Then he starts to translate more of Annika's words. "'Diamond earrings. Pearl strand. Brass candlesticks.'"

Five minutes have passed now, but Dr. Nemeth seems to have forgotten about both the time and the crowd of students waiting behind him. Finally he closes the book, but instead of handing it to me, he pulls it closer to his chest. "I'm leaving Sunday for the Salzkammergut," he says. "I have a grant to take six students with me, and we'll spend almost a month searching for items like these that the Nazis dumped or hid."

Charlotte inches toward him. "It's been eighty years . . ."

"It seems impossible, but divers continue to find things under the rock ledges and submerged forests in these lakes." Dr. Nemeth slowly lowers the book. "And the water is cold enough to preserve what's been left behind."

What would it be like to dive into the depths of one of those lakes and search for hidden candlesticks and jewelry among the ledges and forests? Of course I'd never go, but it must be magical to explore where few people have ever been. A treasure hunt on an entirely new scale.

He glances back down at the podium before looking at me again. "Can I borrow this book?"

I shake my head. "I want to return it to Annika's family."

"I'll get it back to you by the end of the week," he assures me, but it feels as if someone is taking something valuable—priceless, even—from me, like one of the items listed inside the book.

"I don't know—"

"We're a lot alike, Callie," he says, but I can't imagine that I have much in common with this professor of history. "You want to return books to their original owners, and I want to return stolen heirlooms to the descendants of those who lost their things during the war."

The pieces seem to fall into place, this mutual quest of ours to reconcile the past.

"You'll tell me what you find about Annika?"

He glances down at the forlorn deer on the cover, standing in the forest alone. "I'll pass along everything I can."

His best offer—a book loan for the week to help us both reunite things with their owners.

Dr. Nemeth turns, the *Bambi* book in hand, and pierces the chatter in the rows below us with a low-pitched whistle. And I want to stay here, learning more about the history of these lakes.

I lean toward Charlotte, whispering, "Should we listen to the rest of the lecture?"

She checks her phone. "We don't have time."

"The mall is open until ten."

Charlotte shakes her head. "I need to be home for dinner."

"You have a date?" I ask, eyebrows cresting.

"I can't tell you."

Dr. Nemeth has started talking about where various Nazi members hid near the end of the war, including the Austrian Alps. I wish we could stay a bit longer to hear his stories, but Charlotte is determined, and now I'm intrigued by her urgency to return home.

Outside we both slip on our sunglasses, and as we walk to the car, my phone buzzes.

"Who is it?" Charlotte asks.

"The researcher in Vienna." I scan the email. "She's going to look for the newspaper photograph from 1938. When she finds it, she'll email it along with the caption so we know whose picture Annika taped in her book."

"You think there's a love story there, don't you?"

I shrug. "Perhaps."

Charlotte knows I'm a romantic. An undercover romantic, but a hopeless one nonetheless.

"When did you start keeping secrets from me?" I ask as Charlotte checks her phone again.

"It's not actually a secret. . . ."

"Then tell me."

She smiles over at me as one who knows me well, better even than I know myself. "Sometimes surprises can be good, Calisandra."

"Not in my experience."

"Then perhaps we'll have to change your experience."

But I don't want to change. The steadiness of my life, the nest I've built around myself, keeps me safe. Other people, like Dr. Nemeth and my sister and Charlotte, could step outside their walls and experience life on the outside, but me, I'm quite secure inside the twigs and leaves I've plucked for myself. No surprises necessary.

CHAPTER 12

ANNIKA

LAKE HALLSTATT, AUSTRIA
JUNE 1938

The sky had collapsed onto Lake Hallstatt during the night, a soft quilt settling over the water like a blanket, hiding the flicker of sun. At dawn's break, Annika plodded back toward the barn to milk the goats, swimming through white waves of fog instead of the blue ones lapping against the dock.

After chores, she prepared eggs and fruit along with coffee in an attempt to revive Vati after his previous night's dance with the lager, but he didn't answer when she knocked on his door.

Around nine, Hermann arrived with a toolbox in one hand, a lunch pail in the other. *"Guten Morgen,"* he said, setting down his toolbox so he could tip his cap.

She glanced back toward the closed door down the corridor, embarrassed that Vati wasn't awake to meet him. "He's still sleeping."

Hermann looked down at his boots, and she hated him, or anyone, thinking that her father was a drunk.

"He's been feeling a bit under the weather lately."

"Of course."

Hermann stood a foot taller than Annika, and his blond hair, more white than yellow, was in need of a cut. He wore the same attire he'd worn every day he came to work with Vati, a flannel shirt over thick arms, denim overalls. Carried the same silver pail and toolbox. With everything changing in their country, this sameness comforted her in a way. Now that Sarah was gone, and with Max still in Vienna, Hermann was her only friend.

"Did Sarah find you before she left?"

Hermann seemed surprised at the question. "I don't know why she'd be looking for me."

Annika shrugged. "She wanted to give you something."

Instead of inquiring about Sarah, Hermann nodded toward the window. "Should I start working?" he asked as if she were directing the chapel project in her father's absence.

"I suppose."

The aluminum percolator whistled on the stove, and she poured him a cup of steaming coffee. They had no sugar in the house, and while she'd gladly offer him goat milk, Hermann preferred to drink his coffee black. He downed it quickly, as if he welcomed the heat, and thanked her for it.

Hermann lived on a farm on the other side of Obertraun, the youngest of five children. When they were in primary school, he'd often joined Max, Annika, and Sarah for swimming and boating.

Once she'd even dreamed about them spending a lifetime as friends, Sarah and Hermann marrying in the village and, of course, her and Max becoming husband and wife, living here part of the year and the rest either in Vienna or traveling the world together.

Now Hermann visited three days a week, though time for swimming was past for him as well. He was a year older than Max and spent his summers working here and at his family's farm. She'd asked Sarah once what she thought of marrying Hermann, but her friend said her parents would never allow her to marry a Gentile boy.

Annika snatched the chapel key off the hook by the front door, and Hermann followed her silently out of the cottage, to the family chapel set against the mountain. She'd visited the chapel almost every day this past week to deliver lunch or help her father and Hermann work on the platform they were building near the altar, but she didn't linger as she used to in the library or Frau Dornbach's dressing room.

While the plaster walls were supposed to house God in this chapel, she didn't think one could box Him up, though Sarah told her that God once lived in a gold-plated box. In the Bible, people carried God around with them as they wandered through the wilderness. God traveling in a case of gold, Annika could imagine that, but not trapped between walls of gray plaster with a dusty tapestry and dirt-smeared windows, two wooden pews and a stone floor.

Mama taught her all about Jesus before she died. She used to speak of God's presence like it was a song, stealing across the lake and the trees, over the Alps and up into the sky.

Did a song ever die, or did it keep traveling?

Surely it kept traveling, she thought, all the way up into the heavens, threading through stars and knotting itself around the fullness of the moon.

She'd volunteered last year to clean the chapel, but Vati insisted that the Dornbachs wanted to leave it in its dismal state. If they demanded a clean house, but not a clean chapel, it made her wonder what Herr and Frau Dornbach thought about God.

"Do you know why they're adding the platform?" she asked.

"Didn't your father tell you?"

She shook her head. "He never talks to me about such things."

"It's for the casket of Christoph Eyssl." The salt manager from centuries ago who'd built this castle.

"Why do they want his casket here?"

"His testament states that pallbearers should bring his body back to his home every fifty years. The Dornbachs are a decade late, but Frau Dornbach has agreed to accommodate this."

Annika shivered at the thought of the man's casket displayed here. "I wonder why they are just now agreeing."

"Because they, like everyone, are trying to maintain a sense of normalcy."

And, she suspected, they wanted to maintain good standing with the local parish.

Perhaps, when the platform was complete, the Dornbachs would add a new tapestry in here, something vibrant and cheery, a garden scene or one with the lake. If Vati would let her borrow the key, she'd collect wild daffodils and primroses during the spring months to brighten the chapel and cover the musty scent.

God must live in flowers as He did in a bird's song.

The engine of a car startled her, and she rushed to the window. The fog was still so thick that she couldn't see past the trees that separated this chapel from their cottage, but seconds later a black-and-burgundy automobile broke through the fog, rumbling toward the chapel.

Had the Dornbachs finally returned? Her mind rushed to take an inventory of the house. She'd restacked all of Frau Dornbach's shoe boxes beside the armoire and cleaned the rooms. But what would Frau Dornbach do when she realized her necklace was missing?

Annika slipped away from the glass as the car parked beside the castle's front steps. She didn't recognize the vehicle, but that wasn't unusual. The Dornbachs purchased a new car at least once a year.

"I must get my father," she said. The family usually sent a telegram before a visit, but the last two times they'd arrived unexpectedly, almost as if they were trying to catch her father in a lethargic state. Not that it was difficult to do these days. It was well after ten now, and Vati was still in bed.

She raced out into the fog and through the trees, flinging open the cottage door.

"Vati!" she shouted, running down the short corridor into his room. He was still asleep, one arm hanging off the side of the bed, fully dressed, except he'd somehow managed to remove his shoes.

Instead of opening his eyes, he made a growling sound. "Go away."

"Get up, Vati." She shook the covers. "Someone is here."

He swore as he lifted his head, his skin a grayish color. "The Dornbachs?"

"I don't know."

"They should warn a man before coming." His legs wobbled when they hit the rug, two columns trying to balance his massive frame.

"I'll heat the coffee," she said, stepping back into the hallway.

He shook his head, trying to steady himself on the bedpost. "Go tell them I was up late working on their chapel."

Stopping in the bathroom, Annika rinsed off her face and ran a brush through her brown hair, frizzy from the damp air. There was no time to change clothes, but her work skirt and blouse were an improvement on the worn winter coat she'd been wearing the last time she saw Max.

She braided her hair as she strode across the living room and then out through the strip of trees, into the courtyard that separated their cottage from the manor home. No one was inside the car when she returned to the courtyard, but she heard male voices in the chapel. Someone was talking to Hermann.

Had Herr Dornbach come alone?

A man stepped out of the chapel, and a moment passed before she realized it was Max, his light-brown hair hidden under his hat. His eyes met hers, and even as she straightened her shoulders, her heart pounded so hard it made her chest quiver.

"Hello, Annika."

"Hello." She glanced at the empty car again. "Where are your parents?"

"They stayed in Vienna."

Max was still six months shy of being old enough to obtain his driver's license, but then again, perhaps no one cared about such things these days.

"Vati's been detained," she said. She could lie to Herr and Frau Dornbach, saying that he'd been working late, but she could never lie to Max no matter what her father asked of her.

"I'm not here to see your father." He opened the back door of the vehicle. "I wanted to see you."

Annika caught her breath, her heart feeling as if it might puncture a hole straight through her chest. She could see herself again in a beautiful gown, dancing with Max across a polished floor. "Really?"

He nodded before turning toward the backseat of his car, retrieving a small cage with a gray cat enclosed inside. "I'd like you to meet Frederica," he said, his smile sheepish. "I was hoping you could take care of her."

The beating of her heart plummeted as she reached for the cage, his words dissolving the foolish vision of him smiling at her as he'd done with Luzia. She would do just about anything for him, and she was fairly certain he knew this. "Of course."

"She's not the sort of cat that likes to stay inside." He lowered the cage to the grass. "In a way, she reminds me of you, *Kätzchen*."

"I'm not a kitten, Max."

Frederica clawed at the door of the cage. When Max opened it, the cat scampered toward the barn.

"She won't stay away for long," he said, watching the cat race through the door.

Annika turned back to him. "You drove all that way to bring me a cat?"

"I have other reasons as well."

She smiled again, brushing her hands over her skirt. Perhaps he had missed her as much as she'd missed him.

His gaze wandered to the trees that hid the caretaker's cottage. "Where's your father?"

"He's—" she started, searching for her next words, but the stomping of boots on leaves interrupted them. Vati no longer looked down at Max, at least not physically, but he was twice Max's girth, and the sneer on his face reminded Annika of a steely samlet from the lake with its many teeth.

Max held Vati's gaze, not wavering, like he'd stepped into his father's shoes as lord of this estate.

"I wasn't expecting you." Her father's words seemed to drag along with his feet. He eyed the cage at Max's feet but didn't say anything. He was used to Max bringing a variety of pets with him.

"I've only come for the night." Max unlocked the trunk of the car. "I have to return to school in the morning."

"Does your father know that you've taken the car?" Vati asked.

"He's much too distracted to realize either the car or his son is gone."

Vati's eyes narrowed. "It seems now is the time to be focused."

"Vienna has changed overnight, Herr Knopf. We're all still trying to find our footing."

"We've found our footing quite well here."

Something crossed Max's face that Annika didn't understand. Sadness or perhaps anger. "I suppose you have."

Vati took a step back. "Tell your father that the platform in the chapel is close to completion."

Annika didn't contradict her father, but she doubted Herr Dornbach would think the platform was almost finished.

"And tell him that it's most urgent I speak with him soon. I've found something of his . . ."

She waited for him to tell Max about the necklace, but he disappeared toward the rear of the castle. Max lifted a satchel off the backseat.

"Do you want me to help with your suitcase?" she asked.

"No, *Kätzchen*." He looped the satchel's strap over his shoulder before he slammed the trunk closed.

Annika sighed, wishing she owned a sequined dress like Luzia's after all, so brilliant that Max couldn't take his eyes off her. Perhaps then he'd realize she had grown into a woman or at least a cat. Not a kitten that needed rescuing.

She may not be able to impress him with her clothing, but perhaps she could regain some of his admiration with her cooking. She'd saved enough schillings to buy the supplies for *Tafelspitz*—a meal traditionally made with boiled beef. Max had stopped eating meat long ago, but she could make it from whatever vegetables she could obtain from the grocer.

"Are you hungry?" she asked as Max lifted the cage from the ground and stepped toward the castle.

"I suppose I am."

"I'll make you Tafelspitz for dinner."

He eyed her curiously, as if surprised that she could cook.

"With parsnips and potatoes and—"

"Thank you," he said, stopping her before she rattled off every ingredient in the meal.

"I'll use whatever fresh vegetables the grocer has in stock."

He reached into his coat pocket and retrieved several silver coins.

She shook her head. "I have the money, Max."

"Schillings?"

"Of course."

"You can no longer use your schillings in Austria," he said sadly, holding out the coins again.

"But what will we use?"

"The grocer will need Reichsmarks."

He dumped several coins into her open palm, and she stared down at the black-webbed swastikas looking back up at her. Perhaps the storm of this Third Reich was rolling into their lakes after all.

"Everything's changing," she whispered.

He turned back toward her before he climbed the steps to the front door. "Hitler's changed much more than our money."

"I don't like it, Max."

She'd hoped he would reassure her, say that she was being silly in her concerns, but he shook his head instead. "I don't either."

"What are we to do?" she asked.

"Fight, in our own way."

But there was nothing she could do to fight the mighty Hitler. She was only a young woman. A kitten, in Max's eyes.

Hours later, after she'd prepared the meal, she delivered the Tafelspitz to the castle. The front door was unlocked, and she found Max in the library, a book and what looked like a letter in his lap.

She set the tray on the circular table. "What are you reading?"

"*Bambi.*"

She sat on the chair opposite him. "My mother gave me that book before she died."

He slipped the paper into the book and closed the cover, his eyes turning toward the dark window as if he could see the cottage behind the trees. "These days it feels as if we are all being hunted."

Perhaps he saw his own dreams of escaping in those pages about the deer.

"If you could run, Max, where would you go?"

"To my aunt's home in Paris," he said. "Or someplace else where the Nazis aren't allowed to hunt people like they are prey."

"It makes me sad to think of people hurting someone who's weaker instead of protecting those who have already been wounded."

Max placed one hand on the book. "People hurt others because they are afraid."

Fear, Annika thought, was a curious thing. Motivating some to hurt and others to heal.

She almost told him about the necklace, but it seemed that Vati had forgotten about it now. Max had enough to worry about without her adding to his heavy load.

When he reopened his book, the words that had once slipped easily between them turned into an awkward silence, bricking up a wall that separated them instead. They could talk here for hours tonight without his parents or her father to disturb them, and yet it seemed as if he were more interested in the silence found inside these walls than conversation.

As Annika returned to the cottage, loneliness engulfed her once again. A bird sang out in the darkness, and she wished she could fly away with the songbirds until Hitler was gone. And Max had returned to her.

CHAPTER 13

The front yard of my sister's home smells like charcoal and grilled meat. Charlotte and I step out of the Prius, onto the sidewalk, and I brace myself for the front door to spring open, my nephews attempting to tackle me with their hugs.

On the way home from Columbus, Brie texted and asked us to join her family for dinner. Charlotte seemed to forget her own plans for the night, readily agreeing to a meal of barbecued chicken, fried potatoes, and fruit salad.

I scan the narrow driveway that leads to an attached garage before glancing up toward two stories and attic dormers of the Victorian house. Typically my nephews are either playing in the drive or watching for me from the windows, but I don't see them peeking down at me this evening.

Did Brie forget to tell the twins I was coming? Or maybe she wanted to surprise them.

Charlotte glances at her watch. "Perhaps we should wait a few minutes."

"Brie won't care if we're early." After our excursion today, I was glad to be ten minutes ahead of schedule. "And Ethan already has meat on the grill."

After flipping the latch on their picket fence, I open it wide for Charlotte and we stroll up the pebbly path that divides the lawn in two, giving my nephews extra time to tumble out. But when we step up onto the porch, the front door is still closed and, oddly enough, locked. I ring the doorbell and wait.

Charlotte checks her cell phone. "Perhaps Brie is still at the store."

"I know where the key is." Tucked away on the corner of their porch in a tiny pop-up box that Ethan rigged up after Brie locked herself out one afternoon, their boys napping upstairs. Before the locksmith arrived, she'd busted the window on the back door and let herself in.

"I'll text her," Charlotte says as I retrieve the key. "We won't want to scare her if she's inside."

Seconds later, my sister's face appears in the narrow window that lines the evergreen door. She waves at us, but it takes her way too long to open the door. An image flashes in my mind of Miss Clavel in Madeline's Parisian boardinghouse.

"In the middle of one night Miss Clavel turned on her light and said, 'Something is not right!'"

Except there's no disaster at the end of the *Madeline* book, only a roomful of little girls wanting what they don't have.

I take a deep breath, pushing Miss Clavel and her girls back to Paris. Dissatisfaction can lead to disaster almost as much as panicking when nothing is wrong.

Brie cracks open the door. "You're early." She looks at Charlotte and then me as if we've made a major faux pas.

"Just a couple minutes." I point back toward the sidewalk. "Should we wait in the car?"

"No, that would be silly."

"It's all starting to seem a little silly to me."

"Give me a minute." But Brie doesn't move, standing in front of us as if she's guarding the entry into the foyer. She's a few inches shorter than me so I glance over her shoulder, wondering where Oscar and Owen are. Something moves behind her, but I don't see either boy.

Charlotte turns toward me. "Let's go get a cup of coffee."

"You don't drink coffee." I tilt my head. "What's going on?"

"Nothing." My sister steps onto the porch, and when she inches the door closed behind her, I know something is definitely not right. A horrific thought pierces my mind, my imagination succumbing to the worst possible scenario.

Are the boys and even Ethan inside with some sort of intruder? Perhaps Brie can't say anything or someone will hurt her family.

I lower my voice. "Is everyone safe?"

"Yes," she assures me, "just not quite ready for dinner."

"I'll help you get ready."

A minivan pulls into the driveway beside the house, parking in front of the garage. Brie groans when the passenger door opens and a petite woman steps out—Jenna Sainte, a friend from church. Her husband walks around to the back of the van.

Brie swipes her hand over her head. "Now they've spoiled it."

"Spoiled what?" I ask, exasperated. Then slowly, like sap

trickling down a tapped maple tree, it hits me. Brie's secrecy and her strangeness when I told her I needed to go to Columbus today. Charlotte's insistence that we return home for dinner instead of going to the mall.

I turn back toward my sister, my words processing the slow revelation. "You've planned a party."

"Of course I've planned a party!"

Anxiety clenches my chest. "But my birthday's not for another week."

"I wouldn't have been able to surprise you next week."

My legs feel wobbly. She probably would have still surprised me, but not like this.

"I know you're not big on surprises," Brie says, apologizing in one sense, but not relenting. *Not big on surprises* is stating it quite mildly.

"I'll be fine," I say, but the quaking has traveled into my voice as I eye the door. Exactly how many people are waiting on the other side?

Charlotte reaches for my arm, this time steadying me. "Everyone needs a surprise party once in her life."

Jenna steps to the porch and gives me a hug. "Happy birthday."

"Thank you."

Brie plants both fists on her hips. "You were supposed to park around the back."

"Oh no." Jenna's smile falls. "Have we ruined it?"

"No," I assure her. "I'm still going to act surprised."

Jenna nods to her husband, and he slides a large white box from the back of the van. "The bakery was running behind."

"Still go around back," Brie says, shooing Jenna off the porch. "The kids have been practicing all day how they are going to surprise their aunt."

Yet another reason that I'm grateful for the preparation.

Once Jenna is gone, Brie reopens the door, and with Charlotte at my side, I tentatively step over the threshold, my arms wrapped across my chest to brace myself.

Owen springs out of the crawl space under the wide stairs. "Surprise!"

The word echoes off the wood paneling, followed by a chorus of voices, the shouts reverberating around the foyer and out the door still open behind me. While I'm not really intending to run, I'm glad I left it open. Unlike my sister, I'm not enamored of being in the center of anything, at least not without a book in my hand.

People seem to step right out of the paneling, like ghosts of all sizes in the hours after dark. I, on the other hand, wish I could fold myself back into the wall so they aren't all staring at me.

And they are staring, waiting for me to say something brilliant, I suppose. My mouth hangs instead. Catching flies, my father used to say when I couldn't find words. Oh, for a book to supply them for me.

Both my nephews race toward me, elbowing each other in the process. In seconds Owen is beside me, clinging to my leg. And Oscar—he's yanking on my hand, pulling me toward the kitchen. "Come on, Aunt Callie."

I glance back at Charlotte as the sea of people parts, and she's smiling at me.

The sea follows us into the kitchen, filling the shared living and dining space. Jenna is beside the counter with her husband, both of them frantically lighting the last of thirty candles on the expanse of cake, like Piglet and Tigger lighting so many candles that Pooh loses sight of the cake.

"Would you care for a piece of my oh-what-a-surprise birthday cake?"

Like the candlelight, Pooh's words flicker in my brain.

Some of the guests circled around us are from church and my college years; others are my story-time kids with their parents. I don't see Devon or his father in the crowd, and at first, I'm relieved they haven't come, but the guilt quickly follows. I should be thrilled to see Devon here even if he's with his father. I should be thrilled to see everyone.

I suspect I'll be feeling guilty a lot tonight.

Jenna rushes around the counter and gives me another hug as if she didn't see me on the porch. "Come blow out your candles before we start the house on fire."

"It might take all night," someone quips from the back.

I glare in their direction. "Very funny."

Jenna props up the flickering cake, the white icing framing a photograph of me in my Story Girl attire. The edges of the cake are frosted with books that look like bricks, the whole display reminding me of a fireplace glowing with flames.

Charlotte begins singing from the back of the room, her beautiful alto inviting the others to join her in the familiar song. As they sing, I read the words written in red icing to match my story-time attire.

Happy 30th, Callie
Our Favorite Story Girl

"Blow them out!" Owen shouts when the song ends, and everyone laughs.

I take a deep breath, but Brie stops me. "You have to make a wish first."

My eyes close, but I can't think of a single thing I'd wish for—it seems I have everything I could ever need here in this room. Then I wish for the only thing that comes to mind in that blur of a moment, that I could have my own family one day. A wish I'll tell no one because I don't want anyone in search of a man for me.

If only I could have a family without the heartache.

With a deep breath, I blow out every last candle, and the room erupts in applause. Then one by one, as if they're teasing me, the flames reignite. In seconds, the entire cake is glowing again.

I groan. The children laugh. And I hear a few adults snicker as well.

When I look around the room this time, I'm smiling along with everyone else. "Who's going to blow these out now?"

"Someone get a bowl of water," Jenna shouts, but Brie already has a bowl ready. The kids slowly realize I'm serious—I am not blowing out thirty candles a second time—and a horde of them jump in to help me, blowing and then drowning the germ-infested wicks in the bowl before licking off the icing and strawberry cake clinging to the wax.

"Wait until you turn thirty," I threaten my sister, but she just laughs and takes a photograph.

So I dive in. Not into the cake, but into Brie's party. Charlotte is sitting on a chair in the living room, gleaming as if someone is celebrating the birth of her own daughter, and her pride strengthens me.

"Can I have a piece of cake?" It's Michael, the boy who educated everyone in the store about his new underpants. His mother nods to signal her consent.

"I believe there's a piece of cake just for you," I say, ruffling his hair.

"Cake for everyone," Brie announces like it's a story-time snack, and the kids around us cheer. I'm thankful that the spotlight has turned and the cake is right smack in the center.

A red paper plate in hand, I scoop up a corner piece and lower it to Michael with much pomp and circumstance. Then Brie slices, I serve the cake along with a scoop of ice cream for each plate, and everyone seems happy. My sister is right in her element, entertaining this crowd in her home.

Charlotte steps up to the counter and serves herself two scoops of chocolate ice cream, no cake. "Surprise," she says, kissing my cheek. "The best in your life is yet to come."

If she weren't holding a plate of ice cream, I'd hug her. "I think I've already had the best, thanks to you and Brie."

"Thanks to the Lord. It's hard to imagine, but He loves you even more than I ever could." She takes a bite of the ice cream and nods toward the small group circled around Brie. "I think having a sister who loves you must be one of the greatest blessings of all."

"She's certainly a blessing to me."

Around nine, the guests begin to fade away like clams claimed by the sea, the tide calling them home. Charlotte kisses my cheek again before driving her Prius away on her own, and Ethan wrangles each twin upstairs for bed.

Once everyone is gone, Brie slides down to the crumb-covered floor, leaning her head back against the wall. "That was a disaster."

I shove a plate out of the way with my toe before sitting beside her. Instead of flowing away with the tide, I want to dig myself deep into the sand. "It was fabulous."

"Are you certain?"

"I loved it. Truly."

She sighs. "That's the important thing."

"And I love that you did this for me. Award for best sister ever goes to you."

"I wish we had more family here who could celebrate with you."

"Our family would have only caused chaos."

I've never had any contact with my mother's relatives, and no one on our father's side of the family seemed to care much about us—or him, for that matter, while he was alive. When he died, Brie reached out to his family with the news that Arthur Randall was gone, his arteries clogged by smoke. She courageously reached out, but no one in the family reached back in. I figured they were afraid Arthur's daughters would ask them for money.

Ethan has a large extended family who bicker among themselves and debate about everything from who should win the Super Bowl to what sort of sauce belongs on ravioli. Ultimately, they love each other to pieces, no holds barred. For Brie, joining the Goretti family was like finding her way home. She slipped easily into their chaos, contributing quite well to it all.

"I wanted to give you something special for your birthday," Brie says.

"You outdid yourself."

"This was a party, not a gift."

I lean my head back against a cabinet. "You don't need to give me a gift."

"That's good because you already have the *Bambi* book I bought for you. Or at least, the professor has it."

"He's going to bring it back."

Ethan slips into the kitchen, standing beside his wife. When Brie glances up at him, a look passes between them. Love in the deepest of forms, grounded in crumbs and kids and complete exhaustion.

I'm envious of their relationship, but also insanely happy that my sister found a man who clearly adores her, a man who has given her what she desired most in life. And he's given her plenty of other good things along with a family—a beautiful home, security, a love that will undoubtedly last a lifetime.

She wants the same for me, but I've told her repeatedly that I don't thrive on noise, that I'm plenty satisfied with the blessing of my small family—a sister in Brie, my amazing nephews, an aunt in Charlotte.

Brie looks back at me, a tentative smile crossing her lips. "Ethan and I have one more thing for you."

I wave my hands in front of me, shaking my head. "You've already given me too much."

Ethan hands Brie an envelope, and she tosses it over to me. "Before you open it," she says, "we are absolutely, positively sure that we want to give this to you."

Anxiety begins to bubble inside me again, and I want to dig myself deeper into my hole. Or have the salty tide sweep me out of my home in the sand, into the vast hiding places of the sea.

But my sister won't let me hide. She and Ethan both watch as I open the envelope, waiting for my reaction. I'm sure it will be about as good as when everyone yelled "surprise" a few hours earlier.

Inside is a birthday card with a woman on the cover lounging on a hot-pink chaise, engrossed in a novel. The front reads, *Some people live by the book.*

Looking up, I glance at the two of them, at the expectation on their faces. There's no turning back now. I open the card.

Others write their own story.

Under the words is a hand-drawn picture of a stick woman wearing a pair of green boots, a brownish structure that resembles the Eiffel Tower looming behind her. Oscar, I assume, drew it in crayon for me. He likes to draw and wants me to read *Henri's Walk to Paris* almost every night I'm here.

Underneath is a note from Brie. *Happy birthday, Sis. It's time for you to write a chapter or two of your own.*

I shake my head, eyeing her, then my brother-in-law. "I don't understand."

Ethan steps forward, handing me a slip of folded paper. "We want you to go away."

"Go away?" My words fall out in a violent rush. It feels as if I've been slapped.

Brie laughs. "Not for good or anything."

Relieved, I take a breath. "I still don't understand."

"You were so full of life when we were kids, Callie, always talking about the places you were going to explore when you grew up. I wanted to be just like you one day."

"And now?"

Brie exchanges a glance with Ethan before continuing. "It's like you've climbed up on the edge of the pool in the past two years, and I—we—want you to dive into life again. Fly to Paris or go swim in the Caribbean or take a Hawaiian cruise like Ethan and I did last year."

The next words pour out before I can censor them. "Except I don't have anyone to go with me."

When I see Brie's face, I feel rotten. Guilty, once again, for making my sister feel bad.

"Nor will you," she insists, "if you don't try to meet some new friends . . ."

Who aren't married—I know what she's thinking, but the thought dangles out there. My high school, college, and church friends have either moved or married by now. Most of them have children of their own, which isn't very conducive to flying away for a week or two, at least not with an old friend. And even if Brie didn't have kids, she couldn't vacate with me. One of us needs to stay at the store.

Opening the check, I gasp at the number. "That's too much."

The smile returns to Brie's face. "The money we find in our used books adds up."

"We haven't found three thousand dollars!"

"Charlotte contributed some to your travel fund, and Ethan and I threw in a little extra as well." She shrugs. "Consider it payment for the many hours you've helped in the store."

"I already get paid." Not to mention my apartment . . .

"Please take it," Ethan says in a way that deflects any argument. "And spend a few weeks traveling this summer."

"Perhaps Charlotte would want to see Paris."

Brie shook her head. "This is an adventure she wants you to have on your own."

When I was a child, I wanted to explore the places I read about in my books, but I don't want to go away anymore, at least not by myself. But the two of them look so happy about their gift that I can't possibly refuse. "I appreciate it."

"No, you don't." Brie laughs. "But you can thank me when you return."

Hours later, after falling onto my bed, I think about what it would be like to visit the islands of Hawaii, but I'm terrified to go someplace like that alone.

Before I turn off my lamp, I make one more wish.

I wish I had someone special to share a trip like this with me.

CHAPTER 14

MAX

"It won't be long until it's over."

His back pressed against the papered wall of the hallway, Max heard his father's declaration in the salon. Instead of shouting this morning, Wilhelm Dornbach's voice was hushed, but like so many secrets, his words drifted away, clinging to the smoke from his Woodbine cigarette.

Max peeked around the corner and saw both parents—his mother sitting quite properly on a stiff-backed chair, hands folded in her lap, his father pacing across the rug nearby, the Woodbine shaking in his hand.

Neither of them had discovered that he'd left two weeks ago to visit the lake. They, like most everyone in Vienna, were distracted by all the new mandates that the Nazi Party brought with them.

"It's like you're talking in code," Klara replied. "It won't be long until what's over?"

"The transformation of our city. Our entire country. In a matter of months, we'll be rid of them."

"Rid of whom?"

"Don't be absurd, Klara." His father tapped his cigarette on the ashtray, embers raining down inside the green glass.

His mother knew exactly whom this city was striving to rid itself of. Windows in shops across Vienna displayed signs that their Jewish customers were no longer welcome, and the Gestapo were raiding Jewish businesses across the city, examining their cash books, warning Gentile customers to find another place to shop, another coffeehouse to sip their *café au lait*, another doctor to see.

And Luzi—how he had missed her since their dance in May. Frau Weiss was furious when she discovered what happened, and his parents had been angry as well, lecturing him in the hours after they left the ball about his indiscretion, as if dancing with Luzi had blemished them all. As if they hadn't been friends with the Weiss family since long before Max and Luzi were born.

Rubbish. That's what he thought about this madness. A dance with Luzi Weiss was something to be prized, not regretted. He was a lucky man that she'd agreed to a dance with him at all, and when the people of Vienna returned to their senses, most of them would agree. They'd fling open the doors to their shops and restaurants and hotels, welcome the Jewish people back as their neighbors.

The grandfather clock in the sitting room chimed four times.

"Why is everyone so obsessed with the Jews?" his mother asked, exasperated.

"It's not an obsession. It's vindication. They've plundered our city for long enough now."

Anger blasted through Max as he stepped away from the wall, his fist grinding into his palm. Luzi and her family were hardly plundering Vienna, contributing music and medical care to their city instead. This new mantra about vindication had been passed down from on high, a ghastly song everyone was supposed to sing whether or not they agreed with the lyrics.

Was his father angry at someone in particular? Some of his top customers at the bank were Jewish, and some of his colleagues in the Viennese banking world as well. The Rothschilds, for heaven's sake, were Jewish. At one time, they'd been the biggest banking family in Vienna.

His father had always been jealous of the Rothschilds' success, but even if he weren't, how could he—how could anyone—speak about the Jewish population as if they were dirt needing to be scrubbed off Vienna's elegant walls?

"Hitler will do here what he's done in Germany," his father said.

His mother shifted on the chair. "Require the Jews to leave?"

"Prompt them to go."

"Not everyone wants to leave," his mother said.

"They will."

"And if they don't listen to Hitler's men?"

"There are ways to convince them."

"You have to stay out of this," his mother begged. "Let others fight the war this time if they must, but not you."

Max stepped onto the Persian rug in the salon, a red carpet stitched with golden thread. "Other people like me?"

His mother waved her hand. "Not you either!"

"Of course him." His father flicked ashes into the tray. "Every man able to join will be fighting for the Reich."

"I won't fight for Hitler."

His father's eyes narrowed, eyebrows punctuating his words with a rigid line. "You will fight."

"No—"

"They'll kill any man who refuses to join."

His mother's hand slipped up to her mouth, unsuccessfully muffling her gasp as his father's declaration hung in the air.

"I still won't fight . . . at least not with them." Max's words seemed to ripple out across the room, slamming into the hutch of china plates, shaking the portraits on the walls.

He was no martyr. He didn't want to die, didn't even know if he was truly brave enough to resist. But how could he spread this hatred born from a man obsessed? A man stirring up the deep-seated animosities already in their country, stomping all over people in his scramble to the top?

Exactly how high was high enough for Adolf Hitler? Max suspected that each time the man climbed to the top of the ladder he would add another rung. And then another. Even if Hitler conquered the entire world, Max doubted it would be enough.

He inhaled deeply, trying to calm his racing heart. "A herd, that's what Hitler calls the people of Germany and now Austria. As if we're animals capable of being led straight to slaughter."

"That's not true," his father retorted.

But his mother inched to the edge of her chair. "Where did you hear that?"

"From Herr Ebner," he said, recalling yesterday's lesson. "Or actually, from Hitler himself. All the students are required to read

Mein Kampf. According to Hitler, whoever owns the youth owns the future."

"That's true about the youth," his mother said quietly.

His father crushed his cigarette against the glass. "But not about the herd."

"Have you read *Mein Kampf*?" Max asked.

His father shook his head.

"Hitler believes ridding ourselves of the Jewish people is the only solution to what he terms a problem. He's created an enemy for everyone to rally against."

"He doesn't have to create an enemy." His father paced toward the window that overlooked Ringstrasse before he turned back to them. "The enemy is already here."

"The Jews are not our enemy," Max insisted.

"They are everyone's enemy."

His mother blanched. "Wilhelm!"

Max needed to make his father understand. "The Weiss family—"

"We cannot align ourselves with such people."

"They are our friends."

His father shook his head. "They are not friends of the Reich."

Max's stomach burned. "And we are?"

"Not friends," his mother said, avoiding her husband's gaze. "But we must collaborate with the new government, for the sake of your father's job."

It felt like they were being mowed down, run completely into the ground without speaking out. Or pushing back.

And at times, it felt as if he were just as guilty as his parents.

"The priest just spoke about loving our neighbor."

His father reached for his pack of Woodbines and dumped

them onto the coffee table, a dozen gray branches falling off a tree. He lit another one, and its smoke clouded the room again. "We're only asking that our Jewish neighbors return to their homes."

"Luzi Weiss is as Austrian as me."

"She's an Austrian Jew."

"Luzi was born and raised in this city. So were her parents."

"But her father's parents were born in Hungary," his father said. "They will find a good home there."

He and his father—they would never see eye to eye on this. Max looked at his mother, hoping for support. "You know the Weiss family belongs here."

His mother reached for one of the cigarettes, clinging to it as she shook her head sadly. "I don't know who belongs where anymore."

Max wished he could shake them both out of their stupor. The world was going mad, following a madman. They couldn't just sit in their chairs, smoking cigarettes, as if nothing had happened.

"If you want them gone—" Max turned back to his father now—"you could speak with one of the consulates and obtain visas for them."

"I must keep myself focused on cooperating with this new regime, or they will decide to take over the bank."

"You care more about your job than about the Weiss family."

"I care more about *my* family! It is my chief duty before God and man."

"Mother?"

She shook her head, seemingly helpless to offer any support as she'd done in the past when his father was angry about one of the injured or abandoned animals Max rescued from the streets of Vienna or the woods around Hallstatt. She, like him, hated seeing any creature in pain.

"Then perhaps I should go as well."

"Don't be ridiculous," she said.

Turning, Max rushed back down the hallway, toward the front door of the house.

"Where are you going?" his father shouted, but he didn't respond. They should know exactly where he was headed.

And he wished he didn't have to return home.

☙

"Frau Weiss," Max called, knocking again on the apartment door.

Someone moved inside. He could see a shadow behind the frosted glass, but no one answered.

"Nina?" he shouted as he jostled the handle. "Please open the door."

He'd already apologized to Dr. and Frau Weiss for distracting their daughter at the ball, but while he'd visited Dr. Weiss in the past weeks, Frau Weiss hadn't let him see Luzi.

This morning Dr. Weiss's office was closed.

He tugged a paper bag out of his rucksack, the contents a loaf of rye, some salami, cheese, and cherries imported from Greece. He didn't know much about caring for people, not like the pets he'd collected over the years, but he wanted to be faithful in helping the Weiss family and anyone else he could until God made right this world that had turned upside down. Then he could help restore some of what had been lost.

He pressed his ear against the door, hoping to catch the melody of Luzi's violin, but he heard nothing now. Not even the shuffling of feet.

"Nina?" He pounded on the door again. "Luzi?"

His voice echoed off the walls on the landing and trailed down the steps, fading away. He wanted to kick the door down, if only to make sure Luzi was well, but even if he was able to manage it, it would only make her parents more angry at him.

Just as he stepped away, the doorknob began to turn. He froze on the landing, waiting for it to open, hoping Luzi was waiting for him on the other side. Instead it was Frau Weiss, her normally groomed hair a frightening sight matted to her scalp, her neat attire replaced by a housedress like Nina wore.

He rushed forward. "Are you ill?"

She shook her head slowly, her shoulders slumped. "What do you want from us, Max?"

"You're still angry at me. . . ."

"Of course I'm angry. That ball was supposed to be a crowning moment for Luzia, to show Vienna that she is talented and bright and—" her voice broke—"unique."

"Everyone knows she's talented."

"But it didn't change anything. They released her from the conservatory last week."

He swore. "Because of the dance?"

She shook her head. "They expelled all the Jewish students. The walls are closing in around us. . . ."

If only he could assure her that the Viennese would come together soon and fight for all their citizens. "I want to help."

"You must stay away from her, Max."

But staying away was the last thing he could do. "We will find a way for you to leave Vienna."

"No country has welcomed us yet, and the Nazis, they are making it difficult for us to go."

Max clenched his fists. His father said that Hitler wanted the

Jews out of Vienna, but why wouldn't he let them leave? "If Luzi and I married, we could obtain visas for your whole family."

"Oh, Max. It's no longer legal for her to marry an Aryan man, even if she converts."

His chest seemed to collapse at her words. How could it be illegal for them to marry?

"Some of our friends have received visas into England and China. Dr. Weiss is at the American consulate today, hoping to obtain a visa to work there. Luzia's received a letter of acceptance into Juilliard—"

"Surely one of Dr. Weiss's patients could speak for your family."

Frau Weiss seemed to look through him, her gaze traveling someplace else for the moment. "The Nazis closed his practice."

"That's not possible—"

"We're all cursed, it seems, in their eyes."

"What about Hungary?" he asked. "You must still have relatives there."

She shook her head. "My family fled from the anti-Semitism."

He picked up the paper bag with food and held it out. She eyed it but didn't reach out. "Please take it."

He listened carefully, hoping to hear the violin or at least Luzi's voice, but all he heard was a clock ticking inside. "May I see her while I'm here?"

"Luzia is out for the day."

He wrung his hands together. "I would never do anything to harm her. You know that."

"You're a threat, Max, whether or not you want to be. Your . . . *persistence* draws attention that's dangerous for all of us in these times."

The words stung. "I want nothing but the best for her."

"Then you must let her go, at least for this season."

Max stumbled back from the door, catching himself on the banister as he tried to process her words. How could he avoid the woman he loved? The woman he would marry, no matter what the Nazis said.

He'd never actually spoken the words to Luzi, told her of his love, but she must know it. And it seemed that she loved him too. Her smile as they'd danced, it had been spellbinding. He knew during their waltz, just as he knew right now, that he'd never be able to love anyone like he loved her.

"Go home, Max," Frau Weiss said. "You've been a good friend to us, but for your sake and for ours, we must say good-bye."

"Only for a season," he reminded her.

"A season . . ." The word trailed off as she shut the door.

He stared at the light grain of the oak, the flower etched on the beveled glass. He couldn't fathom a future without Luzi, didn't want to imagine his life without her. The violin breathed life into her, but to him, she was like the beautiful music that fed her soul. A melody that energized, inspired, and haunted him at the same time.

Max left the food in the hallway, and a taxi delivered him to the baroque building on Boltzmanngasse, a building that housed both the American General Consulate and the Consular Academy for international students. He'd studied the architecture of this formidable building in school—it was built at the turn of the century in the classical style. Visitors usually waited inside the consulate, but a long line trickled out the front door this afternoon and wrapped around the white plaster wall. Across the street hung a banner at least five feet tall with a Nazi slogan embroidered in black on the cloth.

Might Comes Before Right!

As if those who were in power were always right. Or perhaps they meant power was more important than being right.

Dr. Weiss stood about two meters away from the steps of the consulate, his head bowed and formal coat buttoned as if it were December instead of July. Max had hoped that Luzi might have accompanied him, but most of the people waiting were middle-aged men, probably trying to obtain visas for their entire family.

Max stepped up beside Dr. Weiss. *"Grüss Gott."*

Someone tapped him on the shoulder with a cane, the voice gravelly. "The queue begins around the corner."

Max glanced back at an elderly man. "I'm not here for a visa."

"You'll have a riot on your hands if you walk through the door," the man said.

Max inched forward beside Dr. Weiss. "I wanted to speak with you."

Dr. Weiss pressed his hands into his pockets, resigned instead of welcoming the conversation. "Talk means nothing these days."

"I'm your friend, Herr Doktor, even when others have turned away."

"Jawohl, a friend is good, but I think you are only friends with me because of my daughter."

"I want to help your entire family." Max thought of the new Mercedes in the garage under his family's home, waiting to be used, and he lowered his voice so the other men around them couldn't hear. "I could drive you to Hungary in our automobile."

Dr. Weiss shook his head. "There are checkpoints at every road along the border, and the guards require visas and baptismal certificates to prove that we're Aryan."

And hefty bribes as well, Max suspected.

Would the guards accept money in lieu of the certificates? There must be a way for them to leave Austria without the mounds of paperwork.

"You'll get the visas," Max insisted. "Today, perhaps."

"I've filled out all the paperwork. Received all the stamps."

Surely Luzi's invitation to attend school in New York would convince the consul to let the Weiss family emigrate.

The sun was warm, beating down on them. "Have you been here all day?"

Dr. Weiss nodded. "I'm doing everything possible . . ."

"I know," Max assured. He couldn't imagine how crippling it must feel to be stuck in a country that didn't want you there, with no place else to go.

The door to the consulate opened, and a small man in a suit stepped out. "I'm sorry, gentlemen," he said. "The consulate is closing for the night."

Groans rippled down the line.

"We'll reopen at nine."

The crowd began to disperse around them. "You have everything—safe?" the doctor asked Max in a whisper.

Max nodded. "I can try to retrieve your things before you leave."

Dr. Weiss shook his head. "The only valuables we're allowed to bring with us are wedding bands."

He slipped something into Max's hand, but Max didn't dare look down. He put it into his rucksack instead.

"I will keep everything safe for you."

"Thank you," Dr. Weiss said before tipping his hat.

The doctor crossed the street, and then Max saw Luzi, sitting on a bench. She wore a plain yellow blouse and skirt, a small hat pinned over her hair, but there was nothing plain about her, even on a seemingly ordinary day like this one.

Had she been waiting all day?

She opened a silver thermos and poured a cup of something warm for her father. Without thinking, Max stepped off the curb, wanting to speak with her, but before he moved closer, the words of Frau Weiss echoed in his mind.

Was his presence really a threat to Luzi?

He would never hurt her. And he couldn't possibly ignore her when she was right in front of him.

Luzi glanced over her father's shoulder, met Max's eye. The slightest nod from her, and then she looked away, but he saw the fear in her eyes.

Luzi was afraid of him.

Heart raw, he ducked behind the trunk of an oak tree and watched her walk away as he'd done at the ball, except this time she walked arm in arm with her father. She held her head high, as if she dared anyone to defy them as they walked home, but Dr. Weiss's head was bowed in defeat.

Max had to find a way to rescue Luzi and her family before Hitler followed through with his threat to solve what he believed to be a problem. If the Weiss family didn't leave Austria soon, it wouldn't be long, he feared, before it would be too late to help them at all.

CHAPTER 15

Wednesday, Thursday, Friday. The days pass achingly slowly without a word from Dr. Nemeth about finding Annika and no email from Sophie with the newspaper photograph and caption. I've checked my inbox about a hundred times, and not even the bookseller from Idaho has returned my email.

I climb up on my story-time stool this morning like a red cardinal on a perch ring. Michael is back this week, though he's refrained so far from blurting out about his underwear, much to the dismay, I imagine, of most of my audience. Several of the kids keep looking his way, but I suspect his mom had a proper talking-to with him before they stepped into the store.

Devon and his dad have joined us, and while I smile at Devon, I try to avoid Mr. Baker's gaze. Cracking the cover of a Karma Wilson book, I begin to read her story about a bear who feels scared, but even as I read, a conversation with Devon's father loops through my mind, preventative measures that sharpen as I carve through the words.

I'll tell him that I have another date tonight if he asks me to dinner—technically true since I'm headed over to Brie's house. And if he asks me if I'm in a relationship, I'll tell him yes—technically true once again even if it's not the kind of relationship he's probably referring to.

I turn another page.

"'Bear trembles in the wind,'" I read. When I pause, the kids shiver with me. "'How he longs for a friend.'"

The children shout out the next line in unison. "'And the bear feels scared!'"

I nod. "Exactly."

Then I read about the other animals who trudge through rain and darkness to find Bear, how they won't let anything stop them from finding their friend.

The front door chimes, and I can't help but glance up, thinking Kathleen might have brought her son again this week. Instead a tall man walks into the store, his presence taking up a sizable amount of space. He's accompanied by a seven- or eight-year-old girl wearing a sailor dress and white sandals embellished with silver bling, her pale-blonde hair brushed back into a ponytail.

My eyes refocus on the book, but I'm relieved to see Dr. Nemeth, hoping that he also has my book and some news. Then my relief turns to slight embarrassment that I'm wearing my striped socks and cape. I shouldn't care what he thinks—he and I are both teachers in our own way, but his teaching is probably done in a classroom with students who don't blurt out about their new underwear.

After adjusting my cape, I finish the story about Bear and then peruse the three books that remain unread on the table beside me. "We only have time for one more."

The kids begin shouting out the names of their favorite books.

Smiling, I glance at the girl with Dr. Nemeth—his daughter, I assume—as she maneuvers through the children to find herself a seat. Then I pick up *Stephanie's Ponytail,* another Robert Munsch classic. When I read the title, the girl smiles back at me.

I tell the story of Stephanie, a girl who wants to be different from all her classmates, wearing her ponytail different ways because each time she changes the style, everyone in the school copies her. Catastrophic for an independent girl like her.

"Time for hot chocolate," Brie calls after I finish this story. Kids roll away like tumbleweeds, and I'm left in a quiet desert, the observer of a wild storm on the other side of the room.

Dr. Nemeth takes his daughter's hand and moves toward me. While she has dressed up for story time, he's wearing jeans, a lime T-shirt, and rather worn flip-flops.

I slip the pile of books beside me back into the crate. "It's nice to see you again."

"You too," he says. "I read about the story time online. I just didn't realize you'd be doing the reading."

"Every Saturday morning." I bat my cape back over my right shoulder. "Story Girl, the kids call me."

The girl in the sailor dress inches up on her toes beside me. "I like it."

"Thanks."

She flings her ponytail back and forth. "And I liked the story about Stephanie."

"I hope you don't shave off your ponytail."

She laughs. "Never."

"This is my daughter," Dr. Nemeth says. "Ellabean."

She rolls her eyes. "It's Ella, Dad."

He shrugs before smiling back at me. "I always mess it up."

"It's a beautiful name."

She fidgets with the bow on her dress. "My mom picked it."

"She did a fine job."

Dr. Nemeth nudges Ella's shoulder. "Why don't you have some hot chocolate?"

Instead of turning toward the pack of kids, Ella eyes the castle, and I admire the way she chooses adventure over chocolate. A bold move.

"It's fine with me if she'd like to explore inside. There's even a slide."

He scrutinizes the castle as if it might be in jeopardy of falling. "I'm not sure . . ."

"My brother-in-law built it," I say. "He's a carpenter."

One of his eyebrows slides up. "A good one?"

"Journeyman," I assure him.

Ella looks at her father with wide blue eyes that match her dress, begging him with her gaze. "No one's in it right now, Dad."

"Oh, go ahead," he says, shooing her away.

I laugh as she disappears through the front gate. "She's a lovely girl."

"Precocious."

"Precocious gets a bad rap."

He swings a worn courier bag from behind his back and opens it. "I have your book."

"Thank you," I say, anxious to hear what he has to report. "Were you able to find out where it came from?"

I shake my head. "I'm still waiting to hear back from the bookseller."

He lifts the book out of his bag, clinging to it even as he scans the hectic room. "Could we talk in a quieter space?"

"Of course," I say. "Do you mind waiting about fifteen minutes? Most of the families will head to the farmers' market soon."

"I'll catch up on my reading," he quips before adding *Bambi* to the stack of books in my arms. Then he lifts *Hatschi Bratschis Luftballon* from the German section of used books, and I glance down at the man on the familiar cover. Hatschi Bratschi looks a bit like Genie in the *Aladdin* movie except he is clothed in a long robe, riding in a hot air balloon. In his hands is a telescope fixed on some exotic location below the basket, searching for children.

As Dr. Nemeth flips through the colorful pages, I stow my books in the office and help out several parents, stealthily avoiding Mr. Baker, who seems to be following me around the shop. When I return to Dr. Nemeth, he holds out the magic balloon book. "This is a terrible story for kids."

My arms bristle, as if he's offending me personally. I almost start lecturing him on the three kinds of children's books, along with the importance of developing a child's critical thinking skills as they enter a story world very different from their own. But no parent likes advice from someone who doesn't actually have children. "It's not ter—"

"And violent," he continues.

"Only if you're an evil wizard or a witch."

"The witch burns up in a fire!"

"This was published to an audience used to reading the works of the Brothers Grimm."

"It's certainly grim."

"The greater the struggle, the more triumphant the ending." He looks at me curiously, and I squirm under his gaze before continuing. "Besides, Fritz has the adventure of a lifetime before he rescues the other kids."

"Still, it makes you wonder what kind of person writes a book like this, railing against people from another culture."

I glance around the room, at the shelves of books filled with stories about antagonists who threaten the hero or heroine. "A man who's trying to confront his own fears."

Dr. Nemeth's gaze wanders back to the castle. I think about the bear in the book we just read, afraid of the wind, and I wonder—what is this man afraid of?

Ella peeks out between the white columns on the second-story window, in the room that Brie painted lavender, silver, and pink for the many princesses who visit our store. The other room has a mural with a suit of armor and a black horse for the knights.

"Franz Ginzkey was from Vienna," I say. "He published this about a decade before World War I."

"I wonder what he was doing during World War II."

"Unfortunately, he ended up joining the Nazi Party. Many people did, I guess, for survival."

Dr. Nemeth glances down at the wizard and his balloon on the cover. "I suppose it's impossible to assign motive almost a century after the fact."

I pull my stack closer to me. "Unless someone left their story behind for us to read."

"But even on paper," he says, "people can clean up their motives. Often you have to hear from a loved one to learn what someone was truly like."

"What if the loved one decides to communicate their own version of the truth?"

Mr. Baker steps up beside me, eying Dr. Nemeth as if he might go to battle himself. A married man with a lovely daughter is hardly competition, but Mr. Baker doesn't know that the man in front of me is married.

I ignore Devon's dad, talking directly to Dr. Nemeth. "Actually, I believe now is a good time to talk. Perhaps Ella can play while we step outside?"

As the other children begin to fill the castle, Ella slides down and races toward her father, taking his hand. "I like it here," she tells me.

"I'm glad."

She looks at the refreshment table. "Do you think there's any hot chocolate left?"

"If not, I know where my sister keeps her stash."

"You have plans again tonight?" Mr. Baker asks, seconds after Dr. Nemeth and Ella step toward the table.

"I do." I glance toward the professor and his daughter as if they're spending the rest of the day with me. And I wonder if Mrs. Nemeth is shopping nearby or if she's waiting for them at home.

"I have plans as well. A date." Mr. Baker studies my face, gauging my reaction.

"I'm glad for you."

He's disappointed at my enthusiasm, but I really am happy.

I motion Dr. Nemeth toward the door, and he follows me outside to a wrought-iron table under the awning where people typically congregate to enjoy their ice cream. He's balancing a cup of coffee and another of hot chocolate in one hand, the balloon book under his arm, and in the other hand, a mug of tea that he sets before me. "Your sister said you'd need this."

"Thank you." I unlatch my cape and drape it over the back of my seat. One of my kids comes bounding out of the store with his parents and bumps my fist before continuing on toward the square. "Are you ready for your trip?"

"Everything's done except the packing," he says.

"Were you able to translate the handwriting in Annika's book?"

He nods. "One of my TAs helped me verify the items to make sure I translated them correctly. I've never seen anything quite like it."

"Me either, and I've found all sorts of things in books."

He pulls out a computer tablet from his bag and opens a document with the translated list. It looks the same as what Charlotte and I have worked together to translate—necklaces, jewels, candlesticks, small pieces of artwork. And the initials at the end of each line.

"It's like a catalog," he says.

"Or a wish list."

"It seems too specific to be wishful thinking." The chair creaks when he shifts his legs. "My assistant thinks this Annika was a very creative child who developed some sort of code with her friends. Perhaps they passed around their books with the notes to read."

"But you don't think that."

He shakes his head.

"What about the teenager in the photograph?"

His eyebrows rise. "Her brother?"

I laugh. "I'm pretty sure it was a crush. Maybe she was writing something to him. . . ."

"Perhaps," he replies in a somewhat-polite way of disagreeing with me.

"You said that Nazis were hiding things in this district."

He nods. "Sometimes they forced locals to help them."

"I can't imagine . . ." I run my fingers down the edge of my cape. "You said Annika told your uncle a story."

Dr. Nemeth glances away, looking at the display window of the stationery store across the street before turning back to me. "My uncle Leo was sent to Austria's lake country as a military photographer in 1945. His job was to document some of the valuable items and artwork that the Nazis dumped when they were fleeing from the Allies." He takes a sip of his coffee. "They stayed at one of Hitler's former youth camps, on the banks of Lake Hallstatt."

I lean forward. "Schloss Schwansee?"

"Exactly." He takes a small photo album out of his bag and sets it on the balloon book. "Uncle Leo took a number of photographs for Uncle Sam in the 1940s. Before his death, he gave his personal photographs to me."

I open the cover and begin scanning through the black-and-white photos. Most are pictures of uniformed soldiers smiling—over their recent victory, I suspect. Several are of the mountains; one appears to be the entrance to a mine.

And then there's a woman holding the hand of a young child, an old manor house behind them with a medieval-looking turret and wall mottled with black. The woman is standing in the shadows as if she's unaware that Leo is taking her picture. Her hair is short, cut above her shoulders, her eyes covered with sunglasses, and she's wearing a skirt and short-sleeved blouse, a handkerchief around the collar.

I point to the charred side of the house. "Was there a fire?"

"It was probably bombed during the war."

I look back up at Dr. Nemeth. "Is this—?"

He slips the photograph out of the sleeve, and when he turns it over, I catch my breath. One word is scrawled in ink across the back.

Annika.

Goosebumps ripple across my arms.

"Her father had been the caretaker of the castle, and after his death, her husband took over the care of the estate."

"What was her husband's name?"

"I don't know," he says. "If Uncle Leo found out, he never told me."

Dr. Nemeth slides the photo back under its protective covering. "Annika said two Nazi officials came to Schloss Schwansee near the end of the war. They dumped boxes of valuable items into the lake."

My heart beats faster. "She kept a record of what they were trying to hide."

"Perhaps."

"Did your uncle's company find anything in Lake Hallstatt?"

"They discovered a number of items hidden in a local mine, but his division never found anything in the water. Their diving equipment wasn't nearly as sophisticated as it is today."

More kids pour from the store, but my focus remains on the professor. "And you've been wondering about it ever since."

He nods. "I wrote my dissertation about ownerless treasure in Austria."

"Ownerless?"

"It's what the Nazis called everything they stole from the Jewish people." He takes another sip of coffee. "I've wanted to search for what they dumped in this lake since I was about Ella's age, but Annika, I think, is the key to finding it."

"Why haven't you searched for the treasure before?" I ask.

"I was supposed to go, about ten years ago. My journey since then has been a bit . . . complicated." He glances down at the photograph. "Have you ever been to Austria?"

I shake my head. "I've never been out of the United States."

"But you know German?"

"Ein bisschen."

Ella steps outside, and Dr. Nemeth pulls out a chair for his daughter. She sits like a proper adult except her legs keep swinging under the table, back and forth as if they're keeping time. She reaches for the balloon book, but her father pulls it away and nods toward the chocolate that's no longer hot.

"I think you'd like all the Austrian castles and music and mountain lakes."

I sip my tea. "Perhaps one day I'll go."

"You should fly over with our team," he says. "Maybe you can help search for Annika while we dive."

I blink, shocked at first at this suggestion; then I mull over his words. He might as well have suggested I visit the moon. What would it be like to visit a place like Austria, reunite golden watches and other heirlooms with their owners?

"I don't know . . ."

"Why not?"

A reasonable question, but I don't have a reasonable answer, at least not one he would understand. I have the money to travel now, thanks to Brie and Charlotte, but the truth is, I'm afraid. Dr. Nemeth probably travels all the time. I can't very well tell him that I've dropped the anchor of my life right here and don't want to leave.

"Hate flying?" he asks, breaking the silence that has grown awkward between us.

"I've never actually been on an airplane before."

"Really?"

"Scout's honor," I say, holding up three fingers.

He studies me as if I'm a relic in a museum. "You've never left Ohio?"

"Yes, I've left Ohio, but I can drive just fine to almost anyplace I want to go."

He nods, quick and businesslike. Not understanding but acknowledging my words. I could tell him that I travel plenty, that the books in the shop and in my flat overhead are my transportation to exotic locations, traveling across time even, but I suspect he won't understand that either.

"Grammy and I are going to Austria soon," Ella says as she lowers her drink. "Dad's taking me to the ice caves, and Grammy wants to see the music stuff."

Dr. Nemeth smiles. "All the places around Salzburg where *The Sound of Music* was filmed."

Ella's not smiling, though. When tears puddle in the corners of her eyes, her dad reaches for her hand. "You'll hardly blink, and we'll be in Austria together."

Ella studies him skeptically.

"Okay," he concurs. "Several blinks."

"A hundred million of them," she says. "Maybe more."

"What if we count the days, not the blinks?"

She straightens in her chair. "Twenty-one days."

"Team Nemeth," he says, holding out his fist.

She bumps it. "Team Nemeth." But after she says this, her smile fades again. "Except Mom—"

"We have to head out." Dr. Nemeth glances at his watch, interrupting her.

The pretty woman pictured in his office flashes through my mind, and I'm curious to know what Ella was going to say about her mother. But she's sufficiently distracted now as she hops out of her chair. Her dad slides his tablet back into his bag before reaching for the album.

I nod down at the photograph. "Do you mind if I take a picture of this?"

"Not at all."

After snapping it, I stand up beside him. "Please let me know what you find about Annika."

"Of course."

He and Ella both shake my hand, and then they're gone.

I study the photograph again on my phone. The woman's face is partially shadowed by the gray shade of a tree, and her arms and legs look pencil thin. I wish I could see her eyes. Hear her story.

I hope Dr. Nemeth finds this treasure for the people who lost it. Perhaps, if he finds Annika's family, I can return the *Bambi* book and its list directly to them.

I scoop up *Hutschi Bratschis Luftballon* to return to the store.

The magic balloon book is about reuniting people, Fritz and the other children miraculously returning to their families after the wicked man takes them away.

This is a much newer version than the one that Charlotte has on her shelf at home, the one with another name inscribed inside, but instinctively I open the front cover, as if the name is recorded in this magic balloon book as well.

Luzia Weiss.

It's not there, of course. The only place I've ever found her name is in the book in Charlotte's condo. Weiss is a common surname in Germany, but in our years of searching, neither Charlotte nor I have found the birth record for a Luzia.

And I wonder again, as I've done over the years, how the record of someone's life can simply disappear.

Anyone who saves a life is as if
he saved an entire world.

MISHNAH SANHEDRIN
(THE TALMUD)

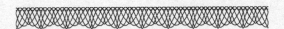

CHAPTER 16

LUZI

Luzi lifted her violin to her shoulder and drew her bow across the strings. *Largo.* The music called for a slow rendition of the piece, but each note she played, whether slow or fast, seemed to cry out in pain. The music, it wanted her to run away like she'd done that night at the Rathaus, flee from this city that had replaced its own music with a seething hatred against many of its musicians. As if the ears of Vienna were being tainted by the notes played through Jewish hands.

Her father was still trying to obtain visas for them, from any country that would take their family, but as the weeks passed, even fewer Jews were able to obtain visas, and those who left weren't allowed to carry anything of value with them. Certainly not enough money to support themselves when they arrived in their new homes. She felt as if they were trying to sail in a wild gust of wind, no stretch of land in sight.

Now her father wanted Luzi to obtain a visa on her own—some countries were still allowing Jewish students to attend school abroad—but she didn't think she could bear to leave her family in Austria.

She collapsed into her chair as if she'd been playing for hours upon hours and rested the violin in her lap. Mutti no longer shouted at her to continue playing, for there was no reason for her to practice. No concerts or balls or even a piece to prepare for school. Music symbolized hope, and these days hope was fleeting in their home.

Her mother had locked herself in her room, sedating the plague of her anxiety with the pills Father prescribed. A dark cloud had settled over their apartment and the increasing fragility of her mother's mind.

On nights like this, Luzi wished she could take a walk along the Danube, smell the flowers in the palace garden at Schönbrunn, clear the threatening clouds in her own mind. The streets of Vienna, at least those in her district, used to beckon pedestrians outside during the summer evening hours to listen to music in the plazas or sip coffee at an outdoor café. But it wasn't safe to go out at night anymore. Nor would she after what happened with Ernst in May. Things were only worse now with Hitler's storm troopers patrolling the streets both day and night.

Still she went out in the morning to find food while Father was visiting the consulate. Her mother refused to leave the apartment, and Luzi was glad Mutti didn't have to see what had happened to their city. Miriam Weiss was a beautiful woman who loved beauty. She should not be exposed to the vile words written on the windows and walls of Jewish businesses. Mutti wasn't a whore, and while men like Ernst might think otherwise, neither was Luzi.

Their Gentile friends had abandoned them in the past weeks. Even Max, it seemed, had finally given up after her mother refused to let him visit. Luzi had considered going to his house, knocking on his door as he had done with her, but Herr and Frau Dornbach were no longer friendly to her family. Frau Dornbach once referred to Luzi as her niece, but she hadn't even acknowledged her at the Opera Ball.

Perhaps Max was as afraid as she was about what might happen if they dared to be seen together. Or had he begun to believe that she was nothing but trash as well?

Sometimes she was beginning to believe that she was trash. Someone to be tossed away. Nothing, in the eyes of this new regime, could redeem her and her inferior race.

Luzi locked the violin back into its case and checked the clock. And she pretended that she had a concert to attend tonight. Or school tomorrow. Or that her father, after standing in line today at the consulate, would be able to obtain a visa out of this country for their entire family.

"My God, the soul You have given me is pure. You created it, You formed it, and You breathed it into me."

She lit a candle near the window and repeated the blessing her grandfather had taught her in Hebrew. Then she said the prayer in German and one more time in the English she'd learned in school.

God had breathed life into her. He had made her and gifted

her with a deep love for the music that spilled out of her hands, her heart. What was she supposed to do when it felt as if the very breath He'd breathed into her was being smothered? When she could no longer even play her music?

She switched off the lamp and pressed her hand against the window. Lightning flashed in the distance, and the roll of thunder shook the glass, as if it were announcing its presence. And then she heard something else. The cry of a baby. Her sister had been awakened by the thunder.

Luzi stole out of the library to her parents' bedroom.

"Mutti," she called out, twisting the doorknob, but it was locked. The sedatives seemed to deafen her mother's ears to both the thunder and Marta's cries. But Frau Dichter would most certainly hear upstairs, and Frau Dichter was an Aryan woman who didn't care much for children. She'd already complained to the superintendent about the crying, and the super had warned Mutti that she must keep her child quiet if they wanted to remain in this building.

Luzi slipped past the locked door to the nursery. Marta had pulled herself up in her crib, her cries growing louder when she saw her sister. Luzi picked her up, gently rubbed her back, and Marta melted into her like soft butter on toast. Her sister may only have lived ten months, but she was scared, just like the rest of them.

No matter how much Luzi wanted to flee to America to attend Juilliard, she could never leave her parents or her baby sister behind. Together they would run, far away from here.

She paced up and down the corridor, Marta fading back to sleep on her shoulder.

Mutti couldn't give up now. None of them could. If nothing

else, they needed to come together to save Marta. No child, especially a Jewish one, should grow up under the hopelessness of this regime.

⁂

Annika knelt by the narrow garden bed with her trowel and began replanting flowers in the blanket of soil that covered her mother's grave—alpine roses, lilies, and tiny clusters of yellow stars known as edelweiss, each star bursting with white-petaled rays.

She'd carefully transported the flowers from the mountain to this hillside cemetery of wooden crosses, iron lanterns, and colorful pocket gardens. Her mother had loved the flowers that bloomed wild in these Alps and the lakes that flowed wild between the forests and peaks. She'd loved the birds and meadows and the sky that changed by the hour, proving, she'd once said, that God prized artistry.

After the last tender roots were planted, Annika kissed her stained palm and held it against her mother's name, etched deeply into the wood.

Kathrin Knopf
1902–1934
Made Beautiful in His Time

A shadow stole over the garden, and she turned to look out at the view, at the sun painting pale orange and pink across the canvas of blue, the final spray of light before dusk. On the far side of the lake was Schloss Schwansee, a faint watermark stamped onto a masterpiece.

In her collage of memories, Annika remembered tramping up this hill beside her mother as a girl, delivering flowers to a friend's grave or lighting a candle in one of the lanterns. This was the closest place, her mother had once said, to stepping into paradise on earth.

She couldn't bear to think of her beautiful mother trapped under the soil. Mama, she prayed, was in an eternal paradise now, safe and healthy with the Father she loved, her heart following the treasure burnished in her life.

Annika's father had paid the rent for Kathrin's body to rest in this soil for another six years. Instead of saving the money to renew this lease, her father drank away most of their income, but somehow Annika would earn enough to keep her mother's body here, along with the two books she'd snuck into the wooden casket when her father wasn't looking, as if her mother would have to remember her because she had the stories they'd shared.

Her stomach turned each time she thought of the caretaker digging up her mother's bones to transplant them to the Beinhaus for everyone to see. She would do almost anything to keep her mother in this soil, planted like the flowers she loved, even ask Herr Dornbach for the money.

If Herr Dornbach ever came back to the estate.

Last week she heard Vati tell Hermann that the Dornbachs wouldn't own Schloss Schwansee much longer. It was the strangest thing to say. Frau Dornbach's family had owned it for generations. Max not returning to the castle—she couldn't bear to think about it. Her father was wrong, but still she would ask Hermann about the conversation. He would tell her the truth.

The shadows lengthened until they crept into the back edges of the gardens, and she gathered her trowel and pail that carried the lake water needed for the flowers. Then she climbed down the steps to the shore and paddled her wooden boat toward home.

A sliver of moon, curved in an elegant script, lit the span of indigo sky. Night had already settled over the estate; her father was probably preparing to drive to the beer hall in Obertraun if he hadn't left already.

Max's cat was waiting near the boathouse to escort Annika to the barn. After Annika milked the goat, she would reward Frederica with a small bowl of her own, and then the cat would snuggle beside her in bed as she read from her mother's Bible.

Annika secured the boat and hurried toward the barn before the goats started bleating. But when she turned toward the cottage, her heart began to race at the sight of a sedan parked nearby.

Had Max and his family finally returned? Perhaps they were looking for her.

With Frederica at her heels, she hurried across the lane, toward the solitary cottage light that beckoned her, but before she reached the door, the car engine started and the driver backed into the courtyard, rushing past her.

In the dim light, she saw her father's face in the backseat. He must have seen her standing beside the trees, but the car didn't stop.

The sound of the car engine faded, but Annika still didn't move. Who had taken her father away?

CHAPTER 17

The clock ticks past five in the morning, but sleep continues to play its wicked game of hide-and-seek. Light from the streetlamp carves a channel through my bedroom, trailing across my comforter, settling on the books stacked on my nightstand, but I refuse to surrender my day to sleep deprivation yet.

Flinging the pillow over my head, I roll away from the light, hoping to find rest in this space. But waves, a midnight wash of blue, slip through the darkness of my mind, stirring up the silt on the banks. My thoughts, they won't let me rest. And the rush of water begins to build, a flood of pictures about to crash against the banks.

A girl dumps something near the edge of a lake—a rope made of gold, like one of the necklaces recorded in her book. Smiling, she is oblivious to the threat streaming toward her.

I open my eyes, afraid of what my imagination might do against my will.

Dr. Nemeth's face appears in my mind, replacing the girl, his eyes curious about Annika's list and later appalled at the magic balloon book for children. He emailed when they landed in Salzburg on Monday, but he didn't have any more information yet about Annika. His team is diving in two other lakes before they travel to Hallstatt.

Did Mrs. Nemeth join her husband in Austria? We would be friends, I think, enjoying tea together while the others are scuba diving. But then again, Mrs. Nemeth probably likes to scuba dive. And travel around the world instead of stay at home.

Dr. Nemeth looked at me as if I were an oddity when I said I'd never been on an airplane. I don't understand what's wrong with being content at home, blooming right where I'm planted. Of course, some might argue that while I was planted just fine, I'm not exactly blooming. Some days I might even argue that as well.

The truth is—and I can only confront the truth in these early hours—I'm not as content as I would like Dr. Nemeth and others to believe. I love my apartment, the security of being grounded in this town, but some days I long for the courage to get on an airplane and experience another place outside my books, just for a week or two. Like my sister's birthday card said so eloquently, to write a chapter or two of my own story.

My passport is unstamped but ready to use, tucked far back in my filing cabinet alongside the receipt for my wedding gown and a brochure from the Quarry Chapel, the place where I'd intended to become Mrs. Faulkner.

Scott planned to take me on a grand excursion to the Cayman Islands for our honeymoon, saying he never wanted me to forget our wedding day or the week following.

I'll certainly never forget either.

The month before our wedding, I spent a long weekend with Brie in Columbus shopping for shoes and jewelry and flowery summer dresses made for the islands. While I was gone, Scott visited a friend in Fredericktown who introduced him to Kathleen. It must have been quite the introduction because three weeks later, after our rehearsal dinner, Brie saw Scott and Kathleen in his Mustang. Deep in conversation, she said.

Brie confronted him. He called me. And in seconds, everything changed.

Instead of swimming in the Caribbean, I spent the next week balled up on my bed, Charlotte and Brie both heating up bowls of chicken soup as if I had a cold or the flu. Chicken soup, to my knowledge, has never healed a broken heart, but their love for me, poured into that soup—and Charlotte's steady reminder that God loved me even more—eventually brought me out of my state of shock, back into a new reality. As the months passed, I tried—and continue trying—to embrace God's love on my own instead of relying on Charlotte to remind me.

Inching up on my mattress, I hug a pillow close to my chest. I don't want to think about the Cayman Islands or Scott or those days of despair, but this room sometimes sparks the theater of my mind, looping memories in slow motion, pausing on frames I'd rather not see yet again.

Capture every thought, that's what it says in the second book of Corinthians. Lock the fugitive ones away in captivity.

A new picture begins sketching itself in my head. Thoughts— hundreds of them—going rogue. Bent on destruction. I want to imprison them, but I can't seem to cram them back into their cell.

The best place to round them up is on my feet, dressed for battle. Or at least dressed to move.

I change quickly into yoga pants and a T-shirt, lace up my bike shoes, and tie back my shoulder-length hair. About a mile from the shop is a paved trail for cyclists and walkers alike, fourteen miles to pedal out my thoughts.

A water bottle in hand, I retrieve my road bike from the storage unit behind the shop, attach my cell phone to the mount between the handlebars, and begin pedaling south and then east on the empty roads, past the manufactured house on Howard Street that was once my home. I've only moved four blocks since childhood, but it feels as if I moved a thousand miles away.

In minutes I'm biking along the Kokosing, a much more placid river than the one that plagued my mind. Sunlight flickers through the oak and maple leaves, sprinkling light onto an asphalt path that was once a railroad track. Hope—that's what I experience every time I take this river trail, basking in the reminder of something old and abandoned re-created into something new. *Progress* is what they might have called it when the workers first laid the track, but no one calls this trail progress now. More like conservation.

Today is June 6. My thirtieth birthday.

This hits me as I embrace the rhythm of cycling, the pedaling a comfort as it empowers me to fight the thoughts in my head. In my work, the fugitives begin to cower back in their cages, giving me the strength to embrace this new decade of life as well.

The river flows quietly beside me, soothing my mind. The water is going somewhere, sometimes in a rush. Other spots it's almost still, more of a pool than a forward thrust. On a journey and yet content to be settled in one place at times. Home.

It's never occurred to me before, the quest of life being one of rapids and quiet pools. The same journey with both highs and lows. Is it possible to be content both in travel and at home, deeply grounded in something far beyond a place?

"On your left," I call before passing a runner. Someone else, perhaps, who wasn't able to sleep.

Another image plays in my mind—one of a Bavarian village and mountain water that hides treasures of its own.

What would it be like to use my birthday money for a real adventure? To celebrate, even, by spending a week or two in Austria instead of Hawaii or Paris? I could go to Vienna, finish my research on Felix Salten, and then join Team Nemeth for a few days, inquiring about Annika as they work.

Team—it's a cozy word to some people, but being part of a team has never been in my comfort zone. Leagues away, actually. I've always felt a bit awkward, as if I wasn't sure of my place inside the boundaries.

It wouldn't take a crackerjack psychologist to figure out the root of that issue. Most kids, I assume, learn how to find a place in their family first, learning how to work together. My early years were about survival, not teamwork.

I failed miserably to partner with Scott, but I partner with my sister every day. We are a small but mighty team. One built on a mutual history, respect, and hope for the future.

Small teams, perhaps, are my forte.

A white-tailed deer leaps across the asphalt, followed by a fawn. When the deer stops to look at me, the fawn stops as well and waits for his mother's cue. Danger, in this fawn's eyes, is only danger if she signals to him. He has complete trust in this doe that cares for him.

Trust, I think, is the greatest gift someone can give.

I cycle past a cornfield, the green stalks already several feet taller than the coveted knee-high by the Fourth of July, and turn left at a cross path that leads into Gambier, an exclusive college town built of clapboard and stone.

Distracted, I've taken the wrong turn off the trail; I realize it the moment I see a sandstone chapel beside the road instead of the college buildings. I bicycle often into Gambier, but I haven't been on this country road, visited this chapel, since Scott and I rehearsed our wedding vows.

Initially I look away from the old church, trying to avoid the memory of the man I trusted completely, the man I thought loved me for exactly who I was. He didn't love me, at least not for a lifetime. I helped him pass the time. Kathleen stole his heart.

I stop in front of the chapel, every stone in its walls excavated from a nearby quarry and laid by the masons who relocated from England in the 1800s to build Kenyon College. A revival swept through the college, stirring students and town residents alike, and together they built this place of worship that has lasted for a hundred and fifty years.

Maybe it's finally time to leave my memories behind, the ones that seem to keep me chained to the past, and start on a new journey. Build something new.

My phone flashes, notifying me of an email, and I tap the screen to read a note from the bookseller in Boise.

Dear Ms. Randall,
Thank you for your purchase of Bambi: A Life in the
Woods. *This book was from an estate sale near Sandpoint.*
I'm sorry that I'm not able to provide you with
more information. Unless something of a critical

*nature is found in a book, it's our policy to keep our
client names confidential.*

> *Sincerely,*
> *Leah Lowe*

Annika's notes are more intriguing than critical, I suppose, but if the list recorded some sort of treasure hidden by the Nazis . . . Ms. Lowe might consider that critical.

A quick search on my phone reveals that Sandpoint is a small town in the mountains of Idaho, on the shore of Lake Pend Oreille—pronounced *Pond Ah-Ray* according to the website. I hunt for someone with the surname of Knopf in the area, but no results are shown.

Perhaps it's just wishful thinking, but I want to believe that whoever sold this book might have known Annika. Or at least known about her.

The meaning of this list might have been family lore, passed down through her relatives in Idaho. Answers easily resolved if only I can find the right person to ask.

Ms. Lowe, I hope, is one of those booksellers who can't resist a good story.

CHAPTER 18

Max spooned the soup into his mouth, but he barely tasted the white asparagus or cream. Hans, a friend from school, had stopped by an hour ago to collect the money needed to purchase an official, albeit forged, marriage certificate for Maximilian Dornbach and Luzia Weiss along with a baptismal certificate into the Catholic Church for Luzia Weiss.

It had cost Max the sale of his motorbike, but Hans promised he could obtain these papers in the next two weeks. And with the certificates, Max would apply for Aryan visas into Switzerland or France for a honeymoon.

He hadn't returned to Luzi's flat for the past month, but

yesterday Dr. Weiss had knocked on the door while Max's parents were gone. Frau Weiss didn't know he'd come, but he asked Max to obtain these papers and escort Luzi out of Austria as soon as possible. With Max and Luzi established in the new country, the rest of the family would be able to follow, he said.

Max gladly complied.

A canary serenaded their tense family meal from the floor above, the song spilling through the vent from Max's room. Dr. Weiss had brought the bird with him when he visited, the prized pet of a former patient who'd obtained a visa to Shanghai. His canary, a rare bronze-colored bird he'd named Beethoven, had to stay behind as well as the bag of jewels hidden in a compartment at the base of his cage. The jewels Max would bury when his family returned to Schloss Schwansee in the morning. The owner asked that Beethoven be released into the wild.

He and his father hadn't spoken beyond occasional formalities since Max had informed him that he wouldn't be joining the Wehrmacht. When Hans obtained the certificates, Max would be leaving Austria for good.

"That bird has to find another home," his father said, glaring at Max as if he and the bird were collaborating to disrupt his meal.

"I'm going to release him at the lake tomorrow." Max took another spoonful of his soup, trying to calm his voice in spite of the racing in his mind.

His father shook his head. "We can't go now, not with everything in turmoil."

Max glanced between his parents. They were supposed to have left weeks ago for their summer retreat. After delays with the bank, his father had assured them they would finally leave in the morning.

He turned toward his mother. "Perhaps we can go on our own."

"Why do you want to go to Hallstatt?" she asked.

The last two summers he'd begged to stay here in Vienna after school released, hoping to spend more time with Luzi, but in the past his parents always insisted that he join them at the lake.

In the past—words that now defined their country's future.

"I want to spend some time with Hermann and Annika." And he needed to speak to Annika. He hoped she would help him again.

"You must tread carefully on that poor girl's heart." His mother stirred her soup, the white cream lapping slowly against the sides of the bowl.

"There's nothing wrong with her heart."

"She's our servant, Max."

"And a friend."

"She considers you to be more than—"

"It doesn't matter," his father interrupted. "None of us are leaving Vienna this summer."

Max glanced up at the ceiling. The canary he could release in the Vienna Woods west of the city, but what would he do with the jewels?

If they wouldn't leave as a family, he'd have to borrow the Mercedes again and take one last trip to Hallstatt on his own.

The doorbell chimed, the sound echoing across the dining room. It was a quarter after six—visitors rarely stopped by their house during the dinner hour.

Their housekeeper served each of them plates filled with *Schinkenfleckerln*, a ham dish baked with cheese, and then rushed into the next room to answer the door. Max's parents began to eat, waiting to see if she would announce a guest or return with a message for one of them. And Max did what he always did—picked out the meat and set it to the side before eating the noodles and cheese.

"You're wasting perfectly good pork," his father said.

Max dumped the meat into his empty bowl and slid it toward him. "You can have it."

Before his father replied, their housekeeper stepped back into the room and deposited the letter opener along with a brown envelope inscribed *Telegramm* in red across the top.

"It's probably Emil again," his father said, referring to Herr Knopf.

His mother glanced at the telegram. "You should respond to him."

"I did respond, but he said that he must speak with me in person."

"Perhaps something is wrong with the Schloss," Max said. "Or Annika."

His father shook his head. "The man wants an increase in salary, but he doesn't deserve another penny."

He slit open the envelope, and they waited for him to speak.

"What is it?" his mother asked.

His father's face flushed as he scanned the typed words, a slow burn crawling up to his ears until they flickered like torches. Then he raised his chin, and Max thought for certain his ruse was up—his father had found out about the hidden jewels or the marriage certificate or both.

But his father's eyes, narrowed into darts, were aimed straight at his wife.

She turned toward the housekeeper. "We'll need coffee with our dessert."

"I have a pot brewing right now," the woman said before retreating into the kitchen.

His father didn't seem to notice their housekeeper's departure. "You—" He wrapped his hand around the telegram before balling it up. "You gave money to Kurt Schuschnigg!"

Each syllable pounded out of his mouth, a hammer flattening a nail. Then nothing. The clock ticking behind them divided the breadth of silence into sections. One. Two. Three. Max counted the seconds in his head, twenty of them before his mother spoke again.

Unlike his father's splotched face, hers had blanched white.

"Why wouldn't I donate money to Chancellor Schuschnigg?" she asked, the tremble in her voice negating any attempt to dispute the accusation.

"Ex-chancellor," his father fumed. "Don't be coy with me, Klara. They are questioning our loyalty."

Max slumped farther into his chair. The darts flew back and forth across their dinner table more frequently these days, especially when they discussed their former chancellor and others who dared to stand up against the regime.

"We have been nothing but loyal," his mother said.

"To Hitler," his father insisted. "Not the old Austria."

"Change is a process," she said. "And you thought Schuschnigg was a good chancellor."

"But I wouldn't donate money to him, right before the plebiscite. Only Jews donated—"

"My donation was private information."

"Nothing is private anymore."

"It was when I donated it." His mother's voice sounded hollow, like she'd lost the strength of it. "They're like parasites."

His father stood and shoved his chair back underneath the table. "They're requiring my presence at the Hotel Metropole, first thing in the morning."

The new Gestapo headquarters.

"I'll explain—"

"No." He drummed the table, as if he were trying to pound out a solution. Then he gave a sharp nod. "You and Max were already planning to leave for Schloss Schwansee. I don't want to detain you."

"Of course," his mother said, smoothing her hands across the tablecloth. "We always visit Schloss Schwansee in the summer."

His father stepped toward the corridor, probably to lock himself in his study for the evening.

She called out to him. "What will you say to the Gestapo?"

He turned back, his eyes still hard. "That my wife made a foolish error. She knows nothing of politics."

Max leaned back as the housekeeper filled his coffee cup. He'd never heard anyone accuse his mother of being a fool.

The telephone rang.

"Don't answer that," his father commanded, and they waited until the ringing ceased. Then he glanced back toward the salon. "You will leave for Hallstatt tonight instead."

"I've done nothing wrong, Wilhelm."

"Innocence is secondary in this Reich."

The telephone began ringing again.

His mother stood. "We'll leave within the hour."

※

"Annika," Max whispered as he rapped on the glass, praying he wouldn't wake up Herr Knopf. Not only was her father a drunkard, Max doubted he could keep a secret. And he suspected that the man would do whatever benefited him the most.

Annika, however, he could trust.

He tapped again and waited in the darkness instead of turning on his flashlight. If only he could speak with Annika during the daylight hours, but he couldn't risk Herr Knopf's wrath or the man's nosiness. And his mother—she'd thought it fine that he and Annika were friends in their youth, but she clearly didn't want him to spend time with Annika now that he was almost eighteen.

Annika was loyal, like a sister to him. And he desperately needed her help.

Max eyed the walls of the castle across the yard. The light in his mother's room was still lit. She was probably playing one of her records, trying to fall asleep after their four-hour crawl through the city and then the mountains after dark. They'd been stopped near the edge of Vienna by guards asking for their papers.

Thankfully, his mother had the foresight to pack both birth certificates and baptismal papers. The uniformed man had given the paperwork a cursory glance, but he studied the canary in their backseat for a long time, fascinated by it. At first, Max had been terrified, but the guard was a kindred soul with his interest in birds. He stayed by the window until Max was able to coax Beethoven to sing.

Neither the guard nor his colleagues searched their Mercedes, but other vehicles had been pulled to the side, their doors open as the guards pulled out luggage, rifled through glove compartments, pulled up the car mats.

Even though his father was furious about the donation, Max had been proud of his mother, supporting their Austrian chancellor even after Hitler had ousted him. But she hadn't wanted to talk about it on their trip. It seemed that Herr Dornbach's impending visit with the Gestapo had depleted her.

No matter how angry his father was, the man would stand behind his wife's innocence in the morning. His reputation and clout in Vienna, and perhaps additional funding if necessary, would clear any suspicion of their family.

Annika's window slowly inched up. "Max?"

Her hair was all tousled, and she looked as if she were still a girl, wide-eyed and innocent, marveling at the world around, embracing her youth even as the new Reich was forcing most of their young people into adulthood.

The years had passed quickly as they both grew, and yet it seemed to him that Annika had stayed the same, as if she would always be the girl who shadowed him like a kitten when they swam and boated in the lake, hiked through the forests and mountains around them. One day, he hoped, she would marry a kind man who would move her far away from her father.

"What's wrong?" she asked.

"Where is Herr Knopf?"

She glanced behind her, as if her father might be waiting at the door. "I don't know."

"Is he home?"

She scampered away from the window and returned seconds later. "He's not here."

Max took a deep breath, relieved. "I need your help."

"I'll be out in a moment."

He waited at the edge of the forest, grateful that the clouds enveloped the moon tonight. They were far from the guards in Vienna, yet he still felt edgy, as if Hitler's henchmen had followed him here.

What would have happened if they'd found his bag of loose jewels in the bottom of the birdcage?

This was the first bird he'd brought to the lake, but months ago, he'd begun using the animals he rescued and their cages to help him courier things for Dr. Weiss. On one hand, he felt guilty about using these animals, but then again, he liked to think they were willing partners. In their innocence they were able to help others.

And he hoped that Annika, in her innocence, would help him too.

Something moved in the trees, and he tensed until he saw Frederica step out beside him, as if she'd heard his voice. He leaned down and petted her behind the ears like he used to do when he'd find her near his home in Vienna.

When he looked back up, he saw Annika. "You're spoiling her."

"All I give her is goat milk. She finds plenty to eat around here on her own." Annika tied back the tendrils that curled like the wild blossoms of a mountain lily around her head. "Did you bring me another animal?"

"I brought a canary with me, but I've already released him into the forest."

Annika squinted at the trees as if she might be able to spot the feathers among the branches.

"He lit off like a flame on a match when I opened the cage door."

Annika looked back at him. "How did you get a canary?"

"A friend gave him to me."

"Someone will think he escaped from the salt mine."

He hoped anyone curious *would* think this canary escaped from Salzwelten, the mine above Hallstatt. One of the many canaries singing for the miners in the darkness. If their song ever stopped, the miners fled, the lives of those birds sacrificed to protect their caregivers.

Annika looped a rogue curl back over her ear. "I didn't think you were coming home this summer."

"We were detained."

"I've been reading the papers," she said. "Hitler seems to be changing everything. Even Sarah is gone. . . ."

He nodded slowly. "The Jewish people who haven't been able to leave are afraid."

"What about you?" she asked.

"I—" He paused to consider his words. "I fear for the people I love."

She nodded solemnly.

"I need to tell you a secret, Annika. A secret you must swear never to tell anyone. Not even your father."

Especially not her father.

"What is it?" she asked.

"Do you swear?"

"I swear."

"Come with me." He took her hand and led her back into the forest, to the place in the woods where he'd found sanctuary for himself. And where he found it still, in the mountain shadow of Sarstein.

Decades ago, when the cool of autumn began to settle over these mountains, his father had hunted chamois, red stag, and black grouse with Max's grandfather, Herr Bettauer. After his father-in-law died, Wilhelm Dornbach expected that he and his son would hunt each autumn as well, but their first hunting expedition ended in a flood of tears. Max would rather shoot himself than kill an animal.

Dogs were an entirely different matter to his father. Wilhelm treated his prized hounds as if they were children, pampering them inside the house during their lives and then burying them on the plot of land where Herr Bettauer and perhaps generations before him had buried their dogs. Max had never known his father to be sentimental about anything except those dogs.

Annika eyed the shovel in his hand as they walked through the trees in the faint moonlight, onto the patch of land hemmed in by scrub brush and a sentry of pine trees, the grass and weeds kept short by the Knopfs' wandering goats. "Have you lost another animal?"

He shook his head. "This place—it's a burial ground for something else now."

"I don't understand, Max."

"The Nazis keep threatening . . . ," Max started. "Many Jewish people fear that the Nazis will take or damage their valuable things."

"My father thinks the Nazis are heroes."

He cringed. "Your father is wrong."

"I know," she said quietly.

He held up a moss-draped pine branch, and Annika ducked under it. Then he leaned his shovel against the wide girth of a tree. Hidden inside his jacket pocket was a small burlap bag, insignificant in appearance but the perfect cloak to camouflage its contents, worth thousands of the new Reichsmarks if the guard had found it.

He had to do more than tell Annika what he did with these jewels and other valuables he collected. He needed to show her.

"You and I can't fight the Nazis on our own, *Kätzchen*, but there's something we can do together to help Sarah's family and the other Jewish people in these lakes." Annika's eyes widened as he took out the bag. "We can keep their family things safe until they return."

"But they can't return until the Nazis leave," she said.

"One day they'll be gone." Hitler and his party thought they were here to stay—a Thousand-Year Reich—but Max couldn't bear to think about evil settling into their country for another year. A thousand years was unfathomable.

Annika glanced into the bag and gasped when she saw the jewels inside. Then Max placed the onionskin list in her hand, folded into a square. Her fingers curled over it.

"Hermann will bring the things to you secretly. You will record them on this paper, using only the initials that he gives you, and then hide the paper away."

"Hermann?" She sounded shocked.

"I'll tell him tomorrow that you'll be helping us."

She scanned the grass between the trees. "Does Hermann know where you bury these things?"

"No—it's safer for all of us if he doesn't know."

"Are you leaving?" In her voice was a sadness that he felt as well, not in leaving Vienna but this lake and his friends here.

"For only a short while." He leaned toward her. "No one knows I've buried things here, Annika, except me and now you."

"I'll keep your secret," she swore.

"I know," he said solemnly. "That's why—"

A rattling sound, the worn engine of a car, echoed through the forest.

Annika reached for his arm. "It's Vati!"

"We'll tell him that . . ." But he couldn't think of a valid reason why he and Annika would be out in the woods together at night unless he was trying to proposition the man's daughter. He glanced down at Annika's hand, but it seemed she'd already slipped the list into her pocket. He hid the jewels back in his bag.

"Run to your house," Annika urged. "I'll tell him I was out walking."

He was tired of feeling like a coward, even more so on his own property. Herr Knopf couldn't suspect what he'd been doing, but if he left Annika here alone, he'd feel as if he were throwing her into the den of a lion, one hungry enough to eat her alive.

"I can't leave you."

"It will be worse if he sees us—"

A crash interrupted her words. Then a blaze of light.

"Annika?" Herr Knopf shouted.

Max felt her hand tremble before she ripped it away. "He can't find us together."

But it was too late. Herr Knopf came thundering through the forest like a bloodhound that smelled a doe.

Annika backed up against the branches of a fir tree as Max shaded his eyes, turning to confront the beam of the man's flashlight. Herr Knopf glanced between him and Annika, gasping for breath before he spoke.

"What are you doing with my daughter?" His words sloshed together like lager against the sides of a Weizen glass.

"We were taking a walk," Max said, praying that the man wouldn't remember their confrontation come morning.

"Go home, Annika," her father commanded.

She stepped up to him. "I'll go home with you."

"I must speak with Herr Dornbach alone." His words dripped with sarcasm even as they slurred. The man had never liked Max; he clearly hated the thought of reporting to Wilhelm Dornbach's son.

Max didn't move. "What is it?"

"I have something to show you."

"Tomorrow, Vati," Annika insisted. "Right now we must rest."

"No." His voice steadied. "I have to show him now."

What would this man, half-drunk, need to show him so late at night? Max glanced at Annika in the dim glow of the flashlight, but she kept her distance as they followed Herr Knopf to the cottage. Anger boiled inside Max at the fear—that he was afraid of his father and Annika was afraid of hers.

He may not be able to challenge his own father, but one day he would be master of this estate. And when he was, he would release Herr Knopf to the wild like he'd released the canary, and keep Annika to care for the property. If she'd stay.

"Inside, Annika." Herr Knopf held open the cottage door, and she stepped through it, her father lumbering close behind. The canary sung out in the darkness above Max, and seconds later the cottage door banged open again. Herr Knopf stumbled back outside.

"I know your secret," the man said.

Max struggled for his next breath. Everything would be ruined if Herr Knopf found out about the burial ground. The man would dig up all the heirlooms, Max feared, and sell them off. Or he would tell Herr Dornbach what Max had done.

His father might fight for his wife, but if he found out what Max was doing, he'd turn his only son in to the Gestapo.

"What secret?" he asked, much more strongly than he felt.

Herr Knopf held up a chain and dangled it in front of Max, the gold reflecting in the light.

Anger roared inside Max again, spilling out. "That's not yours."

"Annika found it."

"Vati!" Annika exclaimed as she stepped out behind him, her eyes wide. Had she been digging in the old cemetery while he was gone? Perhaps he shouldn't have trusted her with his secret.

He would recover the rest of the items in the ground and hide them someplace else.

Herr Knopf motioned toward his daughter. "Tell him where you found it."

Max shook his head. "It's not nec—"

Herr Knopf interrupted him. "She found it in one of your mother's shoe boxes."

"You stole it?" he asked Annika. But even as he said those words, relief washed over him. His secret—the secret he'd shared with the girl in front of him—was still safe.

"I'd never steal from you!"

"*I* took it," Herr Knopf said with a disconcerting pride.

Max leaned closer, his hand outstretched until the pendant on the end settled into it. The golden star was like the ones Herr Weiss had given to him. A *Magen David*.

Perhaps his mother was helping their Jewish friends hide things as well.

Herr Knopf rolled his shoulders back. "I suspected it all along."

"Suspected what?" Max began to close his fingers around the necklace, but Herr Knopf snatched it away.

Herr Knopf reached for Annika's arm and yanked her back toward the door. "Ask your mother."

CHAPTER 19

"Story Girl!"

Ella Nemeth races toward me. I'm standing on a stool instead of reading from one, placing a boxful of new arrivals in their proper place.

As I climb down, Ella twirls to display the pink ribbon around her ponytail, then motions toward a couple in their sixties standing near the door behind her.

The man is dressed in neatly pressed khaki shorts with a button-down shirt, his brown hair graying at the temples. The woman beside him has on a paisley sundress, the hem nearly reaching her tan-colored sandals. Her copper hair is clipped short, her nose the same shade as her hair, as if she's plagued by a cold.

The woman sneezes into the crook of her arm, confirming my thoughts.

"Who are these fine people?" I ask as Ella reaches for my hand, tugging me toward them.

"Grammy and Gramps."

"It's better than Grumps," the man says with a smile before he shakes my hand. "Peter and Lottie Nemeth."

"It's nice to meet you, Mr. and Mrs. Nemeth."

"Likewise," he says. "And please call us Peter and Lottie. It makes us feel younger."

I decide right then that I like Dr. Nemeth's parents. "Are you from Columbus?"

"Atlanta is our official home, but Ella is our only grandchild, so Columbus is like home for us as well."

"Josh said he emailed you a few days ago about their adventure," Lottie says.

I nod. "He told me they found a wooden box in Lake Grundlsee that looked promising, but when they recovered it, all they found inside were milk bottles."

"I never believed Leo's story," Peter says, "but he convinced Josh and my other two sons that Hallstatt and those other Austrian lakes were stocked with treasure."

Lottie blows her nose. "Josh and his team are arriving in Hallstatt today."

I already know this but don't say so, worried that they might wonder about the relationship between their son and me. Dr. Nemeth has been keeping me informed about the team's expeditions in the surrounding lakes and his search for Annika's family.

Ella tugs on my shirt. "Are you reading a story soon?"

"No." I stack the books onto an empty shelf. "We have story time on Saturdays."

Her lower lip trembles as if this is catastrophic news, and when she wipes her sleeve across her eyes, my heart begins to plunge.

Lottie leans over, whispering to me. "She's missing her dad."

Ah. Sad and sweet alike that she misses her dad. At her age, I'd always been thrilled to see mine walking out the door.

And it makes me wonder—why isn't she missing her mother as well? Dr. Nemeth has yet to mention his wife in our correspondence. If she stayed behind with Ella, where is she today when her daughter's heart is breaking?

I glance at the empty rug near the back of the store. "Any day is a good day for a story, isn't it?"

Ella pumps her head slowly at first and then deliberately, rubbing the back of her hand over her eyes again.

"Would you like me to read one right now?" I ask her.

"Yes, please."

I look up at her grandparents. "Do you have time?"

"Of course," Peter says, and his wife nods in agreement. This time she's smiling at me.

I hold out one jean-clad leg and strappy sandal, displaying them to Ella. "I'll need to get my socks and cape."

Ella grinned. "You can read without socks."

"I'm not certain that I can."

I scan the room, looking over at Brie, who's working fervently at the counter, and then at the dozen or so children with their adults, flipping through book pages and utilizing the slide. My sister won't mind if I slip in an extra story or two on a Friday afternoon.

"Why don't you spread the word to the other children," I tell Ella. "I'll meet you at the back of the room in about five minutes."

Ella rushes to one of the children nearby, and Lottie mouths a thank-you. I retrieve Story Girl's cape and socks upstairs, and when I return, Brie catches my eye, holding up the store's landline. "There's a phone call for you."

Ella is still busy rounding up an audience, so I step to the counter and answer the call.

"Is this Callie Randall?" a woman asks.

"It is."

"My name is Liberty—" She hesitates as if she's trying to decide whether or not to tell me her last name. "A bookseller from Boise called and said that you found some sort of list in one of my parents' books."

My heart pumps harder as the chatter and laughter around me seem to dull. "I'm sorry for your loss."

"My mom and dad have both been gone for several years, but my brother and I have had a hard time parting with their things."

"I understand." Not because of my own parents, but one day Charlotte will be gone and I can't imagine selling anything of hers to strangers.

"We don't have enough room between us to keep everything, but still it's tough. . . ."

"Did your parents collect a lot of books?" I ask, hoping Annika was her mother.

"My father was the collector, though most of his books were scientific in nature."

"Was he a doctor?"

"A veterinarian," she says. "He was much more fond of animals than people."

"What were your parents' names?" Perhaps the question is too personal, especially since she still hasn't told me her last name, but I can't think of a more tactful way to ask about Annika.

"Why don't you tell me first what you found in his book?" She sounds nice enough, just suspicious.

I tell her about the list embedded in the pages. "The name Annika Knopf was inside the cover along with *Schloss Schwansee* and a photograph of a young man."

She doesn't respond, so I ask, "Have you heard of Annika?"

"My father talked often about the castle, but not about the people."

My heart begins to speed up again. "What did he tell you?"

"My father—" She stops. "I need to speak to my brother before I say anything else."

"Of course."

I give her my cell phone number so she can contact me after she talks to him. If she'd known what was in this book, perhaps she wouldn't have let it go. These special books, I think, should be cherished like the treasures they are.

Then again, what if I was opening something that her parents deliberately closed? It could be that Annika didn't want her children to know about her past. Who was I to step into their family and rearrange their secrets if her parents were trying to keep secrets?

Someone tugs on my shirt, and I look down to see Ella. She doesn't say anything, simply nods toward a small group of children who have assembled in the back corner.

"Pick out a book for us to read," I say.

Ella scans the shelf and pulls out a book as I take my place in front of the audience.

Where the Wild Things Are. Another old story about a naughty child on an adventure, a book that a lot of parents didn't want their children to read when it was published. Perhaps some parents still don't want their children to travel where the wild things reside, though I like the journey of this boy named Max, who realizes that home is an awfully good place to be.

I glance over at Peter and Lottie, but they don't seem the least bit concerned about the selection. So I begin to read about Max meeting all sorts of fierce creatures along the way.

Several years ago, I researched the author, Maurice Sendak, for a blog post. Sendak based the wild things in his book on childhood memories of his relatives—the ultimate writer payback, I suppose. Max is grounded in the memories and imagination of Sendak's childhood, and the kids in front of me seem as mesmerized by Max's rumpus as generations before them, trailing this boy through an adventure of epic proportions.

I continue reading about his voyage, how he confronts his fears and, in a sense, tames the monsters who wanted to eat him. They play for a season until he's ready to go home. "'And Max—'" I lower my voice so the children lean in—"'the king of all wild things, was lonely and wanted to be where someone loved him best of all.'"

When I glance up, Ella is grinning at me. Who in the room, young or old, doesn't want to be with someone who loves them? Nothing wipes away loneliness like genuine love, the promise of it overcoming the thrill of the greatest adventure. Making an adventure a joy, not an escape.

As our hero begins his voyage home, my mind wanders to the adventure of little Fritz in the magic balloon book, another boy who travels around the world until he ultimately reunites with his parents. Perhaps one of the best parts of a grand journey is knowing you have someone to come home to when you're done.

I read two more books to the children before several parents begin stepping toward the door, clearly ready to head to their own homes. My little audience groans when I tell them we're finished.

"Come back tomorrow if you'd like to hear more," I say before they disperse. Then I stand to reshelve the wild things.

Lottie steps forward again. "It's such a joy to see someone who still delights in a good story."

I smile—that's me, I suppose, finding meaning and delight in the musings of someone else's adventure.

"Max reminds me of Josh when he was young."

"Really?" I don't mean to sound shocked, but Dr. Nemeth doesn't seem like the kind of person who would lose himself in the world of pretend.

"He's changed a lot since Grace died."

"Grace?"

"His wife," she says, seemingly surprised that this is news to me.

I collapse back onto my stool, my legs trembling as the weight of her words bear down. The conversations between Dr. Nemeth and me, they've been focused mainly on finding Annika and the missing treasure. He's had no reason to mention the loss of his wife.

Poor Ella. I never should have criticized Mrs. Nemeth for her daughter's sadness, like she was my mother abandoning me. Every girl should have a mom to talk to, a woman who cares about what she thinks. Who's there when her body—or her heart—is hurting.

Who loves her when she feels alone.

"Losing someone changes everything," I say.

She nods. "Josh is just now starting to live again."

Ella slips up beside me. "Do you think there are any wild things in Austria?"

"I doubt it."

She grins. "Except my dad."

"You're a blessed girl, Ella, to have a father who loves you."

When she takes her grandparents to the slide, I lean back against a shelf, processing Lottie's words. And my heart breaks for Dr. Nemeth. How sad to lose his wife, the mom of their sweet daughter. What appeared to me as cool and calculated is perhaps someone trying to venture back out of his shell.

"Story Girl!" Ella calls, and I watch her lunge down the slide one more time before her grandparents say good-bye.

Hours later, as I'm trying to craft an email to Dr. Nemeth about the woman who called from Idaho, a new message appears on my screen. It's from Sophie in Vienna.

Unfortunately, I haven't found any records that mention an Annika Knopf. Austria didn't have a central birth registry before 1938, but if you know where Annika attended church, you can search for her baptismal certificate, and perhaps a wedding and death certificate through them.

I finally located the photograph that you requested from the *Neues Wiener Tagblatt*. Attached is the scanned picture along with the caption from the society column.

I click on the first attachment, and the newspaper photograph expands on my screen. Now I know whom this young man is smiling at—a beautiful young lady who's dressed as if she descended from royalty. The admiration in his face is clear, not a care in the world beyond the woman across from him. I can't see the front of her face, but her gaze is focused back on him, as if she could spend the rest of the evening dancing in his arms.

If this is Annika . . . why would she cut herself out of the picture?

I click on the second document. Sophie has circled a paragraph for me.

Maximilian Dornbach and . . .

My iPad screen seems to gray, and I blink hard, trying to focus again on the second name.

Maximilian Dornbach and Luzia Weiss, Opera Ball.

Maximilian Dornbach. Max. The king of the wild things.

And Luzia Weiss . . . the name in Charlotte's book.

My heart races again. Charlotte thought her birth name was Luzia, but clearly this woman was born years before 1938.

Is it possible that Luzia Weiss was her mother?

Stunned, I read the name again, afraid that I might have mistaken the spelling, but the caption is identical to the name written in the book about Hatschi Bratschi.

Charlotte was adopted from an orphanage in France, not Austria, and yet . . .

I surf online for Luzia Weiss and Luzia Dornbach in both Vienna and Idaho, but nothing comes up. Then I search for Maximilian Dornbach in Idaho.

This time an obituary fills my screen.

Max Dornbach. Veterinarian. Resident of Sandpoint. Winner of the AVMA Animal Welfare Award. Father of two children. Husband of Renee Dornbach for almost fifty years.

A hundred questions spring into my mind for Liberty—Liberty Dornbach, I assume. I try to call her back, but she doesn't answer.

Why is the picture of Max and Luzia in the back of Annika's book? Did Max know about her list?

And most important to me at the moment, what happened to the woman in Max Dornbach's arms?

CHAPTER 20

Max collapsed onto a chair in the ancient entry hall, the faint strains of music sprinkling down from the second floor of the Schloss. Herr Knopf had refused to return the necklace to him even though Annika had found it in Frau Dornbach's room. He didn't blame Annika for being curious, but her father . . . It was thievery, taking something from one's employer.

Herr Knopf didn't seem to care when Max called him a thief. Collateral, that's what the man had said.

But collateral for what?

Herr Knopf had shaken his head, refusing to answer the question. Max's mother could probably answer it, but he wasn't entirely sure that he wanted to know why Herr Knopf had been smirking when he delivered that news. Had he discovered that Klara Dornbach was helping the Jewish people as well?

A door creaked farther down the corridor, and his mother emerged into the foyer, flipping the switch that powered their chandelier light.

"Why are you still awake?" she asked, a porcelain cup nestled in her palm. The steam from chamomile tea billowed into a cloud around her dark hair, hanging loose over the shoulders of her robe. Her face was scrubbed clean of rouge and the burgundy-colored lipstick she usually wore.

"Herr Knopf wanted to speak with me," he said.

"Whatever could Emil need at this hour?"

Max closed his eyes, a dull ache creeping up the back of his neck, shooting pain through his head.

He'd lost track of the hours since they'd arrived from Vienna. Was it three in the morning now? Later even? Neither of them would have much rest tonight.

"Herr Knopf found a necklace in your room."

She slid into a chair beside him, across from the grand stone fireplace that lay dormant in the summer months.

"With a Star of David."

She stared at him, dumbfounded, and then the shock of the find began to slowly register in her eyes. "It was hidden away. . . ."

"Not anymore."

His mother's gaze trailed up the carpeted steps to the first floor of their home. "He was rummaging through my things."

Max didn't reply, not ready to incriminate Annika, who seemed as stunned as he had been by the discovery.

"Did you get it from a friend?"

"It was a gift from my mother." Her hands trembled as she tried to sip her drink, splashing tea onto the marble tile. "No one else must find out, Max."

"Who gave her the star?"

"Her mother," she whispered.

Max leaned his head back against the wood paneling, the ache behind his eyes pounding with her words. "My grandmother was Jewish."

"She was baptized in the Catholic Church as an infant, but according to the new laws in Aus—Ostmark, she would still be Jewish."

His grandparents had died more than two decades ago, leaving his parents—the newly wed Wilhelm and Klara—the estate of Schloss Schwansee as their inheritance. He'd never met his grandparents, but people in town remembered them. Unlike the Dornbach family, who used the castle as a holiday residence, his grandparents had lived at Schloss Schwansee year-round.

His grandparents had two daughters—Klara and Annabel. Tante Annabel had married a French artist years ago and relocated with him to Paris.

"I will give Emil money," his mother said. "It will keep him quiet."

"Not for long." The man would take the money and keep asking for more.

He scooted his chair toward her, the legs screeching across tile. "Does Father know?"

"He never asked."

"But he suspects."

"I don't know," she said. "My grandparents converted before

my mother was born. Your Oma didn't know about her heritage until long after she'd married."

"But you knew before you married."

"I loved your father, and he loved me for who I was. An Austrian Catholic girl."

"From a prominent family." He hated the bitterness in his voice, the cruelty in his words, but if his mother had been an Austrian girl without an inheritance, he doubted his father would have married her.

What would his father have done—what would he do now— if he discovered the truth? Wilhelm Dornbach's identity was grounded in his work and the purity of his blood.

"Our marriage was suitable for both of us."

"But not if he knew you were Jewish."

"Partially Jewish," she insisted. "My father and his parents were Aryan."

"It shouldn't have mattered either way."

"It didn't matter twenty years ago," she said, her head bowing again to the cup in her hands. "But now it matters very much."

"Is that why Tante Annabel moved to Paris?"

She nodded. "The changes in Germany worried her."

"What about Uncle Félix?"

His mother shrugged. "We never spoke of such things."

Silence. It seemed to be what kept all of them sealed away in their private spaces, afraid of what might happen when the truth came out. Because speaking the truth now could be ugly, labeling people like they were cans of soup at the grocer's. Selecting who was worthy to be in Hitler's Third Reich based on their ancestry or faith.

People—good people—like Luzi, who had to leave school

because of a lineage established long before she was born. Her father, a respected doctor just weeks ago, now without a position, the respect for all his work gone.

Max walked toward the front door to lock it. "Father will find out."

"Not if you don't tell him."

He'd never betray either of them.

CHAPTER 21

The rumble of a car engine drowned the chorus of birds who'd nestled themselves between green conifer boughs and crisp leaves turned auburn and orange by the autumn winds. Annika hopped off her bicycle and hid behind one of the giant pines, watching between branches as a black sedan moved slowly toward her, bumping over the rocks and tree limbs that littered the dirt.

A long lane, the width more accommodating to an oxcart than an automobile, stretched from Schloss Schwansee east, to an unlocked gate about half a kilometer away and on into the town of Obertraun. Every few months, lost or curious drivers would venture through the gate and find themselves on the estate with no place to turn around until they reached the courtyard by the castle.

The estate had been built to be accessed by water, but this path, hidden under the trees, gave the Dornbachs and the occasional visitor opportunity to drive. These days she wished they could lock the gate and block anyone from coming onto the property. Except Max, of course, and Sarah and Hermann. How she missed all of them. Sarah had left for Bolivia months ago, and Annika's father no longer needed Hermann's help with the platform. It still needed to be painted, but Vati didn't seem to care.

The men in uniforms came to visit her father several evenings a week now and sometimes during the day, often taking him away with them. At first she thought they were friends of his, going to the pub, but he no longer stumbled home in a stupor, smelling like sour beer. In fact, he seemed much more focused, like the sharp prick of a pin, though she didn't know exactly what held his attention.

She was furious at him for telling Max that she'd found his mother's necklace, as if she had been trying to steal from the Dornbach family. It was almost as if he were intent on ruining the Dornbachs out of pure jealousy for their wealth and prestige. And ruining her as well.

Where would she and her father go when Herr and Frau Dornbach decided they had enough of Vati's rage?

The black sedan crawled past her, and she saw two men in the front seat wearing the stormy gray tunics of the SS men she'd seen in the village of Obertraun.

What did these men want with her father?

The Dornbachs, she suspected, wouldn't want Hitler's men on their estate, but Vati didn't care what they thought anymore. He'd stopped their work in the chapel, and he didn't even bother to lock the front door to the castle, coming and going as if he owned the place.

As if he didn't expect the Dornbachs to return.

Max and his mother had left hours after Vati showed him the necklace. The next day Annika had cleaned the castle, but she didn't linger, afraid of what she might find. Max hadn't contacted her even though she'd written a letter of apology, saying that she'd never intended to harm him or his family. It had been stupid of her to go through Frau Dornbach's things.

When the forest sounds returned, she pushed her bike back on the lane and began pedaling again, careful to maneuver around the rocks. She'd told Vati that she needed to go to the grocer's, and if these men returned before she was in the village, she didn't want them to offer her a ride.

She'd waited weeks for Hermann to bring her valuables to hide, but he hadn't returned to the estate after Vati stopped building the platform. Hermann needed to know that she wanted to help. That she would do whatever she could to protect what her father and these men were trying to steal.

She unlatched the iron gate that stretched like a spiderweb between the stone walls and pedaled to the road that followed the train tracks into town. The chalets and barns ahead of her rambled through the threads of valley, hemmed in between the Alps. In addition to its five hundred residents, Obertraun had been filled in summers past with tourists from across Austria and Germany who boated and swam on the lake or hiked through the mountains. Other visitors arrived in the winter for skiing.

In autumn and spring, this town consisted mainly of residents like her who'd been living here their entire lives. Most people knew one another, Hermann once told her, but since Vati had forbidden her to attend school or church, her world rarely expanded past the iron gates. Now that Max and Sarah were gone, her only connection to life outside was Hermann, along with the grocer and the butcher and the regular visits from Pastor Dietz, asking Vati if she could return to the evangelical church.

She'd waited long enough to help Max and the others hide their valuables from the Nazis. The papers no longer reported anything negative about Hitler or his party, but she'd heard something on the BBC last night that terrified her. The Jewish people in Germany were disappearing, it seemed. Taken away to work camps. Their things confiscated.

What would happen if people in Austria started disappearing as well?

The air on the other side of the village smelled like fallen leaves and the newly chopped wood that had been stacked in bins near the country homes and lined up neatly against barn walls. Cows wandered toward a fence along the bike path to watch her, their bells clanging like chimes in the breeze.

The Stadler family farmed in a valley east of Obertraun, at the foot of the Dachstein Mountains, and Annika found Hermann in his overalls and work gloves, loading shovelfuls of manure into a cart inside their barn.

He leaned his shovel against the door. "You're a long way from home."

She felt awkward for a moment, interrupting his work instead of answering his knock at her cottage. "I've come for a reason."

"Of course. Would you like some coffee?" He nodded toward his family's house on the other side of the barn door, a chalet backed against the hillside. Autumn leaves dangled low on heavy branches, framing the sloped roof and heavy shutters and empty window boxes.

"Perhaps in a bit," she said. The house would be quiet with

Hermann's siblings gone, off starting families of their own, but she still wanted to speak with him outside so his mother wouldn't hear. "Did you see Max when he visited in August?"

Hermann shook his head slowly. "I didn't know he was here."

"My father scared him away."

"Did he say when he would return?"

"No, but . . . Max spoke with me."

Hermann propped one of his boots on the blade of his shovel, waiting for her to continue.

"I know where he hides your things, Hermann."

Hermann's eyes flashed. Not an admission of guilt, but enough that she knew he understood. "What things?"

"The things you're keeping from the Nazis."

He glanced over at the chalet and then reached for the handle of his shovel before turning away from her. "I don't know what you're referring to—"

"He asked me to help you, Hermann."

"He didn't tell me."

She lowered her voice to a whisper. "I want to help."

He ground the metal tip of his shovel into the floor of dirt and hay, looking through the door again. "This isn't child's play, Annika."

She straightened her back, her head held high. "I'm no longer a child."

He studied her for a moment, and she wished that she'd worn a scarf over her hair instead of plaiting it into braids. "I suppose you aren't."

"What happens if the Nazis search your home? They will find these things, and your family—"

"I've already counted the cost," he said, his voice sober. "There's always a cost for standing up against evil, Annika. You have to do it for the right reasons."

"Max asked me to do this."

"You can't help people because of Max."

Annika considered his words. Was she helping hide the valuables because of Max or because she thought it was right?

The image of Sarah flashed in her mind. Her friend carrying the bag with treasures for Hermann. The items were probably somewhere on Hermann's farm, waiting to be buried in the land behind Annika's cottage. Max said that not even Hermann knew what he'd done with them.

She had to do something to help those who were being plundered by the evil in their country. It would be the greatest honor to care for Sarah's heirlooms and to do the same for others in their community until they returned.

"Please, Hermann. These things—they will be safe on the estate."

"Your father has become quite friendly with Hitler's friends."

"Then they will never suspect that we're hiding things."

He filled his shovel with the manure and piled it into the cart. "I'll come to the boathouse tonight, while your father is gone."

Hermann kept his promise, rowing his boat under the catkins and into the boathouse before her father returned. The sky was ablaze with yellow sparks of sun and red-ember clouds that coiled like flames above the lake before the cold blues of night soaked up the fire.

He handed Annika a seed bag, and she cradled it in her arms.

"I've listed the items and the initials of each owner inside the bag," he said. "Burn my list when you're done."

She nodded.

"I'll bring you more when I get them."

"Thank you."

"Take care, Annika," he said before rowing away.

She hurried up the bank, and as she neared the cottage, she heard the rumble of a car engine again. She rushed into her bedroom, sliding the bolt across the door, and minutes later, her father's boots clapped down the hallway, the slam of his door shaking her room.

When his snores finally rattled the thin walls, she turned on the lamp and dumped the contents of the bag onto her bed. Some pieces were wrapped in brown paper, rolled in so much masking tape that they looked like one of the boulders along the lake. She brushed her hands across the loose pieces. Gold necklace. Ruby brooch. Six silver teacups with saucers.

Teacups that she'd seen displayed in Sarah's dining room hutch.

If her father found this, she had no doubt he'd sell the items and return to the tavern, drinking away the profits. Or he'd use the items to bribe other people in their community. She couldn't let either happen, for his sake or the sake of the families who valued these things.

Annika retrieved her *Bambi* book from under the bed. Inside, stuffed between the pages with Max's photograph, was the onionskin list from Max. But if Vati or someone else ever opened the book, the paper would slide to the floor.

As she sat cross-legged on her bed, Annika began to meticulously record the items that Hermann brought for her, but instead of putting the words on onionskin, she wrote them inside the pages of *Bambi*. Her father might open the cover, searching for paper, but he'd never think to scan through the text.

After she finished recording each item from Hermann's list,

she transcribed Max's records into the book as well. Tomorrow afternoon, when her father was gone, she'd take Max's place in the forest and bury these items between the animals in the ground. Then she'd burn both Max's and Hermann's lists. These treasures, they would be safe in her care.

CHAPTER 22

"May I look through the Hatschi Bratschi story?" I ask Charlotte before settling into one of her two living room chairs. We have less than an hour before story time begins—and she's my featured guest—but it's enough time to look at this old book.

"Of course," she says, nodding toward the bookcase. "Would you like some hot tea?"

"Yes, please." Usually I help her brew the tea, but I want to examine the book while she's in the other room.

When she slips into the kitchen, I inch *Hatschi Bratschis Luftballon* carefully off the shelf. The blue spine is cracked, ready to split, and the last thing I want to do is damage Charlotte's only connection with her past.

Inside the cover is the name I remember well.

Luzia Weiss.

White light.

I skim the pages, hoping that whoever this Luzia was, she wrote something in the pages like Annika did, but the only handwriting is the fancy script recording her name.

What would Charlotte say if I told her that perhaps the name Luzia originally belonged to her mother instead of her? I'll hold that information close to my heart until I find out what happened to her family, if I can find out. Annika's story somehow connects with this Luzia Weiss's story; I desperately hope it also connects with Charlotte's.

It seems impossible, but like Mrs. Murry told Meg in *A Wrinkle in Time*, you don't have to understand things for them to *be*.

I don't understand all that is happening, but I'll search until I can find answers. And I pray that I find a thread of joy stitched into the sorrow and agony of war.

Liberty hasn't returned my calls, but I have a list of questions ready for when she does and some new information as well. Early this morning, Dr. Nemeth sent me a photograph of Schloss Schwansee, and then the birth and marriage certificates for Annika Knopf from the *Evangelische Pfarrkirche*, the evangelical church in Hallstatt. They didn't have a death certificate on record for her.

The Dornbach family, Dr. Nemeth said, owned Schloss Schwansee before the war, but according to the certificates on my iPad, Annika was only sixteen when she married the caretaker of the castle, a man named Hermann Stadler.

One of the students on Dr. Nemeth's team is taking the train to Salzburg tomorrow to find out who owns Schloss Schwansee now.

Charlotte places a mug of green tea in front of me.

"Thank you." I take a sip as she glances out the window at two songbirds perched on a slender branch.

"Listen," she whispers.

"What is it?"

"They're singing for us."

I quiet my racing thoughts and listen with her to the melody of these birds, simple yet sacred in a sense as they embrace this gifting of song. Charlotte's gaze travels down to the book with the wicked wizard on the cover searching for children to steal.

"Do you mind if I borrow this a few days?" I ask.

"What do you want with old Hatschi Bratschi?"

"It's for my research."

"Of course." She reaches out to touch the cover as if it might transport her as well before looking back up at me. "How is our Dr. Nemeth?"

He's not exactly ours, but I decide not to debate the topic. I haven't told either Charlotte or Brie that he's a widower. It doesn't change anything between Dr. Nemeth and me, but they might drop hints about our relationship when it's strictly a professional one. "He and his team are starting to dive today in Lake Hallstatt."

"Have they discovered any treasure?"

"Not the treasure they've been hoping to find, but they recovered a Nazi dagger from Lake Grundlsee." He sent me a picture of it along with pictures of several smaller items they discovered in the depths of the lake. All of it would be turned over to the Austrian government.

"And Annika?" she asks.

"He confirmed that she lived there during the war, but he doesn't know where she went after. The gates to the estate are locked, and he said no one that he's asked remembers her."

"It's very difficult to talk about what happened then. The

memories . . ." Charlotte's hands shake as she reaches for the porcelain mug that holds her tea, taking a sip before she continues. "You have to relive the pain to tell the stories."

"I can't imagine," I say. "I still wish someone had told Nadine who brought you to the orphanage."

"By the time she needed that information, everyone was gone."

I lower my tea. She's answered my questions over the years when I was searching for her family, but she rarely talked about her memories of France. "What do you mean, they were gone?"

Her green eyes are clear when she looks at me. Her mind might want to run, but she presses forward. "The Nazis came to our orphanage; did I ever tell you that?"

"No—"

"Near the end of the war. The Gestapo decided to clear it out before the Allied soldiers arrived." She looks at the book cover again, a new sadness stitching her words together. "Nadine had been volunteering to help with the children. I was sick that week, before the Nazis came, so she . . . she'd taken me to her home."

"Were the children Jewish?"

"Most of them." She glances out the window, and I turn with her to see a red-winged blackbird on the branch. "But it shouldn't matter."

"No, it shouldn't."

"The Nazis killed all the children and caregivers except Nadine and me. As if it were a crime to be young or help a child." When her voice breaks, I reach for her hand, clasping it. "I was seven by the time the Nazis left France. Nadine and I returned to the abandoned orphanage, and almost everything had been taken or destroyed, including my baptismal certificate. But we found my book. What was worthless to the Nazis was priceless to me."

My phone buzzes, and I scan a text from Brie.

Thirty children are here, asking about Story Girl. Any idea where she went?

To France, I want to tell her, more than seventy years ago.

We're coming, I reply.

Charlotte picks up the mugs, the interruption from my phone bringing her back, but it takes me longer to process the threads of this story. What a burden Charlotte has borne her entire life, surviving the invasion of the Nazis while almost everyone close to her was killed.

Did everyone in her biological family die during the war as well? If most of the children in the orphanage were Jewish, Luzia and her daughter might've been too.

How did Luzia Weiss transport her baby from Vienna to France?

So many missing pages between the covers of their story, if there is a story connecting Charlotte and the Luzia who danced at the Opera Ball.

When we reach the store, I introduce the kids who don't know Charlotte to the matron of our story hour, and she surprises them by selecting a modern book, the one about cows that type. They listen, mesmerized by her ability to click and clack and moo without a red cape.

I step back into a row of books, watching her work her magic for both the children and the dozens of parents standing behind them. And I scan the small crowd for Ella Nemeth, disappointed that her grandparents weren't able to bring her back today.

Charlotte smiles at me before turning the page, content in who she is even though her past is muddied. I admire her courage and grace with children and adults alike.

Did she inherit these qualities from Luzia, or did she learn them from Nadine?

Last night I asked Sophie to look for Luzia's name in the

archives, but I may never find anything else about Luzia until I get myself on an airplane to Austria to search through the records of the many churches and synagogues in Vienna.

How do other people do it with such ease, the traveling away from all they know to a place of total unknowns?

"Callie," Brie whispers as she steps beside me, "I'm afraid we have an unexpected visitor."

I glance over at her. "Why are you afraid?"

"It's Scott."

I stay frozen beside the row of Star Wars books, feeling as if I've been invaded in my safest of places. Scott and Kathleen join the adults in the back while Jack squeezes between the other children to create a new seat.

Scott has gained a few pounds since the night before our wedding, his midsection expanding within the comfort of marriage. The last time I saw him was at The Alcove, during our rehearsal dinner. I distinctly remember thinking how handsome he was. And how lucky I was that he'd picked me to be his wife.

I suppose there's a chance—albeit slight—that he would have been faithful after we said our vows, but his heart wouldn't have been mine. I hope for both Kathleen's and Jack's sake that he chooses to remain faithful to them.

As Brie slips back to the refreshment table, Scott catches my eye, and I respond with a quick nod before looking away, any fondness between us gone.

I've wondered often in the past two years what would happen when I saw him again. I'm greatly relieved to realize that I feel nothing at all. The longing in my heart, the regret, is gone. I can't change my past—I'm well aware of that—but I can change the course of my future. Like Charlotte, my past doesn't have to define me.

"I am with you always, even to the end of the age."

The words from the Bible—the most powerful book of all—flood through me. I might sequester myself in my room, trying to hide away, but God is with me here just as He would be on an airplane across the ocean and into Austria.

I know I must go now—to help Charlotte find her family. And if this Luzia isn't related, Charlotte will never know. She'll just be pleased that I was courageous enough to fly to Europe on my own.

❧

Hours later I slip into the office at the back of the store. I've agreed to work the evening shift so Brie can transport her boys to the pool, but before she leaves, I want to search for plane tickets to Salzburg, the nearest airport to Hallstatt.

A message from Dr. Nemeth appears in my inbox. It's a long note detailing their find in Lake Hallstatt this morning, a watertight box with a list and silver coins inside. The World Jewish Congress is extremely interested in it, he says. Sadly the list he found is very different from the one in Annika's book. It's the names of Austrians who were taken to a concentration camp.

My stomach turns. Not only did the Nazis try to rid themselves of the people on this list, like the children at Charlotte's orphanage; they tried to hide any record of their imprisonment and, presumably, their deaths.

The evil that raged during that time . . . it still rages all over the world today. How can people be so cruel to others? This is one thing I don't want to ever understand.

I read the rest of Dr. Nemeth's email.

No one we've asked seems to remember Annika Knopf or Annika Stadler, though we've discovered the current owner of the property, a man named Jonas Stadler. Probably her son or grandson. Tomorrow I'm going to the estate to see if anyone is at home.

My fingers hover over the keyboard, trying to form the words in my head before I type. He invited me to join their search when he visited the bookstore. There's nothing wrong with accepting the invite.

I type a short email back to him.

If the invitation is still open, I'd like to join you and your team in Hallstatt this week.

I stare at the message for a moment and then hit Send before I change my mind, expecting it to take hours before Dr. Nemeth contacts me in return.

Minutes later, my cell phone rings.

"You're really coming?" he asks, clearly surprised.

"I believe I am." I'm not ready to tell him or anyone except Brie about Luzia yet. I'll just search while his team is diving.

"We'll be in Hallstatt all week, but you should stay in Europe as long as you can."

An idea slowly occurs to me—Ella and her grandmother are planning to visit him soon. Perhaps they wouldn't mind if I join them on the plane. "When are Ella and Lottie flying over?"

He's silent for a moment before responding. "Unfortunately, my mom was just diagnosed with pneumonia."

"Oh no—"

"The doctor caught it before any serious complications, but no traveling for her until she's recovered."

His daughter's face appears in my mind, those tears of sadness on her cheeks yesterday. "Ella must be devastated."

"I'm coming home the day my team finishes here."

I hear the concern in his voice, and I understand—I've spent much of my adult life afraid to travel in case something bad happens while I'm gone. But then I remember my birthday wish, that I would have someone to share my trip. Ella would be good company . . . and insurance that I would actually step onto that plane.

"Why don't I bring Ella with me?" I ask. "We can come after your team leaves."

He's quiet again, and I chide myself for asking. For all he knows, I'm like Hatschi Bratschi, waiting to steal children away.

"I wasn't trying to hint—" he starts.

"I know."

"You like children, right?"

I burst out laughing. "Of course I like children."

"Stupid question."

My laughter stops, but still I'm smiling. "In all my years as Story Girl, no one's actually asked me that before, Dr. Nemeth. They just assume I like kids."

"You have to start calling me Josh."

I hesitate. Names are important and changing what I call him means tearing down a wall.

But then again, if I'm flying to Austria, perhaps it's a wall that must come down.

"Josh," I finally say.

"Having you bring her . . . it's a lot for me to ask."

"You didn't ask. I volunteered."

He pauses again. "Honestly?"

"Yes." Kids and books, both of them energize me.

"If we haven't found Annika yet, you and I can search for her together."

And I like this idea of searching for Annika with him, after I find what I need about Luzia.

"I bought traveler's insurance for my mom's flight. I'll just transfer her ticket into your name."

I stiffen, not wanting to be obligated to him. "I can purchase my own ticket."

"Please, Callie."

I wish I could see his face, understand his motivation. "It's hard for me to be away," he says. "If you are taking care of my daughter, then I want to make sure I'm taking care of you, too."

How can I argue with that? I'm not entirely certain what to say, but I relent.

"They were supposed to fly out this Thursday."

"I can meet Ella and your father at the airport."

"You'll need a passport," he says suddenly, as if he's just thought of this glitch.

"I already have one."

Brie peeks her head into the office. "The pool closes in two hours."

"I have to go," I tell Josh.

"Thank you, Callie."

After I disconnect the call, Brie asks, "Why are you smiling?"

"Do I have to use my birthday money for Hawaii or France?"

She eyes me curiously. "No."

"Because I'd like to go to Austria."

Her scream rocks the books on our walls. And probably scares away any customers left in the store.

CHAPTER 23

Divorce.

That's how his honorable father chose to deal with his wife's Jewish problem: by ending a marriage that had lasted more than twenty years.

Neither Max nor his mother told him about the necklace or that Herr Knopf knew her secret. The Gestapo were quite adept at uncovering information about the Jewish people on their own. Weeks after they returned to Vienna, the Gestapo discovered what his mother had paid Herr Knopf handsomely to ignore. The records of Klara Bettauer Dornbach's heritage were buried, but like the jewelry at his family's estate, they weren't buried very deep.

The relentless Gestapo exhumed her family's records with the precision of trained grave robbers and then issued her husband an ultimatum: either divorce his half-Jewish wife, or Wilhelm Dornbach would be considered a Jew as well. And eventually, they explained, he would lose everything, including his position at the bank.

But with a divorce, Wilhelm could keep his job, their home, and the many assets—including the Schloss—that his wife had brought into their marriage. All Jewish property, they explained, was being redistributed to Aryan owners, and his Aryan pedigree had been documented and certified.

Max wanted to think that his father proceeded with the divorce to protect his wife, but if he considered leaving Austria for her sake, Max never heard of it. Instead his father visited the French consulate, a loyal customer of his bank, and was able to expedite the process for his wife to visit her sister in Paris. She would leave tomorrow, using the baptismal certificate that the Gestapo hadn't confiscated to travel through Switzerland and then up through France. If she stayed any longer in Vienna, Max suspected the vision in the Gestapo's blind eye would clear.

His father had promised to cooperate in full with the new government. And someone at the headquarters said Max would be protected as the son of an Aryan.

Ever since they'd returned from the lake, his mother had refused to talk about anything of significance at home. The walls had grown ears, she said, and silence was all the Gestapo deserved.

So they slipped away this evening, she and Max eating Emmental cheese sandwiches and sipping ersatz coffee at a dingy café in the Judenstrasse, the only restaurant they could find that didn't have some sort of sign out front stating that Jews were no longer welcome in their establishment. Yet the rest of Austria seemed to be moving along as if nothing had happened, eating and shopping where they pleased as long as the restaurants and shops weren't owned by Jews. Several of those elite Vienna establishments had closed until further notice.

Max's own ancestors, he now knew, were Jewish, but it changed nothing about him. He believed that Jesus Christ was God's Son, attended Mass faithfully every Sunday, though he wondered why his bishop wasn't decrying the whole state of affairs. The church leaders, he prayed, wouldn't begin bowing to a new god.

His father had said the discrimination against Jews would only get worse; that was why his mother must leave. In Germany, they were shipping Jewish people off to internment camps.

Soon, Max feared, they would begin sending Austrian Jews away as well.

His mother's fingers pressed into the silver rim around her plate instead of her sandwich. "I wish you could come with me."

"They would never let me leave the country now." In December, he would be required to join the Wehrmacht.

They wouldn't let him go, but perhaps the guards would allow Luzi to leave with the certificates he'd finally obtained. She could go to France via train with his mother, and he could join them soon, traveling by foot over the mountains if he must. Both Luzi and his mother would be safe from whatever was to come.

She spooned sugar into her coffee and stirred. "I don't want to leave."

"But you must," Max said, leaning forward. "And perhaps you could take Luzi Weiss with you. She would be a good companion—"

"Does she have a visa?"

"I was able to . . . obtain paperwork for a visa." He paused. The details of his transaction must remain secret. "I have a marriage certificate for Luzi and me. And a new baptismal certificate for her."

"Oh, Max . . ."

"She doesn't know, nor has she agreed to marry me, but her father knows. He wants her to leave the country."

"She is a lucky girl, Max, for you to love her so much." Her words seemed to float like the cigarette smoke in this place, a sad reminder that her own husband hadn't been faithful to his promises.

"Father only wants you to leave because he loves you as well."

"Of course."

"When this is over, he will destroy the divorce certificate, and you'll remarry," he said, though his words lacked conviction. But hope, no matter how false, was necessary to take the next step. One foot in front of the other until his mother was so far along the path that the motivation to begin her journey was long forgotten.

"Please take Luzi with you," he begged.

"The French consulate only gave me a visa because of your father's urging. They won't make an exception for Luzia."

"Before you leave tomorrow, you can speak to them about your daughter-in-law."

"It's not that simple, Max."

He knew it wasn't simple. The Nazis, it seemed, thrived on both complication and confusion when it came to ridding their country of the Jewish people. They changed the rules at random, created new processes and then changed them again to confound anyone trying to leave.

"Have you talked with Luzia?" his mother asked.

"I'll speak with her tonight."

Max stole over to Luzi's apartment after darkness fell, dodging the bands of storm troopers that patrolled the streets by ducking behind trash bins and into familiar alleyways.

In the back of her apartment, the lamp glowed in the library, the window open. He listened for music, but none stole out into the night.

Cupping his hands around his mouth, his voice hushed, he called her name. If Dr. or Frau Weiss or their neighbor upstairs came to the window, he'd duck back into the shadows, blending again into the night.

But then he saw Luzi by the curtain, her hair cascading in curls over the shoulders of her white sweater, and his heart quickened.

"Max?" she whispered through the screen.

"I need to speak with you."

"I don't know—"

"Please, Luzi."

He heard the cry of a baby in the background. "I must bring Marta," she said. "I fear she has the croup."

"The night air will do her good, then."

He leaned against a tree, waiting. It had been too long since he'd spoken to Luzi, since the night of their dance, but she lived boldly, beautifully, inside his head, waltzing across the hardwood floor.

His breath caught when she stepped into the light of a streetlamp. She'd tied her hair back into a ponytail, making her look much younger than her seventeen years. And yet she'd aged in another sense. Perhaps it was her stooped shoulders, an invisible burden weighing her down.

Marta coughed, and Luzi patted her back, bouncing her gently as Max joined her in the light.

"Where's your father?" he asked.

"Out. I don't know where he goes."

He nodded toward Marta. "Will she let me hold her?"

"Perhaps."

Marta resisted at first, squirming in his arms, but she settled quickly against his chest as her cough subsided. Sometimes the simple things, like the breath of fresh air, were the best cure for an ailment.

Luzi collapsed onto a bench, her shoulders drooped forward as if the burden was too much to bear.

Max paced beside her. "You are exhausted."

"Marta cries often, and my mother . . ."

"Is your mother ill?"

"Ill with worry. She's taken to her bed."

He couldn't imagine the spirited Frau Weiss confined to her room.

"I fear she's lost all hope."

"Your father hasn't been able to get a visa?"

She shook her head. "Even if we're able, my mother could never make the journey."

Tears filled her eyes, shocking Max. In all the years he'd known Luzi, he realized that he'd never seen her cry.

"If you went now, your mother could come later."

She shook her head. "If we don't leave as a family, we're not leaving at all."

He glanced around at the trees as if someone might be listening, but he didn't see anyone. "My mother is traveling to France tomorrow."

"Why is she going away?"

He almost told Luzi the truth about his Jewish ancestry, but he didn't want to burden her further now. "She's visiting her sister."

"You should go with her, Max."

Those were words he didn't want to hear. Did she want him to leave Vienna without her?

"If we can obtain a visa, my mother would like you to join her."

"I can't—"

"Once you're there, you can send for your entire family. And I will come as soon as I'm able."

"The consulate won't give me a visa."

"We have to try."

"I can't leave Mutti or Father in this state. Or Marta."

"Your father asked me to get you out, Luzi. If we can't fight the Nazis, we must flee."

"I'm not going," she insisted.

"I will speak with him."

"Please, Max," she said. "I don't want to leave without my family."

And with those words, he felt trapped inside a box that kept shrinking. He'd thought Luzi would go if he secured the papers.

"Then we must find a way to get you and your family out together."

Marta stirred, reaching her arms out for Luzi. He handed the baby back as she began to cry.

Luzi nodded toward the upper windows on her building. "I have to feed her before our neighbor complains."

When Max leaned forward to kiss Luzi's cheek, Marta gripped his ear. Her cries stopped for a moment, distracted by her find. Luzi laughed, and Max smiled at the glimpse of joy a child could bring.

He took the folded paper out of his rucksack and handed it to Luzi. "Take this."

"What is it?"

"Your baptismal certificate in the Catholic Church."

She looked at the paper as if it were powdered with poison. She and her parents may not be practicing Jews, but they were grounded in the heritage of their ancestors' faith. "I can't take that."

"You might need it, Luzi. And your father wanted you to have it."

When Marta began to cry again, Luzi reached for the certificate.

"Good-bye, Max," she said before escaping back inside.

He didn't like how she'd said her good-bye, so final. As if she thought she might not see him again.

He stayed in place, underneath the light of the Weiss library. After it turned off, another light flicked on, farther down the apartment. Luzi's bedroom? She'd yet to draw the curtains, and it took every ounce of strength for him to turn away.

"I see you're enjoying the view here as well."

Max swiveled at the sound of the voice behind him. It was Ernst Schmid, except the man was wearing a brown shirt and red armband with a black swastika emblazoned on the white circle. He'd gained weight since Max had seen him last, feasting, perhaps, at the table of his commander.

"What are you doing here?" Max demanded.

"Same as you," Ernst said, nodding toward the lit window.

Max pounded his fist into his hand, wishing that he could knock the smirk off this man's face. "You'd best keep walking."

"And you'd best straighten up your priorities, Max." Ernst glanced at the window again before looking back at him. "I heard a rumor at headquarters . . . ," he started. "Something to do with your mother."

Max cringed.

"Heard she was a—" The word he said was so terrible, so vile, that Max didn't think; he flung out both hands and shoved Ernst back.

Ernst's hand dropped to his holster and he pulled out a black pistol, aiming it at Max's head. "Don't touch me again."

Max backed away, his hands up. If the Gestapo found out one of their cronies shot the son of Herr Dornbach, surely there'd be hell to pay. Then again, if they'd already begun to spread the rumors about his mother, maybe they'd spin his death as the son of a Jewess, another piece of trash the Nazis had heroically cleaned from their city. Or Ernst would say that Max attacked him first.

He wouldn't be much help to Luzi dead.

"Go home," Ernst said.

Max stepped into the trees, but he didn't go far. He waited until the light in the window was extinguished. And Ernst Schmid walked away.

⁂

Tears, they caked Luzi's cheeks like rosin on the hair of her bow. A violin wouldn't play without rosin; some people didn't know that. No music, not a single sound, came from the strings without the rosin to gently coax it out. A violinist, no matter how good, relied on this amber block made from pines.

She brushed the tears away as she hurried through the mist-laced streets. She couldn't play her music without rosin, and how—how was she going to live without her sister?

Marta stirred in her arms and then settled back against her chest. The lingering aroma of sausage and sautéed potatoes, sauerkraut and schnitzel crept out from alleyways between buildings that housed apartments and offices, but besides the smells of Vienna, she and Marta were alone.

She couldn't go to France as Max had asked of her, but she must get Marta to a safe place until she and her parents were able to follow.

A poster was tacked to a newspaper stand—the same poster she'd seen across Vienna in the past weeks. It was the photograph of an adorable baby boy and girl, faces one might see on a box of wheat flakes at the grocer's, except this piece of Hitler's propaganda was selling something much different. Underneath the faces of these sweet children were the words *Future Criminals*.

As if they'd already indicted Marta and the thousands of other *Kinder* in their city for the crime of being Jewish.

An SS officer stopped her near the Schönbrunn Palace, asking why she was out before dawn. She told him her sister was sick. They needed a doctor.

Marta coughed spectacularly in that moment, as if she were auditioning for a part at the Burgtheater. The officer stepped back, concerned, it seemed, for his own health.

The truth was, Luzi was the one who was sick. Her own breath had been stolen away.

The housekeeper at the Dornbach house answered her knock and invited her into the salon. Luzi asked for Frau Dornbach, hoping that both Max and his father were still asleep.

Marta, with her brown curls and rose-red cheeks and runny nose, fell asleep again in the pleasant warmth. Luzi kissed her forehead and began humming Beethoven's "7 Ländler," a song meant to accompany Austrians across the dance floor. The music, she prayed, would carry Marta wherever she went. And she prayed her sister would go far from here.

Even though it wasn't yet six, Klara Dornbach was fully dressed in a neat ivory and black traveling suit and matching gloves. When she was a child, Luzi had called her Tante Klara, but she stood beside Klara as an adult this morning. An equal. Klara may be Aryan and an aristocrat in this diverse city, but they had the common bond of music. And of Max.

Klara glanced back at the hallway before looking at Luzi again. "Why are you here?" she whispered.

Luzi stood carefully, holding Marta close to her chest so she wouldn't wake. "I need your help."

"I fear that you won't be able to get a visa to France."

"We haven't been able to get a visa anywhere, Klara."

The woman took off her gloves and pulled them through her hands as if she were wringing out excess water. "How is your mother?"

"Not well, I'm afraid."

Klara's gaze stole to the window, to the first rays that lightened the room. "So many are hurting."

"She can no longer care for Marta, and I—I don't know what is going to happen to our family."

"I wish there were something I could do."

Luzi hugged her sister closer to her chest, not wanting to let go and yet knowing that she must. "You once had a baby girl, long ago."

Surprise blazed through Klara's eyes, and her lips opened, but no words came out.

"I was young, but I remember her, Klara. She looked just like Max."

Klara reached for an armchair to steady herself. Perhaps Luzi was pressing too hard, but Klara must understand that while her daughter was gone, she could still rescue a child.

"I cried at her service and for months after," Luzi said, rubbing her hand softly across Marta's back. "Whenever I saw a pram on the street, I would mourn your loss."

"You should leave—"

"Please take Marta with you." Each word shot pain through her chest, but she couldn't turn back. "You will save her life."

"I can't—"

"Please, Klara. I fear what will happen to her."

"They won't hurt a baby," she said, but neither of them believed her words.

"It will be on our hands—both of our hands—if we do nothing."

Klara slid a cigarette out of a carton, her hands trembling as she tried to start the lighter. Finally she gave up and threw both the lighter and cigarette back on the table.

Luzi stepped toward her. "A long time ago, you said I was like a niece to you."

Klara's eyes filled with tears. "You have always been like a niece. Your mother like my sister."

"Then Marta is like your niece as well, except she can't fend for herself. We must fight for her."

Klara's gaze dropped to Marta, and Luzi saw the sadness in her eyes. "Your parents want her to leave?"

"My mother is too sick to care for her."

"But your father—"

"He will be pleased to know she is safe," Luzi said softly.

"The agents will never believe me."

"I have a baptismal certificate." Luzi dug into the satchel between diapers and money, a bottle of milk along with an engraved rattle from Luzi's childhood and a book with her name inside—weak evidence, perhaps, but she hoped they might help Klara in case anyone disputed Marta's new name.

She laid the baptismal certificate on the coffee table. The details that Max had forged were impeccable. Luzi only had to alter, very carefully, the date of January 1923 to January 1938. The guards, she prayed, would only scan it, their interest focused on the money in her bag instead of the baby.

Klara pointed at the top line of the paper. "Your name is on this."

"The guards won't know Luzia is not her birth name. You can tell them that she's your granddaughter."

"But Karl Weiss is not my son," Klara said, pointing to the father's name on the certificate.

"Luzia is the child of your daughter, not your son. Your daughter married a Weiss."

"The guards will never believe me—"

"With enough money, they'll believe almost anything."

Klara knitted her fingers together and rocked up on her toes. "What if they won't let me through?"

"Then you bring her back to me tomorrow and board the next train headed to Paris alone."

Klara walked to the window and fingered the curtains. "I will consider it."

"We don't have long to consider, Klara."

"Wait here," the older woman said.

Marta began to stir, and Luzi gently brushed her hand over her curls. "I will come for you," she whispered. "If only you will wait for me."

She did this because Marta needed food and milk and a safe place to rest at night. She did this because she loved her baby sister more than anyone else in the world.

She did this because Hitler and his men had given her no other choice.

CHAPTER 24

Ella clings to my hand as we board the jet. Or perhaps I'm clinging to her, ready to embark on my very first flight, an entire box of Dramamine stored in my carry-on and my cell phone upgraded to an international plan so I can call my sister or Charlotte whenever I'd like.

Charlotte kissed my cheek an hour ago, after she and Brie escorted me to the security line. "Courage, dear heart," she said, quoting Aslan, and I saw the pride in her eyes. In two weeks, they both promised to be back at the Columbus airport, waiting for me.

Ella and I loaded up on extra snacks, just in case, and after we find our seats on the plane, she gazes out the window, waiting for the other passengers to board. "Do you think we'll be able to see the ocean?"

"I'm certain of it, and I read something about seeing icebergs near Greenland too."

"I'm not going to sleep a wink," she says with all the confidence of a seven-year-old who knows exactly what she thinks.

"I hope you'll sleep some. If not, you'll be too tired to play with your dad when we land."

"I'm never too tired to play with him."

"I'm sure he's never too tired to play with you either."

She fidgets in her seat. "How long do we have to sit?"

"Awhile, but I brought something for us to read." I reach into my handbag as if it's a magician's hat and pull out three books. Ella picks *Bloom*, a story about an ordinary subject living in a kingdom of glass, a girl named Genevieve who must save everyone in her land.

As the airplane backs away from the gate, Ella reaches for my hand, and I gladly hold it, checking both of our seat belts before we begin rolling down the runway and then lift off into the air. As we climb higher, the city that confounds me seems so small, minuscule. We have a clear view of the entire place instead of trying to maneuver through all the confusion on the ground.

Once we're above the clouds, Ella removes her nose from the window, and I release her hand. Together we begin to read about Genevieve's quest in this fairy-tale world.

"They will never believe that an ordinary girl could do such an extraordinary thing," Genevieve worried. "What would I tell them?"

"Tell them there is no such thing as an ordinary girl," said Bloom.

"See, you can read without your socks," Ella says when we finish the story, as if I've accomplished a feat.

"I guess I can."

She gives a firm nod of affirmation and picks up another book, this one about a treasure hunt.

"If you could hide a treasure, where would you hide it?" I ask.

"Someplace no one would ever find it."

"A wise choice."

"Like in my shoes."

I glance down at the sparkly silver and teal shoes on her feet, Velcro strapping them together instead of laces. "Interesting . . ."

"My mom said that you can tell a lot about a girl by her shoes."

"I believe you must have had the smartest mom in the world."

"Smart and pretty," she says before glancing over at me. "Was your mom smart and pretty?"

"I don't remember much about her."

Ella reaches for my hand, and I hold it, both of us lost for a moment in our own thoughts. My mother seems pretty enough, I think, on Facebook. I decide that she must be smart, too. Extraordinary.

"None of us are ordinary girls," I say.

Ella and I read about the grand treasure hunt, a brain candy kind of book, and as she drifts off to sleep, I realize that I've forgotten to take my Dramamine. But after our layover in New York, I fall asleep just fine, waking again on Friday morning when the rays from a Parisian sun flood through the window.

Uniformed French agents check our bags and passports on the ground before I grab a pastry for Ella and a latte for me. Two hours later, Ella reaches for my hand one more time as our plane descends over Austria, this time landing in Salzburg.

The fortress of salt.

Josh beams when he sees his daughter. He swings her in his arms, and then he reaches out toward me.

My mouth drops open. "You're not going to try and swing me . . ."

He laughs. "I can if you'd like."

"No, thank you."

He takes my carry-on bag instead.

Ella chatters about our flight and the Sprite that I let her drink and all the books we read. When she races forward to collect her suitcase from the belt, Josh turns to me again, the intensity in his brown eyes tempered into a welcoming gaze.

"I'm glad you're here, Callie."

"Me too."

"Thank you for bringing her."

"She's a joy," I say, and he grins at my words.

As a taxi drives us to Salzburg Hauptbahnhof, I feel as if I've entered another world with the cathedrals and abbey and the faint strains of music that have lingered here for hundreds of years. My own fairy-tale kingdom.

While we wait for the next train to Hallstatt, my cell phone rings.

"It's an Idaho number," I tell Josh, taking a sip of my second latte.

"You'd better take it."

I walk toward a quieter space, away from the crowds, before I answer Liberty's call.

"I've spoken with my brother," she says. "Neither of us knew about this list."

An announcement blasts overhead in German, but Liberty doesn't acknowledge it.

"Did your father ever speak to him about Annika Knopf or the Stadlers?" I ask.

"In the years before my father's death, he spoke often to both of us about his memories in Austria, but my brother doesn't remember him mentioning anyone named Annika."

"What sort of things did your father tell you?"

"He liked to talk about the dances in Vienna and the animals he would rescue from the streets. And the castle, of course. He loved that place as a boy. I asked him several times about the conflict in Austria, but he only wanted to talk about his escape over the mountains and his work for the Allies until the end of the war."

I glance over at Josh and Ella, and they are huddled together, engaged in conversation. The familiar pang of jealousy rips through my heart. Once again, I'm alone.

I turn away. "Was your father named Max?"

She pauses. "How did you find his name?"

"There was a photograph in the book."

"Can you text it to me?" she asks.

Seconds later, I send it off. Her voice shakes when she speaks again. "He was a handsome young man, wasn't he?"

"Very."

"Do you know the name of the woman with him?"

"Luzia," I say slowly, hoping that she knows this name. "Luzia Weiss."

"I wish I knew who she was."

And the thought occurs to me—if Charlotte is Max and Luzia's daughter, Liberty would be her half sister.

"I'm trying to find out," I tell her. "Did Max return to Austria after the war?"

"Once, my mother said, before they married, but he never talked to my brother or me about it. On one hand, I think he was trying to protect his family from the horror, but I also think the memories were incredibly painful. My father wanted to help people and animals alike. What he must have seen during the war—I'm surprised it didn't kill him."

"I can't imagine."

"After he died, my mother told us a little more of his story. I think she wanted us to understand why he slipped away sometimes in his mind. *Fugue* is what she called those times, from the Latin word that means 'flee.'"

Like Charlotte when she slipped away.

"Everything changed for my dad when he was arrested." Liberty's voice sounds hollow, as if an echo from the depths of a tunnel. "During Kristallnacht."

"The night . . . ," I begin, but the words seem to lodge in my throat.

Liberty finishes it for me. "The night of broken glass."

CHAPTER 25

A whole lot more than glass shattered on the ninth of November, during Vienna's night hours. Men, a horde of them with axes and knives, broke down doors in the darkness. They smashed windows, started fires, arrested thousands of innocent Jewish men. A pogrom, they called it. As if naming the event justified the horrific things they did to the people across Austria.

When Hitler's men began pounding on the Weiss family's locked door, everyone except Dr. Weiss was asleep in their beds. The crack of steel, ripping through wood, woke Luzi from her fitful sleep, and she reached for Marta in the crib that still stood at the base of her bed. But Marta was gone, only a memory dimmed by the violent stomping of feet, the raucous laughter of men who'd reverted to the bullies of youth.

She lifted a tattered bear from Marta's crib and reached for a robe to cover her nightgown. Perhaps, if the men weren't inside the apartment, it wasn't too late. They could escape downstairs, hide in her father's office.

She found her father fully dressed in the music room, an old Austrian novel called *The City Without Jews* in his lap. As if he were waiting for the Nazis to come.

The men were in the kitchen now. She could hear them, crashing pots together, shattering her mother's china.

Their floors had trembled several days ago when the earth under Vienna quaked, as if nature itself had been warning them to flee, but they could do nothing. They couldn't leave then, nor could they leave now.

"Go back to your bedroom," her father said, his voice strangely calm. "And lock the door."

"A locked door won't stop them!"

Four men stomped into the music room, their eyes wild as they scanned the books on the shelves, the music on her stand. The teddy bear clutched in her arms, Luzi cowered in the corner as the men pulled out drawers, swiped the shelves clean of their contents. One of them opened her violin case and ripped out the prized instrument that her father had commissioned for her. Then he smashed it over his knee. With the crack of the violin's neck, her heart seemed to split in two.

When her father followed them into the hallway, begging them to stop this madness, Luzi reached for the phone, her entire body trembling so hard that it pounded against her ear. She phoned the police station, telling them they had intruders.

"Are you Aryan?" the dispatcher asked.

"No, but—" Something else crashed in the hallway, deafening her for a moment, and when she could hear the line again, she realized the dispatcher had hung up.

Smoke flowed through the window, and she wondered if the Nazis had set the entire city on fire. Screams echoed through the room, intruding from outside. Her family wasn't alone tonight, but there was no consolation in this brotherhood. No comfort in the communal wounding of bodies and souls.

The men stuffed their pockets full, stealing what little her family had left, but she didn't start screaming until they seized her father, tying his hands behind his back.

"He's a doctor," she cried after them. "An honorable man."

But these thugs didn't respect things like honor.

Luzi followed them downstairs, into the frigid air, pleading as they forced her father into an open-air truck with a host of other respectable men, some of them wearing nightcaps and dressing gowns, others in fancy suits as if they'd been pulled from a performance at the Vienna State Opera.

Her father glanced at her, his eyes sad. He forced a smile before they drove him away, and the pieces left of her heart splintered like her violin.

Turning, she raced back up the stairs, into her apartment. "Mother," she yelled.

The lock, the entire knob, from her parents' door was lying on the carpet. She flung back the wood door and switched on the light before scanning the room. The men had forced themselves inside, but they hadn't harmed her mother. At least, not her body. She was still in her bed, her vacant eyes focused on the dark window.

"We must do something," Luzi shouted, trying to rouse her.

When she finally spoke, Mutti's voice was as vacant as her eyes. "There is nothing we can do," she said before she fainted away.

Luzi collapsed on the mattress beside her mother. She—*they*—couldn't give up now.

Closing her eyes, Luzi forced the music of Strauss, the composition about the village swallows, to flood into the darkness and tears. The music, it was the only salve against the pain. Against the atrocity. Even without her violin, the melody anchored her. *Da capo.* Playing again and again.

Where had that truck taken her father?

More shouting outside now as acrid smoke bled into Mutti's bedroom, the sulfur burning Luzi's nose, coating her mouth. She closed the window, but it didn't block out the screams that shook the glass. Someone else was hurting in the darkness. Probably one of the tens of thousands in this city who dared to be Jews.

These men were like bloodhounds, never relenting from the hunt.

Luzi looked back at her mother. Her eyes were closed, her breathing shallow. And she felt torn between the two people she loved.

Perhaps she and her mother could go together; they could find her father at the police station. The men who'd arrested him, they had made a terrible mistake. Her father, she would make them understand, had done nothing wrong.

When her mother cried out, Luzi reached for her hand.

Her mother wouldn't be able to make it to the police station, and her father would be angry if she left alone. What if the men returned while she was gone?

She couldn't leave her mother to fend for herself.

Someone else cried out from another building. Or perhaps the park below their apartment.

God help them all.

Or had God left Vienna?

If He hadn't, it seemed as if He'd looked away.

"Run, Max," his father commanded, pushing his son toward the hallway when he saw the officers through the spyhole.

Max ran down the back staircase of their home in his nightclothes, but it was too late. The Gestapo was waiting for him outside.

His father joined them, swearing at the uniformed men, saying that Max was the son of a party leader, heir to the Dornbach fortune and estate. But the Gestapo had a list of men to arrest in Vienna, and Max was on it. There was no arguing with the list.

Two men waited as Max dressed and then dragged him to the police station as if he were a criminal. He knew the police captain, a friend of his father's. And the man apologized profusely as one of his officers searched Max, saying he had to do his job. A miserable job it was, Max replied, arresting innocent citizens in the middle of the night.

They drove Max away from the station in an army truck with a dozen other men, a guard and his gun watching over them. The streets were pandemonium. Windows broken, walls streaked bloodred with hateful slurs, a mob of pigeons squawking in the chaos. Smoke poured from the synagogue they passed, and two women chased after their truck, calling out names of men who weren't among them.

The Nazis took Max and their other prisoners to the elite Spanish Riding School, next to the Hofburg Palace. The men awaiting them inside shoved him into the crowded arena, beating a fellow passenger for inquiring about a *Toilette*.

Scanning the room, he found a familiar face. Luzi's father was kneeling on the clay floor, trying to care for an elderly rabbi who was clutching his chest, his face blackened with bruises. Max knelt beside Dr. Weiss, but they couldn't save the rabbi's life.

When the man slipped away, Dr. Weiss's head collapsed into his hands. "It's meaningless, all of this destruction."

God created man to care for the earth, Max believed, and care for each other. This evil was the work of the serpent in the garden, the enemy who wanted to kill instead of care. All these guards around them, they'd made a pact with a snake. Revenge was what they sought, but neither Max nor Dr. Weiss had tried to harm any of these men.

The guards lifted the rabbi and hauled him away.

Dr. Weiss focused on Max. "Why are you here?"

"The Gestapo discovered that my mother is Jewish."

"Does Luzia know?" Dr. Weiss asked.

He shook his head. Then he dared to ask the question that had haunted him all night. "How is Luzi?"

"She was unharmed when the agents took me away."

Max's voice broke when he spoke again. "She didn't want to leave your family behind."

"When they release us . . . I will convince her to go."

Max eyed the large doorway into the riding school, flanked by four guards. There'd be no running past them, no matter how much he wanted to rescue her.

Dr. Weiss lowered his head, leaning over as if he were going to tie his shoe. He spoke quietly instead. "They are asking about my patients' things."

Max glanced up at the guards again, rifles molded from wood and metal in their hands. "How do they know?"

"I pray none of my patients . . ." Dr. Weiss rubbed his hands over the clay. "I told the agents that I didn't take anything."

Max prayed the items would be safe at Schloss Schwansee, in Annika's care. That she would keep this secret from her father. If the Gestapo found out the truth about Max and Dr. Weiss, they would surely kill both of them and, heaven forbid, the Weiss family and even Annika.

If he'd thought the Nazis would suspect his hiding place, he never would have asked Annika to help him.

"Have you heard from your mother?" Dr. Weiss asked.

"Not yet."

"I think about Marta, every hour of the day."

"My mother will care well for her."

"And will you care for Luzi and Frau Weiss as well, if they don't release me?"

"They will release you."

"Please—"

"*Aufstehen,*" one of the guards shouted into a megaphone. All the men stood.

"I'll take care of them," Max promised.

The men stood for hours, all day and most of the night, their legs throbbing. Those who fell asleep were awakened by the butt of a gun. Others, like the rabbi, never awoke.

They'd grown into a crowd of hundreds now, standing in awkward lines under the chandelier light. Some of them were dressed in the nightclothes they'd been wearing when the Nazis arrested them. Others were dressed in suits or long cloaks or the black caftans of rabbis.

Guards stood between the white columns that encircled the arena and on top of the balcony as if they were spectators of a sport, as if their captives were the school's white Lipizzaner stallions on display. Except Austrians treated their horses with much more dignity than they afforded their Jewish compatriots.

The cruelty that Max saw in those hours would haunt him the rest of his life, but he never put into words what he saw there, never spoke of it to his wife or children. To put words to it would give respect to the men inflicting cruelty on all of them. And pour shame deep into his wounds.

When they finally rested, he sat beside Dr. Weiss, drinking cloudy water from a bucket passed around for the men to share. The doctor had tried to care for the men around them who'd collapsed from exhaustion or illness, but he had no medicine, no supplies of any kind. This inability to act was taking a deep toll on him.

On his fourth day in the arena, one of the guards called Max's name through a megaphone.

Max stood tentatively.

"Come with me." The guard yanked him away from the others.

He glanced back at Dr. Weiss, who nodded his way.

"Geh mit Gott," he mouthed.

And so Max went with the blessing, relieved in one sense to flee from this horrific place even as he feared leaving Dr. Weiss behind.

Later he learned that Dr. Weiss and many of the others were taken away hours later.

But instead of going home, they were shipped off to a place called Dachau.

CHAPTER 26

Glacier water laps against the sides of the ferryboat as Josh, Ella, and I cross between the train station and the glowing lights of Hallstatt village. Ella's already asleep, resting against her dad's shoulder, the masked rays of sunlight settling orange and pink over the snow-dusted mountains and clear lake.

Between the caffeine and mountain air, I'm wide awake, mesmerized by the gold that sparks like fireflies on the lake's surface. Then I see it, on my left. Schloss Schwansee stands like a worn sentry on the bank, its rear guard a fortified rock wall that sweeps up like a wave about to tumble over the house, into the lake.

A spruce forest spreads out on both sides of the castle. The train station is on the west, and to the east, hidden behind a jetty of pines, is the town called Obertraun. The lake, Josh said, is five miles in length, plunging down into four hundred feet of hiding spaces—log piles, shifting sands, and a vat of mud.

He and his team already scanned the water in front of the castle with a remote-operated vehicle before they dove about fifty feet to hunt in the underwater ledges, but they never found any evidence of the rumored treasure.

His students have scattered now, off to explore Europe on their own. I've told him that I'll be doing some personal research in Vienna while I'm here. Until Jonas Stadler returns his calls, Josh is planning to take Ella to explore the ice caves and snorkel in the water near shore.

When I glance at Josh again, he's watching me. I turn back to the castle.

"It's been standing there since the 1600s," he says.

"Just think of the stories it could tell." Like the book that once resided there.

"A salt administrator built the house. An eccentric man by the name of Christoph Eyssl von Eysselsberg."

"How do you know this Christoph Eyssl was eccentric?" I ask.

Ella squirms, and Josh gently rubs her back until she's resting again. "The man also built a mausoleum for himself in Hallstatt's Catholic church. Then he mandated that his casket be transported back to the castle every fifty years."

"Like he's returning home?"

"Exactly."

I rub my arms. "That is creepy!"

"The curator at the local museum said the last time his casket traveled across the lake was before the war. The spring of 1939."

"War changes everything, I suppose."

The castle seems to fold into the trees as we near the center of the lake. How many Austrian boys were schooled under Hitler's regime at this place? And had the Nazis stored jewelry and other valuables here before they dumped them into the lake? Even with the help of sonar, the treasure could be lost in these deep waters and silt forever if someone like Annika or her descendants can't point out where the fleeing Nazis threw it.

If Annika told Leo about the treasure, surely she would have told her children where the Nazis tried to hide it.

My mind wanders to Annika and Max. According to his daughter, Max left Austria before the Americans entered the arena of World War II. Did he know about the treasure? Perhaps that's why he took Annika's book to Idaho with him.

But if he knew about the treasure, why didn't he tell his children?

"I found the deed of transfer from the Dornbach family to Hermann Stadler in 1955. It was transferred to Sigmund Stadler in 1962 and then to Jonas Stadler in 1992," Josh says. "I haven't found anything else about Annika."

"Maybe there's a death certificate for her in Salzburg."

"Maybe," he says. "I found her mother's grave in the Hallstatt cemetery but not one for any other member of the Knopf family."

The ferry nears Hallstatt, and the buildings seem to cling to the mountain behind them. The first road to this village, I read online, wasn't built until 1890. For centuries, the access between many of the houses was by boat or what locals called the upper path, a small corridor that passed through the attics. Now I understand—the ancient buildings are so close to the water's edge, they look like they are about to tumble into the lake.

When the boat docks, Josh reaches for the suitcases, and Ella snuggles close to me as I carry her across the cobblestone plaza to the peach-and-white guesthouse along the waterfront, a three-story inn planted right here for half a millennium.

The staircase inside winds three times before stopping at the top floor, and Josh opens two doors across the landing from each other, setting my suitcase inside the room on the left.

I slip into his and Ella's room, carefully lowering Ella onto one of the twin beds. She wakes with a start, searching until she finds her dad behind me.

She smiles before closing her eyes again, and he takes her hand, prays a blessing over her, and I'm stunned at the sight of this strong man who would humble himself to pray for his child. When he finishes, he kisses his daughter's forehead.

The two of us step out onto the narrow balcony that stretches across to my room on the other side, about twenty feet above the lake.

"Are you tired?" he asks.

"More like wired."

He points toward a small round table in the center of the balcony, the tabletop a colorful mosaic made from pieces of broken tile. "You want to stay up for a bit?" I hear the trepidation in his voice, as if he's asking me out on a dinner date.

I glance toward the dim lightbulb flickering over my sliding-glass door. Part of me longs to nest inside, but a bigger part of me wants to stay right here with him.

"For a bit," I say.

"I'll be right back," he says before turning toward his room.

I lean against the wrought-iron railing and look down at the lights of town reflecting back as if the lake were a mirror. Across the water is Schloss Schwansee, but I can't see it anymore. Darkness, it seems, has curtained it for the night.

Four hundred years of stories in that place, many of them lost in the unyielding hourglass of time. But somehow, I think, Josh and I will unearth the story of what happened there during the war.

CHAPTER 27

A dozen men converged on Schloss Schwansee with blazing torches, like a band of pirates from years past in their boats. Their savage cries ricocheted off the stone crevices in the mountain behind the house and roared across the water.

Annika hid her shovel behind the cottage and raced into the trees, watching the men in the faint starlight from her fortress of pine needles and bark. They looked like a black cloud of bats, wings pulsing madly, red eyes piercing the night.

Had they come for the silver and jewelry and candlesticks buried in the land behind her home?

She shivered in the night air, afraid of what these men would do if they discovered what she'd buried. And she prayed that God would be with her in the darkness, not locked away behind chapel walls.

Frederica crawled up beside her, and she lifted the cat, clutching her close.

Were these men drunk or only intoxicated by what they had planned?

She was glad the Dornbach family was safe in Vienna tonight. From her hiding place, she prayed that the things she'd hidden, dozens of items now, would stay safe in the ground.

Glass shattered, a window on the stalwart castle victim to a rock or brick.

Why must they break the glass when they could simply walk through the front door?

For a moment, she thought about running all the way to Obertraun, finding her father, but then she saw Vati in the crowd, carrying a torch like the rest of the men. And she trembled again.

More glass breaking—the castle, the barn, her cottage, the sound rippling through the trees, shattering her heart. Then she smelled kerosene, saw the flames. Their little cottage captured by the fire.

She had to stop these men before the castle was consumed as well.

Frederica leapt out of her arms when she started to run across the yard.

"Vati," she hollered, racing up to him.

Her father turned to her, a crazed look in his eyes and then hatred. The same look that he'd given her the night her mother died, bitter and cold, as if Annika had taken her life.

One of the men opened the front door to Schloss Schwansee and rushed inside.

"What are you doing?" she shouted above the roar.

"Serving justice."

"But what . . ." she started. "What did the Dornbachs do?"

"Klara Dornbach is a Jew."

He said the word as if she were a criminal. As if Frau Dornbach had committed a terrible crime.

And then Annika understood. The necklace wasn't a gift for Frau Dornbach or something she'd purchased, like her shoes from Paris. Like Sarah's, this necklace was a symbol of her heritage. Vati had been forced to work for someone he thought less than him. Someone he believed should be serving him instead.

Her heart wrenched, the pain of it threading down her limbs. She, in her nosiness, had convicted the entire Dornbach family.

Through the castle window she saw the flash of flames in the salon, smoke pouring through the portal of broken glass, extinguishing the starlight. If they didn't douse this now, the fire would devour the castle. Perhaps every building on the estate.

She yanked on her father's coat. "We have to stop this!"

They had a lake full of water behind them and a fire hose. They could pump out every drop of the lake if they must to stop these flames.

But instead of racing for the hose, her father ran toward the front door.

An upstairs window shattered, raining down glass from the castle, and the mob of men poured back into the courtyard. One, two, three—she counted only eleven now. Her father wasn't among them.

The men rushed back to their boats and disappeared into the darkness, leaving the fire to spread behind them.

"Vati!" Annika yelled, running toward the castle. She had to get him out before the flaming walls, the roof collapsed on him.

But the heat—it lashed at her skin when she stepped through the front door. And she couldn't see through the smoke.

Surely her father would retreat out one of the back doors. Or she could enter through the chapel.

Across the courtyard, her cottage buckled under the weight of flames, shuddered to the ground, but the storage shed near it remained intact. The doors behind the castle were locked, so she retrieved the hose in the storage shed and began dragging it toward the main house.

Through the smoke, she saw someone else rushing up the bank. Had more men arrived to finish the destruction?

But then she heard the man call her name.

"Hook it up," Hermann commanded, pointing toward a tap.

Her hands trembling, Annika screwed in the brass connector, and cold water poured out of the nozzle as they dragged the hose to the front of the house.

"Vati!" she screamed again as the flames blazed inside the window.

But he never answered her cries.

CHAPTER 28

"I thought it might help you sleep," Josh says, lifting a bottle of Riesling.

I step back from the railing and sit on one of the two wrought-iron chairs. "I'd love a glass."

He sets a paper bag on the small table between us and fills the two wineglasses that he brought out of his room. "Apparently they grow these grapes at a vineyard nearby."

I sip the sweet drink. "Is Ella asleep?"

"Like someone conked her over the head."

"I swear I didn't do it."

He laughs. "I know. She said that you read to her until she fell asleep on the plane."

I lift my feet, showing off my black sandals. "She was quite proud of me for being able to read without my Story Girl socks."

"You're a marvel."

"Or my cape."

"A true achievement," he quips. "But I'm not joking about your being a marvel. Thank you for bringing Ella and for taking great care of her along the way."

"It was a selfish move on my part." I roll the stem of the glass between my fingers. "I was worried about coming on my own."

"I'm glad you came," he says. "And not just because you brought Ella."

Heat flushes up my neck, and I turn back toward the lake, glad for the dim lights. "Thank you."

He nods toward the castle across the lake. "We can rent a boat tomorrow so you can see it up close."

"I'm going to spend most of the day in Vienna." I have a list of churches and synagogues on my iPad, and I'll visit as many as I can to inquire about Luzia's birth or baptismal certificate.

"Are you spending the night there?" he asks.

"No. There's a train coming back late tomorrow."

"Perhaps I can take you to the station in the morning after I show you the castle."

"I'd like that." My face flushes again, and I wish someone would challenge me to dunk my head in a bucket of ice right here. "If only we could go onto the estate . . ."

"There's a big sign on the dock threatening prosecution for anyone caught trespassing."

"You let a sign stop you?"

"My team was diving here with special permits from the Austrian government. If I was caught trespassing, it would jeopardize everything we've worked for."

"And now?" I press.

"We could knock on the front door together and see if anyone is home."

I can't imagine stepping onto someone's property without an invitation, but if it brings me closer to Luzia . . . "How long have you been trying to find Annika?"

"I started more than ten years ago, but then—" he rips open the paper bag and serves soft white cheese and rye crackers on it like it's a platter—"I had to take a break."

Because of his wife, I assume, but it's not my business to ask. Our friendship is safe as long as we keep it focused on what we're both searching for, not what's happened to either of us in the past.

"When I was in graduate school, I found records confirming what Uncle Leo had said about the Nazis dumping ownerless treasure in these lakes. I also discovered a memo from a Nazi official who had been searching Schloss Schwansee for items formerly owned by the Jewish people in this area.

"If the Nazis ever found these items, no one recorded it—not that they would have. Treasure seemed to stick to Nazi fingers, especially those of officers who were supposed to hand over everything they stole to the Reich. Even American soldiers sent some of the valuable things they found home, calling them the spoils of war."

"Were the Nazis searching the estate or the water in front of it?"

He gives me a curious look. "The memo says the property, but what has been found in this area was located in the caves or lake."

"I wish you could search inside Schloss Schwansee."

He glances down at his phone. "Herr Stadler still hasn't responded to any of my inquiries."

I take another sip of the wine and wonder about the Stadlers. Did Hermann take over the house from the Dornbachs because he was a Nazi? Or because he married Annika?

Josh leans back in his chair, dangling his flip-flops over the edge of the railing. "What else did Liberty say?"

My gaze travels back to a light flickering across the water. A window from the castle or perhaps a boat. "Max Dornbach loved this house and lake when he was a child, but he never told her what happened here during or after the war. Perhaps it was too painful to remember."

He slices through the cheese with the edge of his cracker and eats it. "The pain I understand."

I decide to step out on a limb, hoping it won't crack under me. "Lottie told me that you lost your wife," I say softly. "It must have been devastating."

"Four years have passed, and I still miss her." He leans back against his chair, his gaze forward as if he can see inside the castle walls. "When your heart is yanked out, it's hard to cram it back into your chest again."

I nod slowly. After Scott's deception, I wasn't sure if my heart would ever be whole again. "What was Grace like?"

He thinks for a moment. "Charming and smart and confident in just about everything except when it came to saying good-bye. She was a fighter like Ella, but the cancer, it devoured her from the inside out." He glances over at me, his eyes sad. "I've never told Ella about her mom's excruciating pain. I want her to remember the laughter and love that Grace poured over her instead of the pain."

I lower my wineglass to the table. "Sometimes I wonder where God is in the midst of such heartache."

"I think God's in the center of it all."

My eyes grow wide. "That sounds so cruel."

"I don't mean it to be cruel. It's just . . . I spent years wrestling through the question of why God would allow harm to come to His children, like Jacob in the Bible wrestled with God, I suppose."

The weight of his memories seems to bear down on him, his gaze refocusing on the lake. "In the midst of Grace's suffering, I saw glimpses of hope. She believed that a renewed and restored body awaited her on the other side of death's veil. Sickness might have taken her from this earth, but I believe her soul is resting now, hidden away with a compassionate God. He doesn't run from pain like humans often do. He's not afraid of it because He knows what's beyond the grave. No more suffering for those who cling to Him."

My eyes focus on the lights below us. "But so much suffering right now."

"I believe God refines us over the fire at times, purifying us like gold, but if the account of Creation is true, then God's original plan for all His children was beauty and peace and daily walks with Him—not cancer or gas chambers or kids being shot when they attend school. This purity, I think, often stings deep inside, but what freedom to know that God never forces anyone to love or serve Him. Even if it breaks His heart, He allows people to walk away."

Josh takes a sip of wine. That book by L. M. Montgomery changed my perspective on God and His love for me, but it's one thing to refine someone and another to . . .

I mold my thoughts into words. "I don't know if I'll ever understand how God can allow so much devastation in this world."

"I don't know if I'll ever fully understand the complexities of the spiritual realm either, at least in this life, but I think the Bible gives us plenty of clues about the freedom that humans have to choose good or evil. Many choose darkness over the light, though I can't imagine how anyone who holds a baby or watches a sunrise or sips something as simple as this Austrian wine can deny the Creator of all things good."

I shift in the hard seat. "Some people think that God caused the Holocaust—"

"Hitler and a whole host of men caused the Holocaust. I don't believe that was ever God's will." He taps on the edge of his wineglass. "So often God is blamed when things go wrong, but people don't usually give Him credit when things go right. Jesus said that a time is coming when the prince of this world will be driven out.

"Life is hard, but He promises victory in the end. And if we believe what the Bible says, we have to focus on what we know to be true—that God loved this world and that His son was moved with compassion by the suffering here."

My heart seems to somersault. "Like with Grace . . ."

He nods slowly, studying me. "I don't believe it was God's will for her to die, but I do think He used her life and, I pray, her death for good."

"Because He is good."

"To the core."

I glance over at the shadowed mountains to the west. "Liberty's mother said that Max spent a year roaming these Alps, fighting against the evil here. When the war started, he was able to make it over the border to Switzerland. Eventually he joined up with the Allied forces and fought alongside them."

"Everyone has a choice," Josh says. "Be strong enough to do what is right or be consumed by evil."

And I wonder what I would do if given the choice. I pray that I would choose what is good.

When Josh lifts his wineglass, I reach for mine. He toasts to the hope of tomorrow. A place where possibilities abound. A place where one day evil will be destroyed for good.

*The L*ORD *is my light and my*
salvation; whom shall I fear?
*the L*ORD *is the strength of my*
life; of whom shall I be afraid?

PSALM 27:1
(OLD TESTAMENT)

CHAPTER 29

Ernst entered Luzi's apartment more than a week after they'd taken her father away, kicking down the broken front door, cornering her in the parlor.

The Nazis had stolen anything she could use to defend herself, and her Aryan friends had grown deaf to her pleas. The Jewish neighbors who remained were hidden in the fragile threads of their walls, powerless to help.

She wished for a cocoon to protect her tonight. Wished she could sprout wings and fly.

When Ernst forced himself on her, the world blackened, sending her to a place far from the shattered pieces of her home.

Color emerged again in her mind, bright and steady. She and Marta were together, playing in Max's swan lake, laughing as they rolled in the meadows of wildflowers. The songbirds sang a beautiful melody, calling her and her sister far away from the lowlands of Austria, to a place high in the Alps where no man ever went.

They flew with the birds, Marta's hand secured in hers. Instead of cigarette smoke, she could smell the blossoming jasmine in the breeze.

A sound ripped through the mountains, seared through her mind as the birds fluttered away. It was Ernst, zipping up his breeches. And her body felt as shattered as the glass around her feet.

"Max can have you now," Ernst said. He towered over her with his knife, disgusted. As if she had driven him to do this.

Oh, Max. He could never find out what happened.

"Luzi?" Ernst sneered.

When she didn't respond, he threw his dagger onto the couch and grabbed her by the throat, his fingers strangling her. She opened her mouth, trying to speak, but nothing came out.

Pain raked through her body again, everything within her collapsing.

And the music, even in her head, was gone.

❧

Max rushed through the apartment's open door, but the moment he saw Ernst clutching Luzi's neck, he feared it was too late.

The sitting room was a wreck—legs of her family's chairs hacked off, the sofa's upholstery sliced, elegant drapes torn down. And Luzi's face was the color of the cement floor in the basement of the Hotel Metropole, his residence for the past week.

"Let her go," Max shouted.

Ernst released Luzi, and relief flooded through Max when she gasped for air. Thank God, Ernst hadn't killed her . . . but what had he done to Luzi while Max was gone?

His mind reeled with possibilities, blurring his vision, and he struggled to regain focus. For almost two weeks he'd been imprisoned—first at the arena and then at the hotel. The lack of food and sleep had depleted every ounce of strength, but right now he had to concentrate the little energy the Gestapo had left him on freeing Luzi.

On the sofa was a dagger, and Ernst reached for it, his face flushed red. "Go home, Max."

"I won't leave," he said, though without a weapon, he couldn't fight this man.

Ernst held the knife in front of him, steady. "I told you that you'd have to choose."

Max could see the etching on the silver blade. *Alles für Deutschland.*

Everything for Germany. Everything for might.

"I choose what is right," Max said.

"Right or wrong, it's irrelevant."

"Not in my eyes."

Luzi didn't speak, as if Ernst had siphoned out the spirit, the music, that once breathed life inside her.

"Come with me now, Max, and I'll leave her alone." The words slid off the man's tongue, like the serpent in the garden.

Max eyed Ernst's holster on the sofa, next to where his dagger once sat, but it would be impossible to wrestle Ernst for it in his weakened state. Broken.

There must be another option.

The agent at the Hotel Metropole made him swear never to tell anyone what happened during his time in the Nazis' care or they would arrest the people he loved. Starting, Max feared, with Luzi.

He'd have to leave with Ernst, to protect Luzi's life, but Ernst would have to take him to Dachau. No matter what they did to him, Max could never join the Wehrmacht.

He prayed that while they were gone, Luzi and her mother would run away.

Ernst waved his knife toward the front door, motioning Max to the stairs outside.

Max took a step back, but his eyes were still on Luzi. And he watched as she reached for Ernst's holster, slipped out the gun. Ernst never saw her pull the trigger. When the gun blasted, his knife clattered to the floor, and Ernst collapsed beside it, hitting his head on an end table as he fell.

Stunned, Max stared at the man for a moment, at the blood that puddled around his arm.

Luzi lowered the gun, but clutched it in both of her hands. "They killed my father."

"I saw him just a week ago. . . ."

"There was an accident, the postcard said. Regrettably. They arrested him and then said they regretted his heart failing." She turned to Max, her eyes cold. "He's never had trouble with his heart."

"I know."

"They killed an innocent man. A doctor who lived to help others."

His skin seared hot, boiling blood beneath the surface. "They hate anyone who dares to help a fellow Jew."

He stepped over Ernst and took the gun from her hands, sliding it back into the holster.

"Where did you see him last?" she begged.

But he couldn't bear to tell her what the Gestapo had done to her father and the other men in the arena, stealing their dignity before they took their lives. Sometimes, he supposed, the best way to protect someone you loved was to protect her from the truth.

"He was helping others when I saw him, and he—he wanted me to tell you that you must be strong as well, for Marta's and your mother's sake." Max glanced down the hallway. "Where is your mother?"

"Resting." Luzi didn't move toward the hall, her gaze on the blackened fireplace before her now, a shell of the woman who'd once loved nothing more than to bring life to an instrument, grace the world with its beauty. Tonight Ernst had harmed her, and she needed her mother's help to heal.

After she heard the gun blast . . . Frau Weiss must have been mad with worry. "Shall I see to her?"

Luzi shook her head. "There's nothing left to see."

"I don't understand."

"My mother is no longer with us."

A sword seemed to pierce Max again, stabbing his heart and soul. "They killed her as well."

"I suppose they did."

"I don't understand, Luzi."

"Vati's tablets were supposed to help her. . . ." She looked at him, and he saw the glint in her eyes. "But it wasn't the medicine, not really. The Nazis stole away her hope, and without hope, how can one really live?"

"Luzi, I'm—" He stopped. What was he? *Sorry* seemed much too tidy, much too shallow a sentiment to communicate the sorrow that burrowed into his soul.

"I tried to revive her, but her grief . . . I think it was too much."

So much loss, and for what gain? "I'll call for an undertaker."

"The superintendent already hired someone to take her away."

Max stepped toward the broken window, cold air pouring in from the autumn winds.

"Ernst came with a warning," she said. "If I don't leave the apartment tonight, the SS will escort me out. Someone else is supposed to occupy these rooms in the morning."

He swore.

"They can have the apartment, but I—" Her voice faltered as she fell into the chair. "I don't know where I'll go."

"You'll come with me," he said. "Right now."

When she didn't say anything, he lowered himself beside her, his knees centimeters above the glass. "Please, Luzi."

"I don't think I can walk." Her eyes fell to her light-brown skirt, and that's when he saw the blood, soaking through her clothes. She flinched when he lifted the hem but didn't stop him. A gash cut from her ankle up to her knee. She needed stitches, but no hospital in Austria would take her now.

Ernst was unconscious beside them, but Max still heard his breath.

He should take the knife, the gun. Finish what Luzi started.

But no matter how much he hated the man, he couldn't kill another human being. Instead he tied Ernst's hands behind him with a cord from the drapes lest he wake and try to hurt Luzi again.

"I'll return," he told her.

He hurried down the back steps, into the private entrance of her father's office. The storm troopers had thrown dozens of the medicine bottles on the floor, a sea of glass, but they hadn't destroyed everything. He packed one of Dr. Weiss's bags with a needle and suture thread, antibacterial medication and painkillers.

If only he'd come straight here after they'd released him from the hotel instead of going home. But his skin and clothing had smelled like the stench in the riding school and basement, and he was hungry, cold. What he'd longed for most beyond a bed and food these past two weeks was a hot shower and clean clothes.

He had stood in the shower until the water ran cold, trying to soothe muscles that ached, wash the memories down the drain. He'd intended to go to Luzi's immediately, but the weakness of his body overpowered the call of his heart, and he had lain down on the sofa, not waking again for another day.

And now he hated himself for it.

He had no animals to carry with him tonight, but he'd taken the cage from his house and hidden hundreds of Reichsmarks in the compartment underneath and then stuffed his papers and some warm clothing into a rucksack. His father wasn't at the house—if he had petitioned for Max's release, no one told Max. He'd put another hundred in his wallet before he took the Mercedes, hoping the money and car would suffice as a ticket out of this town.

Headlights gleamed through the window, and Max ducked back toward the stairwell. The SS were here, but neither he nor Luzi would be going with them tonight.

He ran back up the stairs. "We have to leave," he told her.

Car doors slammed outside, and seconds later, he heard the stomping of boots on the main staircase, below the smashed front door.

How many men had they sent to arrest one broken woman?

Luzi tried to stand but wobbled on her feet, not able to put any weight on her right leg. "You must go without me," she insisted.

He'd lost weight in the past two weeks, his strength waning, but adrenaline pumped through his veins like water in a hose, a surge to stop the fire. He scooped Luzi off the chair, carrying her down to her father's office. She trembled in his arms, and he was thankful for her fear in one sense. It meant that she still had life in her. That she could fight.

A man shouted for him to halt as they ran out into the small park, toward his mother's prized Mercedes on the other side of the trees. But he wouldn't halt for anyone.

After lowering Luzi into the passenger's seat, he drove away, praying no one would stop him until they reached the edge of town. And that Luzi would be safe at the estate until they could find a way out of Austria.

Herr Knopf's face flitted into his mind, and he pushed it right back out. The man knew about his family's heritage, but he couldn't think about that now. Annika, he prayed, would help.

Several cars lined up on Hauptstrasse, guards checking vehicles and papers before the drivers and their passengers left Vienna. Luzi had hesitated when he gave her the pain medicine, but he promised her that the powder would help, not harm her as it had done with her mother. He wanted to relieve some of her pain, but even more, he feared it would make her grimace at the guards when they both needed to smile.

The pain went much deeper than her skin—no medicine could relieve the sorrow underneath—but right now, to save her life, they both needed to pretend.

As they crept forward, Max reached over and took her hand. The last time he'd held it was the night of their dance.

Oh, to be able to go back and watch her play her violin and

waltz with her across the floor, inspired by the hope of the future, not the fear.

"Please smile, Luzi," he begged as a young border guard stepped toward his window, and she forced her mouth to move, though it wasn't exactly a smile.

"I remember you," the man said. "You're the fellow with the canary."

Max smiled in return. "No animals with me tonight, but I'd like to introduce you to my lovely wife."

Luzi lifted her hand, waving.

"It's a late hour for you to be driving."

"We're only able to get away for a few days before I join the Wehrmacht. We're honeymooning at my family's estate—"

"You have all your papers in order?"

"I believe so."

He dug into his rucksack and handed the man his baptismal certificate and the forged paper saying that he and Luzi were husband and wife. As the man studied them, Max glanced in his rearview mirror. No sign yet of anyone following them.

"This says you married in August."

Max nodded. "And we are quite anxious now to depart."

"Where is your wife's baptismal certificate?"

Max opened his rucksack again. "Surely I packed it. . . ."

When he looked back up, the guard's eyes had narrowed.

Instead of showing him the certificate, Max slipped the marks out of his wallet and slid them across the door. "I only want to honeymoon with my wife before I leave. . . ."

The guard eyed the money for a moment before taking it. Then he returned the papers. "Enjoy the estate."

Luzi leaned back against the seat as they drove out of Vienna, cruising through mountains and valleys. And anger raged inside Max.

He'd been faithfully hiding things for his Jewish friends, thinking they would recover them later, but what value did these items have when lives were being stolen? Luzi had lost both her parents this week, and he feared she was fading away as well.

An hour later, Luzi tugged at his shoulder, and he stopped the car, waiting as she vomited in the weeds.

"My stomach must not like the medication," she said, though he suspected her body was erupting from the fear that crested inside her.

"We'll be there soon," he promised.

Hitler had ruined his plans for him and Luzi, but for now, at least she was safe with him.

CHAPTER 30

Annika hadn't been through the doors of Hallstatt's *Evangelische Pfarrkirche* since her mother died, but she crept into the gray stone church early this morning, her heart aching. The bells rang in the tower above her, resonating down to the floor and streaming through her veins like the brine that flowed through the pipeline above town to the salt factory below.

Every Sunday when Annika was a child, her mother had brought her over to this simple sanctuary settled along the lake. Her mother would sit with her Bible in her lap, and they'd worship together with the small congregation on wooden pews.

As a girl, she had felt peace inside these walls, like she felt in the woods. So different from the cold, stark chapel beside Schloss Schwansee. She could see, through the clear windows, the castle across the water, a place that looked tranquil from afar. But today, even though the flames were long gone, the ashes that had rained down over the forest were piled into blackened mounds. And a tendril of smoke still curled up through the trees.

She touched the gold and diamond star that hung around her neck, concealed under her sweater. Few things had survived the fire in her cottage, but Frau Dornbach's necklace along with Annika's metal box defied the flames. She would wear this star until she could return it to either Max or his mother.

The cottage was destroyed, but she and Hermann had been able to stop the fire in the castle before it traveled outside the salon. Hermann had gotten her father out as well, but it was too late to save his life. The fire had consumed Vati inside and out.

Whenever she tried to close her eyes, flames licked at the corners of her mind, the rawness of her father's screams echoing in her memory. Vati hadn't been good to her, especially in recent years, but he was still her father. She couldn't say she missed him, but she missed what had once been. A family who had cared for one another. A job for her father on a beautiful estate. Friendships she had thought would last a lifetime.

Hermann had broken his arm trying to help Vati, but still he helped bury her father in the woods, in a plot marked only by a cross. The memory of her home lingered with the smell of the charred stone and wood. She'd never tell anyone, but she silently mourned the loss of her cottage more than her father.

Knotting her fingers together, Annika bowed her head to pray. Her eyes remained open so the flames wouldn't lick the darkness.

How she had missed coming to this church each Sunday. The

rhythm of the songs and the Bible reading and the curate who spoke with confidence about a God who loved people so much that He was willing to die for them.

She buried her head between her arms, draped over the bench in front of her. Hatred had driven her father to his death, and she feared that the hatred in her heart might kill all the good left inside her.

"Hello, Fräulein."

Annika glanced up into the kind eyes of Pastor Dietz. He wore a long white robe, starkly clean compared to the state of her heart, and his balding head gleamed in the light of the wooden chandelier that hung as a crown of sorts over the sanctuary. He'd come to the cottage multiple times since her mother passed, but Vati never let him stay long and certainly didn't allow Annika to return to church.

"I was going to visit you this evening," he said. "It's a tragedy. . . ."

She nodded slowly, not able to tell him that her own father was responsible for the fire. She couldn't tell him, or anyone, what Vati had done. Those who still believed in Austria would run her out of town.

"Do you have a place to stay?" he asked.

She nodded. Until the Dornbachs returned, she planned to borrow the rooms in their home that the fire hadn't destroyed.

The pastor glanced up at the wooden cross at the front of the sanctuary, the windows overlooking Lake Hallstatt on each side. "It is wise of you to seek solace."

"It's desperation that drives me, Herr Pastor."

"The Scriptures will be of comfort to you."

"I'd been reading Mother's Bible, before I lost it in the fire, but I found no peace in it," she said. "Only violence."

"Ahh," he said. "The Old Testament books reflect God's justice when people chose to follow evil, but He overcame the violence and evil in our world when Jesus rose from the grave."

"So many people were killed back then and today—"

"Don't you see," the man said gently. "Death is no longer a threat to those who believe in Him. The ultimate weapon of our enemy has been stolen away."

His words washed over her like salt water, stinging at first before they began to heal. Death had always terrified her, but if God had overcome death, perhaps she didn't have to be afraid.

"Jesus sacrificed Himself like a lamb to atone for all of our sins. His death conquered the fear of it for all who put their faith in Him."

"I believe, Herr Pastor, but so many people are hurting. . . ."

"The Scriptures say, 'Greater love hath no man than this, that a man lay down his life for his friends.'" The pastor glanced out the window at the *fuhr* boat rowing by the church, its long nose curled up like an elephant's trunk. "May I pray with you, Annika, that you will find peace in Him as you love those around you?"

When he prayed, a flood of peace surged through her. The fire—the evil—may have destroyed her home, her Bible, but she wouldn't let it destroy her heart.

Late that night, Annika prayed again for peace as the castle walls creaked and groaned, the cold wind rattling the windows. What would Herr and Frau Dornbach do once they realized their caretaker was gone, their beautiful living space charred?

They'd stopped mailing their weekly check after Vati confronted Max, and now they'd probably think her father had gotten exactly what he deserved, especially after threatening them, but still they would grieve over the destruction of their home.

The stench of smoke had settled into the threads of carpets and curtains and the upholstery on every piece of furniture. Even the books in the library had absorbed the pungent memory of fire.

She'd tried to sleep first inside the familiar walls of Frau Dornbach's dressing room, but the space was too tight, the fear too strong that someone might start another fire while she was locked away. The guest room wasn't much better, but at least she could breathe here.

She didn't know if the Dornbachs would approve of her sleeping in this room, under their fine bedcoverings, but she must sleep somewhere, and the barn and chapel were much too cold.

God, she'd read in her mother's Bible, saw all things that were done in secret. He exposed the heart of the wicked. If God could see things done in secret, then His gaze must roam outside the tiny chapel on the Dornbachs' property and the churches across the lake. He saw what her father had done, saw what she and Hermann were doing as well, their attempt to save what they could. He knew that she was trying to love those who needed it most.

A door slammed outside, and Annika's heart plunged. Hermann always came by boat or motorbike, during the day now, so no one would suspect. He told the truth to anyone who asked—he was helping Annika now that her father had passed on.

She crept to the window. The Nazis, she feared, had returned for her father, not knowing he was dead. What would they do when they discovered he was gone?

Hitler had a group for young women—the League of German Girls. She didn't want to join Hitler's group, but how could she refuse if they insisted?

In the dim light of the stars, the body of the car came into focus, and she realized it was the Dornbachs' black Mercedes. Her heart leapt when she saw Max step out into the courtyard. Finally, after all these months, he was home.

She prayed that he didn't hate her for what she had done.

He opened the passenger door, and at first she thought he was helping his mother, but a much smaller woman emerged beside him, bent over as if she needed a cane.

She rushed outside, wanting to explain what had happened with the necklace, what had happened with the house.

"Annika," Max said sadly when she joined his side, as if her name was a burden. "I'd like you to meet Luzi."

Annika stared at the young woman before her who looked so frail, her cheeks gaunt, her dark hair a tangled mess. Luzia Weiss, the woman she'd cut out from the newspaper picture. The one she'd burned in the stove.

But the glamour was gone from this woman. She looked more like Frederica the cat, when she'd first arrived, than a debutante from Vienna.

"She's been injured," Max said.

"Should I prepare a bath?"

Max nodded. "I have salts for you to put in it. Will you help me clean her wound?"

"I'll do my best, but I'll have to use the bathroom in the castle. Our cottage has burnt down."

Max glanced over at the trees, at the charred remains of the building, but he didn't seem surprised. "Is Herr Knopf in town?"

She shook her head. "He died . . . in the fire."

Luzi's head rose slightly, her eyes dull. "My father is gone as well."

Annika reached for Luzi's other arm. "You will be safe here."

"Thank you, *Kätzchen*," Max said.

The jealousy in her heart roared, but he must know that she'd never intentionally harm him. Nor would she hurt Luzi.

The woman cringed when Annika helped lower her into the warm bath.

She didn't ask what had slit Luzi's leg. Soon they would have to be honest with one another, the three of them, but they would keep their secrets tonight.

Luzi wasn't her friend, but Max was, and her love for him ran deep.

For Max, she would lay down her life.

※

In the hour before dawn, Max stood on the dock beside the boat-house, wondering what had happened to all of them. And what would happen to them now.

His arms and legs were weak, as if one of the military trucks had driven over him and then backed up for a second round. His body was spent, but his mind was as alert as it had ever been.

The Gestapo, he feared, wouldn't stop looking for Luzi. After finding Ernst's body in her apartment, they would surely continue their search.

No one knew where Max had taken Luzi, but Schloss Schwansee could only be a temporary resting place until she was able to travel again. His family owned a mountain hut up on Sarstein, but the trail was steep, treacherous, even for those physically able.

Luzi wouldn't be able to climb with her injured leg, but perhaps in the weeks ahead he could help her up to the hut. Then in the summer, they could hike through the mountains into Switzerland and up to find his mother and Marta in Paris.

A boat puttered along the bank, and he turned to run again. Luzi could hide in the crevice in the library, the space his ancestors had built to stash money and people alike. Then he'd find another hiding place on the estate for himself. Unless the Gestapo brought dogs, they'd never find him hiding in the trees.

But before he stepped off the dock, a flashlight beam crossed over him, and he froze until he heard Hermann's voice, calling his name.

Relieved, Max helped his friend dock inside the boathouse before Hermann climbed onto the platform, his right arm bound in a cast.

"Annika told me about the fire," Max said as they walked toward the castle. "Thank you for helping her save the Schloss."

"I was too late to save Herr Knopf," Hermann said.

"I suspect Herr Knopf might have had something to do with the fire."

Hermann nodded slowly. "He told the Gestapo in Salzburg that your family is Jewish."

"My mother is Jewish," Max replied, but in that moment, he decided to embrace this heritage of his ancestors. The men he'd stood with in the arena had tried to maintain their dignity, unlike the men who tormented them. "Which means I am Jewish as well."

"You can't stay here," Hermann said as they walked toward the house. "Tempers in town are raging strong."

Max thought of all he'd left behind: a city in shambles, a father who seemed to disown his flesh and blood. "I can't go back to Vienna either."

"There's a group of men who have gone into the mountains. Some are Jewish and others are Aryan men who have refused to join the Wehrmacht."

"I brought a woman with me," Max said. "I must get her to safety before I leave."

"Does anyone know she's here?"

Max shook his head.

"Then she will be safe."

"No one knows that I'm here either."

"Someone saw your car in Obertraun last night. You need to drive away in today's light so people will see you. They'll never know about her."

"I can't leave Luzi."

"You have to leave her to keep her safe."

Max nodded to the towering mountain behind them. "There's wood and some food and a Sterno oven in my family's hut. I'll hide up there for now."

Together they concocted a plan. He would drive the Mercedes slowly through town so anyone curious would know he was leaving. Then he'd hide the car in the abandoned barn on Sarah's property before hiking up the mountain on snowshoes after dark. It might take hours in his condition, but he would do it for Luzi's sake.

When it was safe, he'd hike back down.

"I've been giving the treasure to Annika," Hermann said, "but I don't know where she is hiding it. If something happens . . ."

"I know where it's hidden," Max said.

"But what if something happens to both of you?"

"Nothing will happen to Annika." The Gestapo would never suspect her, but many of the Jewish people nearby knew about Hermann's involvement. One day the Nazis might arrest him or Hermann for taking these things, and while Hermann was loyal, Max feared he would buckle under an interrogation.

"If I knew—"

"Someone might kill you for it." Max directed him up the steps. "Please come inside."

Annika was drinking coffee in the library, and Luzi was on the couch, a blanket wrapped around her.

"Hermann, this is Luzi," Max said.

Hermann's eyes focused on his shoes. "Hello, Luzi."

"I have to leave for a few days," Max told her. "Annika and Hermann will care for you here, but I will return whenever I can to check on you."

Annika handed him a cup of coffee. "Where will you go?"

"It's not safe for me to tell either of you, but if you need me, Hermann can find me."

"I will take care of her and your . . . other things."

"Thank you, Annika."

Max showed them the hiding place beside the fireplace, the panel built by his ancestors that opened with the push of a thumb. Then he kissed the cheeks of both women and was gone.

CHAPTER 31

The waters of Hallstatt are an inky blue in this early morning hour, captured by a net of mist as Josh steers us toward the castle in an electric boat.

I was planning to visit a number of churches in Vienna, but I received an email from Sophie last night. She still hasn't found anything about a Luzia Weiss in the archives, but she found several papers that mentioned a Luzi. I've arranged to meet with her this afternoon to review them.

"What's it like to dive under the surface?" I ask, trailing my fingers through the icy wake.

"Have you heard of the German word *Abstand*?"

I lean back against the seat, searching my brain for the meaning. "It has something to do with travel."

He nods. "It's also used to explain the space between us and the world. A distance that a diver can find under the water."

"You dive to escape?"

"Escape from the noise of our world while I'm searching for treasure."

"My space is the wall of my room back in Ohio."

"There's a wall down here," Josh says, pointing to an area not far from Annika's former estate. "It's ribbed with stone for about forty feet and then it drops out. I can take you sometime to see it."

Curiosity wars again with my fears of the unknown. "I much prefer the world up here, even with the noise."

"You won't—not after you experience what's underneath."

It's just the two of us out on the lake—Josh called one of his students who'd decided to stay a couple extra days near Hallstatt, and she agreed to hang out with Ella this morning while Josh took me to the train station. I suspect Ella might still be sleeping when he returns.

"Why haven't you dived here before?" I ask.

A breeze sweeps across the lake, stirring the blue, and I zip up my jacket. At first I don't think he's heard my question, but then he responds.

"I'd planned to dive before Grace and I were married, but when she discovered that seven divers had drowned searching for treasure near here, she begged me not to come. She was afraid the water would take me from her." The gentle buzz of the electric motor fills the space between us, his words settling over me. "Instead of my drowning, the cancer stole her from me."

"She must have loved you deeply."

He glances toward the castle. "And I loved her more than this dream of mine, but before she died, Grace said that she didn't want me to live in fear like she had once done. I still battled with whether or not to come this time, for Ella's sake. My chair at the university said it was time for me to stop researching ownerless treasure and start searching for it."

"You would lose your job?"

"Possibly. If I didn't bring a team here this summer and write about our findings, he was going to consider someone else for full professor and tenure. It wouldn't be good for either Ella or me if I lost this position."

I hear the doubt in his voice, the wanting to do the right thing but not being certain what was best for his daughter.

"You take good care of her, Josh."

He looks away again, but if nothing else, I want him to know this. "Even the fact that you're concerned is . . ." What is it? Admirable. Kind. Compassionate. Perhaps his care for her is simply what the word *father* is supposed to mean.

"I don't want her to grow up afraid," he says, "but now I'm the one scared for her."

Fear—I pray it doesn't plague Ella like it has me. Sometimes it seems like I am afraid of almost everything, including the man right in front of me. "She won't be afraid, not with you there to tell her that she doesn't have to worry. That she can leap over every roadblock in her path."

"Except when you don't. Because, sometimes, you won't." Dr. Seuss was right on that account, but just this morning, I wish he would stop speaking to me.

I dip my hand back into the frigid water and fling the droplets away. "If for some reason she can't leap over those roadblocks, you'll tell her that you love her no matter what."

"Did your father tell you that?" he asks.

I feel the ice creeping up inside me, no bucket challenge

needed. I've talked too much, exposed the brokenness of my heart, the pieces that were supposed to be neatly swept under the shell.

"We're almost there," I say.

Even with the mist, I see the indisputable *Kein Durchgang*—No Entry—on the dock, but my gaze quickly wanders to the medieval Schloss behind it. Online pictures don't do the castle justice, at least not with the mist circled around the turrets and hovering over the slate roof. Or perhaps it's smoke. The smell from a woodstove wafts down the bank.

A stone retaining wall stretches in front of the main house and the five outbuildings on the estate, the rocks protecting the shoreline but also, I suspect, keeping away unwelcome visitors. Like us.

Undeterred, Josh motors toward the forest on the east side and pulls his boat up through the tall weeds, beaching it between the pine trees.

"*Wegefreiheit,*" he says as he eyes the wall of trees in front of us.

"What does that word mean?"

"An Austrian's universal freedom to roam around."

That thought makes me smile. "I suspect that doesn't apply to private property."

"No. Locals are rather strict about keeping tourists off their land."

I wrap my arms across my chest. "Then why are we here?"

"Because it's the only way to find information about Annika. Now that my dive is done—"

"We're still trespassing."

"We'll simply knock," he says. "Herr Stadler will either invite us into his home or he'll ask us to leave. We won't stick around if we're not welcome."

My desire for information wins out over my reluctance. Together we cross through the forest, past the remains of a small house, the wood and stone blackened, the roof caved in. Then the forest breaks into field, and before us are several gardens, ablaze with flowers.

Someone cares well for this land.

A barn stands close to the water, a small fortress made of stucco and stone. Inside the doorway is a middle-aged man dressed in brown trousers and a white T-shirt, his graying hair tucked partly under a cap, a milk pail in hand. He doesn't appear to be very pleased about having guests.

"This property is private," he says in German.

"*Ja,*" Josh replies. "We are looking for someone who once lived here. Do you speak English?"

Irritation flares on the man's face. "This is my home. Not an attraction."

"My name is Josh," he says. "My uncle stayed here in 1945, right after the war ended."

"An Allied soldier, I presume?" the man asks with a mixture of German and English.

Josh nods.

"Most people here want to forget about the war."

"In the United States, we want to remember. So it never happens again."

"With the remembering, the stories can get twisted, *ja?*"

The man is looking at me now so I answer. "It is our job to unwind them. So we remember the truth."

"Even when we do remember, we can't seem to stop men in our world from killing each other," the man says, and his English—at least when he is angry—is quite good. He's at least three decades too young to have fought in World War II, but I wonder if he's fought in another war. "Why are you in Austria?"

Josh introduces us properly, shaking his hand as if we are meeting at a dinner party. "I brought some students to dive the lake with me."

"Treasure hunting?" the man asks as if it's an accusation.

"I'm looking for what the Nazis would have called ownerless treasure."

"There's nothing left to be found in this lake."

Josh isn't ready to be dismissed, especially after he already found a list of names and the silver coins. "My uncle met a woman while he was here who told him about things that were hidden."

The man is paying closer attention now. "What was her name?"

"Annika Stadler."

The man swings his pail into his other hand. "Frau Stadler doesn't live here anymore."

My pulse speeds up. "But you know her?"

"*Ja*, but the memories here, they are hard."

A glance over at Josh and I see the interest pique on his face too. I don't think either of us truly thought Annika would still be alive.

"Callie has found a book of Annika's from her childhood. We thought Frau Stadler might want it returned."

"What book is that?" the man asks.

Josh glances at me.

"An early edition of *Bambi*," I say, carefully guarding my words. "It contains some sort of list."

"I will ask her about it. Where are you staying?"

"At Gasthof Simony," Josh says.

"I am Jonas Stadler."

"Is Frau Stadler your grandmother?" I ask.

The man gazes out at the lake, toward the village of Hallstatt. "Do either of you have children?"

Josh slips his phone out of his jacket pocket, and I glimpse a recent picture of Ella holding her stuffed bunny, sitting in front of a bowl of Cheerios and glass of orange juice. He turns it to show Herr Stadler. "This is my daughter."

"She looks like she is full of life."

"In abundance."

"And you would do anything for your daughter, would you not?" Herr Stadler asks.

"I'd give my life for her."

"I would give my life for my family as well." The man steps away. "I will contact you at Gasthof Simony if Frau Stadler would like to speak with you."

Josh nods. "Fair enough."

"Auf Wiedersehen," Herr Stadler says, tipping his cap.

We wander back to the boat, the smell of wood smoke wafting through the trees.

Frau Stadler would be well into her ninth decade of life by now. If she's willing to speak with us, will she remember what was lost? And where it went? Will she remember the man whose photo she taped in her book or the woman who'd been cut away?

The clock, I fear, is working against us all.

CHAPTER 32

Ernst Schmid spent more than three torturous months in Vienna's General Hospital, recovering first from his bullet wound and then from the infection that infiltrated his body. He'd heard the doctors whispering when he pretended to sleep, saying the infection would kill him, but he'd conquered it. Just as he would conquer Max Dornbach when he got out of this prison.

Major Rosch didn't acknowledge Ernst's return to the Hotel Metropole, but he cared nothing about recognition. The doctors thought they and their medicines had cured him, but no medicine could cure like the drive of revenge. His focus, sharper than the tip of his knife, killed the infection.

The Gestapo commander didn't speak to him, but the other agents whispered as he stepped off the elevator to the upper floor of their headquarters, wondering who had shot him and why. When Major Rosch visited him in the hospital, Ernst had told the man that he didn't know who wounded him, that he was checking on a complaint about a Jewish family who'd refused to leave their home and someone shot him from behind.

The office windows overlooked the streetcars and pedestrians and parades of tanks and soldiers that marched up Morzinplatz every day. Life in Vienna was much more ordered now, the things of frivolity in the past. Their Führer was focused on conquering the world, but Ernst wanted to conquer only one man.

He would find Max Dornbach and make him pay.

Ernst picked up the telephone on his desk and called the commandants at Dachau and Mauthausen. Dr. Weiss had died at Dachau, but no one could tell him if they'd taken Max to one of the camps. Or where Luzi had gone.

Next he tried to phone his mother at the house where she worked in Munich, but no one answered. He hadn't told her that Max tried to kill him, but she would cooperate with any investigation against the Dornbach family.

When Ernst was younger, his mother hoped each summer that the Dornbachs would extend an invitation for her and Ernst to join their staff at the family estate near Salzburg, but they never did. Instead his mother waited faithfully for them to return, taking in ironing to support herself and her son through those hot summer months.

They hadn't been nearly as faithful to her.

He sent a telegram to Munich.

Need to find the Dornbach family. What is the name of
their summer house?

Ernst spent the rest of his morning addressing memorandums
to commandants across the Third Reich. If they found a man
named Max Dornbach from Vienna or a woman named Luzi
Weiss, he wanted to know. Then he spent his afternoon visiting
the new tenants in the Weiss apartment, the rooms all clean and
tidy now.

They left him alone in their parlor as he tried to replay what
happened that night he'd come for Luzi. His expectations had been
high—he'd waited so long to have her—and she'd disappointed
him. The disappointment he remembered well, but the moments
after were a blur.

Max had shuffled through the door, interrupting him, and
Ernst had been livid until it occurred to him that he could have
two things he wanted that very night—Luzi and the life of this
man who loved her.

And he would've had both if Max hadn't shot him first.

Ernst pinched the bridge of his nose, trying to remember. Luzi
had distracted him—he hadn't even seen the gun in Max's hand.
But he remembered the shock of it, the explosion of pain.

Next he took a taxi to the fancy *Stadtpalais* off Ringstrasse
where Max and his family lived, the small palace where his mother
had scrubbed floors until her hands swelled, set silverware for
the finest of meals while she was eating leftover schnitzel in the
kitchen. The apartment where she'd washed laundry for a family who soiled their clothing like the common man but wouldn't
remove their own dirt.

The upper floor was vacant, and the neighbor below said that

Klara Dornbach was visiting her sister in France. Herr Dornbach had been reassigned to Berlin.

In the morning, Ernst sent a telegram to Germany, but Herr Dornbach's short reply was clear. He didn't know the whereabouts of his son, though he suspected Max had joined Klara in Paris.

If Max had made it to France, had he taken Luzi with him?

Ernst riffled through files. The paperwork was a beast of its own, thousands upon thousands of records trying to track who'd left Austria and who'd stayed behind. Luzi, he discovered, had been approved for a visa to America, to attend Juilliard, but the permit had come after Max had shot him. He couldn't find any record of her leaving Vienna.

A messenger found him amid the files, delivering a two-word reply from his mother.

Schloss Schwansee.

The name of the Dornbach estate.

Ernst smoothed the yellow paper on his desk. Then he called the headquarters office in Salzburg and asked them to pay a visit to the castle of swans.

He wouldn't hurt Max when he found him, at least not at first.

First he would eliminate what Max prized most.

CHAPTER 33

Life grew inside her.

She hadn't told Annika about the baby, but while her friend slept, Luzi spent the midnight hours ripping seams from Frau Dornbach's borrowed clothing to accommodate her growth. She had altered several dresses and a skirt for Annika too, replacing her friend's worn clothing. Unlike Luzi, Annika grew thinner as the months passed.

Luzi wanted to hate this baby inside her, the offspring of a man who'd stolen what he had no right to take, but each time she felt the baby move, she clung to a new hope. This child was hers, not Ernst Schmid's. She would raise him or her in these lakes, far away from the evil in Vienna.

This castle was her new home. Annika her sister, of sorts.

The two of them had worked with Hermann to clean up some of what the fire had destroyed, though they'd closed the door to the parlor—it was beyond their ability to repair.

She whispered quietly to her baby at night, quoting the passages of Scripture she remembered in lieu of a song. But on the days her chest felt as if it were gasping for air, those days she missed her sister and parents so much that she wished her life had been stolen away as well, she'd walk down to the shore and watch the strands of mist linger over the lake.

A warm foehn blew down from the mountains this morning, bringing with it the damp fog and wreaking havoc on Luzi's muscles and her mind. She'd already milked the goats, the handle of the tin pail cold in her hands, but she wasn't ready to return to the castle. Life was a mist of sorts, she decided. It blew between two shores, never really going anywhere, and when the sun came out, the mist disappeared. In the light, everything became clear.

One day, when the madness ended, she would find Marta and raise her alongside the child growing within her—that hope drove her out of bed each morning, waiting for the sun.

Passover began today, the celebration of God's passing over their people and their freedom from oppression in Egypt. Her parents had never celebrated the Jewish holidays, but Luzi's grandparents remembered each one. Annika wanted to remember these holidays as they waited for Max, to celebrate the God who loved His people.

But how could she celebrate freedom today when her people were still being oppressed?

Last December, she and Annika had lit candles for Chanukah, remembering how God had provided to defeat the enemies of the

Jewish people. Annika had celebrated God's miracles with her, and Luzi helped Annika celebrate the birth of her Christ with the turkey Hermann had brought for them and the small tree they'd found in the forest. They'd decorated the pine boughs with ribbons from Frau Dornbach's bureau, glass balls, and miniature candles.

On Christmas Day, they'd read from the Dornbachs' Bible, and Luzi hadn't stopped reading it since. The New Testament was a story of a Jewish man, a righteous man who claimed to be the Messiah. As she read through the story of His crucifixion, she felt His wounds keenly. And she longed for the freedom He offered, no matter what the people around her took away.

On her left, Hermann's motorboat streamed toward the estate, and he waved to her as he approached the boathouse. He joined them more often now, repairing things that were broken or bringing them meat from the fertile hunting grounds.

Annika had taught her how to fish and milk their goats, and Luzi had taught her how to sew. Annika had also cut Luzi's hair and bathed it in hydrogen peroxide so she resembled a younger Aryan girl, a resident of these lakes. Together they'd raided the Dornbachs' library during the winter months and read books that took them far from here.

For these months, the Nazis had left them mostly alone.

The Gestapo in the black cars had arrived at the estate last month, searching for Max. Luzi had hid in the space near the library's fireplace while Annika told them the truth—that she hadn't seen Max in a long time.

Annika hadn't seen him since the day he left Luzi here, but some mornings the two women would wake up and find a note under their door. He didn't give them much information, only a line or two, but it was enough to know he was safe. Twice he'd come into the house while Annika was asleep. He'd kissed Luzi's cheek, promised that he would return for her, and then he was gone.

His love for her never seemed to waver, and she wished with everything inside her that her heart didn't feel so cold. Empty. As if she had nothing left to give except life to the one person who remained in her care.

If only Max could see how much Annika adored him. How she would do anything for him. If only he knew that Luzi was as broken and charred as the parlor in his family's castle.

Hermann began crossing the bank toward her, and she released arms that had wrapped themselves around her chest.

Some nights, Hermann would come, and she'd hear him and Annika whispering together. Annika hid whatever was in Hermann's bags in a plot between the trees, but Luzi harbored their secret for them. Just as they faithfully harbored hers.

She wanted to control her life, as she'd once controlled the music pouring from her violin, but life wasn't a neat set of notes, composed by Strauss or Bach. It was much more messy, chaotic, like an orchestra tuning their instruments before the concert began.

Oh, she craved a concert. Musicians working together to create something beautiful that brought joy to the listeners, not something ugly to tear people apart.

Waiting was all she had now.

Waiting until she could find Marta.

Waiting until someone stopped Hitler.

Waiting the four months until her baby was born.

Annika wanted to hate Luzi Weiss because Max loved her, but she couldn't do it. Luzi's beauty on the outside, the beauty that

Annika had tried to burn away when she clipped the newspaper photograph, was embedded inside her as well. And now she was expecting Max's child.

Annika had known it for a few weeks, but she hadn't dared voice the truth, for voicing it would make it into a reality. She kept hoping that she was wrong, that Luzi had gained weight as the gash on her leg had healed, but each day it became more apparent that Luzi was pregnant.

Annika's heart had shattered at first, knowing that Max would always see her as a kitten, but there was more to care about in this world than her heart. She still loved him, always would. She just couldn't tell Luzi—or anyone else—of her feelings.

"When do you expect the baby to arrive?" Annika asked as they ate their dinner of broiled trout on the veranda. The air was cold, but neither of them wanted to be inside. No matter how big the house was, the walls seemed to close in on them.

"In August, I think," Luzi said quietly, her voice sad. "Why do you care for me, Annika?"

She almost said because Max asked her to, like he'd asked her to hide the heirlooms for their Jewish neighbors, but it was about more than Max. The words in Mama's Bible swept back to her. "Jesus said to love our neighbor as we love ourselves."

"Aren't you afraid?" Luzi asked, her voice trembling with the question.

"Terribly."

Luzi rested her hands on her stomach. "Do you think Jesus was afraid when He died?"

In her heart, Annika believed that this man who loved and healed would be deeply grieved by what was happening in their world. Like Pastor Dietz said, He came to heal, not to kill. But she didn't know if He was afraid.

"I'm not certain, but I don't think we have to fear if we serve a God who can conquer death," Annika said, trying to cling again to those words.

Hermann joined them on the veranda as he often did in the evenings, sitting beside Luzi. He blushed when she looked at him, and Annika's defenses flared again. He shouldn't be watching Luzi like that. Surely he must know that Max's baby was coming soon.

Hermann nodded toward Annika. "Herr Pfarrer needs to speak with you."

She glanced over at the parish church perched on the hill across the water. The Dornbachs had attended Mass there, but she'd never been inside. "Why would he want to talk to me?"

"He has to arrange a time to transport the Eyssl casket."

Annika cringed. With the changes in their country, the Dornbachs gone, she'd thought the church would surely forgo those plans.

Hermann scooted his chair toward her. "The Nazis want parishes to go about their business as if nothing has changed in our country. Herr Pfarrer thinks this will help with morale."

"But everything has already changed," Annika insisted. Their lakes, her family, her home. In the past year, Germany had swallowed up the heart of her country. She no longer recognized the parts that remained.

Moving a box of old bones across the lake wouldn't rejuvenate anyone.

"Annika—"

She shook her head.

"It's only for one night."

The thought of having the man's bones in the chapel . . . She would never sleep until they took them back to the church.

"If you refuse, the Gestapo will ask questions. Maybe even return for another visit."

A *Kuddlemuddel*—that's what her mother would have called this.

"I don't want his remains here."

"It's necessary, Annika."

Luzi glanced between the two of them, her eyes wide. "What casket?"

And Annika began to explain the tradition of old.

CHAPTER 34

Sophie meets me in the lobby of the gold-and-white baroque-style building in Minoritenplatz that houses the state archives. She's a slight wisp of a woman, drowning in her black pants and baggy blouse, but she doesn't need stature to command respect. She seems to be an institution of her own in this place that records the institutions from Austria's history.

Light filters around the edges of the heavy drapes in the reading room, across dozens of tables with cylinder lamps and researchers huddled over mounds of boxed materials and stuffed manila folders. Sophie motions to a table with two folders, and we sit across from each other.

"Why do you want to find Luzia Weiss?" she asks, and I hear the concern in her voice, as if she's not quite certain that she wants to pass along the information in these files.

Her hands link together, a chain of sorts across the top of the folders, and I begin to tell her the tale of two books and their owners, stories that didn't end between the covers. About Annika and her list of heirlooms, Josh's uncle Leo and what Annika told him about the treasure. I tell her about Charlotte and the orphanage in France, about the name I suspect to be her mother's. And I tell her that I want to know the endings, whether happy or sad.

Besides Brie, Sophie is the first person I tell about the possible connection between Charlotte and Luzia. It's sacred, I think, this story of theirs, but I'll never know for certain what happened unless someone in Austria helps me.

"This Frau Stadler . . . ," Sophie says slowly. "Why do you think she found treasure on the estate?"

"What else would she be record—" I stop.

"Perhaps she took things from the homes of Jewish people who'd already been sent away."

I take off my glasses and set them on the table. Annika, in my mind, is a hero, but what if she was really the perpetrator of a crime? What if she and Hermann stole heirlooms from the Nazis' collection or even from her Jewish neighbors after they were gone? Frau Stadler could have been trying to steer Josh's uncle *away from* some sort of treasure instead of to it.

"People were prosecuted across Austria and Germany after the war for keeping things that had belonged to people killed in the camps."

"What if, in some way, they were trying to help?"

"After the war, no one in Austria would have believed them," she says. "Help was a rare commodity back then."

I glance down at the folders again. "What's in the files?"

"A memorandum," she says as she opens the first folder. "It mentions a Luzi Weiss from Vienna."

I skim the typed document from across the table, but it's all in German.

"It's written by a Gestapo agent," Sophie explains. "A *Kriminalassistent* by the name of Ernst Schmid. He's lost track of Luzi, it seems, and he's inquiring about her whereabouts."

The warmth in this room doesn't stop my shiver. "Why was a Gestapo agent searching for her?"

Instead of answering my question, Sophie turns the memo around, and I see Luzi's name in the midst of the writing.

Is this the same person as Luzia Weiss from the article? And Luzia Weiss from Charlotte's book? I don't know that either woman is related to Charlotte, but seeing Luzi's name in print here, even recorded by the Gestapo agent, gives me hope.

Perhaps Luzia hid with Charlotte in France while Ernst Schmid was looking for her.

The other folder contains a second memo and a newspaper photograph of a young Luzia playing with an ensemble. This caption says *Luzi Weiss*, but it's clearly the same woman who danced with Max at the ball.

"The Gestapo reported that they found a Luzi Weiss." Sophie inches another paper across the table to me.

My glasses are on again, and I'm trying desperately to decipher the words. "Where did they find her?"

"Hiding inside a castle on Hallstättersee."

I suck in air so loudly that several researchers turn to look at me.

"They arrested her in April of 1939." She points down at the paper, and I see the name of the lake clearly, no need for translation.

Where was Max Dornbach when they arrested the woman he seemed to love?

"Perhaps Annika decided to turn Luzi in to the Gestapo," Sophie says, and even though eighty years have passed, I feel the wounds. Betrayal—one of the worst kinds of pain.

"Was Luzia a Jewish woman?" Sophie asks.

"I believe so." I glance down at my handbag as if the photocopy of Luzia's name inscribed in the magic balloon story might talk. As if it would lead me to the truth.

But to what end? If Luzia was Jewish, if the Gestapo sent her away, there was no hope for reconciliation. No healing to be had in the truth of what might have happened to her. Reunion would need to happen on the other side of this life.

I take a picture of the memo before Sophie closes the folder. "I've searched everything that is public here. You must rely on the private sources now or the records kept by religious communities in Vienna and perhaps in Hallstatt."

I reach for my handbag. I don't want to stop until I'm able to at least link Luzia with Charlotte.

"Many died during the war," Sophie says, trying to comfort me.

"I know. I'm just holding on to the hope . . ."

"There's nothing wrong with grieving your loss."

But I'm not ready to grieve yet. "I need to search . . . to see if Luzia died in a camp."

She nods. "The Holocaust Memorial Museum keeps a record of victims online."

There's no WiFi access in the reading room, so I wander back outside and across cobbles of gray stone that wind between buildings and through a park. My thoughts are as flighty as my feet, not certain of exactly which direction to go, but I know, even if I don't want to check, that I must search the database to see if the Nazis killed Luzi or Luzia Weiss from Vienna.

A sign in the window of a coffeehouse promises WiFi gratis, so I order a cappuccino and find a marble-covered table. Outside the window is a white statue of a horse and packs of students, professionals, and tourists.

Typing Luzia's name and birthplace into my iPad is tremendously painful, each letter a hammer to my heart. It's only a screen in front of me, only words, but words that carry significance far beyond this room.

Nothing is recorded in the database for Luzia Weiss, but when I input *Luzi*, the screen flashes, opens to a new window. And I see the truth of what happened to her.

Ravensbrück.

The word slams against my chest, the pieces of my heart splintering.

A hundred thousand women, I read, were killed in that German camp alone, each with a family and perhaps children as well. I never knew Luzia Weiss, yet for Charlotte's sake, I feel keenly the pain of losing her. All those years Charlotte searched, Luzia was already gone. Exterminated.

This wasn't God. Isn't God. A beautiful young woman dying for who He created her to be. I didn't know Luzia, but tears, I think, are one of the greatest tributes of all. Perhaps that was why Jesus wept for the loss of his friend in the Bible, before He raised him from the grave. Perhaps, even when we know there is life in the *after*, we can still grieve for the *now*.

I may be the only one left to grieve for Luzia. To remember. And so I cry for her tragic death, mourn in that coffeehouse what might have been.

I'd hoped to be able to bring Charlotte information about what happened to her mother, but this news . . .

As I walk back to the train station, along the regal lanes with shops and restaurants and houses built for opera, I wonder how many people in Vienna remember what happened in the war. My world of books confronts the realities of life, but the endings—at least the ones I prefer—clean up the mess at the end. Everything is resolved when I close the cover, but the ugly realities of this world—what man does to man—bleeds right off the page.

Tears flow down my cheeks again, and I decide in that moment that Sophie is right—there's nothing wrong with the sadness. With remembering a dance of life that ended much too soon. A star captured from the freedom of sky.

Perhaps this woman wasn't Charlotte's mother, but even if she was, I don't have anyplace else to look. The search for Luzia Weiss has ended for me, the final page closing at the gates of Ravensbrück. And I can almost hear the slam of those gates echoing in my head.

CHAPTER 35

The information Ernst had been waiting for finally arrived. The Salzburg agents hadn't found anyone except the caretaker's daughter at Schloss Schwansee, but an agent at Dachau had convinced Herr Fischer, one of Dr. Weiss's patients, to speak.

When the Gestapo arrested this man in November, they'd searched his lavish home for the jewelry his wife once displayed, but nothing of value remained. They'd interrogated Frau Fischer at length before taking her to jail. She'd seemed shocked at the disappearance of her jewels, but Jews lied about everything, especially their valuables.

The men who'd survived the roundup returned home with

directions to leave Austria immediately, but the Gestapo held a few, like Herr Fischer, who refused to answer the simplest of questions. The Jew had kept his secrets for months, but they'd finally extracted the information they needed. And it was much more valuable than anything they could have found in his house.

Herr Fischer had been a regular patient of Dr. Weiss, a victim of chronic bronchitis, and he'd trusted the doctor with his health at first and then the jewelry that he'd wanted to keep safe, he said, for his wife and children. He claimed that he didn't know where Dr. Weiss had hidden the things, but eventually, after a brief reunion with his wife, he recalled a fact that intrigued Ernst most of all.

Several times during Herr Fischer's medical examinations, Max Dornbach had paid the good doctor a visit even though he'd been in excellent health. Once Herr Fischer heard them talking about Schloss Schwansee.

Ernst tapped on the edge of his desk, his arm throbbing. A constant reminder of what he needed to do.

Hands trembling, he removed a glass bottle and spoon from the bottom drawer of his desk. The doctor had prescribed tablets to relieve his pain, but the tablets had done nothing to take it away. He poured the clear liquid into his spoon and chased the bitter taste of morphine with a cup of coffee.

Had Max taken the jewels to his fancy castle? Perhaps he was hiding even more than jewels there. Perhaps he was hiding a certain woman as well.

His commander wouldn't let him leave Vienna to search for Luzi, but if these jewels were hidden at Schloss Schwansee, surely the man would let him take the train west. He'd find the jewels, and then he'd find her.

An elevator delivered Ernst to the third floor, to the office of Major Rosch. The commander was two decades older than Ernst, a man of impeccable grooming with his pale-gray tunic, hair shaved short above his ears, Iron Cross that hung in the middle of his stiff collar. He'd been ruthless in Vienna, a perfectionist who wanted the city as pressed and starched as his uniform.

Ernst read him the report on Herr Fischer.

"Call the headquarters in Salzburg," Major Rosch said, tapping the silver nib of his pen impatiently on the desk.

"I've already been in contact with their agents, but they haven't found anything of significance in the house."

"Have them search both the house and the grounds this time."

"This time—" Ernst lowered the paper—"I want to search instead."

"They are competent, Officer Schmid."

"Of course," he complied, trying to find another angle. "But I'm the only one who knows what Luzi Weiss looks like."

Major Rosch waved his arm. "She's of no interest to us."

"I suspect she will be of great interest if she's been helping Max Dornbach hide this treasure."

The commander stopped tapping, his eyes narrowing. "Then send a photograph."

Ernst's heart quickened. If they found something, he doubted they would leave any for him. "This is my find."

"It's a few trinkets and a girl, Ernst. We have plenty of both here in Vienna."

"Major—"

"If they find something of value, then you can go."

Ernst stewed in his office for an hour before he finally called Salzburg and asked them to search Schloss Schwansee one more time.

"If you find a woman named Luzi Weiss, phone me right away." He swallowed another spoonful of morphine. "And don't touch her until I arrive."

CHAPTER 36

A fishing boat creeps below the inn, trawling for the day's catch, and the air—it smells like roasted coffee and sweet pine, rose petals and alpine snow, mountain wind and memories.

Most of the lake is hidden in these early morning hours before the fog slips back up the mountains, settling into crevices and caverns to hide for the day. I sip from one of the two coffee mugs that I retrieved down in the lobby, the caffeine slowly clearing the fog from my mind even as it lingers in the air around me.

No one seems to be awake in the room across the balcony, not that I've wandered over to knock. I returned so late last night from Vienna that I didn't see either Josh or Ella. And I miss them.

My feet propped up on the chair across from me, I return an email from Brie. Eventually I'll tell her what happened to Luzia, but not over the phone.

It won't impact Brie like it has me. She'll be sad about the truth, in her way, but then she'll remind me that Charlotte has both of us, and the ties of family can go far beyond blood in one's veins.

Perhaps I will tell Charlotte what happened to Luzia and what I suspect about Max. Perhaps she and Liberty Dornbach could even test to see if they have a DNA match. I want to protect Charlotte, and yet in some way, the information about Luzia might comfort her. At least she would know that her mother wasn't able to return for her in France. And that she might have remaining family in Liberty and her brother.

The glass door slides open on the other side of the balcony, and Josh steps outside, swiping his hand through messy brown hair to push it back from his eyes.

"Good morning." I slip my feet off the chair, and he pulls it out.

I feel self-conscious for a moment in my long-sleeve T-shirt and pajama bottoms, my hair tied back in a knot.

"Good morning to you," he says. "I thought I smelled coffee."

I push the second mug toward him. "I wasn't sure what you wanted in it, so I gambled with cream and a packet of sugar."

He takes a long sip. "Perfect."

Pink light spreads slowly across the water until it illuminates the Alpine houses and stone church to our right, driving away the fog.

"Did you and Ella enjoy the ice caves?"

He nods. "She didn't want to leave."

"The girl embraces every moment," I say, my fingers wrapped around the warm mug. "Like her dad."

"Like I used to."

"You don't fool me, Dr. Nemeth."

"I wasn't trying to."

"Right . . ."

He laughs before taking another sip of coffee. "I thought you were shy, back when I first met you in Columbus, but you aren't shy at all." When he stares at me, I pull my sleeves over my hands, trying to ward off the cold. "You are afraid of something, though."

I roll my eyes. "Everyone is afraid of something."

My attempt to deflect doesn't deter him. "I think, Callie Randall, that you are afraid of yourself."

I hate it when people analyze me. Hate it even more when they're right. "That's ridiculous."

"Or perhaps it's more like you're afraid of letting others get to know who you are, beyond the stories that you like to tell."

"There's nothing wrong with stories—"

"Unless you use them as a shield," he says, taking another sip. "We all process differently—I get that—but it's one thing to reflect and mull things over internally, another to crawl into a shell of your own making and hide."

"I'm not hiding."

The sun edges over the mountain, chasing the remaining mist and lamplight away. He unzips his jacket as sunlight sweeps across our balcony. "It's just a theory."

"Why must doctors always theorize?"

He laughs. "Because until you recognize a problem, you can't make a change."

"I don't have a problem— "

"I'm certainly glad to hear that."

My skin begins to warm as well, but not from the sun.

"Did Herr Stadler call you?" I ask, ready to conclude the analysis.

He pulls his phone out of his pocket and glances at it. "Nothing yet."

Josh has questions for Annika about the treasure, but it doesn't matter so much now, at least to me, whether she calls. Except perhaps she could tell me why Luzia was at the estate and if she remembers any stories about a baby who was taken to France. Then I would know . . .

"We missed you at dinner last night," he says. "My date fell asleep over her food. I had to carry her back to the inn."

"You're an amazing dad, Josh."

"Not particularly . . ."

"I'm a bit of an expert in this area."

He eyes me. "You've studied good dads?"

"No . . ." In that moment, I decide to inch a bit further out of my shell. "Let's just say my father wouldn't have carried me home from a restaurant. For that matter, he would never have taken me to a restaurant that didn't have a drive-through."

"Ah . . ."

"It gives me a great appreciation for all the men in this world who are excellent dads."

The Hallstatt ferry embarks from the dock on our left, cruising toward the train station on the other side of the lake.

"What did you find in Vienna?" he asks.

I sigh. "Sadness, I'm afraid."

"It seems as if sadness is stamped all over this place."

"So much beauty and yet so much sorrow."

"It seems to linger here, doesn't it?" Together we watch a swan circle the water below us. "The memories of the many who died seem to cling to these hills."

I reach for my coffee mug again, and even though it's cold now, I wrap my hands around it. "I've uncovered a story that goes beyond just these hills. It relates to Annika's story, but it's a personal journey for me as well."

I wasn't planning to tell him, but it pours out of me, this story about the woman who has journeyed with me for most of my life. I tell him that Charlotte knows me well and loves me for exactly who I am.

"Yesterday I found information about a woman who I think might have been Charlotte's mother," I say. "And then I discovered she was killed at Ravensbrück."

"Does Charlotte know?" he asks.

I shake my head.

"What was her mother's name?"

"Luzia Weiss."

Josh nods slowly, as if he's soaking in this information. Then his eyes grow wide.

"What is it?" I ask.

He turns toward me, but he's looking over my shoulder, at a hill beyond the inn. "There's something I need to show you."

CHAPTER 37

LAKE HALLSTATT, AUSTRIA
APRIL 1939

The ornately carved and worn casket that housed Baron Christoph
Eyssl von Eysselsberg came via boat in the evening hours, the second week in April. It was a strange sight to watch the pallbearers
carry it up the bank on their shoulders, starlight sprinkling the
casket with a silver dust.

Luzi was hidden behind the wall, but Annika watched the odd
procession from a window seat in the library. Herr Pfarrer in his
formal black vestments led the men and the ancient casket across
the estate by candlelight, to the unpainted platform in the chapel.
The church had faithfully kept its promise from centuries past.

If only they could help the people today . . .

No one in this region remembered Christoph or his family, only the reputation of a peculiar salt administrator who had built this castle and ruled over this area as if it were a kingdom. And his strange request to return home every fifty years.

Better, Annika supposed, that his casket visit here than he haunt the place, but she would much rather his remains stay in the crypt where they belonged.

Minutes later, the Catholic priest knocked on the front door, and Annika hurried through the hall to meet him.

"Are you well?" Herr Pfarrer asked.

"I am getting along well enough."

"The casket is secure in the chapel," he said as if he'd brought her a gift. "We'll return in the morning."

She nodded in acknowledgment, her fingers tightened around the iron door handle. Being agreeable was one of the best things she could do to ward off suspicion, but she would be counting down the hours until the body of Baron Eyssl von Eysselsberg returned to his crypt across the lake.

When the priest and men were gone, Annika knocked five times on the panel near the fireplace. Luzi unlocked it from the inside before pulling it open. She had what she needed in the small space to last for days if necessary. Pillow and blanket. A flashlight and chamber pot. A thermos with water, brown bread, and pickled eggs.

Annika's *Bambi* book was now hidden in this space as well, in the metal box that she'd rescued after the fire, but Luzi had never mentioned opening the box or seeing Max's picture taped in the back of the book. Annika almost wished that she had seen it, that she would ask about it, even. They talked about all manner of subjects, but they rarely spoke about the man who'd brought them together.

Luzi scooted out of the space, and Annika reached out, helping her to her feet.

In the past weeks, Luzi's belly had swollen under the clothing she'd managed to alter from Frau Dornbach's wardrobe. Hiding inside this space must be far from comfortable, but Luzi never complained. She knew much better than Annika what might happen if the Gestapo found her here.

"When will they return?" Luzi asked.

"In the morning."

Luzi excused herself to use the bathroom before they began preparing dinner. Nights like this, Annika was even more grateful that Luzi was here with her. She didn't think she could bear to be alone in this huge place, even on the nights when there wasn't a casket behind the house.

She brought a loaf of sourdough *Hausbrot* to the library along with butter and a jug of goat milk for them to drink. Before Annika returned to the kitchen for plates and cups, Luzi stepped back into the room, her skin a pale pink from washing, her peroxide-bleached hair wet around her face.

"Please sit," Luzi said. "I'll bring the rest of the things."

"No—"

"Please," she insisted. "You need to rest, and it's good for me to stretch my legs."

"Thank you." But Annika had sat only for seconds when someone rang their doorbell again. She turned and stared at the archway that separated the library from the hall.

"The priest must have forgotten something," Annika said, trying to drown the familiar pangs of fear inside her.

The bell rang again, and Luzi pressed the edge of the panel, opening it into the wall. "I'll spend the night in here."

Annika shivered. "It shouldn't be necessary."

"My hiding protects us both."

Annika nodded before Luzi pushed the panel closed from the inside. The seams between the panels stitched up neatly.

When the doorbell rang for a third time, Annika took a deep breath, praying that it wasn't another mob returning to finish what they'd started with the fire.

If they barged inside, how would she get Luzi out of here?

Instead of answering the front door, she opened the one to the parlor, the room where Vati had died. She hadn't been back inside since the fire—and she didn't want to go now—but she couldn't answer the door until she saw who was on the other side.

Carefully she stepped over remnants of burnt wood and ash-laden furniture piled on what was once a finely carpeted floor. Through the broken window, she saw Hermann on the stoop, the bell ringing through the house again.

She rushed back into the hall, opening the door. "What is it?"

"I just received a call, from a schoolmate in Salzburg. He said Gestapo agents are coming back here to search for missing treasure from Vienna."

The pounding in her heart resumed. "When are they coming?"

"He didn't know."

The Gestapo agents wouldn't find Luzi's space etched into the wall, but if they searched the grounds, they might find the heirlooms buried in the forest.

"Where is Max?" she asked.

Hermann took off his corduroy cap, his blond hair clumping to his head. "Hiding in the mountains."

"He wouldn't tell anyone."

Hermann shifted his hat. "Not unless something much bigger were at stake."

She reached for the post. Had they forced Max to talk for Luzi's sake?

Her mind raced, trying to determine what to do. "We have to move the things."

"They'll search every crevice in this place."

She turned slowly toward the chapel, an idea brewing in her head. "Can you help me with one more project?"

"Of course."

❧

Annika didn't recognize either man who stood on her doorstep, each dressed in the brown shirt and red band that required no introduction.

The other agents who had visited from Salzburg had been somewhat polite—apologetic, even, when they insisted on searching for Max—but the agents this morning offered no apology. It was quite clear that they and the men waiting outside in their black vehicles, four of them parked in the courtyard, were going to search the estate whether or not she wanted them here.

If she could keep them in the forest, searching, Luzi would be safe inside.

"You are hiding things," the senior agent said. Not a question, a proclamation that he clearly believed to be truth.

Annika steadied her voice. "Your agents already searched the house."

"Where is Herr Dornbach?" the younger man asked, a trickle of grease seeping down his jaw, pooling at his collar.

"Max Dornbach," the elder clarified.

"I don't know," she said. "Perhaps in Vienna."

The younger one moved closer. "Are you Luzi?"

She blanched. "No, I—"

How did they know Luzi's name?

"She's the caretaker's daughter," the elder said as if she hadn't an actual name. Then he turned back toward the other cars and curled his arm up like a hook, as if he'd caught a fish.

The men tumbled out of the cars and began scouring the property. Two more of them stepped toward the house, ignoring Annika when she said their men had already searched every room in the castle. They started in the kitchen, pulling out drawers and rifling through the cabinets as if she'd hidden treasures in the flour or sugar bins.

Luzi, she prayed, would be safe in her hiding place.

As the agents stormed into the dining room, she feared the worst had come to Max. If so, he could no longer protect his things . . . or the child who belonged to him.

Would these men search until they found Luzi? The Nazis, it seemed, would stop at nothing to find those who eluded them.

What would they do to Annika if they didn't find her?

In the library, the men began to search through the hundreds of books, and her heart dropped when one of them plucked a copy of *Bambi* from the shelves. But it was Max's copy, not hers.

Unless Luzi, for some reason, had decided to place the book in the library.

When the younger agent held it up, she prayed he wouldn't begin turning the pages.

"This book has been banned," he said.

She tilted her head, hoping they would see her as a kitten like

Max did, naive and perhaps a little silly. "Why would someone ban a book about deer?"

The men, all four of them, looked confounded by her question.

"Or is it the hunter that they don't like?" she asked.

The elder agent grabbed the book from his partner's hands and tossed it onto the floor near the fireplace. "Because Felix Salten is a Jew."

Sweat glazed Annika's palms, her pores spilling over when she couldn't use words.

One of the agents picked up a lamp and began pounding on the walls with the bronze base. She wiped her palms on her skirt as meters became centimeters. Then his lamp was poised to strike the panel that protected her friend.

An image popped into her head—she and Max sitting on this sofa a decade from now, hand in hand. Remembering Luzi together. Max wouldn't long for Luzi as he once had, not with Annika as his wife.

She didn't even have to tell these men where Luzi was hidden. They would discover it on their own. Nothing she could do would stop them from finding Luzi. Nothing except . . .

Words tumbled from her mouth as she stepped in front of the panel. "What do you want from me?"

"We don't want you," the man with the lamp said. "We want the treasure you've hidden. And the girl."

More pictures flashed in her mind. This time of Luzi and the child that grew within her. Of Max and his love for the woman behind the panel. Even if he never found out about the baby, Annika would know.

These men of Hitler, they would take both mother and child with them, and no matter what Annika did—marry him, even—Max would never recover from this loss. His heart would be broken, the woman he loved gone.

Annika's heart quaked, shooting a tremor up her throat, and her voice fled for a moment.

But if she was going to do this, she would have to be strong.

"I'm Luzi Weiss," she finally said, praying for the strength to press on.

The man studied her appearance as if he didn't quite believe her. She had no photo to prove it, no certificate, but she did have . . .

She reached under her collar and slowly pulled out the Star of David necklace. "Max brought me here."

"You're not Luzi," the elder agent said, but the agent near the wall was distracted now, the lamp at his side.

She didn't refute the agent's words, but all of them were staring at her. As long as they were focused on her, Luzi would be safe.

She couldn't think beyond that.

The elder agent stepped forward and eyed the necklace. Then he ripped it off her neck. "You are stupid to tell us so."

Annika notched her chin up even as the fear swelled within her. "I'm proud of who I am."

"There's no pride in being a Jew." He turned to the man by the wall. "Take her."

Another agent ran into the room. "We found something in the yard."

The agent clenched Annika's arm, forcing her forward. She glanced back at the panel one last time before leaving the castle that she loved.

CHAPTER 38

The faint scent of the pale-pink peonies in my hand perfumes our walk to the cemetery. Ella holds my other hand as we follow her dad up stone steps, seventy of them total before we crest the hill.

Metal and wooden crosses mark dozens of small gardens in this cemetery, each person commemorated with a cross and a unique array of flowers on their grave. Life springs from this soil that buried those who've gone before us, beauty unfolding from the depths of sorrow.

It's a strange concept for Americans, but the residents of Hallstatt rent graves instead of purchasing them. When the ten-year lease expires, Josh told me, the grave is usually reoccupied, but someone—Max Dornbach, I assume—continued renting this grave almost eighty years after Luzi died.

Even if her body isn't here, I want to remember her life as well.

Josh glances over at me and then down at Ella's hand, secure in mine. In his eyes, I see something new, and I wonder if he would have taken my hand if Ella weren't clinging to it.

He stops first in front of a garden plot for Annika's mother, Kathrin Knopf. A woman who died five years before the war began. Tiny white flowers bloom across the garden plot as if the dirt has been glazed with snow. At the base of the wooden cross are two coral-colored asters towering over the kingdom of white, and a red candle hangs in a wrought-iron lantern over the grave, the glass sides blackened as if someone has burned a candle often in her memory.

Does Annika tend to this plot for her mother, or do her children help her?

Josh motions me ahead. He doesn't have to point out Luzia's grave on the next aisle. The carpet of white blossoms and twin coral asters are identical to Kathrin Knopf's.

Confused, I search the other plots nearby, but no other two are alike.

Does Annika tend both of these graves?

Kneeling beside the cross, I read the epitaph. And my eyes fill with tears.

Luzia Weiss
1921–1939
Greater love hath no man than this,
that a man lay down his life for his friends.

"You okay?" Josh asks me, his hand on my back.

"I will be."

"Come on, Ella," Josh says, reaching for his daughter's hand.

Ella squeezes my fingers, and they continue wandering down the aisle of garden plots without me. I know this is a gift he's offering me, an opportunity to process this by myself, but oddly enough I don't want him—them—to leave.

I place the bouquet of peonies near the base of the cross and step back. My own gift feels cheap somehow, this leaving of flowers bought from a florist instead of lovingly planting and tending flowers to grow as a legacy. But it's the only gift I have.

Tears escape from my eyes like they did yesterday, flooding my cheeks. It's so wrong what happened, this separation of families who longed for one another. Charlotte's mother, I assume, sent her child away to protect her like so many desperate parents did. The parents who realized, before it was too late, that letting go was the only way to save their children. The parents who lost their lives.

I reach up to wipe my tears but decide to let them flow like I did in Vienna.

"Grüss Gott," a voice says behind me.

I turn abruptly, not realizing that someone besides Josh and Ella is in the cemetery. It's an older gentleman dressed in a green folk jacket, matching trousers, and a red tie.

Beside him is an elderly woman stooped over slightly, one hand resting firmly on his arm while her other hand carries a tin watering can. Her gray hair is trimmed short, and turquoise-blue earrings dangle from her ears. She's wearing a yellow blouse and gray dress slacks with hiking shoes that just trekked up seventy steps. I can't see her eyes—they are covered with silver-rimmed sunglasses—but I admire her resolve.

For a moment, I feel as if I'm intruding on someone else's story, but then again, Charlotte has invited me into her life, her world. If Luzia is her mother, then I am here as an ambassador of sorts.

The woman stops beside the cross and takes off her sunglasses, her green eyes—the color of jade—studying me. Each wrinkle on her forehead, the tiny lines that spray out from her eyes, are like chapters, I think. She wears part of her story on her face, in a sense, both the hardship and the beauty. If I open the cover, I wonder what I'll find inside.

"Do you know of Luzia?" she asks, her English as good as mine.

This time I swipe the tears away. "Only a bit of her story, but I think I know someone who cared about her very much."

She pats the man's arm, a signal between them, and he moves away with the watering can. And I stand here beside this beautiful Austrian woman and wonder.

"Sigmund is my oldest son," she says, nodding as he fills up the can from the spigot on the chapel wall. "I call him my anchor."

"Are you typically adrift?" I ask.

She sighs. "Some days it feels that way."

"My name is Callie Randall."

She shakes my hand but doesn't offer her name. Josh and Ella have turned back toward us now, and she nods at them. When Ella waves, the woman waves back. "Is that your family?"

"He's a friend," I say, much too quickly. "A friend and his daughter."

"Ah," she replies. "It is good to have friends."

Numbers shuffle in my head, the places where lines from stories usually reside, as I try to calculate her age. "Are you related to Luzia?"

Her gaze falls to the grave. "She was a dear friend to me."

I hear pain from almost eighty years past, the loss still fresh today.

"She never should have died so young," I say.

When I look for Sigmund, I see that he's joined Josh and Ella at the other end of the cemetery. And I'm grateful for these extra moments.

"Do you tend both Luzia's grave and the one for Kathrin Knopf?"

Another flicker in her eyes, something I can't read. "Why do you ask?"

"We've been trying to contact a woman named Annika Stadler, Kathrin's daughter."

The woman hands me her trowel, and I clutch the metal handle, warmed by her glove. "Will you pull the weeds for me?"

And so I kneel and begin to extract the green intruders that have overtaken the white petals, the sunbaked dirt caking on my hands. I pull each weed slowly, and this act of purging feels more honoring than my offering of the peonies.

When I stand up, I hand the trowel back to her, and she nods her approval at my work. "Luzia would like knowing that you cared for her."

The church bells ring out, echoing across the cemetery and lake, keeping time for the people on this hill who still care about such things.

"A legacy, it's like a song, isn't it?" I say when the church bells fade. "The musicians may change, but we can keep it alive."

Her eyes fill with tears, and I apologize for upsetting her.

She waves away the apology. "Who is this person who still cares about Luzia?"

"Her name is Charlotte Trent," I say. "She's been like family to me."

"How does she know Luzia?" The tremble in her voice returns with the question.

My gaze falls to the white-petaled grave. "I believe Luzia might have been her mother."

Breath catches in the woman's throat, and a pale film glazes her eyes before they close. When she teeters forward, I catch her, and she leans into me like a rag doll, limp and worn from years of play.

Sigmund, the anchor, has noticed as well. When I glance over my shoulder, he's rushing toward me with Josh and Ella close behind.

"Mama," he whispers softly, holding her in his arms. And another word, fainter yet. Meant for her ear alone.

He calls her *Annika*.

CHAPTER 39

Luzi spent the night in the sliver of room behind the wall, sleep-ing in fitful stages. Twice she turned on the battery-powered lamp to check the time, but she never opened the panel to check on Annika or see who had come to the door.

By morning, her skin was slathered with sweat. The hiding space was warm, her body radiating heat, but more than that, it was the walls. In the darkness, they felt as if they were inching toward her. Black jaws ready to bite.

The third time she turned on the lamp, the clock read nine.

Baby pressed down against her bladder, and she would need to either leave this hiding place soon or maneuver her body over the chamber pot in this sticky, cramped space.

Leaning against the pillow, her mind wandered, back nearly a year ago when she'd been playing her violin at the Rathaus, entertaining the elite of Austria, dancing with Max around the polished floor. And now, in such a short time, everything had changed. At one time, she'd prided herself on being Luzia Weiss, daughter of the esteemed Dr. and Frau Weiss, but the Nazis had stripped the honor from that name. There was no honor or dignity left for her.

Baby kicked again, and if she didn't move quickly, she'd leave more than sweat on the floor.

She pulled on the panel, cracking it open. Then she heard pounding in the room. The angry voices of men.

Her heart hammering, Luzi sealed up the space in the wall again, praying they hadn't seen her. Her body began to tremble, and she curled up like a caterpillar, wishing again that she had wings. In the darkness, she could see the faces of these men, their brown shirts and badges, the black web etched of their arms. Every one of them looked like Ernst in her mind, wanting to hurt her and now her baby.

She heard them draw closer to her space, the echo of their pounding.

Tears fell onto her belly as she awaited her fate, praying for God's mercy. When they found her, she wanted to go in strength as her father had, without fear marking her face.

Minutes passed—an eternity—and then just as quickly as it had started, the pounding stopped.

Luzi pressed her ear against the wood, straining to hear—she must hear—but the sound eluded her.

One and two and three and . . .

Triple time.

Not the pounding in the room outside, but the beats of her heart. The aching in her emptied soul. The music still escaped her but the measures remained, the steady pace keeping her mind from finding relief in madness.

Another hour passed counting the beats, her bladder long since emptied on the wooden floor.

Sleeping relieved her temporarily from her fear. Then she awakened to more pounding. At first she thought it was the measures beating again in her head, but someone was knocking on the panel. Steady taps.

She pressed her ear to the wood, listened for the voices of men.

Someone knocked again, five times in a row.

The signal for her to slip safely back outside.

Still she didn't unlock the panel. She was safe in this locked shell, or at least as safe as she could be inside a wall. What if the men were trying to trick her? They could be waiting for her on the other side.

Five taps again, slow and deliberate. And then she heard someone call her name.

Luzi tentatively slid back the bolt that held the panel in place, peeking through the crack until she saw Hermann. Relief surged through his eyes, but there was no smile on his face. She crawled out quickly, embarrassed at the stench.

She pushed her wet hair back, and he helped her stand. Her legs wobbled from the cramping in her muscles, but she was no longer focused on herself. The library around her—books scattered across the floor, lamps lying on their sides, one of the windows broken. It looked like her apartment in Vienna, the night they took her father away.

Her eyes wide, she turned to Hermann. "What happened?"

"The Gestapo came."

"They were looking for me," she whispered.

He nodded slowly.

"But they didn't find my hiding place." She stepped forward. "Annika?"

When no one answered, she called Annika's name again.

"Luzi—"

She pushed around Hermann and ran into the foyer, panic rising inside her chest. "Annika!"

Hermann followed her, but he didn't yell for Annika. Instead he collapsed on the front staircase, his head buried deep in the grave of his hands. The entire weight of the Alps seemed to press down on his shoulders, and she feared knowing the reason. She didn't think she could bear to lose someone else. "Where's Annika?" she demanded.

"The Gestapo. They took her away."

Luzi felt as if she might collapse on the floor. "Why would they take her?"

"She claimed to be you."

His words washed over her, slowly at first. Then they nailed themselves to her heart, one at a time.

"Why—?" But she didn't have to ask; she knew why Annika would do this.

Greater love had no man or woman.

Greater love had Annika for her and . . .

Her heart seemed to cave in. She had known Annika loved Max, had seen it clearly in her eyes when Max brought Luzi to her. Max was oblivious, but women—they knew these things.

Still Annika had done the unthinkable for her.

In that moment, Luzi knew that she could never marry Max Dornbach. He belonged with Annika.

"We must stop them," Luzi said.

Hermann shook his head. "They will arrest you, too."

"It doesn't matter anymore."

"It should matter." He looked back up at her. "They will punish her even more severely for hiding you."

"Then you must go." She glanced toward the window. "Or Max."

"We will do everything we can." But any strength left in his voice broke.

She shivered. "What will they do to her?"

"Take her, I fear, to one of their work camps."

She crumpled onto the tile floor, wishing she could crawl back into her hiding place, make it all go away. Wishing she could open the panel one more time and see Annika on the other side.

"I must do something," she said.

"Come home with me, for the sake of your child." Hermann reached for her hand. "It's no longer safe for either of you here."

"It's no longer safe for us anywhere."

* * *

"I told you to wait for me," Ernst yelled into the telephone.

The line buzzed back at him, an awful, whining sound.

"Why must we wait?" the man on the other line finally replied, sounding bored. The tone infuriated Ernst.

"Because I wanted to interrogate the girl."

"She had nothing to tell us."

"You, perhaps, but she had plenty to tell me." He wrapped his fingers around the glass ball of his paperweight and squeezed it. These idiots had sent Luzi away even though he'd never once told them to send her to a camp. She was supposed to be collateral to draw Max out of his hiding place.

"Our commander put her on a train."

"My commander said she was supposed to stay!"

"Then he should have communicated that to Salzburg."

He'd overstepped his bounds, perhaps a meter or two, and as he paced in front of the desk, the phone cord scraping the edge of the wood, Ernst decided to change tactics.

"What else did you find?"

"Nothing of significance."

"Nothing at all?"

"If you are referring to the jewelry and other valuables, there's nothing of worth in that castle."

If it wasn't in the house, it must be nearby. He only needed to retrieve it, and then he would find Max and send him off to a camp like Luzi.

Ernst no longer cared what his commander said. He'd been patient long enough, sending photographs and memos to Salzburg that were promptly ignored. Major Rosch would show his gratitude once Ernst returned with something to line both their pockets.

Early the next morning, Ernst left Vienna via train and traveled almost four hours to the desolate Obertraun *Bahnhof.* No automobiles or even a bicycle were available for hire, so he hiked through the forest until he located the gates of Max's summer estate and walked right through them.

One day he'd own a castle much like this one . . . or perhaps this estate would be his home. He would marry someone much more prominent, more beautiful, than Luzi Weiss. An Aryan, of course, with the purest of blood to make Hitler himself proud. Someone who would show Ernst the honor and respect that he deserved.

Luzi deserved whatever the work camps gave to her.

He searched for a day but found nothing from Max and Dr. Weiss's cache. The Gestapo, it seemed, had emptied the house of anything that would be of value, and they'd dug up a plot of land near the chapel. Perhaps they'd found things there and kept them.

Or perhaps Max was smarter than he imagined and stole the treasure himself.

His return ticket to Vienna was tonight, 22:00 *Uhr*. On the trip home, Ernst concocted and schemed and determined his course forward. Max, he knew, would return eventually to Schloss Schwansee. Ernst could wait for weeks, even months, if he must. He would travel to the castle again and again until he found Max Dornbach and his treasure.

His plans had solidified into stone by the time the train reopened its doors under the iron awning in the Wien Westbahnhof. But when he returned to Hotel Metropole the next morning, his commander wasn't pleased that he had traveled to the lakes without permission.

If he wanted water, Major Rosch said, he could have the entire North Sea. Then he reassigned Ernst to an office in Hamburg, a thousand kilometers north of Hallstättersee.

CHAPTER 40

Hours passed as she sat in the library recliner, staring at the instrument handcrafted from black willow by Karl Lang, a master violin maker from Salzburg. She'd had Sigmund remove it from the dressing room and place it on the upholstered window seat. Then he slipped away to let her rest.

Sleep wouldn't come, though. Not that she wanted it to.

She twisted the ivory chiffon of a handkerchief between fingers that grew stiffer each day as she eyed the violin. Decades ago, when this violin showed up at their door, it had terrified her. Someone knew her secret, and this gift . . . at the time it felt more like a threat than a present, but over the years she'd wondered if it was actually a gift, from the man who had saved her life.

The music had begun returning to her mind in small pieces after Sigmund was born, the notes on her music sheets dancing like ballerinas in her head. God had used that child to breathe life back into her as well. Still she hadn't touched this violin or any other, though every week she attended a concert—outside at Mirabell Gardens, inside the gilded Stiftung Mozarteum, it didn't matter.

She lived in Salzburg now, had for decades. While she came each week to tend the garden plots, she hadn't been inside this castle in more than fifty years.

Hermann's mother had gently cared for her back in 1939, and then she and Hermann had married, a month before Sigmund was born. The pastor in Hallstatt had been quite willing to certify them after Hermann shared a glimpse of their story.

When the war began, the Nazis asked—no, they commanded— the caretaker's daughter and her husband to oversee the estate and their new camp since the caretaker seemed to be missing. She and Hermann built a new cottage by the castle, and he tended the land while she cleaned the house and prepared meals for boys forced to grow up too soon.

Her little family stayed here after the war, having no place else to go in their divided country, a new Austria parceled out for occupation by the United States, France, England, and the Soviet Union. The entire country gained independence again in 1955, more than a decade after the war, but she and Hermann didn't leave the estate until 1962, after Hermann was offered a position in agricultural sciences at the newly reestablished University of Salzburg.

They'd locked the front door and handed the keys over to Sigmund, the year he'd turned twenty-three. Thirty years later, Sigmund gave the keys to his son.

She and Hermann eventually parented four children—three

sons and a daughter—and then added a *grand* to their parenting title for a total of six grandchildren along with an astonishing number of great-grandchildren and seven great-great-grandchildren in recent years, though one *great* was plenty for her. None of her tribe understood why she didn't want to visit this place. All they saw was the beauty and mystique of the mountains and lake, while she . . . All she saw were the ghosts.

For almost eighty years she'd faithfully paid rent for the graves above the lake, and no one had ever asked about Luzia or her story. Most Austrians were too afraid to talk about those lost years between 1938 and 1945, veiling them behind the black drapery of time. The power and strength of the Nazis clouded many a vision during that era, and a whole generation wished they'd made other choices.

But admitting the wrongness took a heart humbled, crippled even, and many in this land, her included, chose a crutch instead of gambling between heartache and healing.

So many times over the years, she wished that she could go back and stop the Gestapo before they took Annika away. Not that she regretted the life Annika had given her, not for one moment; it just wasn't hers to live.

She closed her eyes, remembering again the dance so long ago that she never should have danced. She should have run from Max, like she ran from Ernst in the park. If so, perhaps the woman who had truly loved him would be alive.

It was much too late to change anything from the past now, but that woman—Callie, she'd said—she knew Luzia's name.

What else did she know?

Her body may fail her, but her memory was still as sharp as one of the bevels used to carve a violin. She remembered most everything, including that conversation yesterday, but before her body gave way—or at least, that's how Sigmund described her spell—she couldn't remember if Callie told her where she'd heard about Luzia.

And she desperately needed to remember.

Her hand slipped instinctively down to her leg, tracing the faint scar that no one else could see. Some things she needed to remember, and others she'd spent a lifetime wishing she could forget.

The strains of an orchestra stole into the library. Strauss and his "Village Swallows from Austria"—the waltz that she and Max had danced. She glanced around, thinking perhaps her mind was failing her after all, but she realized that Sigmund must be playing music in another room.

And the melody of Strauss strengthened her.

Her son had vague memories of the youth camp that had taken over the estate, but he didn't remember the evil that ran rampant here before or during the war. He knew all about National Socialism, of course, but knowing was much different than experiencing. She'd prayed for his entire life that the only evil he and his siblings would ever have to fight was that which tried to infiltrate from the inside. And she'd prayed that each of them would fight with all their might.

There was much to lose in telling her story now, and yet . . . perhaps something to gain as well. Hermann had been gone for fourteen years, and she'd read in the papers that Ernst Schmid had died in Berlin a decade after the war, no children surviving him. He was one of many Nazis who'd never gone to trial, cloaking himself as a victim of the past regime.

Only Hermann knew what Ernst had done to her; she'd told

him when he proposed marriage long ago, and he had kept her secret, raising Sigmund as his son. He'd also helped her search for Marta.

She dropped the handkerchief into her lap, remembering the baby she'd held to her chest as they traversed the Vienna streets, kissing her cheeks before she transferred her into Klara Dornbach's care.

Sometimes her arms ached for the violin, but they ached even more for her sister.

After the war and then the years of zoned occupation, she and Hermann had traveled to Paris, searching for Klara and Marta in the ruins of war, but they never found either of them. Her sweet sister, she feared, had suffered as Annika had, while Luzia bore only a single scar on her leg.

Her family was all gone, exterminated by evil, and the guilt of it almost crushed her. But God had kept her on this earth for another season. And with Hermann's help, she decided that she would honor her parents and sister by living, that she would continue Annika's legacy by serving God and her husband and children.

And Max Dornbach—she didn't know what happened to him. Near the end of his life, Hermann told her that he'd sent Max away before they married, afraid that the man's impulsiveness would betray them. He had other motives besides his fear—Luzi knew that—but he had protected her for a lifetime, harbored the secret about her and her child.

She'd prayed for years that God had kept Max on this earth for another season as well.

Sigmund stepped back into the room, his cell phone in hand. He'd turn seventy-nine in August, and unlike his biological father, he had grown into a man of character, a man who wanted to protect those in his care like the father who'd stepped in to raise him. He'd become a doctor, like his grandfather, but he always called a female colleague when it came to his mother's medical care.

"Liselotte just called," he said, sitting on the arm of the chair beside her.

"Did she say that I'm done?"

"She said your body is in perfect working order. The fainting was a fluke."

"My body is far from perfect order."

"You're made of steel, Mama."

She reached out, took his hand. "I want you to call Callie and her friend."

He studied her for a moment. "Jonas said they came to the house on Saturday. They were searching for treasure."

"I don't know about their treasure; please tell them that."

"Of course."

"But I want to apologize for my . . . unusual departure."

"An apology isn't necessary."

"They can come for brunch tomorrow," she said, her mind made up. "But first . . ."

"What is it?"

"Before they come, I have a story to tell you."

CHAPTER 41

We find a shallow cove to the north of Hallstatt, pedaling our rental boat to the place our innkeeper recommended we swim. A stream runs into the lake here, icy water pouring down from the mountains, smoothing out the bed of rocks for a respite in the summer's heat.

I dip my toes into the creek and then recline on the backseat of the pedal boat, the fractured rays of sun trickling down through the leaves as Ella and Josh splash in the water. Birds sing in the forest, and as Ella and Josh wander upstream, jumping from stone to stone, I enjoy the rise and fall of the birdsong, a gentle current like the one that rocks the boat.

I miss my family, but something about this place breathes a gentle contentment inside of me. Peace. I don't miss being home, not like I thought I would. Perhaps it's because of Ella and her dad. I'm away and yet I've found a bit of home here with the two of them.

After our visit to the cemetery yesterday, Josh helped Sigmund Stadler carry his mother down the steps and to the office of a doctor in Hallstatt. Sigmund texted Josh last night to say his mother was awake again, but we haven't heard anything else. So we wait and I worry about this elderly woman who climbed all those steps to care for the graves of her mother and the woman she called a friend.

Dozens of questions continue whirling through my head as I rest in the warmth this afternoon. I want to ask Annika about the listings in her book, about the photograph of Max, about what has happened in these decades since the war. And most of all, I want to ask her about Luzia Weiss.

The story from her *Bambi* book flutters into my mind, the journey of a deer who longed to be with others and yet learned as a young fawn that to survive, he must live in fear. And that he must spend most of his time alone so no one would hurt him, including Faline.

What a sad life, I'm starting to think, to live alone because you're afraid.

Because I'm afraid.

I want to enjoy the stories of others, but I don't want to live solely in their pages any longer. I want to embrace my future, my own story, without fear.

Last night after Josh and Ella settled into their room, I wrote the last paragraphs of my blog about Felix Salten. It seemed fitting to finish the post here in the country he once loved, eighty years after he ran away.

Abstand is a German term that means building an intentional space between an individual and the world around him. In order to protect his life, Felix Salten had to lay a brick wall between himself and the country he loved. He never returned to Austria. Like the roe deer he created on paper, Salten spent his final years roaming until his death on October 8, 1945, months after the Soviet Army liberated Vienna from the Nazis.

Perhaps Salten described his journey best in one of his last books—*Bambi's Children*:

One-Eye spoke in his oiliest tones. "You're very famous, now. The whole forest speaks of you as though you were already a legend. I should be honored that you speak to me at all."

"If it's an honor," Bambi told him, "it's very unwillingly bestowed. What I did, I did because I had to."

"It was heroic of you," said One-Eye with sly flattery.

Bambi shook his head. "Is it heroic to do what necessity demands?" He wheeled and disappeared.

Necessity demanded that Salten disappear from Austria, but he left behind a treasure trove of stories for children and their parents to remember what might be lost today if we don't stand against the evil in our midst.

I reach for my phone and snap a selfie. Me, Calisandra Randall, relaxing in a pedal boat. I text it to Brie, knowing she might go into shock when she sees it.

Ella squeals on my right. Josh has lifted her up, cradling her under her arms as her legs dangle in the water, swinging her from side to side. This is what fathers are supposed to do, I think. Make their children laugh, secure in their arms.

The jet lag weighs down my eyes, and I doze before being awakened by someone pouring cold water over my feet. Ella—laughing as she scoops up the water in her hands, reviving me.

When I look over at Josh, he shrugs. "I couldn't stop her."

"Because she's bigger than you?"

"Her willpower is certainly stronger."

Ella grabs a stick and throws it into the water, watching the current steal it.

"Go away," I murmur to Josh, closing my eyes again.

"Oh no," he says, climbing into one of the bucket seats up front. "No more sleeping, or you'll be up all night."

And it occurs to me that I was sleeping, soundly, on a plastic bench seat, surrounded by noise. The time difference has me a bit upside down, but upside down never improved my sleep before. Josh and Ella—they aren't wearing me out like most people do. Instead, I am utterly content when I'm with them.

For this brief moment, a chapter in the greater story, I feel as if I'm part of their little family.

"I'm used to staying up all night," I say.

Josh stretches out on the front seat, extending his long legs and water sandals to the opposite side of the boat. "Mind if I join you?"

I push up to my elbows. "Are you giving me a choice?"

"Not really." He pulls his ball cap over his eyes and sunglasses.

"If I don't get to sleep, then neither do you."

"I'm just resting my eyes." He doesn't rest them for long, though. I watch him open the storage compartment between the seats and check his phone.

"Nothing yet?"

"No. I keep hoping Sigmund will call with another update."

"I didn't mean to scare her."

"I can only imagine she's spent a lifetime being afraid."

It's a common bond between us, this fear.

"After the war," he says, "about twelve thousand Nazis were detained near here at a place called Camp Orr. They created a group called the Spider to resurrect the Austrian Nazi Party and annex Austria back into Germany."

I shiver at this thought. "Thank God they didn't succeed."

"Many people here thought the Nazis would take over their country again one day. After what they lived through, it must have been a terrifying thought."

"The fear didn't go away," I say. "Perhaps it never went away for Annika."

Josh glances toward Ella; she is quite content now building a fortress with stones and leaves on the riverbank. "'He will wipe every tear from their eyes, and there will be no more death or sorrow or crying or pain. All these things are gone forever.'"

I peek up over his shoulder to see if he's reading the verse from his phone, but the phone's no longer in his hand. "You've memorized it?"

"I clung to it for years."

When I close my eyes again, it's not to sleep. It's a wall of sorts, blocking him out, and yet I see the picture of his wife in my mind, the photograph he had hanging in his office. I can't imagine how hard it must have been for him to watch her suffer and not to be able to take away her pain.

"How did you do that?" I ask, opening my eyes slowly.

He turns toward me now, propping his feet up on the bucket seat. "What?"

"How did you let Grace go?"

"She'll never be completely gone, not from my heart at least, but she's with her Father now, and I know . . ." His voice cracks, confidence melting in his love. "I know that He's taking good care of her."

God as a father is not the picture that I want to see. At least not as my father. But a father like Josh . . . I can see God in him. In men like Ethan and others at church who care well for their children.

"I'm sorry that your dad didn't love you like he should have, Callie."

"No apology necessary."

"That's not how God meant for it to be."

I rub away the knot trying to worm its way into my left shoulder. "It seems that so much in our world is not what God meant for it to be."

"I think we can cling to the goodness we see in the world. To the beauty in these lakes and the laughter of those kids who come every Saturday to hear your stories."

Goodness, the heart and soul of a father. I like that picture, knowing God's character isn't reflected in every dad of this world.

Ella throws a stone into the stream and giggles when it hits the water.

"Does she remind you of your wife?" I ask quietly so Ella doesn't hear.

"In her laughter and her grand outpouring of love, but Ella is branching out with graceful new limbs of her own. She seems unbreakable, but I'm afraid I'll say something to hurt her. . . ."

"What would Grace have told you?"

He thinks for a moment. "To be gentle."

"Gentle and strong," I say.

When he smiles at me, a strange feeling creeps into my heart. A tectonic shift. Josh and I—I think we might make a good team.

"I'm hungry," Ella calls from the bank.

Josh is still smiling when he offers me his hand. "Should we break out the sandwiches?"

He helps me climb over the edge of the boat, and we sit on a log by the shore. Leaves rustle around us, and someone paddles a canoe around our boat, heading upstream. When Josh's phone rings, he pulls it out of his pocket and wanders toward the trees, just far enough away that we can't hear the conversation while Ella and I unwrap the brown paper from our sandwiches and begin eating the turkey and cheddar cheese on sourdough bread.

"I like it here." Ella wipes mustard off her face with the back of her hand.

"Me too."

"My mom wouldn't let Dad dive in this lake."

"Did he tell you that?"

She shrugs. "I hear things."

"I bet you have amazing ears."

She tugs on one of her earlobes. "Like a moth."

"I didn't know moths had such good hearing."

Josh puts one leg over the log as he joins us. "Did you hear what I just said?"

Ella scrunches up her nose. "I wasn't listening to you."

He looks at me. "That was Sigmund."

"Is Annika okay?"

He nods. "The doctor said her body is in good working order, though apparently Annika said that no ninety-seven-year-old's body works all that well."

I smile. "It sounds like she is better."

"Sigmund asked us to come to the castle for brunch tomorrow. His mother would like to hear your story and share a bit of hers, though she doesn't want to talk about lost treasure from the war."

"That puts a damper on your search."

"On *our* search," he says. "But I want to learn about Luzia too."

Ella balls up the brown paper that was wrapped around her sandwich. "C'mon, Dad!" she says, tugging on his hand.

When he stands up, she rushes into the water again, but before he follows her, he offers his hand to me as well. "Come play with us."

I hesitate, looking down at his offering, a palm spread open. I could sit here and mull over my thoughts alone, or I could join them in their laughter.

"Please, Callie."

Ella hops back up to the shore. "Team Nemeth!" she exclaims, a smile lighting her face.

"Team Nemeth," I say before taking Josh's hand.

The three of us splash and laugh, throw twigs and rocks. And as we play, the world seems to right itself again.

When Josh knocks on the castle door, the muscles in my neck fold and ripple down my body. I'm not entirely sure why I'm shaking—we are invited guests this time.

Ella is chattering beside me about glass castles and fairy tales, and I think about what Annika must have been like when she was seven and then a few years after, living on this estate when the Nazis marched into her country. I can't imagine all that she must have seen.

I've dreamed about Annika Knopf this past month, wondered about her story. Though I pray Annika is innocent of any crime, perhaps she is ashamed to tell us what happened when she was younger, if she stole items from her Jewish neighbors. But even if she won't talk about the treasure, I hope she'll tell us how her path intersects with Luzia's journey.

Sigmund answers the door and welcomes us into the house that is now his son's summer home. As we walk through the grand hall, tiled with marble the color of cream, he assures us that his own home in Salzburg is quite modest, as if he's ashamed of the grandeur here.

"Would you like some lemonade?" he asks Ella.

"Yes, please."

"There's a playground out back, where two of my great-grandchildren are currently swinging." He turns to Josh. "May she play with them?"

Josh hesitates, and I understand. He won't always be able to cushion her, but for now, he must.

"Is there a place we could sit outside and talk?" I ask.

"Of course." Sigmund waves us farther into the house. "We have a veranda, and my mother would love nothing more than to enjoy the lake from there while you talk."

Josh tells Ella that she can join the other children.

We follow Sigmund through the foyer, around a white-painted staircase that winds up to the second floor, and past two closed doors. The third one is open, Annika waiting for us inside.

Her chair is backed up against the dark paneling that rounds the library. Sigmund cradles his mother's arm as she stands to greet us and then escorts her outside through French doors.

I clutch my handbag, folded under my arm, as we follow them.

Inside my purse is *Bambi* with Annika's list, the photograph of Max and Luzia, and the photocopy from Charlotte's magic balloon book.

Sigmund helps his mother sit on one of the cushioned patio chairs clustered around a glass table, though it seems to me that she doesn't need much help at all.

"How long did you live here?" I ask Annika as we join her at the table.

"My husband and I cared for this place for more than twenty years. Hermann injured his arm before the war began, which was an unexpected blessing in that he couldn't fight in the Wehrmacht, but the Nazis wouldn't let him—wouldn't let us—remain on his family's farm. Because my father had been the caretaker on this estate, they assigned us the role of caring for this property while it was a camp."

She says the words as if she's rehearsed them many times, as if they've been embroidered into her core for years, frayed and worn.

"Why were you looking for me?" she asks.

I glance at Josh before pulling *Bambi* out of my handbag and scooting it across the table. "It started with this."

I'd expected some sort of emotional reaction. Tears. Laughter. A gasp of surprise or even shock. I may never know if Annika found the items recorded inside these pages—or what, if anything, she did with them—but I'd expected something to commemorate the reunion of a long-lost book with its owner.

Instead, she just stares at it, and I'm disappointed, I admit. Even without the potential of finding treasure, I'd hoped it would be a homecoming, of sorts, this gift from her mother long ago, traveling around the world before it returned here.

Annika's mind seems sharp, but perhaps she's forgotten this season of her life. Or blocked it out.

I open the book and show her the first listing. Annika rubs her hand across the corner of the paper as if it's some sort of talisman to help her remember. "She knew . . ."

Sigmund leans over the book, scanning the line with her.

"What did she know?" Josh asks.

Annika looks up at him before turning to me. "How did you find this book?"

"It seemed to find me," I tell her. "The children of a man named Max Dornbach sold it in an estate sale, and my sister purchased it for me."

Recognition glints in her eyes, followed by a flood of fear. I want to reassure her, not cause any more pain. I show her the inscription at the beginning of the book and then skip ahead to the newspaper clipping of Max.

"I think the book was trying to find its way home," I say.

"Max is gone?"

I nod. "He died three years ago."

Annika traces the edge of the torn clipping. "I never knew if he survived the war."

And so I tell her what I know about his home in Idaho, about his clinic for animals and the daughter who adored him as much as Sigmund clearly adores his mom. As I tell her these things, a tear slips down her cheek.

"My uncle met you, after the war," Josh says, trying not to cross over the established no-treasure-talk line. "He and his men were searching for items that the Nazis dumped in the lake. We thought you might have been writing down some of these items in your book."

"Neither Hermann nor I wanted the Allied soldiers to search the estate," Annika says, her fingers still on the edge of the book. "The Nazis did dump things in our lake, but I don't know where they hid any treasure. People have searched for generations and have found nothing hidden on the estate except bones in a pet cemetery."

Josh sits back in his chair, his gaze focused on his daughter leaning back in her swing as if her toes might really touch the sky. "What were you recording?"

"I never wrote in this book."

I glance over at Josh, wishing I could decipher his eyes. Is Annika lying to us, or did someone else use her book to record stolen items?

From my handbag, I take out the full newspaper clip of Max and Luzia dancing and slide it across the table. She stares down at the couple from so long ago, wiping away her tears. "So you know of Luzia Weiss through the newspaper piece?"

I shake my head. "I've known about Luzia for most of my life."

"But how?"

I retrieve the photocopy of Luzia's name inside the Hatschi Bratschi story. "From another children's book."

This time Annika's eyes grow wide. Instead of touching the photocopy, her body lists to the left. I reach for her shoulder, ready to catch her in case she tumbles again, but she doesn't faint this time.

Slowly she reaches out and takes this paper, clutching it to her chest. The way she curls over it reminds me of Charlotte.

"Where did you find this?" she demands.

"I'm not certain," I say slowly, "but I think the book was with Luzia's daughter."

"Her daughter?"

"During the war, someone took my friend—Charlotte—to an orphanage near Lyon, France. Her paperwork was lost, but this remained."

"Marta," she whispers.

I glance over at Sigmund, but he is focused on his mother. "Would you like to rest?" he asks.

"No," she insists. "I must find out."

I lean toward her. "How did you know Charlotte's mother?"

She reaches across the table and takes my hand. I see more tears building in her eyes before they spill over and flood her cheeks.

"Luzia wasn't your friend's mother." We all wait quietly for her to continue. "I believe Charlotte was Marta—Luzia's sister. Our mother—she died during the war."

"Your mother?"

She looks back at the lake as she releases my hand. "I wasn't born with the name Annika Knopf."

Sigmund's face doesn't change. Whatever she has to say, it seems he already knows.

His mother lowers the paper to her lap. "Once upon a time, many years ago, my name was Luzia Weiss."

Now Josh reaches for my hand. If she is Luzia, then—

"What happened to Annika?" I ask.

CHAPTER 42

Her face pressed against a pollen-cloaked window as the milk-run train snaked through farmlands and forest, pressing north and then west toward the setting sun. She'd longed to travel far away by train, but not now—now she just wanted to return home.

The lake, the cold mountain water, it was waiting to wash the dirt and pollen from her sweltering skin. To swim with Sarah and Max and Hermann like they'd done when they were children.

And her mother—oh, how she'd loved singing and laughing with the woman who'd given her birth and then filled her heart with joy, the two of them carefree like the birds in the trees. Like they could fly all the way up to hide among the stars.

This train didn't stop for milk—it was much too late in the day for that—but it stopped for more women, young and old, packing them into the crowded cars. They clung to each other, these women, holding hands, their tears blending together on shoulders and cheeks. Nameless, each one of them, in the minds of their captors, yet deeply loved by the ladies surrounding them.

The seat beside Annika was still open—the other women chose to huddle on the floor or cram together with their loved ones on plastic seats meant to hold two.

Alone in a crowd—it was a terrible, miserable place to be. She longed for someone to help ease the loneliness in her heart too.

But almost everyone she loved was back in the wilderness of lakes, hidden away so they wouldn't be pressed into a train, transported into the unknown. And Max—was he searching for the treasure, thinking she had taken it like the necklace?

Hermann, she prayed, would tell him the truth.

"Schweigen!" the guard up front commanded, and the car quieted.

If only he would tell them where this train was going, but he only spoke—barked, really—when the aching sounds of grief overpowered the shuddering noise from this metal box around them.

The car would remain quiet until they stopped at another forlorn station for passengers who didn't want to board. Then the crying would resume.

Annika had done nothing wrong, and neither had any of these women around her. Their only real crime was the breath that passed in and out of their lungs. This breath, the one thing the Nazis had yet to take from them.

"There is Another who is over us all, over us and over Him."

That's what Bambi had said: that Someone was greater than the Man with the gun who hunted him and his friends. He never said who, but Annika knew.

Jesus—the Son of the God she'd met in her mother's Bible, the man who conquered death—He was stronger than the guard at the front of this car, than the agents who had interrogated her back in Salzburg, than whatever awaited her when this train stopped for the last time.

He had died for her and the hatred she'd harbored for her father, for her envy of the Dornbach family, for taking the necklace out of Frau Dornbach's shoe box, for bringing Hitler's wrath on their beautiful castle.

Darkness fell over the car like a shroud, steel wheels rumbling beneath her feet, and when she closed her eyes, she could almost hear the sound of Max's shovel pressing into the ground, helping Luzi's family and others to hide the things they valued, not knowing that their things were worth more now than their lives.

Where was Luzi?

Annika had been gone for days, a week maybe. Max would find Luzi, she prayed, in that hiding place. They would care for their baby together, and one day, he would care for the animals that he loved as well.

"But as for me I know that my Redeemer liveth, And at last he will stand up upon the earth: And after my skin, even this body, is destroyed, Then without my flesh shall I see God. . . ."

Her eyes closed, Annika could see Max burying one of his charges, could hear the solemn words from his lips. And this time, no laughter escaped from hers.

God—her Redeemer—He lived. And one day she would see Him. Perhaps one day soon.

MELANIE DOBSON

A promise threaded those words, a hope that He would conquer evil. That she would be with Him. She was lonely, but this time when she thought about death, she wasn't as afraid.

The Nazis might try to take away this whisper of hope, like they wanted to steal the jewels, but she could cling to it deep inside her, in a paneled place where they could never find it—the hidden spaces of her heart.

The squealing of train brakes, the gasp of steam. As the train slowed, Annika looked out at a lamppost spreading a muddied light over one woman—an elderly lady in a housedress—and an armed agent. The guard opened the door, and the woman boarded.

The train pressed forward again, and Annika had closed her eyes, trying to sleep, when she felt someone sit in the seat next to hers.

"You're not alone," the woman whispered.

Annika turned, wide-eyed, and saw the trace of a gentle smile cross the woman's face. She was older than Annika's mother, but in the dull light, Annika saw peace in her eyes, like she'd seen in her mother's before she died.

Annika reached for the woman's hand. Her fingers curled into her palm as if she were plagued by arthritis, but she didn't recoil from Annika's touch.

A train ride bound to nowhere, but peace flooded through Annika's heart as well, sweeping away the last strands of fear.

Neither she nor this dear woman next to her was alone.

CHAPTER 43

"Reader, nothing is sweeter in this sad world than the sound of someone you love calling your name."

Words, oh so true, of Kate DiCamillo in her story about goodness and forgiveness, about broken hearts and the fight against evil. The tale of a courageous mouse called Despereaux.

We pack so much into the confines of a name, the padded walls sheltering character and faith, work and family, history and home. Yet a name can be boundless as well, rich in legacy and fierce with love.

The moment Charlotte says Luzia's name, everything shifts. It doesn't matter that an ocean separates these sisters or that they are staring at screens—Sigmund's laptop in the castle library and Brie's cell phone in Ohio. What matters is that they found each other.

Introductions are short between them, unnecessary really.

Light breathes into the darkness of their stories, shadows fading away, and then the thread of truth begins weaving their lives back together, one strand at a time.

Josh and I slip out onto the patio as they remember together.

Ella waves, quite content playing with Sigmund's "greats" again—kicking around a soccer ball near a guest cottage. Josh and I move down to the bank, a sliver of tall grass and rocks between the water and pine trees.

The journey of these sisters, the story of one life stolen too early while another lived in her place—it's all too much for me to process at once. Luzia told us about the man in Vienna who hurt her, about Max's heroic attempts to save her life, and about that morning forever etched in her mind—April 9, 1939. The day the Gestapo took Annika away.

"Do you think Luzia loved Max?" I ask, the question in my mind spilling out to the man next to me.

"Perhaps," Josh says. "One's first love is hard to lose."

I think of the tears in Luzia's eyes as she told us about Hermann. "Second love is hard to lose too," I say. "She and Hermann were married for sixty-five years."

Josh reaches for my hand, and my fingers seem to melt into his. Even with Scott, I felt on edge at times, like he was expecting something of me and I wasn't certain what to give, but I feel content here beside Josh. Like I can trust him with the pieces of my heart.

I told Josh about Scott late last night, while Ella slept, and he empathized deeply with my loss, different from his and yet we both have had to grieve losing someone we loved. And we've both had to battle our fears.

We sit on an old wooden bench near the shore, a branch dangling over us. "I wonder if Charlotte and I would have found Luzia years ago, if she kept her name."

"Ernst Schmid would have found her long before you did."

I shift my legs. "An impossible time." Each of them—Luzia and Annika, Hermann and Max—they fought evil the best way they could.

The pattern of sky is changing as white layers itself upon the blue, and a breeze stirs up the water in front of us, the lake layered with its own secrets.

"Will you keep diving?" I ask.

"Perhaps."

"I'm sorry you didn't find the treasure."

"We found something more important," he says. "And, I hope, a second chance."

"For Luzia and Charlotte?" I ask quietly.

"Yes." When he turns to me, the fierceness in his eyes matches the storm building overhead. "And perhaps a second chance for both of us, too."

I like the thought of that—no pressure, just the possibilities.

"What happened to that German wall built firmly around you?" I ask.

"You're breaking it down, Callie."

Just like he's been breaking down the wall I built around my heart. "Sometimes, I suppose, we have to give up that distance to welcome others into our lives."

He releases my hand and props his arm across the back of the bench. I settle into that space of strength between his arm and chest. A protected place like the depths of this lake before us.

My gaze, in the rest of contentment, falls across this strand of water to the hillside where the grave stands to honor Annika's life, though the name on it, Luzia, is the one Annika took as hers long ago, Luzi and Annika's secrets hidden away.

"And above all, watch with glittering eyes the whole world around you because the greatest secrets are always hidden in the most unlikely places."

These words from the bizarre story about a girl named Matilda who loved books, written by Roald Dahl—a man whose imagination seemed unfettered by any chains.

And then I think of another strange story—this one about the salt administrator and his casket that used to travel across these waters every fifty years to visit his home, the last time in 1939 before the war began.

The number does the strangest thing in my mind. It blurs out and then refocuses like the autorefractor at my optometrist's, crystal clear the second time. According to Luzi, the Gestapo took Annika away in the spring of 1939 as well.

"What if—?" I start, struggling for words so that this man I've grown to admire doesn't think I'm completely crazy. Then again, his willingness to think outside the proverbial box, like Annika once did, has brought us to this place. "What if you can still return the treasure to its owners?"

"I don't think this lake is ever going to relent."

I take a deep breath, calming the craziness. "What if the treasure isn't in the lake?"

He glances behind us at an estate that would have been thoroughly searched by the Gestapo and the teenage boys who resided here under the Nazi regime. "Where else would it be?"

I tell him my idea, and he pulls out his phone to dial a contact in Vienna.

And I realize he doesn't think I'm crazy at all.

CHAPTER 44

More than a decade after the war, when the Russian soldiers along with the Americans, British, and French finally left Austria, Max returned to Lake Hallstatt.

The newly reunited government of Austria was trying to return property to any Jewish owners left to claim it, but he had no desire to keep the estate that had been used by the Nazis. The place where the Gestapo had stolen Luzi away.

And the treasure that he'd taken such great care to hide with Hermann and Annika—it seemed there was no one left to claim that either.

The front gate into Schloss Schwansee was locked, but he

found the collapsed portion of the wall that he'd climbed over often before the war, between the forest and the sheer cliff at the foot of Sarstein.

He hadn't thought he would ever come back here, not after that night in 1939 when he'd crept down and found both his home and his heart in ruins. When he discovered the house ransacked, Annika and Luzi gone, he'd snuck over to Hermann's house in the dark. His friend told him the news that haunted him for the past fifteen years. The Gestapo had found Luzi, hiding in the wall, and they'd taken her away to a place where he could no longer protect her. A place of no return.

He'd sobbed then, like a wounded animal, and the thought of Luzi, suffering at their hands, still flooded his eyes with tears. For days he hadn't been able to eat. And he'd wished he were dead, begged God for the ultimate mercy of taking his life.

God's mercy proved to be different from his own.

Over his shoulder this morning was a rucksack, one that he'd purchased in America, and inside was all the paperwork for the estate. He was transferring this place to Annika. Frau Stadler now, he'd learned.

He hoped Annika was as happy as possible in these tumultuous years after the war, while their entire country tried to right itself after it fell. Hitler had marched into their country without a fight in 1938, but oh, the war that had been waged to get him back out again. The man had stripped this country bare, though Max could still see the beauty as he'd taken the train from Salzburg. The soul of Austria—it was still here.

His family's old home rose in the distance, above the pine trees. These past years he'd traveled plenty and seen castles much older— and much larger—than Schloss Schwansee, but if the original owner had wanted to call his home a castle instead of a manor, then who was Max or anyone else to stop him? His family, and those before the Bettauer and Dornbach families, had certainly played along with the game, pretending that this place was meant for royalty.

If only he could pretend again and bring Luzi back to him. Unlike what Frau Weiss told him, he never should have let her go.

After multiple inquiries, he'd discovered that Luzi had died at Ravensbrück days after she arrived at that camp. She had suffered—how could she not?—but it comforted him in one sense that she hadn't suffered for long.

After years of searching, he found his mother in New York. She had remarried before the Germans occupied France, and she'd been able to hide her secret with her forged paperwork and newly acquired last name. Her husband, a French professor, hadn't been enamored of the Nazi Party. He led a group of resisters in their village, thwarting the Nazis whenever possible while married to an Austrian woman no one knew was a Jewess.

Max's father had died in the weeks when Berlin was gasping for its last breath, when the city was being slowly suffocated by the Russians in the east and the Allies pressing in from the west.

He'd searched and searched for Marta, after his mother told him that she had taken the child to an orphanage when she'd crossed into France, unable to care for her after the border guards took most of her money. She'd feared for both of their lives.

He'd traveled to the orphanage, but the place was closed now, any records destroyed. Then he'd learned the sad, awful truth. Most of the children had been sent to Auschwitz in April 1944, near the end of the war. He refused to believe that Marta was among them; he'd spend his life pretending, if he must. Taking solace in the unknown.

Before he finished his walk to the castle, he stopped at the old pet cemetery. People had relied on him—him and Dr. Weiss—but how naive he had been. Thinking of himself as some sort of hero when the enemy wasn't really after the heirlooms of their Jewish friends. The enemy was after their lives.

A white cottage had been built on the land where all the treasure was once stored, a neat-looking place with geraniums trimming each window and a garden plot that stretched across the land where he'd buried the heirlooms.

What had Annika done with the items hidden there?

Not that there was anyone left to return them to, but he wanted to ask her that question today, along with many others that had haunted him for the past fifteen years.

He knocked tentatively at the castle's front door, hoping Annika would greet him, but a housekeeper opened it instead, directing him back toward a renovated library. As he waited for the Stadlers, he crossed the room to the secret panel and pressed, but the seam had been sealed shut.

The books were in good order on the shelves; some of them he recognized from his youth. This place had been a refuge for him and Annika in their younger days, and he hoped it would be a refuge for generations to come.

He and Annika had been the best of friends as children and then awkward acquaintances of youth. But he'd trusted her with his greatest secrets. The treasure and then Luzi. He didn't know what happened to their treasure, but she hadn't failed him on Luzi's account—no one could stop the Gestapo.

He wandered to the bookshelf and perused the familiar titles, some new ones among the old books that his parents had collected over the years. Among them, he found *Bambi*, the story he'd loved as a boy.

He was beginning to open the cover when someone walked into the room.

"Max?"

Turning, he saw Hermann, but if he had expected a warm welcome—and if he were truly honest, he'd hoped for one—the doubt in his friend's eyes was more like a chill.

Was Hermann afraid that Max would take this old place from him? Hermann could have it. Could have everything inside it as well.

He glanced down at the book in his hands. Except, perhaps, this.

"I only have a short time," Hermann said. "I have business to attend to."

"Of course." Today's order was all about business.

"You are well?" Hermann asked.

"I am settled. On an American lake that reminds me of Hallstatt."

"Much has changed here since you've been gone."

"The entire world has changed in the past fifteen years."

Hermann glanced out the window as if he were looking for someone, and Max turned with him.

"Where is Annika?" he asked.

"Not far."

"May I see her?"

"I don't believe it's a good idea," Hermann said. "The memories are hard for her."

"They are hard for all of us."

But Hermann didn't relent. Max had wanted to ask Annika about the treasure, but he'd also wanted to thank her for caring for Luzi until the end.

Was this why Hermann was acting strange? Was he worried that Max would somehow steal Annika away? He'd loved her, like a sister, but he couldn't imagine loving anyone else like he'd loved Luzi.

"Did you ever find your mother?" Hermann asked as he stepped toward the door. Max followed him.

"I followed her to America, after the war." He didn't tell the man how he'd helped the Allies, escorting messages and people alike across borders that were supposed to be secured. Many here in Austria might hate him if they knew what he had done.

He hadn't told anyone about the treasure either. People were being indicted today for stealing valuables from Jewish families during the war. He hadn't wanted to steal anything. He'd wanted to keep their belongings safe. Be a banker, in one sense, like his father, with holdings for the future. But it would be difficult to convince a judge of his innocence when he couldn't give an account for the things he'd hidden away.

"What happened to the things I buried?" he asked, his voice low so neither the housekeeper nor anyone else could hear.

"I don't know."

"But Annika would—"

"When the Gestapo came to search," Hermann said slowly, scratching his cheek, "they took all the heirlooms."

Max studied the man's face, the perspiration beading along his hairline. He'd never been any good at lying—one of the reasons Max hadn't told him where the treasure was hidden. But Annika had known. If Herr and Frau Stadler sold the items that they'd safeguarded, the guilt was on their heads.

Max held up the *Bambi* book. "This used to be my favorite."

"What the Nazis didn't destroy, Annika wanted to keep in honor of your family."

"May I keep this one now?" He may never read the story again, but the book reminded him of all that was once happy in his home.

"Of course."

He thought Hermann might ask if there was anything else he wanted from his family's things, but his former friend was silent. Max tucked the book in his satchel, and Hermann watched him from the door until he crossed into the forest.

He'd already arranged passage to New York Harbor—he should go directly back to the station, take the next train out to the port at Caen, but it wasn't right for Hermann to keep him from seeing Annika one last time. He wasn't a threat. Only an old friend.

He'd learned how to stay hidden during the war, and he hid now in the trees, watching the courtyard and the gardens. As morning turned into afternoon, a BMW drove up the lane. A woman dressed in a yellow blouse and denim capri pants emerged from the vehicle, a wide-brimmed summer hat on her head. Three children tumbled out behind her, a toddler and two girls around eight and ten, he surmised, and then an older youth, a young man about fifteen or sixteen, stepped out of the passenger door.

Annika was no longer a kitten. She'd grown into an elegant woman who seemed to have aged well in the past fifteen years. The little boy took one of her hands. Then the girls and the young man joined them as they spun in a circle, laughing together until they fell onto the grass. Annika's hat tumbled off her head, and when she reached for it, Max saw her face. Saw what he never imagined he would see again.

It was Luzi there before him, her smile the one that had enchanted him the night of their dance, the eyes that stole his heart.

Luzia Weiss was alive.

But the Nazis had logged her name meticulously in their extermination records at Ravensbrück.

Whom had they taken away in 1939?

A tremor coiled down Max's spine. In that moment, he knew, or at least he thought he knew, what Annika—and Hermann—had done. He collapsed onto the floor of pine needles and dried leaves, sick as the day when Hermann told him that Luzi had been taken away. And he held the book closer to his chest, trying to connect the scattered pieces in his memory.

Annika hadn't stolen the heirlooms. His friend had been taken away that day in April. And Luzi, perhaps she had thought Max ran away.

It was much too late to change any of it now, but still the questions flooded his mind.

Hermann had told him Luzi was gone, taken away by the Gestapo, and then he'd married her.

Did anyone else know their secret?

Surely some of the people in town must, but perhaps they'd buried it with the destruction from the war.

He didn't speak to Luzi, though everything within him wanted to tell her that he was okay. They'd never dance again, but this time he could leave with a final good-bye.

But the good-bye would only be good for him. Not for Luzi or Hermann or their children. So much of her life already lay in ruins. He wouldn't shake the foundation of what remained.

Before he returned to his ship, Max found the finest maker of violins in Salzburg and commissioned him to craft an instrument and hand-deliver it to a certain woman who had once lived for music. And then he went home.

EPILOGUE

Snow sticks to the clear fragments of a stained-glass window—the picture inside, a Madonna watching over Christoph Eyssl's tomb. We're an odd group gathered in this chapel above Lake Hallstatt, a week before Christmas. Twenty-three people preparing to open the casket of a man who died nearly four hundred years ago.

It's taken months to gather all the necessary permits, but Sigmund partnered with Josh, and these two men, along with Luzia, managed to convince people across Austrian ranks about the possibilities. The Austrian chancellor, a friend of the Stadler family, is here today along with some other very important people, most of whom think I've spent too much of my life reading fairy tales.

I'm most interested in the VIPs who surround me: Charlotte and her sister, Brie and Ella, and a certain man on the other side of the church, the newest tenured professor at OSU, talking to the chancellor about other places he'd like to dive one day.

"It's a miracle, isn't it?" Charlotte says, and I agree with her. She's gone from having a family of only Brie and me to a crowd of nieces and nephews who've welcomed her into their fold. And a sister who clearly adores her.

"I'm proud of you," Brie whispers to me.

"For what?"

"Your courage."

I smile at her, the person who knows me best of all. Others wouldn't think of flying to Austria as courageous, but it took everything I had to get on that plane six months ago. And my everything was worth it for Charlotte and Luzia. And for Josh . . .

"I'm proud of him too." Brie nods toward the man who became my husband last month. "For luring you out of your cage."

I laugh. "You make him sound so conniving."

"He's a smart man for falling in love with you and inviting you into his world."

"Brie!"

She laughs. "Just saying it like I see it."

"Thank you for my gift," I tell her, sweeping my hand across the crowded room, stopping at Josh. "Without you, this never would have happened."

"Has it been worth it, Callie?"

And I know what she means—not the numerical kind of worth, but has it been worth risking my heart, the safe boundaries of my nest, to accept Josh's invitation to share our lives as a family.

"Indubitably."

Violin music travels in from the narthex as we wait for an

archaeologist representing the World Jewish Congress to arrive. Max Dornbach's great-granddaughter is playing Luzia's violin.

Even though Luzia can no longer play herself, she's caught up in Anna Dornbach's song. And so is Charlotte. The two sisters are sitting beside each other, arms linked. Pity the person, I think, who would try to tear them apart now. I've lost Charlotte in one sense, but my heart doesn't bleed as I thought it might. Instead, it's expanded to make room for more.

Behind Charlotte and Luzia is a row of eight people from Bolivia and Canada, descendants of a family named Leitner who escaped from Obertraun before the Austrian Jewish people were transported to concentration camps. Besides Luzia, they are the only ones we've been able to locate who might have a claim to what, if anything, is hidden in this chapel.

When the archaeologist and her assistant arrive, Josh slips up beside me and takes my hand. I'd expected the archaeologist to use some sort of fancy tool to open the casket, but the two women cover their faces with respirator masks and begin to pry open the box with a crowbar.

The lid tilts up, their success overpowered by the stench that permeates the room. The priest opens two doors, allowing the cold air to sweep through the nave, and I cover my face with my sleeve. Ella glances over at me, and I nod, giving her permission to slip outside with Anna.

The archaeologist reaches inside the casket with gloved hands and lifts out a burlap bag. One extraordinary girl, she confirms, brilliantly recorded the treasure in a place few adults would look and then hid it in the most unexpected of places.

Inside the bag is a gold necklace, the Star of David, engraved with the initials *S. L.* on the back. One of the women from the Leitner family gasps. "It's Aunt Sarah's star," she says, and I smile.

The *Bambi* book and I—we've found our way home. Perhaps more of these items will find their way home as well.

Ella and Anna return to the sanctuary, and we watch quietly as daylight fades into the lilac hour, the archaeologist and her assistant carefully cataloging burlap bags and brown-paper wrappings and feed sacks—all filled with valuables from before the war. Every piece will be recorded, using Annika's book as a reference, and the items will be returned to the Leitners and the descendants of any other families who survived the Holocaust.

If no one remains, the pieces will go to a museum in their memory and to honor all who died under Hitler's regime.

The archaeologist pulls an envelope out of the casket, well preserved in the same salt used for Christoph's remains. Then she reads the handwritten note to her small audience.

Dear Max,
To keep our secret safe, I must hide it away again. I'll guard
it even when I'm afraid, even after you are gone. If I'm
not able to retrieve it, I hope that you will find this one
day and remember what Mama once told me: Our hearts
follow wherever our treasure might be. I hope your heart
follows this treasure home.

When she finishes, I glance at Charlotte and Luzia in the dim light; both are crying. In fact, tears seem to be flowing freely in this space now.

Outside I hear the whisper of a song, then a chorus of birds in their own harmony. Each one is singing a different melody, like each person in this room. Only God knows the entire score of our lives, but we all have our assigned parts, measures to sing solo or with a choir.

Stepping out of the pew, I press my nose against the window and find a rust-colored bird perched on a snowy tree, watching our group through the glass. Quietly I move toward the back door and outside into the winter air.

A flock of stars watches over the lake, and I wonder, perhaps, if these stars are watching over us too.

The door opens again, and Josh slips up beside me, squeezing my hand. As I lean into him, we remember together the precious lives lost, but more than that, we remember their legacy, the majestic voices and instruments blending into a starlit symphony of sorts.

No one can stop this music. Its journey continues, I think, throughout the earth and up into the heavens. An eternal, sacred song.

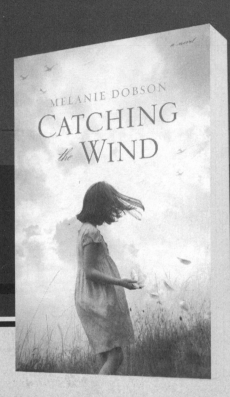

AUTHOR'S NOTE

Fifteen years ago, my husband and I backpacked across seven countries in Europe, savoring the culture and charm in each place. When we stepped off the ferryboat called *Stefanie* and onto the cobblestone streets in Hallstatt, we were completely enamored of the history and quaint beauty in this ancient village. The rugged, snow-capped mountains and pristine lake and the mysterious castle across the water—all of it captured us, and I dreamed about one day writing a story set in this beautiful place marred by evil during World War II.

The magical Hallstättersee with its swans and alpine water, and the other lakes around it, were dustbins of sorts, collecting whatever the Nazis swept into their waters as they fled south from the Allied troops. Schloss Schwansee was inspired by the castle on Hallstättersee called Schloss Grub—the residence of the eccentric salt administrator who wrote in his testament that every fifty years his casket would journey back home. During the war, this estate was used as a Hitler Youth camp.

Much has been written about "ownerless treasure" since Jon and I visited the Salzkammergut, but this story continued to burn inside me until I finally put it on paper—a story about a castle and a treasure, but most of all, about ordinary people who resisted evil in their own, extraordinary way.

I've tried to remain as true as possible to the facts and history of Austria during World War II. After the annexation in 1938, the Nazis began expropriating Austrian Jewish property to use for their war preparations. Many Nazi officials kept a portion of these assets for their own pockets.

Almost two hundred thousand Jewish men and women lived in Austria before Hitler annexed their country to Germany. A UPI article from 1938 said that approximately ten thousand Jewish men were arrested in Vienna after Kristallnacht in November. Some died in camps, but many returned home as broken as the glass in their windows. Their Nazi oppressors swore these men to secrecy, threatening their life and the lives of those they loved if they spoke about what happened during their imprisonment. And they were told to leave Austria immediately—a feat made nearly impossible by changing regulations, closed doors, and the money and heirlooms to pay for such a journey being stolen away.

Another article from the 1950s said that the material loss of Austrian Jewry was estimated at more than one billion dollars. Sadly, not many Austrian Jews were left to reclaim their property. By the end of the war, only about five thousand of the Austrian Jewish people remained.

The Nazis were no respecters of age. In 1944, they also raided an orphanage near Lyon and deported all the Jewish children except one refugee girl who was being nursed by a young French aide in her home.

Up north in Berlin is a powerful memorial to the Holocaust. From the outside, this plaza looks like a forest of concrete slabs, dreary and dull, but if you wander into the wide passages between the columns, you discover that it's something else altogether. The labyrinth of slabs inch closer and closer the farther you walk, deeper and deeper into the ground, until you're trapped in the darkness. Lost and alone.

At the beginning of 1938, Austria was an independent country prepared to fight Germany. Then almost overnight, without firing a gun, they renamed it Ostmark—Eastern March—fully under Nazi control. The poignant demonstration from these slabs, the gradual loss of Germany's liberty as people became trapped in Hitler's web, didn't occur in Austria. Their takeover was more like the clamp of an animal trap, the sudden snap of jaws that offered no warning and little hope for escape.

And yet, even when there's no escape in this life, there is hope, I believe, in the One who burns with eternal goodness and light. Hope in an everlasting life through Him. Through this story, I wanted to remember the many who've been lost in this life but are not forever gone. The hope that God's love and justice conquer evil in the end.

Hidden Among the Stars, like all my novels, was written with the help and support of multiple people who are superheroes to me. While I strive to be as accurate as possible with my facts, sometimes I mess up. Any and all errors are my mine alone.

A special thank-you to:

My amazing agent Natasha Kern and friends at Tyndale, including Stephanie Broene, Shaina Turner, Sarah Rische, Karen Watson, Sharon Leavitt, Maggie Rowe, and Maria Eriksen. I have learned so much from each of you and am continually grateful for the opportunity to partner together to publish stories with our shared mission to both entertain and inspire.

My first readers—Michele Heath, Sandra Byrd, Lyn Beroth, Gerrie Mills, and Ann Menke—for being so generous with your time and for blessing me with your wisdom and encouragement. The wonderful ladies in my writers' group, including Dawn Shipman, Julie Zander, Nicole Miller, and Tracie Heskett. I so look forward to our time together each month and am grateful for every edit and insight along with our laughter.

Cathy Dennis, I thoroughly enjoyed attending a Passover seder with you as we learned more about the Jewish faith and celebrated together our freedom from slavery. Elizabeth Gilbert and the team at my local library for helping me obtain the resources that I needed to write this story. My cousins Josh and Ines Beal for helping me with my many Austrian questions. Josh and Ines had a beautiful baby girl as I finished writing *Hidden Among the Stars*. Josh and Ella in this novel are completely fictional, but what a pleasant— and perhaps providential—surprise to find out that Josh and Ines named their daughter Ella.

Natalie Perrin and her rock star team with Historical Research Associates in Portland for helping me figure out how to break into an ancient casket and warning me not to tamper with any human remains off the pages of this book. Hundreds of scenarios crowded into my brain as I wrote this novel, but attempting to open a casket myself—you'll be glad to know that the thought never once crossed my mind!

Cecilia Greaves from the tourism office Tourismusverband Inneres Salzkammergut for graciously answering my questions and counting the number of stone steps as she climbed up to the Hallstatt cemetery. Hagen Schiffler, a violin maker near Salzburg, for tracking down information about Karl Lang, a brilliant violin maker from that era, to craft Luzi's gift.

Julie Kohl for gifting me with your friendship and faith journey. Authors like Randy Alcorn, Jessica Kelley, and Holocaust survivor Alter Wiener, who've wrestled in their writing with the hard questions about suffering and forgiveness. The dear friends who helped me brainstorm the title for this book and who pray for me on those days when I don't think I can write or edit another word. You know who you are, and your prayers for wisdom and tenacity are exactly what I need to continue on this writing journey.

My family and friends in Mount Vernon, Ohio, who always welcome me home. This small town, with its fabulous Paragraphs Bookstore, is one of my favorite places in the entire world!

My gracious father, Jim Beroth, a lifelong resident of Mount Vernon and regular volunteer on the Kokosing Gap Trail, for not only loving our family well and praying for all of us, but for flying out to Oregon to care for my girls while I was on deadline. Love you, Dad!

My daughters, Karlyn and Kiki, for your inspiration, creativity, and sweet laughter. And my husband, Jon, for exploring Hallstatt with me so many years ago and encouraging me to write this story based on all we learned there. The adventure continues. . . .

And to the Master Creator, who dearly loves and grieves with His children and offers both redemption and the gracious gift of eternal life to each one of us.

CALLIE'S COLLECTION OF CHILDREN'S BOOKS

A Wrinkle in Time by Madeleine L'Engle

Bambi: A Life in the Woods by Felix Salten

Bear Feels Scared by Karma Wilson

Bloom and *Click, Clack, Moo: Cows that Type* by
    Doreen Cronin

Curious George Goes Camping by Margret and H. A. Rey

Disney's Pooh: Happy Birthday, Pooh by Bruce Talkington

Fancy Nancy by Jane O'Connor

Fox in Socks and *Oh, the Places You'll Go* by Dr. Seuss

Hatschi Bratschis Luftballon by Franz Ginzkey

Henri's Walk to Paris by Leonore Klein

Madeline by Ludwig Bemelmans

The Magic Tree House series by Mary Pope Osborne

Matilda by Roald Dahl

Ribbon Rescue and *Stephanie's Ponytail* by Robert Munsch

The Humming Room by Ellen Potter

The Story Girl by L. M. Montgomery

The Tale of Despereaux by Kate DiCamillo

The Voyage of the Dawn Treader by C. S. Lewis

Where the Wild Things Are by Maurice Sendak

ABOUT THE AUTHOR

MELANIE DOBSON is the award-winning author of nearly twenty historical romance, suspense, and time-slip novels, including *Catching the Wind*, *Chateau of Secrets*, and *Shadows of Ladenbrooke Manor*. Three of her novels have won Carol Awards; *Love Finds You in Liberty, Indiana* won Best Novel of Indiana in 2010; and *The Black Cloister* won the *Foreword* magazine Religious Fiction Book of the Year.

Melanie is the former corporate publicity manager at Focus on the Family and owner of the publicity firm Dobson Media Group. When she isn't writing, Melanie enjoys teaching both writing and public relations classes at George Fox University.

Melanie and her husband, Jon, have two daughters. After moving numerous times with work, the Dobson family has settled near Portland, Oregon, and they love to hike and camp in the mountains of the Pacific Northwest and along the Pacific Coast. Melanie also enjoys exploring ghost towns and abandoned homes, helping care for kids in her community, and reading stories with her girls.

Visit Melanie online at www.melaniedobson.com.

DISCUSSION QUESTIONS

1. *"God is infinitely more beautiful and loving and tender and kind than anything we can imagine of Him."* Callie's view of God changed after reading these words in *The Story Girl*. Do you agree with this perspective? How has literature influenced or changed your view on God?

2. Many of the Austrian characters in *Hidden Among the Stars* are trapped in the same seemingly hopeless situation in 1938, but each of them handles the threat of evil differently. Have you ever been trapped in a situation that seemed hopeless? Did you respond like any of these characters?

3. The Nazis banned and even burned literature written by Jewish authors like Felix Salten because of its potential to expose the truth about Nazism. In the contemporary story, Callie discusses the good and bad influences in children's literature (healthy books to build a mind, brain candy, and poison). What do you think about the censorship of literature? How do you sift through different genres and messages in books for you and/or your family?

4. People often hide the wounds of their past and sometimes the emotional pain of their present as well. Why do we hide our pain? How can we help others heal from both past and present wounds?

5. Both Callie and Annika had to confront their fears near the end of the book, but the results of these confrontations were very different. What fears have you had to face in your life, and what happened when you confronted them?

6. Callie often invokes lines and stories from children's books to understand the world around her. How does this mind-set help and perhaps hurt her?

7. What is the significance of music in this story? What sustains you through difficult times?

8. Charlotte invited Callie and Brie to be part of her family after their parents died. Do you think family can extend beyond biology? What does family mean to you?

9. Annika sees the beauty and power of God in flowers and in birdsong. Where do you find God in your daily life?

10. Josh wrestled with the question of why God would allow harm to come to His children. Do you believe that God is in complete control of our world? Where do you think He is when people suffer?

11. In spite of her fears, Annika makes the ultimate sacrifice for Luzi and Max by offering herself instead of allowing the agents to take Luzi away. Do you think Annika made the right decision? How would you have responded?

12. The pastor in Hallstatt says, "Death is no longer a threat to those who believe in Him. The ultimate weapon of our enemy has been stolen away." What do you believe about the afterlife? How does this impact your life today?

TYNDALE HOUSE PUBLISHERS IS CRAZY4FICTION!

Fiction that entertains and inspires

Get to know us! Become a member of the Crazy4Fiction community. Whether you read our blog, like us on Facebook, follow us on Twitter, or receive our e-newsletter, you're sure to get the latest news on the best in Christian fiction. You might even win something along the way!

JOIN IN THE FUN TODAY.

 www.crazy4fiction.com

 Crazy4Fiction

 @Crazy4Fiction